BOOK 1

BEING STILL

Again

TAMBERLY MOTT

Edited by Michelle Striler

For permissions contact: www.Tamberlymott.com

Or write to
Mott
P.O. Box 928
Sloughhouse, CA 95683

This is a work of fiction. Historical events, names, characters, places, and incidents either are the product of the author's imagination or are used fictitiously. Any resemblance to actual persons, living or dead, events, or locales is entirely coincidental.

Portions of this book contain nonfiction. Any identifying characteristics have been changed or are entirely coincidental.

Cover and Interior Design by KUHN Design Group | kuhndesigngroup.com

Edited by Michelle Striler

Printed in the U.S.A.

Library of Congress Cataloging-in-Publication Data
Mott, Tamberly L., 2022
Being Still Again, Book 1, 1st ed.

ISBN 979-8-9871115-0-5 (paperback version)
ISBN 979-8-9871115-1-2 (e-print version)
ISBN 979-8-9871115-2-9 (audible version)

Visit www.tamberlymott.com

For my mother, Nan,

I treasure the memory of rushing home from kindergarten to watch Dark Shadows with you. And, even before my teen years, I can still hear your whispered excitement (always in the wee hours of the night when everyone else was asleep, but I was still reading the newest Nancy Drew mystery you had given me), "Tam, you awake? Come watch a scary movie with me!" We would hide behind the couch pillows, anticipating the howl of the werewolf, and laughing at the drunk old bitties eating tripe through their hairnets. I cannot count the times we watched horror and mystery movies from the 60's and 70's, and other classics, you called them "the oldie moldies," but your love for watching them, together, never got old. I wish you were alive to read this story, the first in a trilogy, birthed from a dream. You would have loved to hear it firsthand, and I would have given you the first draft. Your motivating faith in my story telling and writing has energized this project, and while I am certain to write books in other genres, you're my inspiration for all things dark and eerie, hair-raising, and mysterious! You also have inspired my career in helping those with mental illness, RIP Mom.

Nancy Fleming
1/3/1945 to 1/21/2006

CHAPTER 1

FREE AT LAST

*"I am no bird; and no net ensnares me; I am a free human being
with an independent will; which I now exert to leave you."*

CHARLOTTE BRONTE

The slender woman stirred on the cot where she slept, then her muscles went flaccid. The darkness in the room hummed a song of internment, enticing her heavily lashed lids to remain sealed. Below, the bluest eyes, unaware of the surrounding shelter, began to move back and forth. Breath slowed to the lowest pace her heart would accept without rebelling. Beads of sweat towered among her brows, giving her eye movement permission to pick up the pace. The tingling, prickling at the crown, spread to the top of her head.

The hairbrush, now in control, tenderly pulled through thick locks. The static-like sensation continued down to her shoulders, across her breasts, spreading down to her thighs. The rhythm was slow and purposeful, like the gentle petting of a lover who knows how to push and pull, and where to dally, to elicit the desired responses. The pungent notes of leather and vanilla warmed her senses. Her pleasure became fuller. The waist long golden hair clung to the brush, and then released itself as the stroke found the smooth ends. Strands glistened as they fell free. Cunning hands extended the follow-up strokes upon her head. The petting became more familiar. Awe ceased as the horrifying recognition came to her mind.

Master? He's here? He's found me. The game has begun.

Cortisol suddenly replaced the feel-good endorphins, and terror seized her awareness.

Don't be angry, please don't be angry. Look eager, he wants eager.

She reflexively turned over to her stomach. Her face found the center of the pillow. She felt gauze-like before his eyes. Her expression shifted, all too late. His sneer prompted her panic. A chill shook her body.

The jury he employed judged her shudder as rejection, and refusal of the master was never acceptable. Consequences were eminent. Knowing hands parted the long hair, and before she could raise a defense, he twisted the hair like a rope around her neck. Holding the hair-noose with one hand, he twisted it tightly, showing no mercy. He laughed maniacally. Forming in her anxious stomach was a pit, a giant's magic seed; it mutated, knotting, thickening as it grew to occupy her throat.

No air, stay calm. Stay eager. Still no air.

His other hand covered her nose and mouth, and she sucked in with all her might. He gave in, freeing her face, allowing a breath. Panic urged flight, but she could not move arms or legs; the master had tied her. Straddling the vanity chair, her small breasts sat snug on the top edge of the seatback, she was exposed and vulnerable. He enjoyed her peril. Her shoulders conceded, giving him the answer he wanted.

Now that you have been reminded of your status you can see that I hold your life in my hands, I will free you, but you will do as I say, enthusiastically. Alright my golden girl, touch yourself the way I taught you.

Releasing her arms, he returned to stifling her airway. Allowing some air, but controlling quantity, she would be gifted with longer breaths when she impressed him. Spasmodically, her fingers moved, per his expectations. She numbed herself and faked her delight. Anticipating her act, his attention returned to her hair, gripping tighter as he spoke.

You want this. Sell it to me.

She did as he ordered, and he loosened his grip to reward her.

The choosing comes next.

Her master's eyes glistened with evil intent as he anticipated her choice.

Would you like me to stop? Decide now.

Desperate for comfort, her mind ricocheted from thoughts to rebellious feelings.

Stop, no more, no more. Let go of my hair! No! I won't obey.

Her body shifted and her face turned away from the pillow. Her muscle tone was returning. Her heartrate normalized, her chest rose and fell. The dream colors muted as the oxygen level improved.

Wait, this can't be happening. You are only a ghost in my mind. You are not real. You are dead. I killed you. My long hair was left behind along with your hold on me.

Ariel's hands, now loosed from the dream's bindings, rapidly found her scalp. Her short hair was confirmation; it gave her eyes the courage to open.

I'm in Caroline's house. I'm alone.

Squeezing her eyes closed, the dream, lingering ever so slightly in her thoughts, had one last whisper for her.

Murderer. It is only a matter of time before your deeds catch up to you.

She shook away the remnants of her sleepy nightmare with a spoken declaration, "No! He's dead."

Fully awake now, Ariel sat upright. Knowing he would never again touch her, made the unknown infinitely more manageable. She continued to calm herself by singing the first song that popped into her head.

"Ding-dong the witch is dead, which old witch, the wicked witch, ding-dong, the wicked witch is dead, wake up sleepyhead, rub your eyes, get out of bed, he is really dead."

Her countenance conveyed the possibility of peace. She did not feel whole, but she felt hope, and that seemed infinitely more important than being 100% stable. Beside her cot, the newspaper lay open. She had circled the contact information in red ink. The recollection called her away from the nightmares of the past, bringing her into her present reality. She reread the ad.

Fem Mannequin Models needed for discrete cash paid jobs, no questions asked, no references necessary. Earn up to $10,000 weekly with A to Z Model Agency. Group interview on Thursday @ 11am. 177 Haley Ave., Reno, NV.

It had been four days since discovering the ad, and Thursday had finally arrived. Thoughts whirred around in her head as she got out of bed, rolling her sleeping bag and pillow into the familiar bundle systematically. It was her habit to store her things to allow her to grab-and-go quickly.

Now, what to wear that says this is the right girl for the job, maybe a Hepburn look?

Besides wondering what to wear for her interview, anxiety triggered by her nightmare, continued to entertain a haunting truth, she was a runaway slave, one who had committed murder, and she might be recognized. She tried pushing it away with reason.

There were men who searched for me, but like the master who controlled us all, that slave is dead. I am new and alive. I am my own.

Ariel reminded herself that her current identification was solid. Naturally tanned skin made her photo impeccable. She was nothing like her former image; from what she remembered. In addition to her radically different hair, she had filled out in ways that made her perfectly sculpted beauty more exquisite. She was a stark contrast to her former self, a darker version. Her name, born from ashes of a medicine man's fire, deep in the heart of the Amazon, had been saved, until now.

I have papers. I am an American with a social security card, and no ties to anything prior. I am prepared to be a "living" Ariel Black, a real person, no disguise. I'm ready to be real…wait…am I?

A *toxic think*, which would not be sung away, blanketed her anxious spirit.

I don't know my real name. No one knows the name my parents gave me at birth, no one.

Her earliest memory, weakened by years of brainwashing and abuse, could only recall having been called, "Little Dove." Hearing herself speak the name, misplaced her thoughts further.

But what name did my parents give me? What if my parents had lived? But no, they were killed, and he's dead too. I shot him dead. What if I had not been able to run away? What if I had not been helped or guided by angels?

Her morning ambition was smothered by a wave of what-ifs. Anxiety had won her back, fleetingly at first, then, unleashed. Lily came to mind before panic took charge.

Lily? I miss you. I do wish you were here. I'm free, like you said I would be some day. But do I deserve it? You said, we were not to blame for what we did. Oh, Lily, I wish you could be here, I need you.

Lily was her first true friend, her teacher, and the only one who gave her unconditional love. In secret, Lily called her Little Dove, as proof of their intimate bond. The clandestine act helped them both to hold on to the hope of being "self-owned" someday. The act of disobedience, using a non-slave name, somehow induced a sense of blamelessness for the slaves, and it produced a hope for their future, "where a little dove could be uncaged, and fly free."

Ariel's present mind reeled in fog-filled memories, then moved toward the dank, insanely prolific jungle, where names and gender were irrelevant. She visualized her past non-binary self, and the jungle. They had all rematerialized, she could hear the monkeys and birds, and the natives, whispering to her, "Alma bonita, alma bonita." Her mental miasma, empowered, took her back, before the jungle; to her first days of *freedom*.

Three years prior.

Waves pushed the bubbling salted foam closer to where she sat on the beach. Fear told her to move back from the water's edge, while curiosity urged her forward; she denied them both. To move at all, meant going toward the unfamiliar; freedom and free people were unknown constructs. She had used every bit of creature nerve to make it this far, she had reached the threshold of a living world. A pinching *what-now* question arose out of the gurgle in her stomach and peaked at the tender place between her sculpted eyebrows.

What now? What now?

Her thoughts resounded in rhythm with the nearby waves as they crashed onto the driftwood shore. Her flawless mouth had no answer. Shoes in hand, her alabaster feet met the sand she had imagined for over 20 years. There was no fight in her delicate body, her tangled mane was all she had left to spar with the wind. The *Master's* "Golden Girl," had always understood her place and did what she was told. Now, just hours into an uncaged life, her budding inquisitiveness was wholly disorganized. The action of killing her master had forced the slight bodied being into the immense unknown. No longer a sub-dependent slave, she would have to think and make decisions for herself, and like experiencing the sand and sea for the first time, it was unfathomable, overwhelming, and awe-inspiring all at once.

The sky, like her mind, was fickle. A few lurid clouds passed unnoticed, swiftly moving one direction, and then another; billowing, thinning, and moving on. The cooling yellow ball dipped behind the body of blue-gray water and the tide shifted away, making room for the spindly-legged shorebirds. Unyielding, she stuck to the vastness of the wooded coastal landscape for a sliver of conclusive knowing.

Where now?

The waiting made her worry; she pushed the thought away and focused on the distance between herself and the horizon. The sights and sounds were new, but the old familiar clapping, crashing, lapping sounds gave her constant pause. The master's recorded voice was always accompanied by a busy sea. Like a vessel taking on water, the messages seeped in, threatening to flood her being.

Hope and fear are phantoms arising from thinking of the self. I heard that over and over. I wasn't permitted to be an I, or a me.

The shore smells made her breathe deeper, her skin noted the temperature, and her ears gathered the remaining evidence. This was air winded by sea, it was not pushed by metal paddles and filtered through narrow earth tunnels. There was no musty scent, and no steady hum.

He said self is bad. What about him-self? Is it different for women, are we lessor? Our parts are different, and everyone has different skills, even among the slaves. I don't see why parts matter. What if there is no difference between a man and a woman, only differences between humans? Lily? What say you?

For this fugitive slave, time passed like a litter of pups whelped by a bitch not more than six months herself. Discovery came in spurts; instinct was forced to lead. Eight pups were born and cleaned before her next thought.

Lily's not here. I am. I am here. There is more of me now, enough to be something bigger. Lily said I was only permitted to be a fraction of my worth as a human. She would say the master keeps for himself, what we should have been given to grow. Lily would say, look upward.

Her eyes went skyward. The first brilliant stars of the evening twinkled in her eyes.

That is a real night sky, made not by man. Lily said Mother Nature is the artist of the world, and the sky is a living canvas. Beautifully alive. There you have it, all is not lost.

The divine had reached her thoughts with a medicinal offering. Recognizing the twinkling wish-lights, she drank them in as life preserving elixirs. Then, an endowment from the heavens, the low hanging moon whispered to her, "Your peace is within you, rest Little Dove."

The darkness gave way to the sunrise, and a new day began. Shaking the unwanted sand from her shoes and purposing her feet to move, the fugitive trudged away from the overnight sanctuary among the fallen trees on the beach. The salty breeze and the honied sounds of nature encouraged her onward. New sightings were everywhere, tempting excitement. Seagulls squawked, pigeons cooed, squirrels chattered and played, and multitudes of geese clucked by, over her head. The terror had subsided, and instead of questions, she had a grateful knowing.

I'm alive.

One day into her uncaged status, with no sign of being pursued, the runaway tentatively drew closer to the living beings around her. Deliberately, like a hunter to prey, she watched, and listened, inching her way out of separateness to gain a better view. She was now among free humans. They passed without looking at her.

It looks like they are all in a hurry to be somewhere else.

Recognizing French and English words, Little Dove listened carefully. She hung onto every word, despite many words spoken out of her context.

Some words have more meanings than I have been taught.

In the distance, a group of people hurled a disc back and forth. The activity seemed peculiar to Little Dove. Their laughter reached her ears, and soon, she was smiling. The joy was short lived. Missing her own sense of belonging, she doubted her ability to be carefree and happy.

Will I ever be like them? Will the world ever be safe for me? Will I ever be able to love anyone besides Lily? Is it possible for someone like me to be whole?

From her limited vantage, a shaded grove of trees in a public park, "the normies" as she later named them, were persons who outwardly treated all genders, young and old, as human beings. It was surreal. Since before school age, her existence had been dependent on seeing all things through her owner's darkened prism. The missing filter was spectacular.

Look there, some even give their leashed pets human-like status. These people have freedom of movement, freedom of expression, apparent self-ownership, and there are more free females than I ever imagined. I have missed so much.

Moving to a bench, nearer the flower-lined smooth grey path, she positioned herself like another who had rested, and then moved on. A red and white cup with a straw, and a knitted hat had been left behind. Little Dove gathered her golden hair, twisted it into a ball, and donned the hat to hold it in place. She picked up the cup and removed the lid; her thirst didn't care that it belonged to another. Remnants of sweetened ice were greedily consumed. It kindled her hunger for something more substantial. Looking to her right, she saw a couple of women running on the path, slowly, side-by-side.

They are unafraid.

About that time, a white bearded male with a deeply lined face joined her on the bench. His loose fitted clothing announced an idle lack of importance, it kept her from running. In his hand were papers, folded together, and covered with English words.

Feeling her stare as he held out the paper to read, he glanced over, and with a pleasant tone, said, "Good morning Miss. Eh? I'm only interested in the sport's page; you're welcome to the rest."

The tiny pale hands accepted his offering, not knowing what else to do. "Thank you," was all she could muster. Bracing herself for further contact, she was surprised he wanted nothing in return. She was not accustomed to being regarded as a normie; she relaxed as her face warmed. The man's small act of kindness inundated her soul with awareness.

Open your eyes and see, is this not real? Maybe there are good male persons?

Thinking "free" was like trying a new language, and her vocabulary was negligible. She decided it was like facing light after being blindfolded. Once her thoughts adjusted to her new reality, she felt certain she could learn to make sense of it all. Her peripheral kept a close watch on the male next to her. She imitated the way he held the paper. His calm manners returned her to her body. Neatly written words jumped off the paper and into her comprehension. In real time, she was transformed from fugitive to an owl-eyed student. The paper contained an article about traveling to Toronto by train, among other novelties. She read it repeatedly and studied the pictures. An old childhood dream snuck loose in her mind.

I have been there or perhaps it was a dream? Whether dream or real, a new life calls for me to come. To live, I must be willing to join the living.

The brisk coastal air had inspired her mind; numb legs took her cautiously toward a woman sprawled on the grass. There was no sense of threat. Hunger pressed Little Dove to speak.

She won't hurt me and maybe she can help.

"Pardon, I am a stranger here, and I need to get to the train to Toronto, J'ai besoin d'aide."

The sight of the runaway must have alarmed the woman, who immediately arose to her knees, and removed her lightweight jacket. Offering the covering and a water bottle, she spoke rapidly, "Oh my

God. I'm sorry, eh. Are you injured? Were you mugged, eh? I cannot believe this, has this happened here, eh? Perhaps it is best to get you to the Mounties station?"

She speaks funny, almost a tic. No matter. Safe to proceed.

"Thank you, no, I prefer to go to Toronto. I am not injured, only hungry and abandoned with nothing."

Accepting the water and the jacket, Little Dove felt moved by the woman's concern. Several swallows of delicious clean water caused her eyes to tear up. Her thoughts clung to Lily for stability.

My Lily was right, angels exist in the world, and one is standing next to me; Lily would be so happy to know it. I wish she was still alive.

Asking no further questions, the benevolent woman, now on her feet, pulled out a protein bar.

"Sorry miss. You are shaking, eh, you must eat. It is only a bar, but I think you should eat before you faint, eh." Opening the package and handing it over like a half-peeled banana, the Canadian woman continued. "The hoser left you with nothing, eh? Sorry you weren't treated better. Are you certain you are not injured, eh?" As she spoke, the track pants she was wearing dropped, leaving her in a pair of biking shorts. "Eh, here, put these on your legs. You're half frozen. Gee, this is terrible. Sorry I don't have more to give you, eh. I can see every one of your bones. Poor thing. Eh, I hope you're not one who thinks she's fat. Okay then, see how you are, eh? An American not worried about eating dairy, nuts, or gluten, I like you already, eh. Go ahead, eat it, then I can take the wrapper."

The pants were several sizes too big, but the giver wound an elastic band around a portion of the extra material to keep them from falling off. Hungrily nibling, it did not take Little Dove long to consume the 35-gram bar, hand over the wrapper, and return to sipping the water. Excitable chatter picked up speed as the minutes passed, the speaker was bent on filling in the missing information with her own intuition.

The shaking had stopped, Little Dove's apprehension stayed. Not knowing what else to do or say, she nodded and shrugged in response to questions posed as statements.

I must not say too much.

Remaining quiet, taking small sips of water, and grunting in agreement when there was an awkward silence, Little Dove stayed small.

The fast-talking Canuck had attracted others to gather around the boney stray. The sight of her skimpy clothing and heeled sandals had the group of locals convinced the stray "gave hugs" for an occupation; they were too polite to say prostitution. They surrendered the idea of contacting the police and focused instead on giving her what they could.

Besides the track suit, and the common "sorry to hear, eh," Little Dove was gifted a handful of loonies, two granola bars, another protein bar, an apple, a pear, a bag of banana chips, a bag of chocolate covered nuts, an energy drink, and three water bottles. Another passerby generously donated a warm coat and a purse-size backpack to hold her food items, along with a toque fashioned like the Canadian flag, and a pair of runners. The shoes were too long, but they fit well enough when tightened by the shoestrings and were welcomed by Little Dove's tired feet.

It was disconcerting to be the center of attention, but Little Dove stayed quiet, sipping water to ease her nerves. She was grateful no one asked for her name or where she had come from. The good Samaritans produced their own back-story, based on a lack of correction.

"This woman has been mugged, and left to freeze to death in the park, after her hoser boyfriend broke up with her, and stole her belongings. Now, she needs to get to Toronto to meet her family from New York."

No one knew how the *poor girl* was going to be able to purchase a train ticket, but no one discouraged her. Instead, she was told how to reach the station, the back way; it was not far from where the huddled group had gathered. Thanks and wishes for luck were worn out. As directed, Little Dove left the park to walk toward the train station, smiling shyly after all the kindnesses she received. She crossed a small creek, thankful there were stepping rocks across the entire way; she did not wish to soak her new runners. Determined not to doubt herself, she walked through a field of waist-high weeds until locating the train's track. Following the tracks to the station took less than fifteen minutes. It was long enough for her to decide she needed to avoid further contact; her angels' bounty would keep her alive.

Time to find a way into one of these cargo cars, without being seen.

～

As if she had climbed into a time machine, she was returned to her present moment.

No train cars, no stickers in my clothes, no too big runners. The mirror says I'm here and I'm alive.

Ariel concentrated, using her recently acquired skills from group therapy, and the spiritual growth acquired in the rainforests of the Amazon, she practiced reconciling the remaining ambivalence.

I am alive. I am in control of me. Out there, besides the all-or-nothing, there is the in between. The between is real. I have a purpose. I have skills. Mother earth richly provides for me. No other can own me. Light guides my thoughts and my next steps.

The brief mental-spiritual exercise felt virtuous. She practiced her new name.

"I am Ariel Black, and I'm here to apply for the modeling position. Yes. I am Ariel and I belong to myself. I am not a slave; I will never be enslaved again. His brands are gone, he is dead, and soon, his ghosts will be dead too. I did what I had to do; I had no other choice. He deserved much worse than a bullet in the chest, but at least he will never hurt anyone ever again. I wish I could have saved my love. Lily…I will never forget what you have meant to me, and for all we never got to be, I will be, I must. I promised you."

The sound of a cawing crow came through the window, Ariel acknowledged its message.

A single morning crow from the north indicates something positive.

"Yes, I hear you. And thank you. I will expect good things today." She imagined herself standing in front of a cheeky hiring agent. "What? Can I be steady like a statue, like a posed mannequin? Yes, I can, in fact, I'm quite experienced at being still."

CHAPTER 2

THE PERFECT COVER

*"How easy it is to judge rightly after one sees
what evil comes from judging wrongly."*

ELIZABETH GASKELL

Lily's thought when she saw it: *There are only 346 inhabitants, it's more like a grove than a city. Loyalville, a copse among mountains of well-rooted trees, the home at the end of nowhere.*

Despite births and deaths, Loyalville, California, had not updated their population sign in decades. Lily favored this fact because it proved this was a stubbornly close-knit little town, where most were related, or they had known one another most of their lives. In her words, they had stay-put-ness.

Loyalville once was a booming mining town, like the other neighboring mountain-folk towns edging the Tahoe National Forest in Sierra County. In Lily's rationale, the generational history, coupled with the lack of transient population shifts, meant Loyalville had a kind of mycorrhizal network; a symbiotic self-sustaining "rooted" community. Beyond what Lily had learned about the science of dendrology, spiritually, Lily believed trees were superior spirits, markedly stronger than any single human, with wisdom beyond any other earthly species. She knew the tree spirits would protect her spirit, and guide her, and warn her if danger came to call. There had been other "cover" locations considered, but Loyalville was the only place that met all of Lily's musts.

A home must have trees. It must be a place low in crime, a smaller population, but one where I can blend in. Locality is critical. The monster's lair is located near the ocean, the years of endless wave crashing made that clear. I need to be far from coastal areas. I believe Loyalville is the best name for a home. This is a mountainous region, where hearty-types value family and the second amendment. Also important. I'm not about to give up my guns. Some say the place has more cattle than people, and I read cattle owners tend to be tight-lipped about their own. And there is a Chinese family. Mr. and Mrs. Yan, a fifth-generation thicket, with all the markings of a perfect cover.

As Lily learned from her research, the Yan family were the owners of Loyalville's Hardware and Garden Supply; a business where the pulse of the community was robust. Their only daughter, named Debbi, went missing as a young teenager. Curiously, the parents rejected the idea of foul play, believing their daughter would return in good health, when the time was right. As reported in a local editorial piece, the Yan's fully expected their child to return because their tea leaves had predicted their legacy would be carried on by a daughter. A corresponding police report listed the incident as unsolved.

Lily examined the girl's picture from the paper; a standard school photo, showing her head and shoulders.

Even with a grainy two-tone photo, she has my eyes, and my cheekbones, a pretty girl, and not too tall. Yuanfen? Maybe so. I have a sense of their culture. after all, my birth parents were Chinese too. They will not be disappointed with me. I'm more than ten years older than their daughter, but it doesn't show. Nearly twenty years since the mysterious event, seems like a ripe time for a family reunion. My work dispensing justice for money, must end. I'm ready. I can be the fulfillment of their tea leaf vision, a win-win. Yes, it is decided. The time is right to reunite.

~⁓~

After several months of intel preparation, and off-the-grid travels to conceal her tracks, the *new Debbi* arrived on the Yan's doorstep with a suitcase, and a well-spun prodigal-daughter-returns story ready to tell. There was no turning back. Lily flung herself away from trained hesitation and embraced the couple as a long-lost child would do. They too showed no reserve. The touch and sentiment were at once stabilizing.

The welcoming was unlike anything Lily could have imagined; relief-happy tears, open arm embraces, and a complete lack of judgement. The Yan's aging memories, and the mountebank's size were a great fit; it also helped that Lily had extraordinary beauty, much like the youthful daughter they remembered.

Any shock was tempered by the faith the couple had adhered to, "We've been expecting your return, come inside."

The parents, hand in hand, led Debbi through the home, pointing out changes they had made since she left. With only minutes into the reunion, Lily assessed them.

A humble couple who lovingly gives credits, rather than boasting of their own deeds.

There were slews of prayers emanating from the elderly couple, otherwise viewed as awkward moments of silence. The "prodigal" went with the flow, staying attentive but quiet. The parents were eager to make their daughter feel she had not been forgotten, and they hoped she had not forgotten her youth, but even if she had, they would be patient and allow nature to take its course.

"Papa built the wall niche himself, to make a proper alter. This is where we pray, and see, our incense still burns. Our daughter is home. I must add fresh fruit."

It is time to speak. Their eyes are seeking even if they will not ask.

Debbi knew she could elaborate later, she was prepared, but she could not deny the couple's need to hear *her truth*. She cleared her throat, searching for the right tone, and the proper delivery.

"Papa, Mama, my eyes have seen the Eastern Suns of Mount Longhu rise and set; nature held me in balance. I did not resist. I did nothing. The flow has returned me to you. It was the right time to come home. You have need, and I am here for you. It is my honor to care for you."

"Filial piety is sweeter when natural and not imposed, is it not, Mama?"

The father was more animated than ever before, it made his wife happy to feel his joy.

"Indeed, inaction can be a steep path. Papa and I have taken every step knowing you would return in our time of need."

Mama Yan reached to dab her eyes. Debbi's father proudly continued, cheerily, for her mother's sake.

"See how Mama sewed the cloth? She made it from the dress you wore to school, the day of your announcement. The lotus represents the freedom from the mire of the world."

"Your Papa cut the hole in the sheetrock and did all the finish work after working at the Hardware counter, it was his passion. And see how he has carved your name and your likeness into the wood, a perfect likeness. This triptych represents fifteen years. As he carved, I burned our written prayers, here; all for you. We used our tears to soften the wood, we did not wish them for mourning; we knew you would return."

The beauty and mastery of the alter was inspiring, the threesome lingered to offer quiet prayers of thanks. Finally, stepping to the right of the alter, the home tour had ended in front of Debbi's bedroom door; it was bright red.

"Papa painted your door; red has brought you luck."

Mr. Yan opened the door with a flair of ceremony, it was a long-awaited moment. "Daughter, see, Mama cleaned for you, placing clean sheets on your bed just last evening, as she has done every week since your departure."

"Papa added the double-panes and tint to your window. See how it has kept your things from being bleached with the afternoon sun."

Pointing to a hanging scroll, Debbi's father added more emphasis to his voice, "Your mother made this, she replaced the framing to prepare for you."

Debbi uttered with reverence, "The Mountains of the Immortals, it is beautiful."

It was challenging for the weary traveler to see and accept the unconditional love, and not lose control of the rising emotions. Debbi drew strength from knowing she had not come empty handed, and she intended to repay their kindness. She examined the room. A table in the corner held a display of miniature drums, bells, chime stones, and a zither; musical instruments passed down from Debbi's great-great grandmother. Not knowing the significance, Debbi walked over to the table and studied each object. She felt compelled. Reaching for the pic, inserting her left index finger, she strummed the zither as if she knew it well.

Mrs. Yan looked to her husband conclusively, "Still her favorite."

The blue and green colors of the bedding and furnishings, the paint too, all chosen to represent longevity and harmony; the Taoist philosophy had prevailed in the Yan's lives. The aged couple accepted the woman who presented herself as their grown daughter without a breath of hesitation. An observer might have thought the girl had only returned from boarding school, the simplicity of it was astounding.

The access to belongings and mementos, along with the telling, and re-telling of family stories, as older parents are known to do, set a perfect stage. Two days of shared history gave "the prodigal" enough key information to be able to go confidently out into the community, to shore up her cover. Before arriving, the geography of the area was studied with the help of satellite technology. Lily had memorized the layout of the various retail shops and businesses, the graveyard and the open areas around the Yan's home and business. She had also memorized most of the names and addresses of key residents; she did not wish to appear new to town.

With the help of her parents, Debbi placed flowers on all the graves related to the Yan's and to those who the Yan-child had seen their death coming. It was joyful and sobering all at once. After graveside prayers were completed, Mr. and Mrs. Yan returned to their home, encouraging their daughter to proceed without them. They did not wish to impose their ideas about where she should go, or what she should say to become reacquainted with their little city. Pulling a large flat garden cart fully loaded, walking door to door, Debbi wanted to personally thank those who most supported her parents, she had plants for all of them. She also distributed small cash gifts to those her parents had identified as "good people in need."

Debbi worked her way toward the address of Nan Everette, now Mrs. Nan Barlowe, her best childhood friend. Next to reuniting with her parents, Debbi felt her meeting with Nan could be the trickiest to navigate. Using her breath, Debbi kept her thoughts light and positive, her pace and body language stayed coordinated as well. Waiting to cross the street, toward the famed diner, Debbi spotted a couple walking hand in hand. She needed a closer look. Leaving the cart behind, she crossed over.

Is that her? Petite mousy white woman with tall black football type, I think it might be.

Ten more steps to be face to face, Debbi was preparing to say, "Nan? Is that you?" Before she formed the words, the woman looked up. Their eyes met. Her stroll skidded to a stop.

"Debbi? Debbi? Debbi! Can I believe my eyes? Bud, look! It's the ghost of Debbi Yan, and she's all grown up."

Having dropped her husband's hand, Nan's own arms went straight up to the sky, then back together, palm to palm as if she were beginning a Sun salutation. She squeezed her eyes closed.

No, I am awake. This is real.

When Nan lifted her lids, there she was, Debbi Yan; not a dream, not a ghost, but live spirit, flesh, and blood.

It's her, she's grown up!

The present reality incited exuberance, it exploded with a screech, followed by a squeal. Debbi, instinctively stepped back to give her shrieks more space, but she followed Nan's example, sending her own arms to the air, then shook her hands back down in front to a prayer position; hands balled in fists, left over right, with thumbs tucked to form a Yin-Yang symbol.

Nan, now shaking, cried out, "You remembered. It is really you! Debbi it's you!"

Imitating the Taoist prayer-hands, Nan balled her fists as Debbi had done. They stood for 30 seconds, each examining the other's face, until smiles widened and hands relaxed. Stepping forward, Nan reached out to take hold of Debbi's shoulders. Debbi gave her own best effort at sharing a happy whoop, and then stepped into Nan's reach. The spectacle climaxed as the two women embraced, and twirled round and round until their tears of delight slowed the spin, and sleeves jumped to catch the falling drops. On the street, curtains were pulled back, doors opened, and entrance bells sang their tinkled cheers; Debbi Yan had returned to the place where she grew up.

Bud stood by, not knowing where he fit in, and still uncertain of his wife's declaration. However, all who were in earshot, emerged with certainty, and reignited the welcome hysteria. Hoots, hollers, and OMG's it's Debbi with an i, were heard from one end of Main Street to the other. Within three minutes, 40 or more Loyalvillians were all but mobbing the two women. The scene and the sounds grew in energy, until Nan, now enveloped in throngs of clapping hands and joyous manic shouts, suddenly froze up and shut down. Bud, who had his eye on her every twitch, turned papa bear. He made short work of freeing his wife from the middle of the crowd, pulling her back into his shadow.

Bud's moves were unquestionable, his motive purely protective, but like a cooler filled with ice water being dumped over heads, the crowd was doused with awareness of Nan's overwhelm. Respectfully deaccelerating, some returned to the doorways. Others, coached by Bud's expression, lowered their voices, slowed their pace, and gave way to allow the women some uninvaded space. The whole of downtown Loyalville, mostly the patrons from Betty's Diner who came out to the sidewalk to celebrate the reunion, switched their focus to Nan. With one less heartbreak, all hoped Nan's health might begin to improve.

The robust owner of the diner, Betty, fancied herself a humorist to anyone who could take a joke, and a middle-aged Mami, to those who needed growing-up. After the hubbub died down, and Nan and Bud were on their way home, she offered Debbi a cup of coffee, and came to her point immediately.

"I can tell by your expression, you be wonderin' what is wrong with that one. She's not the same girl she was when you knew her. Eternally heartbroken, that's what we all said, that girl could not get over you leavin' without saying your good-byes. Don't know if she's showed you? Nan's got miniature pictures of you's two, at around thirteen years, be my guess, that she's got hangin' in a gold heart locket around her neck. She's kept it these twenty years you've been gone. For years, she was a fearful frazzled teenager, more than any other I've known. That there little piece of jewelry, to her a prized possession, has allowed her to keep her best friend in reach. I've seen it dozens of times, when she feels stressed, she'll clutch that heart mightily, as if it was your own hand. She found her peace in pretending you never did mysteriously disappear, now she won't have to pretend anymore. After high school she did pretty well being involved in the care of little children, as long as they weren't the snotty types. And who knows, maybe if things had gone different, maybe her nervous condition would have waned in time. I'm no doctor, but I can tell you her condition had to be part biological, and part trauma, even before the big fire."

Mesmerized by Betty's candid insights, Debbi asked if she could say more about the catastrophic fire.

"It was right about five years after you been gone, and life around here was beginnin' to get back to routine for them that missed you, especially your parents. And that was when Nan started dating Bud. About that time, that fancy horse owner, the one with that big place on the mountain, maybe you remember he employed lots of folks around here up at his big estate and horse barns? Well, Nan was among 'em, she was working as a Nanny for his son. Never did learn what was the exact cause of that fire, but she was there, and she turned out to be the only one who survived. The boy, his parents, all the staff, and all 'dem famous horses was burned up like they was kindlin. I don't have to tellya what kind of trauma that spelled for Nan. She recovered some, but she was never the same. Eventually she said yes to marrying Bud. She wasn't worried about mixed race children, but it turned out she couldn't have 'em. And it didn't seem to matter, those two were a happy match, at least for a handful of years. Then, the changes started."

Hanging on every syllable, Debbi nodded, eyes wide, "And Bud? Was he to blame?"

"He wondered that too. Fact is, that big ol' guy came askin' if'n I thought she was regretting marrying a black man? I knew there weren't many mixed-race-couples around these parts, and maybe some were ol' school, but I knew that wasn't an issue for Nan. No, she was sweet as pie, even when her memory started taking long siestas. Bud took her to the doctor and pretty soon, after lots of costly tests, he got his answer. Nan was diagnosed with early onset dementia. Canya believe it? I still have a hard time wrapping my head around that one. And when she gets upset by her confusion, which I'm sorry to say happens a lot, her mind hightails it back to y'all's teen years. Luckily, Bud is still in her world, even when the past jumps into the present. I can tellya, he's one of only two people that girl trusts."

"And who is the other?"

"Well if you din't know it already, ya ought to be able to guess it by now, the other one is you. And Lord knows, she's as protective over you as a momma elephant over her own, even if she can't tell day from night. Guess her protective instincts are still intact. As far as I know, she might not know me tomorrow, but you, Debbi Yan, she will never forget."

~

Contrary to the mostly isolate life of a slave, or a contract killer, Debbi Yan of Loyalville had hundreds of people to know and to be known by; one time meet-ups would be a thing of the past. She was now part of a community where people were seen, valued, hugged, and bid farewell, daily.

Becoming Debbi Yan was opening up a pandora's box of human feelings. Lily had to stretch her capacity by utilizing her "nature intelligence" to make sense of "people" feelings, which had been mostly suppressed all of her life. The process could not be quickened, but she found her discernment was improved when she spent time among the trees.

Being real was a brand-new concept for Lily; as a toddler, she had to act like a boy, as the master's child-sex-doll, she had to be eager and willing to act as many different "dolls," each one unique to the game she was told to play. Lily had played with hundreds of men, though rarely more than once. She obeyed her master despite his cruel demands; not knowing any better, she had loved him for saving her.

Life changed when Lily had grown older, and her master found a new child-doll to adore. He wanted Lily to teach his new doll, and the other young one's he enslaved. However, seeing their innocence and recognizing she had once been as pure, Lily had feelings of loss, guilt, and shame. Ultimately, the change in her role produced a desire to protect the other slaves; particularly the one he called Golden Girl. This internal conflict caused her to see the master as bad, especially when he permanently separated Lily from her "Little Dove," aka Golden Girl.

Slave friendships were forbidden, nonetheless, the two slaves found ways to connect. Of course, the master knew, he had arranged their "secret" meetings in order to have a reason to punish them for disobeying. The punishment was to be treated as dogs. Living as animals did not prevent the slaves from developing a strong emotional joining, if anything, it increased their spiritual connection. And then, when Lily was no longer mentally pliable, she was deemed "permanently tainted," and he sentenced her to death. A death she might have accepted, if it had not been for the relationship she had with Little Dove. Little Dove had given her a reason to live.

I will climb and engage with the trees; their spirits will help me to know how to be a friend to so many different humans. Just as the trees drop their leaves, their needles, their cones, I must drop my pretense and be real.

CHAPTER 3

MANNEQUIN MODELING

*What luxury it would be to have a pet, but not one
that requires a cage. I suppose it will be a cat.*

ARIEL

The long hot shower helped Ariel to feel refreshed and unde-terred by the usual desire to go back to her little cot to hide her head under the blankets. It was a new day, and she could imagine her future; it was bright. A few minutes with a comb, and her short hair fell into place, then it was time to apply her makeup. Unfortunately, sitting at her vanity reminded her of the nightmare. To distract her-self, and for inspiration, she picked up her tablet, and navigated to one of her recent discoveries, *Breakfast at Tiffany's*. The movie had become a healthy guilty pleasure. It transported her away from the disturbing past, taking her to a promising "today;" where she needed and wanted to be.

Focusing her energy on her appearance was positive, as she wanted to look her best. Listening, then imitating Hepburn's tone, Ariel tapped into her acting skills. Echoing the movie line playing on the small screen, "It calms me down right away, the quietness, and the proud look of it; nothing very bad could happen to you there, not with those kind men in their nice suits, and that lovely smell of silver and alligator wallets. If I could find a real-life place that made me feel like Tiffany's, then I'd buy some furniture and give the cat a name."

Wearing unadorned black ballet flats, high-waisted cigarette pants, and a black crew neck sweater-cropped, Ariel presented herself out of costume, as genuine as she had ever dared to be in public. After double-checking the address from the job ad, the *Hepburn* styled seeker entered the windowless office space. Just inside, a large color-ful banner announced, *Welcome to A to Z Modeling Agency.* Beside the six-foot rectangular, black and white polka-dotted office desk, there were about thirty daisy-yellow chairs lined up, side by side, in the windowless room. Restlessly, Ariel joined those already occupying seats, careful to keep her feelings away from her face. As she landed on her chair, the other seated bodies turned, eyed her from head to toe, then watched as her delicate hand drew off her over-sized cat-eyed sunglasses. Ariel returned the favor, with pointed glances and polite smiles.

Within ten minutes, all the bright chairs were filled with women in fashionable attire, job questers all tempted by the promise of part-time work, paying more than most earned with full-time work. Once the homogenous group satisfied their visual curiosity with one another, their attention went to the three closed doors, opposite the entry door. Each door was painted a bright Crayola color.

Vivid tangerine, hot magenta, and royal blue now isn't that curious and wonderful!

Ariel had memorized her ninety-six pack of crayons. She enjoyed the familiar colors and assumed the lack of stark office whites meant the people working there were not afraid to be expressive.

I think I like them already, whoever they are, and I hope they will like me too.

The unoccupied office desk and chair were next in line for the job seeker's attention, she read the framed display sign which was positioned in the center of the desk; it did not have personality. "Please be seated," was far from welcoming, but at least it gave the jittery something to do.

To avoid absorbing the growing impertinence in the room and to distract her from the scented air, Ariel decided on a mind journey. She had aversions to strong odors, and there was more than one in the room.

Why do women insist on dousing themselves with fragrance? To make a lasting impression. And, uh, not necessarily a good one.

The heady perfume made the butterflies in her stomach do backflips, and Ariel feared her face had taken on a pale green color. She was still working to re-train her overactive olfactory receptors. She held her chin up, but her mind had another time and place to visit. In the space of a few seconds, three years evaporated, and she was once again in Toronto, on her third day of freedom, and her first interview…

The Mounties were doing their best to provide aid to the featherweight woman with the incredulous story of human bondage, murder, and escape. She had been found as a stowaway on the train two days into the trip, but they kept her on the train until arriving in Toronto. In the police station, while under the authority's spotlight, the fugitive would not confess to killing the man who had enslaved her since the tender age of three; her maudlin account held that her "owner" had been killed by someone else.

"His client surprised him and threatened him with a gun if I was not set free, he pretended to agree, and my cage was unlocked. Shots were fired. My eyes were squeezed shut, I think it was the client who fired last, then they both fell backward."

Little Dove professed that both the intended client, and her slave owner had died, allowing her to make her break.

"I didn't dare look back, I had to run, it was my only chance. There were others, but they were all locked in their cages at the time. I had no choice but to leave them."

"Do you know where you were held, where you were going or where you came from?"

"We were in Vancouver, about to be shipped, to uh, his clients, the client, uh, appeared out of nowhere. It's impossible for me to say where we were imprisoned, we were kept in cages, and we were always transported under cover. The monster who owned me was careful to keep all whereabouts secret, even among his clients."

The female officer spoke up, unsure how hard to press the frail victim, "And yet, one found you?"

"That is what happened, and I learned where I was by reading posted signs after I, I ran. Otherwise, when in the cages, I had no idea where I was, it was always kept from me. Another slave told me that we have been shipped all over the world and then, uh, shipped back to the place, the prison, where he put me. All I know, it wasn't Canada."

"How's that, eh?"

"The warm humid temperatures, the sounds, and the smells. Very different than here. My prison was near an ocean, a warm one, not like here. Not that I ever saw it. I believe I was kept in a cave near the coastline," her voice had become despondent, "not because I ever saw it. Most times, the crashing waves were all that could be heard for days on end."

"You are doing great, don't worry if you cannot remember everything, it's okay, you're safe now. But eh, are you able to say more about the others? Anything would help."

It was a pull for more details. Still, the lenient officers were mild mannered, hoping not to intimidate the suffering victim. Little Dove's balletic body movements, and expressions, were boundaried and gracious, much like a delicate Chantilly lace curtain, fluttering in the breeze, and never losing its form or elegance. Her naivety was part of her act, careful was all she knew to be, the way Lily had taught her. Displaying timidity, she responded to the non-monsters, while continuously processing her intuition.

They don't want to hurt me. They want to understand. Less is more, it is best I know nothing. They like watching me.

To be persuasive, she maintained her eye-contact even while her lean form shook from weakness. Tearfully, but with obvious restraint, she continued.

"You must understand, I was young when my parents were," she swallowed hard, holding back real tears, "murdered." Reaching up and patting her poignant eyes, she continued with a fearful wonderment, "I barely remember what they looked like, let alone the precise location of my Canadian home, my memories have been clouded over the years."

"Are you able to say how they were murdered?"

"Both were shot in the middle of their foreheads, they died instantly."

The seasoned audience, a male, and a female officer, awestruck, almost forgot to be formal. They were enthralled with her demeanor, despite their unanswered questions.

"Do you know where you were when this happened?"

It was clear the woman could not prove her citizenship and had no one to validate her testimony, yet the police were inclined to believe her without hard evidence.

"It's all so fuzzy, those early memories, it is not easy to distinguish between what I remember, and what was told to me. I think we went to a place called Mexico for a winter holiday. I remember the snow on the windowsill outside, and my mother let me choose a summer sundress from a catalog; I was wearing it, when it happened. My father was driving, laughing. There was happy music playing on the radio, we were singing along. I was in the backseat looking out at the clouds in the sky. The car stopped. There was a whoosh sound, then blood was splashed all over my white dress. My mother screamed. Another whoosh sound, then nothing. My parents were dead, and I was alone. He said I was there for days."

"He?"

"I was found by my captor. Because he saved me, I belonged to him. That is what I grew up believing."

The fluid eloquence with which she spoke was marked by a gloomy persuasiveness. Like a spider spinning a sticky web, Little Dove had methodically unfolded her tale, using words and ideas never articulated distinctly before, yet spoken penetratingly, as if well-rehearsed. She had recognized the significant landmarks in the city; Casa Loma Castle, CN Tower, and the Royal Museum, all places connected to the faint recollection of a lost life.

Although thin, and emotionally damaged, the authorities could see she was intelligent, even if she lacked knowledge of current events and some commonly used words and phrases. However, her appearance perplexed them. Unlike other victims held for significant periods, they noted her teeth and gums were healthy and flawlessly straight and white, they were hardly a testimony of maltreatment.

"How were you able to get to the dentist, eh?"

"I, uh, I do not understand what you are asking. Where is a dentist?"

"No, it's not a place, a dentist is a person. You know, someone who does dental work? A person who fixes cavities, puts on braces?"

"I do not understand what your words are asking."

"I'm sorry Miss, we wondered how you came to have such a perfect smile and how did you take care of your teeth during your imprisonment?"

"Oh. My teeth. If I had use of hands, I was responsible for cleaning my teeth. When I wasn't permitted to be human, I mean, at times he made us act like dogs, and dogs don't have hands, they have paws, so, the master had, uhmm, dentists, clean me, if that's who they were. I mean he had them fit me for, uhmm, sometimes metal devices were put into my mouth to keep me from talking, and to keep my teeth straight. He was a maniac about me being, uh, perfect. I wasn't supposed to be awake or know about those who, uh, cleaned me."

The police were made speechless, but their incredulous eyes wanted more information.

Oh, no, don't share too much, they cannot bear to hear it. Look how they wince, their knowing glances at one another, look how their breath is shallow.

"Are you able to say how many of them there were?"

"He kept many kennels."

"Oh, no, I meant how many other slaves did he keep?"

"I wasn't permitted to know anyone unless you count the teaching slave. But I heard many voices over the years."

She made her final plea, "I can't remember any other details, I've told you all I know, except, here, look here, at my knees. These brands are all that is here to prove I'm telling you the truth." She revealed her scarred knees. "I'm ready to get rid of these marks and leave the past behind me. I'm not looking for anything more than to start over. A home, a place to root, heal, and start a free life."

The police, fully captivated, if not beguiled, were dazed by the scars on her knees, where she had been horribly branded. Her fingerprints and the skin on the bottom of her feet were also burnt to keep her from being identified. Her story and her scars convinced the Mounties, and she was taken to the hospital to be checked for other injuries and given additional care.

Within a 72-hour period, Jolene Johnson was created. The officers who had interviewed her went to give her the good news.

Upon hearing her new name, the pencil-thin woman, smiled from her eyes, coyly batting them for special effect, "Nice to meet you, I'm Jolene Johnson."

Liking how it rolled off her tongue, she decided to have fun with it. Without modesty, enjoying her moment of triumph, she chimed the country song she had heard on the radio earlier that day.

"Jolene, Jolene, Jolene, Jolene, please don't take him just because you can."

Smirking, the officer's reaction spurred her on. She sang a few more words, and then trailed off into giggles. It was her first taste of being silly, and for her, it was fanciful and freeing. The name they gave her mattered not. She guessed that "Jo" would make a good neutral-gender nickname; she liked the thought of identifying as non-binary. The two officers reacted to the melodic tune she sang.

They looked at one another, nodded, and said in unison, "Eh, you sound just like her!"

Grinning with satisfaction, the eager impersonator tried the "Dolly" accent again, paraphrasing something the famed singer said on the radio program.

"Oh my dear, I'm no Dolly, and I ain't no singer, but you'll never do a whole lot unless you're brave enough to try."

"Well, ain't that the truth Miss Jolene Johnson, and perhaps you should seek work in the country music industry, you're a natural, eh."

The starstruck female officer was certain the recovering victim could be an instant success. *Jolene's* newfound bravery had her wishing, not for a singing career, but for her own life to begin.

It is only a name, what about the rest? They can't give me a life. They can't bring Lily back. I have nothing but a name, no child of my own, no love in my life. I know these people are sincere, but they have no idea who I am. And there are many men who know exactly who I am. No. Who I was. How can I know what is true? I guess I'm safe enough, and the doctor here has been positive. She said I am in good health. Good enough to be released. She also said I was well enough to have corrective surgery for my knees.

Maintaining her guard, *Jo* pressed forward, judging her situation to be "safe enough." With reassurance from the supporting officers, and a newly developing mindset prioritizing self-care, she decided to take advantage of the Canadian health benefits being offered. Plastic surgery had been performed on her numerous times during her slave years, this time it would be her choice, not the perfection-driven master's order.

Signing her new name on the authorization forms felt like a necessary milestone to taking control over her life. Arguably, the only exception to being flawless was the monster's mark signifying she was not her own. Designed as a continuous line, a little larger than the size of a quarter, his mark was an imperceptible JON, encircled with spikes. *Jo* wanted it erased.

Sixteen days later, following scar revision surgery for her "branded" knees, *Jo* nervously waited for the final release order to be given. Gone was the warmth from the covering which had been laid over her form, and the stubborn chills gathering on her hands and feet, had taken notice. The dreamy terror, brought on by the familiarity of waking from general anesthesia crept into her stomach and disguised her sense of smell. Knowing it would pass, *Jo* did not bother reporting the sensation.

"Eh, there you are I see, and you're a beauty, eh, according to the doctor. How are you feeling?"

"I feel good, may I leave?"

"Not yet, but soon you'll be moved to the pink chesterfield room, it is much warmer in there."

Picking up the patient's hand to view the wristband, the medical attendant continued, "State your name and date of birth?"

Pulling her hand back, *Jo* wiped tears away with hesitant embarrassment. She was shaking.

"Eh? Just give'er, tearing up and chills are commonplace after surgery, you'll be feeling chipper in no time, eh? Says here you are Jolene Johnson, born on February 29, 1995, eh, does that sound true?"

No one knows what is true about me, I suppose that day and year is as good as any.

Opening her mouth to speak, *Jo* felt uneven and chilled. The nurse must have been briefed of her situation; he went about pulling the intravenous line which had been put into her arm. He was gentle, but it brought back memories from her past. Stuffing her feelings, she focused on the colorless walls that surrounded her.

"I…I am cold, might there be another flannel covering?"

The weight of lingering thoughts was forcing moisture into her blue eyes.

"Yes, I have one ready for you." A warmed blanket was retrieved, unfolded to the chest, and tucked snuggly around *Jo's* feet.

Jo used her newly developed Tennessean twang, "I can tell you I wasn't born yesterday, and you can call me ready to tap right out of this place."

"Them's jokes you got there, eh? Sorry, you won't be dancing too quick for a few weeks."

With no further questions, the nurse completed his tasks and called for an orderly. Before she knew it, the four white walls, begging for an identity, were traded for shades of pink and a TV. Feeling warmed, more alert, and considerably less nervous, *Jo*, idly watched the monitor suspended from the ceiling in the corner of the room. The station, airing news, was reviewing the top early morning stories, among them, a woman kidnapped in Montreal. The event was said to have occurred at a grocery mart, in broad daylight, in front of a handful of customers and employees. The victim, a cashier named Joanne Johnsen.

What?! Joanne Johnsen, Jolene Johnson, how? How could anyone know?

Upon hearing the victim's name, *Jo's* hopeful face turned white, her armpits sweated up, and her heart quickened. Trained intuition seized her widening pupils and spoke up.

Someone has tracked me to my new name, and lucky for me, they chased the wrong person. So much for being hidden in Canada. I should never have trusted a system run by men with unchecked power. Too much power bears bad seeds disguised as good deeds. Lily's words, and true once more. If Lily were alive, she would say what is best to do. A breathy sigh pushed back from the mental weakness. *Wait. No. I can't let myself think that way. She would trust me to decide for myself. She would remind me of my strength. There is strength in tolerating small misfortunes. I must leave but I need not panic.*

～～

Returning to the present day, Ariel was suddenly aware that the sickening perfume had managed to fade away. The flying ribbons over the air vent explained the change. There was another woosh of air when the magenta painted door opened wide, and a spectacular forty-something brunette, wearing a wireless headset, entered the room.

Wow, she's beautiful. Game on.

The brunette was rocking a revealing electric green leather dress, with cutouts, very high-end chic fashion. Her face looked girl-next-door, but her attire, and five-inch stilettos said otherwise. The arresting woman walked past the row of spectators, her pacing, runway-like, with three point turns on each end. Back and forth, rhythmically, she worked the room of onlookers like they were her puppets. Most were guilty of flirting with the high slits in her skirt every time she passed by. The gaps divided the skirt into four sections that were smartly attached to the top bodice with leather loops.

I wonder why she moves like that, like she's tempting us? Oh, and I see she has nothing under her skirt, no pubic hair to tell us her true hair color. Her skin is lovely, tanned, with no tan lines.

The enchantress ceremoniously began, "Please call me Anne. I am here to orient you to the position you are seeking, and I am here to answer your questions. This is a special employment opportunity, and it takes a particular type of lady to fill the requests we receive from our clientele, one must be quite disciplined at ignoring distractions."

"Perhaps," she continued with the slightest hesitation, as if she did not know to whom she wanted to direct her script, "you will be successful in passing the pre-employment prerequisites. If you are chosen, and if you can prove yourself in front of a sampling of our clients during the action-interview, you will be welcomed to our team of accomplished mannequin models. Our clientele has come to expect the highest level of customer service, and my task today is to screen out those who are unable to meet our expectations. Now then, please remain in your seats, and I will come to you for personal introductions."

Ariel found herself tempted to keep looking at the flesh that lay beneath the green leather skirt. It had been many months since she was able to enjoy skin time with another, especially one as flawless as she appeared to be. Not wanting to lose her focus, she forced her eyes to stay on the woman's angular face. The green goddess walked around to greet each of the women, inviting each to state first name and age, then stand and turn for her before returning to their seat.

"I am Ariel, twenty-five."

When all were greeted and minimally assessed, the goddess resumed her pacing.

She keeps looking back at me, she approves, glad I decided on this outfit.

Anne kept her movement methodical, then quickening her steps, working up to a crescendo. When she finally stopped, she made direct eye contact with Ariel, holding her stare, as she articulated more information.

"Some of you may be here as long as two hours this morning, I do hope you ate breakfast before coming. Clients tend to like lean, but never forget, no one wants to hear your stomach gurgling."

Ariel reflexively reached for her tummy, and nodded, affirming she had eaten. This garnered a pleasing smile, before the electric green skirt twisted into an elegant pose. Anne's silhouette, like a Michelangelo sculpture, drew a breathy hush from her captive audience. Then, like a dancer, she gracefully bent forward, reaching out with a flattened back, dropping her gaze to the floor, and pushing her bare bottom out boldly. Anne held her pose for dramatic effect, before adjusting her stride, stepping beyond her shoulder's width. Her mechanical moves were practiced to the point of fluidity, while still being mannequinlike. As she slowly rose, she purposely stepped back into another provocative position, nearly pressing her lady parts into the face of her target. The recipient, at first doe-eyed, leaned back, and dramatically turned her head away. Her snarled lips told of her decided distaste for the unapologetic, if not shameless choreography. Anne sensed the disdain, turned abruptly, squaring herself with her target, and moved to a respectful distance.

Anne started with her eyes, a steel gaze. Her soft voice contradicted the look, "Did you say Bianca? Your name, it was Bianca, correct? Do I offend you?"

The angry-embarrassed woman was fiddling with her bag, and unconsciously shaking her crossed leg. The other women, including Ariel, were mannequin still, as they watched the interaction. All waited for her response. The lull, finally getting her attention, caused the woman to abruptly sit up to speak.

"I, uh, yes, it's Bianca, but I doubt I'm the only one thinking that was, uh, rather unladylike, to show off your, uh, derriere. You nearly sat on my face."

Nodding her head like the woman, the green temptress repeated herself with emphasis, "Did I offend you, Bianca?"

Remembering what was at stake, regretting her denunciation, but not knowing how to unspeak it, the woman stuttered, "Uhh, I, no, I mean, I'm sorry, I have misspoken. You are only doing your job."

Ignoring the guilty apologist, then clearing her throat in an assertive manner, Anne asked the rest of the room, "Is there anyone besides Bianca who is offended by my demonstration? If so, please, let's agree to be honest with one another."

Not waiting for a response, she took another few steps to reach the center of the room. Without hesitation, Anne reached for her hem, pulling off the green layer easily, exposing her beautiful naked form. Dropping the garment, then looking directly at Bianca again, she asked, "Which part most offends you?"

Bianca's face turned such a shade of red, it looked like her head might blow off her neck at any moment. She opened her mouth, as if to say more, then closed it. Clearly shaken, she collected herself, stood, and left the office without looking back.

Anne stood proudly, "Anyone else uncomfortable with nudity? Because there are many customers who prefer their model's nude, or who themselves may choose to be naked during the gig. In fact, be warned, all will be rendered naked for their action-interview."

Her statement caused movement among those assembled, then one by one, another six women clumsily found their way out of the office, as if they could not get away fast enough.

Smiling broadly now, Anne did not hide her pleasure, "For those who choose to continue, I want to be clear, this is not prostitution, the employer is not a pimp, there is no sex involved, ever, but this is not a job for the modest. However, you can be assured, whether you are clothed or not, our clientele understands that touching any of our professional models, at any time-which includes before, during, and after the gig, is strictly forbidden. Touching a model constitutes the breaking of our contract, and there are associated financial consequences. Now then, shall we continue?"

The room was quiet. Most could not help but appreciate Anne's dignified poise, even while wearing only a headset and high heels.

She shows no guile. Getting naked for income is not my first choice, but getting paid in cash, and the strict anonymity, this is ideal, if I can make the cut.

"We pay very well. We ask no questions of you, only that you stay flexible, conform to our standards, and that you keep a healthy appearance. We have hairdressers and make-up artists who will aid you, when we need a more dramatic style, otherwise, we want you to be yourself. We need all body types, but we prefer lean models who have a stable body weight, and who are comfortable in their own skin. Alright. Your completed, signed paperwork should be returned to our receptionist, who will then give you a number. Please stay seated until your number is called for further screening. Thank you, and good luck."

Anne turned and exited behind the magenta door. Before Ariel could think further, the tangerine door opened, birthing a secretary-type, balancing a tall stack of paper filled clipboards. She managed to keep from dropping them on the desk, then looked up, surprised the women were not already moving to get started on their applications.

The paperwork was dissimilar to most other job applications, with few blanks to fill, mostly boxes to check for interests and experience, but the last page captured Ariel's attention.

"There is no speaking or moving allowed during interviews. Breaking silence, and/or discernable movement, may result in imme-diate dismissal. All applicants will be notified when the still period is over, and Q&A time will be provided, if needed, at the end."

Oh, they need to see we can keep still, and questions will only show ignorance.

Intuition was instructing Ariel, she continued reading down the page.

Silent periods, for both pre-employment, and job assignments will not exceed two-hour periods. Applicants must sign the non-disclosure agree-ment before their interview can begin. Specialized training will be pro-vided, as needed for worthy candidates. If hired, each model maintains the right to refuse an assignment, based on personal needs, no more than once per month. We expect our models to do three assignments in a cal-endar month, at a maximum of two hours per gig, with an added paid hour for travel time. We recommend the use of a monophasic combina-tion birth control pill, to support fewer bleeding days, and reduced PMS symptoms, since this can be problematic for most assignments.

The last line left Ariel feeling indignant.

Hmmm, that's presumptuous. I don't bleed.

Ariel looked around the room, then back to the clipboard in her lap.

You know it's death if the wrong people come to recognize me. But who's to say they could recognize me; his brands are gone. I'd be a prop, a deaf mute one. Nothing shameful about it, even naked is no big deal. The types I'm avoiding would never be satisfied with just looking at women. Being still and quiet for only two hours, a cakewalk compared to the wheel or days in cages where I couldn't move. No sex involved, and it promises to pay better than anything I've seen. The don't-ask-don't-tell goes both ways, it feels safe.

CHAPTER 4

A BOX OF JOURNALS

"Preserve your memories, keep them well,
what you forget you can never retell."

LOUISA MAY ALCOTT

There was no such thing as "leisure time" for Lily as she embraced the personality of her new alter. She had accepted a job at the Main Street Postal Store. Accordingly, it became a regular stop for Nan and Bud on their afternoon walks. Each time, Nan would be thrilled to see her friend, her exuberance never failed, even if her memory continued to decline.

"Debbi I'm so happy you were not hurt, I have missed you, I didn't know if you would ever come back. Tell me you won't leave again."

"Please don't worry my friend. I'm here to stay."

"Good. I wrote you lots of notes. You will need to catch up. Tell her Bud, tell her she needs to catch up."

Bud began awkwardly, "I know Nan, I know you're excited Debbi is back, but she is working now. She works here. We can catch up later."

"Bud, not you. No boys allowed. Please, it's Debbi's turn and her Papa made only one key."

An odd-looking key was tied to a braided tri-colored string and held out as an offering to Debbi. When she did not respond, Nan spoke up with urgency, "Take it, go on."

"Thank you, Nan."

Accepting the red, white, and blue loop with some reluctance, Debbi had no idea what it meant. She did not know that Nan had the antique key in her possession the day young-Debbi disappeared, and she had kept it all twenty years, telling no one. Nan watched her friend's face, she did not see what she expected.

"It's your turn." Nan, abruptly distressed, "You have the key now, it is your turn."

"Thank you, Nan, but I am working right now. How about we get together once I am off my shift? I will come over and I will bring dinner. We will catch up on the notes together, won't that be nice?"

"You be nice, Debbi with an i, it is your turn. You need to go." Nan's agitation was growing.

Not wanting to see his wife become upset, Bud tried to assist in helping things make sense. "Nan, listen, she can't go now, she is working. See. She is working."

Bud had pointed to the nametag Debbi was wearing, as if seeing it would help his wife to understand. His effort was in vain.

"Not now, Bud. Debbi? We made a pinky promise. It is your turn. You go and..." Nan stopped mid-sentence and moved to hide behind Bud when other customers entered the shop. Her body language, already juvenile, told Bud that she was becoming overwhelmed. She was uncomfortable around most people, more so when boxed in. He would need to get her out of the shop and back outside before her mood swung too far south. Hiding his breaking heart from his voice as he took hold of his wife's hands and looked squarely into her face.

"Nan, it's okay, we will see Debbi later. You can tell her all about it later when she brings dinner. She is busy now."

Like a scene out of King Kong, Bud's huge, calloused hands

enclosed Nan's, then tenderly, he drew one arm around her, bringing her to his side. "See, she is busy now."

"She is busy?" The frantic blaze of darting eyes, slowed, a new focus began clouding Nan's vision. Concentrating with all of her might, Nan squeezed her eyes closed to process the cyclone of confusion.

What was I saying? What was it? I know it is important, I can feel it. Why can't I remember? Why am I here? Why can't I remember? Think.

Nan's apprehension turned to fear. Although she felt strongly about something, she could not remember what it had been. She tucked herself more deeply into Bud's shoulder, as if in doing so, she could make herself disappear. Debbi remained quiet, keeping her questions to herself. Nan was not well. Nan was not well. Not only did she want to avoid upsetting the frail woman, but she was unclear on where the answers might lead.

Bud turned his wife away from the counter and moved toward the exit. Opening the door with his free hand, Bud looked back over his bulky shoulder, giving Debbi an embarrassed smile. She nodded in return, understanding his pain. A few hours later, Bud called Debbi to ask about the clandestine note sharing with Nan.

"She expects you to write her a note and return the key once the note has been placed into the box, the one your father made for you. She said the two of you made a pact in second grade not to tell anyone else about the box. I seriously don't know how many notes she's written, but she claims she never stopped writing you. She won't tell me anything else."

"My memory is a little foggy on the details of our note exchange ritual. I can't remember where we kept the box, but clearly Nan has not forgotten. How about a girl-only walk after dinner? She could take me to it, and if you want, you can follow us, so you will know too?"

"Sounds like a good plan. Thank you Debbi."

The plan worked beautifully. Learning the location of the lockbox filled with childhood journals was a major game changer, there was much history to read. The school-girl notebooks were filled front to back, edge to edge with handwritten print, and had other scraps of white and colored papers stuffed between the pages. Some notes were written in a secret code, as young diary keepers are prone to do with sensitive topics. Venting about school yard, and neighborhood dramas, often wishing the mean kids would leave them alone, Debbi read her way through the beginning years.

Lily also had experience with bullies, as a child and as a sub-slave. In young Debbi's case, she wrote about being found alone, the children tormentors encircling her, trapping her in their hand-held jail. Their sing-song voices would prattle on until Debbi screamed for help, or until an adult approached them.

"No one wants to play with Debbi with three eyes, she can tell you the day you're gonna die." The bullies were also fond of booing and making graveyard jokes. "Booo-oooo-ooo, Debbi Yan is cursed, she speaks ghost, and she digs graves faster than most."

In response to the bullying, one entry read, "The mean kids were rude to me and Nan today. I cried because Nan cried. They did not get in trouble. Nan was sent home. I was sent to clean the chalkboard. It is not fair. Papa said ignore their words for they are not worth our tears. Mama said they are just afraid of their own shadow. Mama said I was not cursed. She said I was blessed with a special gift, passed down from the first Yan's who came to America and worked in the mine."

Evidently, the bullies were not making it up, Debbi Yan did have a "death knowing." Nan's whispered secrets, together with the diary entries, revealed the greater story. At age four, Debbi Yan innocently collected flowers when she perceived someone was about to die. She went with the memorial bouquets, insisting her parents take her to a specific household, albeit strangers to all of them. Each time, some person had indeed died. At age six, the child seer began to ask if she could say goodbye to the dying, before the death occurred. Her parents did not deny her requests. They did ask those involved to keep the information to themselves, hoping to protect the child from those who would not understand her rare gift; the word got out despite the parent's wishes.

Then, at age thirteen, Debbi Yan made her first public prediction; it would also be her last. Following an uneventful morning with no lingering premonitions, Debbi left for school as she always did, walking with her best friend, Nan. The normalcy of the day vanished when the teacher noticed a sudden change in the young teen during the morning all-school announcements.

According to Nan's journal entry, "Like a robot, Debbi stood up and walked out of the classroom, ignoring our teacher's requests to return to her seat. I could not imagine why she started acting that way. Debbi always did what she was told, but she ignored me when I tried to talk to her. All the kids got restless, so I left the chaos before it made me crazy. I had to know what she was doing. I pleaded for her to stop and talk to me, but it was like she was in a trance. She walked into the principal's office, without knocking on her door. I was afraid, but I followed her. Debbi stared at the microphone held by the principal, she didn't ask, she just grabbed it out of her hand. All I could do was stand there, it happened so fast. Principal Cuevas was so shocked she forgot how to speak. Debbi spoke eerily, as if she had instantly become a grown-up. She said, "Soon, I will leave you. My time on earth has been brief, but my spirit will carry on. Warning to the innocents, be wise about who you trust. Be aware. Don't be still, make noise, be seen, and do not go out alone."

Nan's entry had been underlined and circled with purple ink. Her next note was scribbled in the page border next to the circled quote. "This morning when Debbi finished speaking, she fainted. Mrs. Cuevas called 911 and an ambulance came to take Debbi to the hospital. I hope she does not die!!! My Mom won't let me go to see her. She says Chinese people are weird and smell funny because they eat fish heads. She doesn't know anything. Debbi would never eat a fish head. And the Yan's are the nicest and cleanest people I know."

The next diary entry was dated three days later. "Debbi can't remember the day she fainted. She doesn't even remember talking on the microphone in Mrs. Cuevas' office. She can't remember me and everyone yelling at her to stop. She said she just woke up at the hospital and felt fine, except she didn't know why she was in the hospital. Mama Yan told me I should not worry. She says I worry too much. My mom doesn't care what happened, she doesn't care if my best friend had to go to the hospital. She thinks Debbi was faking, but I know she wasn't. Mama Yan said Western doctors do not understand spiritual health. I am so happy she did not die."

Reading the diary entries made by young-Debbi, it appeared the teenager had no recollection of her "performance" at school, nor her "death knowing." Thereafter, the once timid girl turned into a typical teenager; one who was more interested in having autonomy than being spiritually gifted. A few other entries by Nan made it clear the milestone event had indeed changed Debbi Yan.

"It has been two weeks since Debbi was possessed. I wonder if body snatchers took her and put another girl in her place? She is still my best friend but now she doesn't believe me when I tell her she used to know when people were about to die. Mama Yan told me not to worry. She said it is best to accept that Debbi has forgotten what she used to know. Why do grownups think they know best? Mama Yan said she is the same person, only she is growing up."

Debbi stayed curious about what Nan had to say about the days leading up to the day young-Debbi was taken, as well as after the event.

"Forget everything I've ever written about Mama Yan. I hate her. My life is officially over. How can I ever go to school without my best friend? My mom said homeschooling is best for freaks and geeks, I hate her too! Why does Debbi have to leave school? She is not a freak! She is smarter than me, but I think the Yan's are afraid the mean boys will start bullying her again. My mom says it isn't bullying, it is just boys liking girls, and not knowing how to act. She says Mrs. Yan is afraid her daughter wants to run away with a boy. That is the dumbest thing anyone ever said! Debbi would never leave me, and she doesn't even like boys."

Out of concern for their daughter's safety, based on the past accuracy of her predictions, the Yan's, did in fact, pull Debbi out of school. She was homeschooled by her mother and put into self-defense martial arts, with accelerated lessons; a fortunate parallel for Lily who studied martial arts following her escape from slavery. The Yan's also refused to let their daughter be alone with other youth. They hired an adult guardian to be with her whenever they needed to be at work. Irrespective of their efforts, less than a year after the prediction in the principal's office, Debbi disappeared, having become momentarily separated from her guardian and Nan, while walking through the graveyard.

According to Nan's tear-stained post-disappearance entry, "The body snatchers came back and took her because she knew too much, right? Revenge of ghosts? Evil spirits sucked her down into the earth? What other explanation is there?! I was there and I saw nothing! No one saw or heard anything, one minute she was there, and the next, she was gone. I want to die! Why did I walk away from her? If I had held her hand, maybe they would have taken me too. How can I ever live with myself if I don't dig up every single grave until I find her?"

By reading through Nan's later entries, it was clear the investigating police had been previously acquainted with the "psychic kid," who once had predicted the unexpected death of a fellow officer. The lead officer admitted he thought she had run away, he said as much during a follow-up interview with Nan. Reading that the police were bold enough to speak about the incident, in such a manner, with Nan, a minor at the time, convinced Lily a bias had affected the investigation.

The Yan's had a longer history in the area than most, they were a respectable family who helped to build the town of Loyalville. However, in this situation, Lily could see that their longevity did not win them any favors. The detective told Nan to admit the truth. He believed Debbi Yan had run away. Nan denied knowing anything about her wanting to leave, and she filled five diary pages with her two take-away thoughts, "Debbi would never leave me, she will come back. Debbie would never leave me, she will come back…"

Bent on using their biased logic, in conjunction with the parent's adamant refusal to mourn their missing daughter, and the locals holding on to the idea that one of their own could not possibly have been taken right from under their nose, the police dropped the case. The Yan's went on with their life, always believing their daughter would return.

Staying true to their belief, eighteen years later, hunched in the office of their lawyer and trust officer, the Yan's protected their daughter's future by ensuring their assets would be saved for her return. Mrs. Yan was adamant in retelling the story to her returned daughter.

"I said, unless you can provide a death certificate, my husband and I are of the belief that our daughter is still alive, we expect her soon, and we wish to make her our sole beneficiary. Our lawyer said he understand, but he kept recommending that we reconsider. Then your Papa spoke English to them. Like a stout oak, he would not bend." Mama Yan continued in her energetic way, "He stood up straight, sticking his chin out as he spoke, saying, Gentlemen, lady, and beloved wife, this dialog must cease. My decision is final. We leave all to our daughter, who will return to us in our time of need."

As Debbi came to know, her Papa was a listener, a man of few words. Mama Yan loved to say, "Papa would have the last word on the matter, in English, to be sure there was no misunderstanding."

～⁓

Although Debbi did all she knew to make her *re-claimed parents'* lives easier, the Yan's health had severely declined in their daughter's absence. Two years was all they had together before their hearts failed them; first Mrs. Yan, and nine days later, Mr. Yan. As planned, all was left to their daughter, a marriage dowry, home and property, savings, and a profitable business.

The inheritance did not affect Debbi's simplistic lifestyle. Instead, she became known for her generosity, always giving to any locals in need. To the employees who had faithfully labored for her parents, she gave in equal parts, the family business. All she asked for in return, to be able to take flowers from the garden department whenever she deemed necessary, to keep her families' graves pleasant and cheerful.

～⁓

The ostensible ease of becoming part of the community did not soften the former slave and she had not come empty handed. Besides

Debbi's inheritance, Lily had accumulated considerable wealth of her own. Her assets, hard-earned, gratuities successfully hidden when she was a sex slave, and cash from the in-between years, when she worked as an assassin. It took months to discreetly collect the funds from the agencies, banks, and the other hiding places around the world, but ultimately, she collected a net sum of 10 million.

Needing a secure place to keep her assets, Debbi bought an altar-tomb, built to resemble a Ming tomb, to place over the graves of her parents. It was the largest in the Loyalville cemetery, which caused some older locals to gossip about the prodigal daughter, saying it was a symbol of her guilt for having neglected her parents for twenty years. In fact, the graveyard supplied the *perfect home* for Lily's belongings. As far as she could see, visitors did not linger, and they were too focused on their own grief to be curious about other mourners. The inner part of the tomb had secret overhead compartments to store her cash and her arsenal of weapons, and it had an inner safe room, giving her a place to hide if danger came looking for Lily.

Absorbing the stolen identity, Debbi blended into the community and was accepted as if she had never been gone. However, taking advantage of friendship, without giving back, was not the kind of person Debbi determined to be. At her core, she felt compelled to be "good" so as not to disappoint the Yan's spirits when they came around to see how she was doing. Debbi felt "being good" meant "doing good," she wanted to make right the wrong done to the Yan family. As her Mama Yan had said, without standards no boundaries are set, and Debbi needed her boundaries.

CHAPTER 5

PROTECTIVE CUSTODY

"I cannot fix on the hour, or the spot, or the look or the words, which laid the foundation. It is too long ago. I was in the middle before I knew that I had begun."

JANE AUSTEN

Returning from her first successful job interview, Ariel cautiously rejoiced that she was asked to return for an "action interview."

I have a chance to become a paid model, it means I'm a day closer to becoming a whole, real person. I need to eat. They want models who maintain their size and appearance. I've finally put on enough weight that my bones are not poking through! And not even one person said anything about me being too skinny, and they don't need fingerprints! Ha! I'm on a roll. I'm so happy I don't have to explain my knees, the skin grafts are barely noticeable.

The memory of her surgery back in Toronto returned to her mind. Reaching down to both knees, she touched the smooth skin.

If I had returned for the follow-up appointment, very likely, I would have been caught by the person who had set out to catch a runaway slave.

Revisiting her time in protective custody as Jolene Johnson, Ariel's mind returned to the days after her knees repaired…

When the nurse returned to the recovery room to check Jolene's status, there was no trace of her, only a *forgotten* cell phone. *Jo* had skipped taking the planned transportation, her instincts waved red flags on the driver who sat waiting for her. She found another taxi. It was not an option to run away, not if she wanted her knees to heal. Instead, she made herself return to the hotel room, to concentrate on the healing her knees needed. Sitting in the common space by the elevator on her floor, to keep an eye out for those coming and going, legs extended with the support of a low table, *Jo* felt agitated.

I can't let myself think the worst. I'm stuck here but I don't want to feel like a trapped animal. I need to read, I'm sure there is more to un-learn, where is the newspaper?

Her psychic equilibrium could be somewhat stabilized by attaining information, and there was as much to learn as there was to un-learn about living as a *free* person. Nevertheless, she remained cautious.

Don't oversaturate your mind, this is not a good time to feel over-whelmed. I need to pace my brain exercise as much as I need to pace my movements, and panic does me no good. The cute doctor was right, I get panicky when I am not able bodied. She was funny asking how will I eat an elephant? Yes, good doctor, one bite at a time. She meant take it slow, don't rush to do everything all at once, especially don't rush while my knees are healing.

Learning, too quickly about the world she had been isolated from, was not without consequences. Processing new concepts sometimes produced emotional stormy a-ha realizations, and self-recriminations. Physically, it was like a mental power surge, which activated her pulse rate and accelerated her spinout.

I can't let myself panic, like when the radio clock started that alarm, and started playing music and I couldn't find the right buttons to turn it off, and then housekeeping came pounding at the door, I know it was all the sounds that I could not stop that made me think something bad was coming for me, and all the while it was so simple, just pull the plug. Keep it simple, small bites, one at a time.

Following two uneventful weeks in her room, with no signs of infection and very little pain, her list of unanswered questions had become the size of an elephant. The news reads were no longer sufficient, and although the lobby magazines were added to her reading schedule, she wanted more answers.

Why does a radio clock have so many buttons, how does a coffee maker know how much liquid to drip, how does a freezer stay cold, where do rainbows come from, and whatever happened to the woman with JJ initials, who was kidnapped in Montreal? The housekeeper said I can find answers at the library, she said the bus stops at the Lillian H. Smith Public Library.

The low-rise building, built to resemble a castle, was just as the housekeeper described. There were several thought-provoking architectural aspects, however, *Jo* was spellbound with the large bronze griffins flanking the entrance. They were monster-sized compared to her petite stature, and never having seen such creatures before, she did not know what to make of them. Standing between them, mouth open, *Jo* looked to one and then the other, and then made two figure eight circles around the pair. A group of children approached, and seeing her attention to the statues, stopped to see what held her gaze. Their near proximity distracted Jo's fixation on the unusual sighting, and the adult accompanying the children, made use of the teachable moment.

"Boys and Girls, you know this library was built to house and protect children's literature, and here, we have arrived at the castle entrance. Does anyone know why these bronze creatures would be placed here to welcome us?"

Jo wondered too. No one ventured a hand in the air to respond, but the question had peaked interest.

"These beasts are found in many ancient cultures, they represent strength and intelligence, they are called Griffins. They are legendary creatures with the body of an eagle, see their heads, their wings, and their talons? But look, an eagle head with horse ears, can you see them? See how they stand erect, ready to listen, like you are all doing right now."

Jo was amused by the children, about kindergarten age, and like them, she had been hooked. Lost in her own wonder, *Jolene* listened as if she belonged to the group of young students.

"Now listen children, I know you will all be eager for the puppet show, but once we ascend the dungeon stairs, you will all need to mind your voices and stay in line with your partners until we find our seats in the theatre, we will be using our ears to hear the show…"

There's a dungeon?

The split-second visit to her past almost made *Jo* bolt. She shook her mind back by tapping into the faces of the children. They were lit up, eyes wide, with joyous smiles.

The dungeon is make-believe, not literal. Puppet show, that's pretend play too.

The teacher went on delighting faces with facts about the mythological creatures, while sneaking in tips about how to behave inside the library, preparing the group to be courteous, respectful, and observant. She also told them how to ask the library staff for assistance, and explained group safety, encouraging them to stay together.

I don't know about your parents, but you are lucky to have a grownup who protects you, and who knows how to talk kid-speak.

The puppet show had left *Jo* feeling warm and bittersweet; it was clear she had been prevented from having a normal childhood, though she chose not to dwell on the loss. Finding her way to the computer learning center, she went to the first person she saw wearing a nametag, just as the children had been advised to do if they became separated from the group. Her backstory was inspired by the marionette's performance.

"Karen? Please, are you able to instruct me how to use this computer?"

"You don't know how to use a computer, you're pulling my leg, eh?"

Karen was certain the patron was teasing.

"What? No, I do not. Please. I have a secretary that manages my social networks. I am curious about how it functions. I am not interested in your leg."

The seasoned library volunteer thought it was unbelievable that a young adult, one with such poise and calm, and flawlessly shaped facial features, had never used a computer. Fifteen minutes later, she thought it was even more amazing how quick the humble, articulate woman was to learn. There were others standing in line at the desk, or else the staff volunteer would have enjoyed lingering to see what would be searched.

"Thank you for your assistance, Karen. You have been a brilliant instructor. I wish to continue on my own, now."

Feeling slightly dismissed by the dazzling smile, the volunteer decided the patron had to have come from royal descent. After pointing her out to a like-minded co-worker, the two agreed.

"I think you're right, that woman is stunning, she must have had work done. And look how she carries herself and how she articulates her words. She must come from money, she's a royal if ever I saw one, eh? Perhaps she snuck away like Ann Hathaway in Princess Diaries, remember that movie?"

"Yes, I do. She must be! Look at her posture, and her hands, how dainty she is. I don't think she was faking about not knowing how to use the computer, can you believe she had never used one before?"

"Not shocking if she has servants and a secretary who do the work. She's smart too, she learned quick. I didn't have to tell her anything twice, she got it the first time."

Keeping a grin from her own face, *Jo* had eavesdropped on the conversation about her, and she did not wish to "lose face." She was pleased with herself; her role play had been effective.

They think I'm a royal? When I return to the hotel, I'll ask at the front desk if it is possible to view Princess Diaries from the television in the room.

Using the search engine as instructed, probing crime news about women from the previous week, *Jo* was stunned how easy and fast the technology produced information; it was like magic. There were numerous stories about muggings, domestic violence, workplace violence, and hate crimes; the expansive list suffered no regret.

Being a woman in the free world, is not for the weak bodied, and definitely not for those weak in spirit, it takes physical strength, courage, and mental métier to survive free living.

Jo's newly formed skill set led her to find a story about a French woman from Canada, who had disappeared while traveling in Tokyo. She noted the incident date was the same as the kidnapping in Montreal.

Witnesses said a slight-bodied woman was pulled from a taxi during heavy traffic, by a thug wearing all black.

Jo's head felt light, and her feet felt heavy.

It could be brutes working for the same person, covering all leads for women leaving Canada, or it could be random violence, that does seem possible.

Thinking of the victimized women made her sad and apprehensive about identifying a pattern. Her heart dropped further when she recalled the trusting faces of those who had assured her of "protected anonymity."

They told me I had nothing to worry about. They asked what I would do with my new life. I did say I planned to travel, and I guess I mentioned Tokyo as a possible destination, but that was only because of the framed photo of the Tokyo skyline in the washroom. There were other officers sitting at desks, close enough to overhear me. No one knew, I had no such intention. How could they? And where else did I say I'd go? Oh yeah, New Zealand.

Within the span of a few more clicks, *Jo* found another incident, reading it to herself as she white knuckled the edge of the table.

Jean-Anne Johnston, a French teacher on sabbatical was taken from a public ferry, by armed men, just off the foggy coast of New Zealand. Witnesses said she was standing alone in the aft, when a highspeed vessel appeared out of nowhere. With swiftness and precision, two men jumped aboard and took the woman before anyone could intervene. The fog prevented the witnesses from agreeing on the type of vessel the perpetrators were using. No one could understand why she was targeted, except to say she was too beautiful and petite to be traveling without a companion.

Closing her eyes to process the words on the screen, *Jo's* breath rate was increasing.

How can there be so many similarities and there not be design? This is not chance. Finding a children's library named Lillian and watching a puppet show, that is chance, but seeing another crime committed against a person who looks like me, with a similar name, on the same day, that is not chance. That could have been me. I cannot ignore this; I must report this to the RCMP.

Upon reporting her belief that she had been the intended victim, *Jolene* was again told not to worry. They did not believe she could decipher facts from fiction, given she had been through some traumatic events. To soften the blow of having her concerns dismissed, they took her to *Timmies* for a "Double Double," and offered her a dart. *Jo* thought the coffee was weak and she did not smoke, but the kindness and the efforts made to listen to her were deeply appreciated. She could feel their sincerity when they assured her that the "JJ" name similarities were "mere chance." Their friendliness was cheering.

"Adjustment will take time. You may not feel your Canuck back is safe, but we're here to make certain it is. You have no problem, eh? We are senior officers in good standing with the RCMP Commissioner, ya-know. But, eh, if it will make you feel better, we will get you referred to a counselor. It is good to talk it out with a mental health expert, don't ya-know."

The problem was *Jo's* gut told her differently, it was insistent. She agreed to seeing a counselor, however, she would not cave from her position, declaring she would keep her whereabouts to herself until the matter was fully investigated. Liam, the counselor, initially considered the "JJ" matters an odd coincidence, much like the authorities. However, her story was compelling, and it was obvious she believed she had been compromised in some way. At the end of their third session, Liam accompanied Jo outside of the building. He wanted to speak to her away from the offices, away from the eyes and ears of others. Based on the paperwork which included her testimony to the RCMP, his superior had insisted Jolene was "paranoid and delusional." Liam thought otherwise, he agreed she could be in danger.

"Miss Johnson, if you would like another safe house until your matter is resolved, you can stay with me. I live alone in Brock, among the farmlands, and I don't get visitors, eh, so you would not be bothered while I am working. It is not an official offer you understand, I just thought it would be better for you if no one else knew. I do believe your story."

The sympathetic counselor had honest eyes, a youthful appearance, and an easy manner. *Jo* noted Liam's hairless face, his calloused hands, and the sincerity of his body language. Her assessment was that he was too young and naive to be involved in espionage of any kind, and her instinct was to say yes.

"I, uh, thank you for believing me. I am certain I am in danger here even if I don't know who might be pursuing me; as you admitted, my story is too salacious to be kept a secret. I don't know of Brock, is it near?"

"Oh, yeah, eh, it is north of here a bit, I make the drive, near an hour each way. And I can't say I know any of my neighbors since I spend most of my time here in Toronto, ya-know. Around my place are grain and egg producers, along with a few small farms growing fruits and vegetables. Planting crops and keeping up with laying hens takes up a fair bit-o' time, ya-know, I don't get doorknockers, believe me Miss Johnson." He did not know if he had convinced her, but he continued as if he had. "I've got the old red Beaumont out at the end of the parking strip. After my lunch, I usually go out to my car to store away my meal box and have a dart. I can leave the door unlocked today. And if you can sneak your way into the backseat, and stay low, I can get you out to my place without anyone knowing about it. It is up to you."

Jo accepted the safe house offer; however, each day served an ample amount of worry and anguish over what to do next. The stress of being somewhere in hiding, would not let her rest. Her mind went between obscene sexual desires, and petrifying terrors and paranoia, which left her unable to speak, and often led her to pace for hours. Finally, the repetitive sequence of thinking and feeling was broken up by a deep sleep, and in her sleep, a lifelike dream came to her. In the dream, Liam was hauled off by the police, and she was exposed as a murderer. She did not think it was prophetic, but it left her feeling more constrained.

How can I continue to stay here? I can almost feel the past breathing down my neck. Staying will eventually put Liam in danger.

By week three, *Jo's* nightmares intensified, and she could not make herself to ignore her fears. She could no longer justify putting her secret supporter at risk. In her heart, she knew she could never forget Liam's compassion to her, nor his tender rejection of any sexual payment.

Liam is an angel, there is no doubt, but it is time for me to go.

~~~

The evening dusk of a summer's eve watched *Jo* leaving her secret refuge and her name behind; it was better that way, or so she hoped. Her new mission was to secure hidden transportation, on a private cargo plane, heading to another country. The unalterable sequence of unrepeatable events moved *the nameless* forward, like an arrow in flight, her direction was decided. Bent on self-sufficiency, a new steadiness came while being apart from the company of strangers. Her animal-like survival instincts had kicked in and the learned subtleties of being invisible would determine her movement.

Minus the items she wore at the time of her initial escape, the former Jolene Johnson was clothed well, wearing every item she had been given. Also in her possession, two water bottles, a handbook about survival in the wilderness, a pocketknife, and the backpack gifted by the *Vancouver angels*. From Liam's tool shed, she had taken a flashlight, a handful of black plastic garbage bags, a pair of leather work gloves, and an eight-inch campfire shovel; items she hoped would not be missed. She did not wish for it to be obvious what she had taken or what she planned to do.

Am I crazy? Am I overreacting? No. I'm grateful Liam insisted no one know about me staying with him. I don't know if I would have asked a man for help before meeting him. I just hope the police don't think he helped me, he may not be able to lie to them, he is a good man. The money he gave me, he should have kept for himself, it does me no good. I can't take the chance of being seen by anyone in the area, the money will stay in these oversized shoes.
~~~

The six trash bags were layered inside one another to make one sleeping bag, giving the runner some protection from wind and moisture when resting during the daylight hours, and it provided her with an instant place to hide when nothing else was accessible. She was small enough to fit inside the bags, and it was functional protection from the cool damp elements, and the bags were easily stuffed into her backpack when she was on the move.

~~~

Reaching the pre-identified airport and digging under a security fence to reach the tarmac, the fugitive stayed low, like an angry, resolute dog. Her stomach complained about being empty for two days, as she scoped the area for possible enemies.

There are four sizable aircrafts, surely, I can sneak onto at least one of them.

The growls emitting from her gut did not hinder her, but they could not keep her awake. Waking after a couple hours of rest, she saw her inventory had changed. There was a large sized plane that looked ripe with its cargo door standing wide open, an open invitation. While waiting for the reflective vests to leave the area, another plane sounded overhead. The landing brought several new sets of eyes for the *no-name* to watch, even as sweat stung her eyes.

All the vests are focused on the incoming plane, this is my chance.

Blurred eyes averted toward the glowing reflections, trash bag in hand, and with one foot upon the lowered entry door, she made one last studied glance to be sure no one had seen her.

I'm in! Oh? "Ouch!"

The *no-name* was startled when a man backed into her from the inside of the plane, stepping hard upon her foot.

"Opa! Pardon ma dame je suis terriblement désolé."

The man turned and saw her, a dirty, skinny, beautifully faced, overly clothed wannabe-thief; standing there, sweat drenched, mouth opened, and now with throbbing toes. He assumed she was stiff bodied from getting caught with bag in hand.
~~~

"Yah. Bonjour. Uh, francais ou anglais?"

"Un peu de francais. You speak English? You are the pilot?"

The man perked up.

She speaks, and she is not upset about her smashed toes.

"Why yes! I am Petry Agathanagelou, and this is my plane, Greek Cargo and Air Freight Express, at your service, miss? You are a hungry thief, no?"

"No sir, Petry Agathanagelou, I am no thief."

Petry was impressed with her tongue, she spoke his name as one who spoke Greek.

"Not a thief, hmmmm, you must be lost, yes?"

She threw herself into her role with tear filled eyes.

"I'm not lost, I'm desperate, and I need help to become lost. I have an immensely powerful, husband. He's trying to have me killed. He will not give up until he succeeds."

"I hope you don't mind me asking, why would anyone want to hurt someone as beautiful as you? Did he find you with another lover?"

Her story came from a true crime television show she watched while hiding at Liam's.

"No. It's just, I know things that could ruin his career, and he is a powerfully dangerous man. He wants to kill me, because I," she closed her stinging eyes to push the tears out and down her face, "I will not stay with him. He said if he cannot have me, no one will. He promised he would not stop, until I was dead. Believe me, even telling you this much puts you in danger. He has international connections and friends among the highest ranking RCMP. My only hope is to completely disappear, now, I must leave now, before I can be traced here. I assure you the police cannot help me."

The last part was her truth, she needed to vanish, and her urgency was convincing.

"I see you are telling me the truth. I wish I could offer help, but I have no friends in this country. If you must flee, now, I recommend you hide in a place with a large population, perhaps a big city in Brazil, if you can speak the languages? Mostly Portuguese, German, Spanish, and of course a little English here and there." Petry had fallen in love with her at first glance. "I could help, if you would permit me?"

Petry had deliveries to make in eleven countries, with multiple-day layovers in Benin, Athens, and Argentina, and his timeline could not be altered. Given his itinerary, her destination would not be until the end of his trip.

"Yes, please can I hide on your plane? I do not wish to cause you any trouble nor would I wish to delay your business. If you are willing to give your word never to speak of me, you may be saving my life."

Her eyes were wild, searching every part of the plane. Seeing she was deadly serious, Petry decided to deliver her, without adding her name to the passenger log. He had given rides to a few other desperados in the past, and none as vulnerable as she. Her grit was appreciable, and her delicate features, endearing.

"For you, brave lady, you have my word. I will say prayers for you."

Around his neck, Petry wore a gold cross. He brought it to his lips and kissed the metal. His first prayer had been sent upward.

"We must act quickly, before the men return to fuel my plane. I keep some emergency supplies in a box, see there." He drew her into the spacious belly of the plane.

"In the forward cargo hold here, this is the only space large enough for you to fit inside." He reached for the lid, it was secured with a basic latch, which could be turned from the inside. "There is not much in there, but it should keep you alive. When on layovers, I will leave it up to you if you want to leave the plane to stretch your legs. I won't say anything, but I will leave notes, and when the cargo door is opened partway, it will be safe for you to exit. On the average, you should have two hours on short stops, and overnight on the long layovers. If you return and the door has been widened or closed, you will need to wait and watch for me to arrive. I will say something to give you a clue about what is happening, and I will provide a distraction to give you time to board."

The fugitive did not hesitate, she climbed into the box with her belongings and her plastic bags. It was tight, but she had lived in smaller cages.

"Thank you, this will be sufficient. I owe you my life."

"You owe me nothing, except you must be strong, very strong to stay alive. God be with you. Our journey will begin within the hour. In flight, there will be low temperatures, and much of the ground time will be in high scorching temps. I will bring water aboard at every stop, you will need it. When the engines start, you can retrieve the bottle, stretch your legs, and uh, you will have only a few minutes to return to your place. While the plane is being loaded and unloaded, you will have to remain quiet, there will be no way for you to see if anyone is near. Of course, I will not be able to communicate, anything I say will be recorded in flight."

Petry insisted she accept the cash he had in his pocket and suggested where to start in São Paulo, then he bid her farewell and closed the lid. On the eighth and ninth stops, while checking the load, and between his whistled tunes, Petry was able to offer additional written details to get his no-name in and out of the plane, safely. He left the notes and hand-drawn maps with the water bottles. One message read: When you get there buy an identity card with a common name. Tell them you're a teacher on summer break, you are there to learn the culture, this will get you started on your new life. God Bless You.

When the eleventh stop came, the *no-name* was more than ready to have her feet on the ground, permanently. Painfully thin at the start, she lost an additional five pounds, eating only sardines, saltine crackers, and chocolate bars; it was all Petry had stocked on the plane. Keeping her knees bent after her recent surgery was painstaking, as was staying hidden while trying to relieve herself. She endured it all, making it to the most populous urban agglomeration as an unknown. In addition to the ride, and limited provisions, the benevolent, albeit lovelorn Petry, had given her close to eight hundred U. S. dollars. Together with what Liam had given to her, *no-name* felt a free life was within her grasp.

CHAPTER 6

HOW AN ASSASSIN ASSIMILATES

*As Rumi said, one day you will look back and laugh at yourself.
You'll say, 'I can't believe I was so asleep! How did I ever forget
the truth? How ridiculous to believe that sadness and sickness
are anything other than bad dreams,' so shall it be in my mind.*

LILY

After escaping a death sentence by the one she had served, and before becoming one of the Yan's, a fifth generation Loyalvillian, Lily mastered compartmentalizing while working as an assassin. Known simply as "L," Lily could be hired by worthy, wealthy, women, to eliminate *bad men*, and make it appear as an accident. Her use of disguise, and her intuitive ability to read people, made her highly efficient at remaining anonymous. Like a ninja, she appeared and disappeared in the lives of those she met, in a highly strategic manner. Her emotions and thoughts were treated the same, in this way she shielded her psyche. It could be said that before the Yan's, *freedom* was little more than a scam.

Stingy with faith and optimism, *L* had lived in the shadows, believing herself too different from most people, and judging most men to be unworthy of any kind of trust. Gradually, however, she opened herself to a few grounded relationships, beginning with one of her hired teachers, an effeminate bio-male named Zing. *L's* new decisive schedule, each segment, timed to the second, became her divided reality.

Sleep six hours. Wake and hydrate, read news and people watch. Body care. Make WWW connection. Mind and body exercise. Study identified targets. Body care and home setting chores. Make kill. Study languages. Gardening. Book reading. Meet with Zing. Additional reading. Mind and body exercise. Body care. Sleep.

Using a "they" pronoun, Zing, her tutor, taught Lily about the struggles and ultimate ascension of LGBTQ+ people groups, domestic and abroad; helping expand her own ideas about current non-normative cultural norms, and sexual identification. The lessons *they* offered, began to weaken previously conceived ideas about men, bio-males, in particular. Disciplined beyond measure, a ravenous student of current social sciences, Lily was amazed with the gains made by cultural minorities and by women. Recognizing how she had been isolated, controlled, and kept from knowing about the free-living world, she determined to surround herself with teachers who could teach her "everything" she had missed. The sciences, world geography, the ancient and current histories, musical arts, film, national and international law, and the conventions of modern warfare, all found their way onto her learning schedule.

In Lily's conspirative mind, connections were certain, and meaningful; spirituality and world religion dovetailed with the evolution of science and technology. Furthermore, her biology studies transitioned into self-defense virtually, physically and psychologically. She received the information factually, without animation or emotion. Those who taught her, reasoned her stoic robotic-like ways stemmed from unseen cultural influences. No one had any idea she had lived as a slave her whole life; they thought of her as a strongly defended, shy, private type.

Arriving in Loyalville, regimented as a soldier might be, Lily had shut off "feelings" from the past. Her life from before was blocked behind a heavily guarded emotional wall, even the good feelings from loving her Little Dove, were locked away. Nevertheless, Lily knew assimilation was paramount.

The community welcoming, and the instant love from the Yan's, and other Loyalville residents, began the essential integration. Lily's "Grinch" heart was indeed softening. In the course of a few days, she found herself experiencing a collision of beliefs and priorities, unlike anything she had ever known. Mercifully, over time, Lily morphed into a more natural-like person, approachable and less defensive. The reduction of haughtiness made her emotionally teachable; she absorbed truths and readily applied them to the living. The self-actualizing, together with a truer grasp of humanity, inspired a mental awareness which could be described as supernaturally activated. She had begun to care deeply for the people who, apparently, cared for their own, even the ones who were gone for twenty years; the newly divorced Donald Harrison was among them.

To support her novel way of thinking and feeling, Debbi dug deeper into psychology and sociology studies. The subjects sparked a desire for "genuine" human connections, and she recognized that even if she herself could not be fully authentic, she wanted to practice her fresh perspectives.

Loyalville had become her model of family and community, and she decided they were all worthy of her protection. She would protect them as fiercely as her *freed-life*, and woe to anyone who would try to pull her away from either. As pleasant as her new life was becoming, Debbi's need to know what had happened to the Yan's child was vital. To right the injustice, she first needed to know what had actually transpired.

Research on the taken girl was dirty work, it took the reinvented Debbi back to the dark world she had left behind. With little to go on, she followed a few false leads, but nothing would dissuade her. Focused on her mission, she bravely refused to succumb to the demons telling her to kill anyone who might be involved with hurting others. She kept her distance from current day trafficking *handlers*, connecting only with those remnants from the past, those who could have been active at the time of the kidnapping event.

As Debbi understood it, all involved in trafficking were a lowly bunch, but the set-up cons were the lowest earning serpents, barely making a living. These types were much harder to locate, given they had no status to make them visible. It was apparent to Debbi, she would need to go to the poorest areas, and she would need to pretend she was one of them. She reasoned to herself as if she had been given the job.

They would have been given the child's name and address, or at least the child's school name, and they would have watched from a safe distance, a day or more, to see how the child went and returned from school. And since the child was never alone, their game was to distract the one accompanying the mark, allowing another to take her without being seen.

Familiarity with the business of human trade, helped the snake seeking avenger know which rocks to kick. Debbi persisted, and before long, a couple of old con artists were identified. The Faay's, an older couple, had been named as possible suspects in similar cases, although no one had verified them working in human trade. Debbi decided she would need to speak to them herself if she was ever going to know the truth.

Little had been said about the Faay's, only that they were old cons, they sold drugs, or at least bought them for their own consumption, and if you needed them for anything, they worked cheap. Once she had their names, it was not hard for Debbi to locate them, and it turned out they lived in Virginia City, Nevada, an easy one-hour drive from Loyalville.

It had been a challenge to avoid telling Donald about the activities keeping her away. With all the driving back and forth across state line to Virginia City, it was difficult to make evening dates. Since she did not wish to be deceitful with her new man-friend, omission was her best other option. Her quick and methodical thinking came up with a number of real excuses to drive somewhere on behalf of Nan and Bud, or one of the other homebound residents she had become fond of.

When Debbi spotted the Faay's, she knew by instinct, she had found the right people. As they had been described, the man was skinny and white, and his wife was a voluptuous darker-white woman. Both were approaching their seventh decade and had the wrinkles, and slouched shoulders, to prove it. In Debbi's mind, they were both rancid excuses for humanity, given they had made a living acting as cons, thieves, and potentially much worse.

By waiting and watching patiently during her two separate visits to the area, Debbi caught the couple's evening routine. She guessed that their stubbornly long shelf lives were near the natural expiration date, and likely they were unable to carry out any dangerous cons, at this point in time. On her third visit to the Faay's dirty neighborhood, she caught them all alone. The two were also sufficiently inebriated, as they walked the three blocks home from a local bar. Knowing greed likely decided their morals, the *voice* of Lily reasoned in Debbi's mind.

They will take money to brag on their conquests, give them the drink they smell of and flash some cash, be sure and take a sip yourself, they need to think you're high before they will trust you.

The shared sips from a flask full of whiskey, got the two old cons talking a blue streak. A few hundred dollars later, and Debbi's generosity had them singing about their misdeeds, and speaking boastfully of what trouble they might still cause. They were enjoying the attention of the beautiful and amiable Asian woman, who seemed taken with them. They saw her small size as nothing to fear, and when she unabashedly pulled out money, they thought they could easily take advantage of her.

Debbi, seeing their confidence, primed them further, "It is not easy finding young Asian kids, and that's what my employer wants to buy, don't think this money is mine to just give away for stories, I better find a little one, and quick. Any chance you two want some work?"

The painted-up old woman did not hesitate to respond, "Sure, we can help you catch a youngster, boy or girl, whatever you're looking for. Hey Sal, remember the kid, the psychic Chinese one? For a psychic, she sure was an easy mark. But we ain't cheap though, and we'd expect cash up front."

"My boss is wealthy; you can name your price."

Thinking they had won the lottery, the Faay's dropped their guard further; their confessions would seal their fate. They admitted to being a part of the kidnapping of fourteen-year-old Debbi Yan. The avenger decided she had endured enough; it was time to *party* with the powdered Wolf's bane she had hidden in her pocket.

With Lily's faint voice coaching her in her head, Debbi *drunkenly* declared, "Well, this calls for a celebration. If you have a mirror and a straw, I can share a little nose candy? I also have a Gina tincture that will have you seeing purple elephants, if you like that kind of high?"

"Why didn't you say so earlier, I was starting to wonder if you were for real. Lainey and I are huge fans of G-highs. Not here though, we have a place nearby, our, uhh, home office."

Sal's eyes gleamed as he pointed their steps. Debbi's arm found the middle of the woman who was too drunk to walk far without the support.

"Well, you are a mighty little bitty thing, you got some muscles to you," Lainey leaning onto the friendly woman was giddy, "and I don't mind your a-thith-tance. I don't like these heels, you see, I believe they're uneven, I'm goin' to kick 'em off the second we get to our sth-teps," Lainey slurred as she faltered.

The Faay's did not notice Debbi wore fitted skin-tone gloves, or if they did, they didn't mention them. Debbi preferred caution over confidence when it came to these matters. The setting worked well, a rundown apartment building in a known drug district. Sal and Lainey's place was overrun with trash, dirty dishes, and a coffee table pre-set with all the relevant paraphernalia. With little effort, Debbi could make it appear as if they had overdosed on clean cocaine.

Maybe it was her sincere wish to leave her past fully behind, a mind torn between the two different worlds, but *Lily* overtook her conscious thoughts to watch the painful deaths of Sal and Lainey Faay. Debbi's homegrown poison worked quickly. Once the couple endured the fast-acting side effects, their heartbeat came to an abrupt halt. Lily placed the clean cocaine residue in all the obvious places, including a little between the lower lip and gum.

"All is done, no looking back, and you snakes can be sure, if I see any more of your kind, they will be quickened to their end, just as you have found yours,"

Lily glanced in the mirror as her words found sound, then Debbi was back in control and on the move; a hooded shadow, left unseen.

Secretly, Debbi wondered if her death toll would ever include her worst nightmare, the monster who raised her, profited from her, and then sentenced her to death. As much as she wished him dead, each nerve in her body had been trained and tempered by him; he knew exactly how to elicit whatever it was he wanted from her. She feared her body might betray her in his presence. One slip, one single wrong move, and she could find herself dead, or worse, back in his grip. He was on her list of things *to avoid*; although Lily would add, only *for now*.

Putting the Faay job behind her, Debbi had a new filter for looking at others, and each contemporary experience made her more aware of her maturation. Socially, the "coming out" as the returned version of Debbi Yan, felt like jumping into the deep end of a muddy-bottomed lake. Debbi became fully submerged in a maze of thickened relationships seemingly overnight. New experiences triggered new feelings, and ideas, never considered before, positive regard burst like popcorn in her mind.

Kindness is a true virtue, and some do offer it without a selfish agenda, they give it to be considerate, they behave out of a good spirit, and sometimes out of unconditional love, it's a true wonder of the world.

CHAPTER 7

VISAGE MATCHING

Every face tells a story, some will inspire, some will terrify.

LILY

Taking a cue from her newfound wisdom, Debbi decided a free life should not be as serious as hers had been. She had created a safety zone for efficiency and potential, but she was still working to understand emotional balance. The adoring Donald impressed her, and he was clearly taken with her. She opted to put her new theories into practice, allowing herself to care for a man, for the sake of stable living. Debbi began a new agenda.

If playing, play hard, it will not take away from working hard, it will help me work better, yin and yang, go ahead, say yes to a date the next time the big guy asks.

Donald Harrison did ask her out, and Debbi did say yes, and they both were blown away by their chemistry. The courtship was platonic in the beginning, but once they crossed the physical boundary, they could not be together without having sex. Trust made for hot sex; it was like Independence Day, fireworks every time.

Sexual compatibility was coupled with similar ideas and desires for how to grow old; it seemed neither could imagine growing old alone, and neither ever wanted to leave Loyalville. Almost from the moment they *re-met*, although weighed down with secrets, Debbi felt the connection was authentic enough for her to be passionate and sensual. She had made love to a woman before, but outside of slave work, she had had zero interest in men. Donald was her first, and she considered him her only true male relationship. She let herself have fun, and he responded positively to her offerings. They married after nine months of dating; he wanted to give her his name, and anything else she wanted.

Debbi wanted to make a home for him, feed, love, and protect him, and continue to work at the postal store. Donald adored her smurfy-housekeeper jubilance in having a home that was put into logical order; it had been quite the opposite with his other wives.

Never have I ever known a woman who enjoys keeping a house clean as much as she does, you'd think she's won the lottery when I hand over my laundry bag for wash day. Instead of being treated like a Rodney, like most schmucks, I get nothing but respect!

The admiration that went both ways seemed limitless. Debbi insisted her new husband retire from work; she felt his health was more important than the money. Donald, being a strong believer in community participation was agreeable to quitting his desk job, in order to devote himself more fully to his marriage, and to the community they loved.

Married life agreed with Debbi. Astonished by the breadth of their relationship, she had fallen "hard" for the big guy, and within a year, harder still for her Loyalville "family." Aside from the sparks they threw in bed, the two were compatible souls, both happiest when they were accomplishing their daily "missions," aka making a home together, and making a positive impact on their beloved Loyalville community. Each made a great fit for the other, right from the start.

The morning had been a productive one for the Harrisons. Practiced time management allowed them to complete their routines, and all the household chores with time to spare. Approaching with his signature dopey grin, Donald hoped his wife could be persuaded to have a little fun.

"It's your free afternoon today, do you want to get lucky?"

"The question is, do you want to get lucky?"

Debbi's whispered reply worked like a little blue pill. Donald's manhood had filled his loose shorts, creating a tent. He proudly pushed his groin toward her, then, dropped to a knee.

"I've never been luckier than the day I married a smurf. And since she also has psychic abilities, I'd say she knew what she was doing. She is one smart, fortune cookie, and she's my date for, uh, you already know, don't you?"

He liked the game of teasing his wife, and he loved how quick she was with her own brand of wit.

"Ah, psychic abilities? That is what you're, mmmmm, pulling for isn't it?"

Debbi reached for him, wrapping her hand around his scrotum; she knew just how hard to grip to turn him on.

Adding a little husky to her voice, "I'd say getting out of town for a few hours is good for both of us, we haven't seen a strange face in weeks."

Her hand went naturally to the places her man liked clenched. His breathing deepened purposefully. He would have stopped all time if he was able. She was everything to him, it was evident in his looming blue-green eyes and in his gentle-giant touch.

"Oh, yes. Mmmmmmmm. You know just what to, uh, say, to get your man's engine revving. We do need our strange, and damn, I love that you want it too. How about you pick the, mmmmm, town, and I pick the joint? And might I say you smell good enough to eat. Mmmmmmmm smurfs smell good!"

His arms engulfed Debbi, who was on his knee, and she melted into him. More kissing. More groans. The brief banter and close contact had them both warm with arousal. Leaning back to catch her breath, and offer a coy smile, Debbi had already decided.

"Let's pick a place in Fair Oaks, somewhere with a view?"

"Smurf, anywhere with you, comes with a beautiful view."

They shared another kiss. Donald kept one arm around his wife. The other hand reached for her chin, then lightly, his fingers followed it up her jawline, to her cheekbones, and then, tenderly back down across her cheek, ending the stroke with a light tap on her perfect nose. Debbi weak-kneed by his genuine passion, smiled reflexively, before finding the right words.

"You sure know how to sweep a girl off her feet."

That was his cue. Donald could not delay his need for her any longer. Effortlessly he stood, lifting his little wife as he moved. He carried her over to their bed, ready to take their make-out session to the next level.

The Harrison's private life was sizzling, and their "public" lunches, shared most days in downtown Loyalville, were similarly juicy; gossip was a shared guilty pleasure. Due to Debbi's work constraints, the couple usually ate at local venues, often walking only a short distance from the post office. Donald's job was to secure a table where the chitter-chatter of other patrons could be *scooped*, and to place their order. Debbi preferred fresh food, and Donald enjoyed seeing her eat heartily. Soup, salad, and a sandwich split for two was their habit. Coffee and something sweet for the big guy, completed their meal.

On the days when Debbi was free in the afternoon, the two would take a longer drive, in search of undiscovered people and places, where, instead of gossip, they could play up Debbi's skill of face reading. Places like Carson City, Grass Valley, and Sierraville, were among their choices; they preferred the small-town type hole-in-the-walls, over chain restaurants. Donald was amused by Debbi's "impressions" of strangers, and secretly, Debbi liked to keep an eye out for any bad apples hanging on the perimeter of her protected community.

Having driven to Fair Oaks Village, just outside of Sacramento, the

Harrison's found a new lunch place, landing at the Fair Oaks Coffee House Deli. The place was busy, which was a good sign to Donald, and it was quaint, something Debbi appreciated. The deciding factor was the homestyle baked goods, Donald's favorite. After they had eaten their panini's, and were sipping their espressos, Donald baited his pantomath wife.

"How about that young woman, I think she's single, no ring, nice posture, roundish face, a little fleshy, I bet she'll make a happy wife. Am I close?"

"She's a good one, the sensitive-caring type, and quite possibly she's a tiger in her fantasies, and most men do want a woman with a potential for honeymoon longevity," a grin snuck onto her own face. "You are right in noting her plump face, she will prove to be a good choice for someone. I'd say she's a water-shape, and that means she is the long-term type."

Donald looked around with his boyish grin, hoping for a hook-up for the innocent looking *water-shaped.*

"How about that guy over there? I saw them each smiling at the other, almost flirting when they were waiting for a table, the athletic looking one with a thin face, wouldn't they make a good match, opposites attract, right?"

"Huh, not really an opposite, dear husband, he's a wood-shape face. I'd say, based on the longer face and the bushy eyebrows, bad match. He'd likely take advantage of her good nature. He is a bit more complicated than she deserves."

Questioning for the sake of hearing Debbi's logic, Donald would not let the idea go.

"Okay, why? Oh wait, I think I know, a narcissist type?"

Playing along, Debbi continued, "Very good honorable husband, you are learning very well. Watching him just these couple of minutes, see how he examines everything with raised eyebrows? Then furrowed together. He is a methodical one, practical. He's thinking through lunch, but not happy about it, must be overworked or likes to play that he is for the attention."

Clearing his throat, Donald felt a little male ego coming forward, as his mind was overidentifying with the bushy eyebrows. He decided to let it go for the sake of the game.

"Well, if the oblong faced guy is not right for her, how about that triangular faced guy, the one working behind the grill?"

Debbi did not mind playing along, but today, her thoughts kept remembering like-faces from the past, faces she wanted to forget. The face working behind the grill, instantly reminded her of her former master.

He's more like a monster than a man.

She reacted stiffly, "You want to see her, with him?! Tsh, tsh, I don't think they are a good match. He's got a fiery temper and he's more of an intellectual type, with ego issues, you see, no lines on his forehead, that's a sign that he's a selfish type."

Donald's spirit of inquiry helped to distract Debbi from her darker thoughts. Largely unaware of his usefulness, he persisted, "I don't see the selfish thing, maybe he does Botox for the lines?"

Laughing a little at first, Debbi reminded her man, "We heard him snap a few times when food orders were ready, as if he were above using his words. A guy like that would be called a metal shape. He's too vain, and analytical to be a diner cook, he should have studied his math in school, and gone into accounting."

Unconsciously, Donald reached up to touch his own jaw, then asked, "I guess angular faces have extra dominating personalities?"

"Hmmm, yes, but you have to watch for other signals to know for sure, not all metal faces are the same. See the man behind me?"

Looking, Donald winked, then whispered, "Don't tell me my smurf has eyes on the back of her head?"

"Oh Donald, it's not eyes alone. Listen to how he uses his fork and knife, how he sets his cup down in the saucer. I don't want to turn around, but is he fair haired too?"

Donald's eyes widened, "Uhhhh, yes, how did you know?"

Truthfully responding, Debbi answered, "I can feel his conscientiousness, rare in a blondie man; it was only a guess. He's a rectangular face, I sense the less forceful type, balanced by a little melancholy, and suspended ambition. He'd be overwhelmed by a one-nighter, let alone a relationship."

"Wow, Deb, we should put you on one of those 800-call-a-psychic lines, forget your job at the postal store, we could get you set up."

Donald pulled his hand up to cover his mouth mid-sentence. The look Debbi was giving him made him stop his playful jesting before he could convince his smile to sober up. He was not ready for the game to end, all the same, the look on her face said she had other thoughts. Before he could learn what was on her mind, the barista who had made their coffees, approached their table, and cheerfully interrupted.

"Hi folks, I'm getting ready to go on a 30-minute break, are you okay with your coffee or did you want something else before I leave?"

Quick to answer the pretty woman, Donald's chivalry was evident, "I appreciate you asking. Uh, Deb, you want anything?"

More concerned for her husband's health, Debbi politely squared her eyes with him before responding. "I'm fine, and I'd recommend you stick to one espresso."

Seeing the lecture in her eyes, Donald sidestepped the issue.

"Of course, you would, but I'm a big boy my little Smurf." He turned to smile at the pretty girl, "I'd love a regular cup...of decaf... to keep this little one happy…and then I'd like to have a slice of the chocolate crusted cheesecake."

"Yes, of course, shall we make that two slices?"

The approval of the lady customer seemed important to the server. Giving way to the playful spirit of her hubby, Debbi shook her head as she spoke, "I will leave the sweets to my dear husband, but I will join him with the decaf coffee."

At that moment, Debbi's phone indicated a message had come in.

"I'm sorry Donald, I have to go back in to close the shop tonight," she held up her phone to show her husband.

"Ah, the boss taking off early. Well, no problem. Should we take it to go? I can save the cheesecake for later."

Secretly thrilled that she did not scold for the dessert order, Donald stayed upbeat.

"Yes, honorable husband, that would be good, we do have the drive to get back to Loyalville." Debbi turned to the server, suddenly aware she had not learned her name, "Thank you, Miss?"

"Uh, oh, yes, it's Sandy. Sorry I forgot to wear my nametag. Well, actually, I didn't forget. I just get tired of people thinking I know about the famous soap star, Sandy Silver, just because I have the same name, and live in the same city."

"Ahhh, I understand, people can make the silliest assumptions at times, but what a coincidence," rolling her eyes, Debbi imagined the nuisance of the situation.

Sandy continued, "I have a common name, sometimes I wish it was a little more original. Anyway, I'll put your coffees in to-go cups, and box the cheesecake. It will just take a minute."

Pulling out his wallet, Donald offered a friendly wink, "Thanks Sandy, nice place here, we will surely give you a good yelp review."

Donald was hugely impressed with the deli.

This place is five-star, food prepared well, fresh, hot, and personable service. Cute server, too bad she gets hassled about famous name. It is kinda weird thinking of a TV star living in this area, but it is a short flight to get to So-Cal, and not likely a tough commute for a rich type. Now, for the round-faced lady, she needs a match, but who?

"Sorry, Deb, if this is getting old, but before we leave, can we please find a match for the round-faced lady with great sexual fantasies? I couldn't sleep soundly tonight if I didn't see her have a chance to fulfill her potential."

Donald smiled with endearing eyes. Returning the smile, Debbi felt her own distractions creeping in.

Why do I feel like we are the ones being watched today?

"Donald, this has been fun, but."

She stopped before saying the other lingering impression. Her hesitation was interpreted as something else.

My wee workaholic always worried about taking care of the Loyalvillians. I better get her back before the worry turns to something worse.

"Ah, you've been a great sport Smurf. No worries, I'll finish her story in my dreams. Let's get you back to your post."

Laughing at his silly face, Donald had eased her mood; he was the only one who could pull her from the dark of her past. Still, Debbi's inner voice reminded her play-time was over. As they walked out, a shadowed figure, who had been sitting under an umbrella, nearby, stood and made haste to a car, then sped off. Debbi saw him out of the corner of her eye.

We were being watched. My gut check was on spot. Damn. I didn't get the license plate.

CHAPTER 8

BAD DREAMS

"Never forget the stars."
FRANCES HODGSON BURNETT

Confusion was lingering like the morning mist, as Nan, the middle-aged, gray-eyed, child-like-woman gazed past the windowpane. Her eyes saw the sun peeking in the East, a pure honey glow in her mind, where the day was about to begin, again.

Pretty sky. A good morning to walk over to Main Street and say hello to Debbi.

Aware she was at home, Nan sensed her husband, Bud, was working nearby; the smell of gasoline was incontestable. They had woken early, and she had successfully dressed herself. Bud cooked cheesy-grits, and eggs, and she had eaten more than usual. Attracted to the shade of the sweater she wore, chestnut, like Bud's skin, her pale fingers gently stroked her elbows as if it were him. Seeing her hands against the fabric, Nan briefly considered the contrast and the soothing texture. Contentment was brimming. Nearby, the white sound from a ticking clock was familiar and comforting; it offered a few extra whispers of peace.

The shift was gradual for Nan. The ticking became louder until the hollow tone changed into a reverberating echo, with no silence between the seconds. The resonance joined the sound of the air return, quiet at first, and then it roared, murmuring words Nan could not understand. The commonplace blurred and Nan's limited knowing became camouflaged with subtle doubts.

What was I thinking? It's not safe to go out. That clock is wrong, it's too dark to go. Bud will not like it. No. He wants me here. Why does he keep me here? Oh, what is that noise? Did I do something? Where am I? This isn't my bed? Why won't the noise stop? No, I'm being silly, I'm fine, I just can't remember what I'm supposed to be doing. Where's Bud?

On the nearest table sat her prescription bottles. One stood out. The house was suddenly void of sound and smells.

Aricept, treatment for Dementia. I have dementia? No...do I? I'm too young to have dementia. It's the pills that make me fuzzy. Why do they make me take so much medicine, it only makes me worse.

Nan's mood abruptly turned defensive. Maintaining her momentary clarity suddenly felt like a battle between sanity and insanity. She could not muster the strength to fight both sides. Giving in to the brain fatigue, a muddled sleep enveloped her. Her dream state allowed the remaining lucidness to retrieve memories, tortured ones, embedded with sensory awareness. The reminiscence grew as if she were reliving it. Fully asleep, her dream began in the usual place.

The woman of the house is crying again. She sees me and waves me over to her side. What can I do? I play with her nine-year-old son and clean his room. How can I help her? Her husband doesn't like me since he saw me at the movies, with Bud. He's prejudiced against people of color. She pulls me into a bear hug. "Oh Nan, I can't stand it anymore. My husband cares more about those horses than for me, and his own son. I hoped he would have missed us these past two weeks. I hoped he would spend some time with us, but no, he's already out in the barn. Henry is in his room pouting and he won't come out. He won't talk to me. Will you try talking to him?" Oh yes, I'll cheer the boy to action. He needs to stand up for himself. I tug on Henry's arm. He holds fast to his sheathed play swords, a gift from his father. "Go on Henry, you can't wait for him to come to you. You go on out to the barn, show him what you've been working on, he'll be surprised, he'll be proud. Don't be afraid, I'll be there. I'll duck behind the hay bales. I'll be close. Go on." The boy tries his father, "Dad, Dad, please, I gotta show you something, I gotta surprise for you." Oh, no. Not that face, that face says he doesn't want to be bothered. The father unfolds, rising over his boy, "Son we've got horses to shoe and if you're not going to learn to help, then take your toys and go play somewhere else." The boy looks back to me, his eyes ask, "Nan, what do I tell him? Do I wait?" No. He's wrong to ignore you, I nod to the boy. I wave my hand. Don't give up. Make him listen, make him pay attention to you. Henry hangs the twin ninja swords loosely over his shoulders. His hands on each end, he holds them firmly in the safety of the shared sheath. Bravely, he swells closer to his father, "But Dad, they're not play swords anymore, I've been working on 'em, you gotta see…" The horse, restless, and distracted by the antics of the boy, lifts a hoof, and then steps down on the farrier's foot. After pulling his boot out from under the horse, the shoer snaps, "Damn." Triggering the father's temper, "Damn it." Oh no, no, no, no, noooo, it's not his fault. The father wheels back toward his son, towering over him. He yells, "Now see what you've done? You happy now? All this for attention? You can't entertain yourself with the toys I buy you? Where's that nig-lovin' nanny of yours?" The farrier limps away, not wanting to interrupt the man from disciplining his son. He walks past me. I don't move, I don't want him to see me. I would be in trouble for eavesdropping. Poor Henry. He wants to make his father proud.

Gasping for air, Nan reaches the place in the dream sequence that agitates her. Her hands reach for something solid. She finds her hair. She pulls.

The angry father ensnares the boy's hands and flings the swords apart. It's too late. He didn't know Henry spent two weeks with the sharpening stones…creating real edges.

The realized consequences are too barbarous for the guileless mind to remain inculpable. Nan's dissociated state keeps her from conscious memory of the event, but her dreams, especially when in color, retain the pain and serve as self-punishment. With Nan's eyes still tightly closed, she sees the final act.

The silver glistening of blades exposed, acute, and razor-sharp. They rip easily through the mushroom skin of the neck, slashing deep through the pink flesh. One moment a crude magenta line, behind the boy's head. The next, blood bursting from a cavernous wound. A blue-red color engulfs the back of his t-shirt. The fluid ignites disbelief, but the shirt, a riot of opalescent purples, says it all. The father's horrified jaw locked open. His love and discipline, now forever fused with regret. The boy's last breath escapes his mouth. The deadly steel swords are thrown aside. The ash-faced father throws his arms around his translucent child. But it is too late. The effervescence slips away. The boy falls back, his head falls forward, and a nauseated swoon spins the scene, before the colors turn to a darker purple, then fade to black.

Nan's pain touched her voice, she emitted a garbled grunt. In the other room, Bud was setting down the wire brush, and aiming the choke cleaner into the holes. The spray noise was followed by more sounds coming from his wife.

Oh boy. Sounds like the nightmare is making an early visit, better set this aside before she gets too worked up.

The worried brow pushed away from the kitchen table, finding his way to his wife's side.

"No, no, please no, no…"

With eyes squeezed tight, Nan's frantic hands grasped and pulled hard at her hair. The pained sensation finally ended the dream, Nan, opened her eyes. The amiable face of a man, familiar but distant, came into her view, it began to speak.

"It's alright Nan, wake up, honey, you're having a bad dream, you're okay, I'm here, you're not alone, it's okay. Now, now, don't cry. I'm here. It's me, your husband, it's Bud, I'm here."

Nan accepted his soothing and was glad to allow the dream to fade. She wanted the kind man to help her, but she wished her husband or Debbi were there. She also wished she were home; around her objects appeared broken, ugly, and supersized. Nothing made sense with the cacophony in her head. Shaking herself, she managed to find words that fit together.

"Where's Bud?"

"I'm right here Nan, it's me, I'm Bud. Nothing to worry about, I'm right here."

The confusion became stronger as scenes from the past refused to let Nan go.

"Where's Bud, I've got to find him, he's burning the place down, he's going to burn us all, where's Bud, oh Bud, where are you? Will you help me find him? I don't know where he is?"

"I'm right here. I'm safe. We're both safe. Look, look. See, you found me, yes, it's me, you know me, don't you? Look around, it's our house. See, no fire. No fire anywhere. Nothing's going to hurt us, it's okay. Just rest my love, it will be okay, I won't leave you."

Crying now, an extension of the dream, Nan became a youngster again. She reached for the pendant hanging around her neck. Opening it, the pictures of her and her best friend greeted her; seeing the faces felt like a safe place in a storm. The tears stopped. The man looked on, *a safe distance*, she thought. Nan smiled, then blinking, became fearful again. The man's face had become distorted, his features triggered her underlying emotions.

Whining, "No! It's my Debbi," then softer and bluer, "Oh poor Debbi. She's gone, who took her?" Nan's voice became more childlike as she spoke, "Where is she? Oh, where is she? I need her."

"Nan, look at me. Nan, Debbi's back, she's back, remember? She came back. You visited with her, only two days ago."

Unconvinced, "Nooo, where is she? Are you sure? I want to talk to her."

Nan shrunk under the lap blanket as she peered into unfamiliar territory. Bud pulled his cell phone from his shirt pocket. He found Debbi and Donald Harrison, third on the list, and called. As it rang, he got down low to help his wife see and hear the call.

"There-there, hon, we'll call her, so you can hear for yourself."

Debbi heard her cell phone ring from the bedside table. She and Donald met glances once they saw the caller identification. Donald waited while she answered.

"Hello, Bud? Is Nan, okay?"

"Hi, yeah, it's me and Nan's here too. Sorry to bother you in the morning, but Nan here had a bad dream, and wanted to hear your voice. She's right here, can you say hi?"

The words barely escaped without a sob. Bud had made many similar calls, but today he felt particularly unguarded.

"Hi Nan, it's Debbi, Debbi with an i, I just heard a song that made me think of you. Bud? Does she have her music in reach? Thinking Carpenters, her mellow mix."

"Debbi with an i, you are found, are you coming to see me?"

"Listen Nan, Bud, is going to play a song for you, will you listen to some music?"

"Yes, but are you coming over?"

"I am going to the postal store. I must work. I hope you can understand. Please come in and see me when you take your walk."

The confusion formed an open mouth on Nan's face, then squeezed her eyes closed tight.

"Debbi? Are you here?"

Bud spoke up calmly, "Nan, Debbi must go to work, it's time for her to work, and we can see her there, at the postal store."

"I'm sorry Bud. If she's okay, I am expected at work this morning, sooner than later. Hopefully, you two can come by for a visit while I'm working. Unless you need something more, right now?"

"Uhem, uh, no thanks. Just thanks for always being a call away. I'm grateful she still remembers the sound of your voice. We'll stop by on our walk today. I've got the Carpenters cued up for her, good call on that one."

"Okay, then. I'll see you at the shop later, listen to your music, Nan. Debbi with an i says, see you later, tater."

Returning the phone to his pocket, Bud hoped the music would help where he could not. He also hoped a cheery tone would keep her from additional confusion.

"We will see Debbi later, she's working today. Debbi wants you to listen to this song, listen."

The catch in Bud's throat gave way to a tear. For her sake, he would need to imitate joy. With a little additional effort, he smiled from his eyes.

"Let's put these on, it was Debbi's idea."

Bud moved slowly, so as not to startle her. The woman-turned-girl allowed for the headset to be put over her ears. When the lyric began, she joined in and sang the words. Some of her darkness receded, "... birds suddenly appear, every time you are near, just like me, they long to be, close to you."

The melody and her affect somehow synchronized. Nan held onto the small pictures cupped in her hand, as if it were a delicate butterfly. Forgetting her angst, she looked up at the man, and sang along with the music. The metamorphosis was as fragile as a rainbow. Bud left her side and switched on all the lights in the house. Shadows were enemies for his wife, and they were not welcomed. The song ended, and another began. Nan looked up from a secret hiding place and saw a brightly lit sunny afternoon, the edges of the room became trees, and the furniture, smooth rocks. Nan was content being outside. The sunshine made her feel safe enough to return to childhood, in her mind. Nan remembered a time, long ago, playing hopscotch, using chopsticks as markers. She giggled, then muttered childish words.

"Debbi, it's your turn," Nan speaking directly to her imagined friend.

Bud watched as she curled herself onto a single couch cushion to make room for Debbi. He was grateful to see she had gone to her happy place. He lingered just out of sight, then returned to the dining room table, which was wrapped in newspaper and covered with the parts of a carburetor. He hoped the music would soothe his wife long enough for him to get the rebuild completed. He desperately needed to focus on anything to keep his own tears from falling.

Debbi picked up her pace as she moved toward the walk-in closet, it was time to change into her self-imposed uniform. She tried to imagine a detour, a quick visit with Nan before work, to give Bud a break, but it could easily become an hour, or more. Arriving late to work would set her whole day off. She decided that Bud would let her know if the situation were truly serious; a bad dream was not a reason to change the day's agenda.

CHAPTER 9

BECOMING ARIEL BLACK

"I am lonely, sometimes,
but I dare say it's good for me…"
LOUISA MAY ALCOTT

Having taken the advice given to her by the pilot, Petry, the *no-name* exchanged some of the gifted cash for Brazilian real and used the money to buy an identity card, a "Registro Geral." She purchased the document under the most common name, Maria Silva. She also secured work. Dumping fish parts was far from glamorous, but the residual smell she carried with her kept others at a safe distance. As she had opportunity, she also gathered a variety of items to help her to disguise her look and make her less conspicuous as a *Westerner.*

The worst is behind me, anything is better than being a slave. I belong only to me. A poor, non-caged human in a chaotic big city is far better than being an evil man's pedestaled prostitute. This place is populous and dangerous to be sure, but I have every intention of surviving and finding my purpose to live.

Tolerating mental and physical agony had been her normal everyday living, but the learning curve was far from over. As *Maria* was realizing, belonging to no one was lonely, and often sexually frustrating. She found herself craving sexual contact, at times she felt foolishly desperate for it. Until now, sex had been about pleasing others; it was her slave purpose, her job. Desiring sex for individual pleasure felt confusing, she had been programmed to be self-less.

Am I selfish to want sex? Am I ruined?

The former slave did not immediately realize her torments were not typical. She was judging herself against an ideal which her master had conditioned into her mind. Fortunately, within a few days, her self-incriminations weakened. When natural arousal elicited the sexual shame, she fought it back. She rejected the conditioned thoughts as no longer relevant, trading them for logical ideas.

I am human, self-pleasuring hurts no one, and it eases my tension.

Beyond sexual gratification, *Maria* was becoming aware of her need for socialization. Providentially, her first month of freedom in the new environment offered much to expand her sense of what she needed and how to get it. She watched people living, working, and caring about one another. She found tough and tender souls, often they were one in the same. There were fresh new tastes and original textures. She listened to words, and to the various accents and dialects, and she reasoned with increased sagacity.

Discerning truth from deception was becoming easier, as was identifying other communication subtleties. Even so, the excess of humanity caused the fugitive to shift from high-rise favela to ground level ghetto every few days. Ingrained instincts told her to maintain her anonymity. As each new day passed, and intentional thinking was practiced, *Maria's* comfort with proximity stabilized. She was learning she could live on the sidelines without being completely inconsequential. And by putting reactionary *all or nothing* thinking in check, she could form significant reflections.

Look at the street waifs, see how they stay without chains or taming. They are poor in status, yet they make their place their own. See them smile. They give some and they take some. Even the poor find a reason to be alive. Belonging to themselves gives them meaning. I need mean-ing, I can matter to me, and if I keep mattering to myself, someday, I will have more.

A growing number of "familiars" were treating her as a normie, and she liked how it made her feel. The ability to accurately read peo-ple, and the heightened awareness of others' daily habits, also helped *Maria* to form her own routine. Despite her wariness of being known, the day-to-day social transactions increased her peace of mind.

Social relations come with a certain amount of predictability, and at the same time, flexibility is always in demand. It is not about con-trol; it is about balance.

This new understanding sparked an increasing amount of inspi-ration for *Maria*. The suppleness of her independence incited hopes for one day having her own home and family. It was a feeble belief at times, dangers were everywhere, but on the good days she imag-ined becoming a mother. The thought of mothering helped her to want to eat, and to live a health-filled life; this was nourishing for her mind as much as it was for her body. She was thriving.

It was a sticky Tuesday. The sun had started its afternoon lean, and with her treasured belongings safely stashed in a secret cubby, *Maria* went out into the congested neighborhood toward the Feira. A maze of sights and smells lured her like a cat following a mouse. Unlike the early days in the neighborhood, she purposely waited for the crowds to thin. She was in search of bargains, knowing they could be found after most of the sales of vegetables and fruits had been made for the day. Three reals were clutched in one hand, and in the other, a cloth bag containing items to use for trade, she was ready to shop, and prepared to negotiate deals. Her other monies and iden-tification were sewn into the layered outfit she wore, for safe keep-ing. She had memorized the locations of her preferred venders, and secretly knew most of them by name.

Walking her regular route, *Maria* planned to stop to buy a pastel, and spend a few minutes at her favorite flower stall while she ate it; then it would be time to buy her groceries. As she approached her destination, she noted a large ladder leaning next to the doorway; it stopped her in her tracks. It was as if the unused ladder was a warning that something "unlucky" was near. She checked her gut. It drew her awareness away from what she was seeing, to what she was hearing. Her steps slowed as did the sounds around her. Instinctual signals took over and abruptly, she recognized what she was sensing. She was being followed. Panic rose in her throat and sweat pooled.

I'm being followed. Not safe here. Hide! But where? Oh no, pain in my stomach. No, I can't be sick, I can't be weak, not now.

She swallowed back the revulsive fear, determined to stay conscious, and intentional. She did not want fright to block more precise thinking. In reality, she knew discerning and interpreting sounds was a daily event, she had to believe she could make the next correct decision. In that moment, even as sweat was burning her eyes, she knew her survival depended on right instincts.

Listen. Think.

Having been forced to live with dogs for a time, she had learned a way of noticing the sounds of being followed. Her body retrieved the relative information from unconscious memory, and she found a place to collect herself. There were no dogs around to affirm her instincts, *Maria's* only resource was her own *natural intelligence.* She synthesized past *dog-think* with her present human thoughts.

Once you hear them, even if you cannot isolate their steps, you will notice your hair raising on the back of your neck, it will help you to listen. Once you know the sound of their steps, block out everything else. Stop, then begin a precise pattern of forward moving steps, followed by pre-determined stops. Repeat your exact pattern a few times, then stop, and watch-listen. If what's following, means to surprise-catch you, "it" will step into your pattern, presuming you will not run if they approach carefully; this will be your chance to see or smell your "chase." If you can't see or smell "it," move forward until you find an obscure place to step aside. If you're smart about where and when to stop, the thing following will pass you by, giving you a good look at what "it" means to you. If your hair stands, it means you harm, and you need to run in the opposite direction, and do not return.

Maria found a narrow space to step out of the vein of foot traffic. A carpet vendor, distracted with customers, did not see her slip between the long hanging rugs. Her hair stood in attention, even as she calmed her breathing. Standing between the dusty carpets, she stared at the flow of people passing, not knowing what to notice. A black clad man wearing bulky dark glasses, and a black hat passed. Steps away, she watched the hat moving haltingly, then it turned around. He was skilled at holding his head at such an angle that his face was partially hidden by the brim of the hat, but *Maria* could see he was not a familiar. The high temperatures were expected this time of year, and most wore muted-colored clothing, yet he was in all black. It was obvious the man was a visitor to the region.

Maria receded deeper into the rugs. A splashy printed shirt, small man-sized, and a matching straw brimmed hat, emerged from her bag. She was thankful to be able to change her look. With the items covering her head and clothes, she made an about-face turn from the lingering stranger, moving out of the hanging rugs through the rear opening. Her small size and agility allowed her to slip under some tables to get back around to the shopper's side. Behind him now, she walked deep into the crowd, until she could run undetected. Not knowing who or why she was being followed, instantly made her life more complicated.

What now? Have I been recognized? Or have I become some man's target? How long has he been watching me? Am I safe to return to get my things?

Once *Maria* had put considerable distance between herself and the marketplace, rain had begun to fall, heavily. She was soaked almost immediately. She felt sadness and loss and the rain only made it worse, but only for a few minutes. Knowing sorrow would impede her survival, she made her mind up to feel able.

I am able to give up my new familiars. No more market employment dumping fish parts, and no more stinky hands. No more Feira's, but I have learned about what is safe and good to eat and I can feed myself.

No more grinning and making funny faces with the children who stare up at me between the cracks. No more renting floors, but those places never belonged to me anyway. In place of sorrow, I will focus on finding new items to change my appearance and move on to the next new place. I can do this.

Looking over the Brazilian vista, *Maria* had approached the edge of the Rio Tietê, she had never stood this close to the powerful currents. With rain coming down in heavy sheets, her able-thoughts were doused by one unable knowing, she had not learned to swim.

I am not wood that floats, nor am I a fish who knows how to move through the water. The roads are flooded, and the river is much stronger than it looked from the distance, yet my life depends on leaving this place. It is decided. I refuse to be swallowed; not by the river, and not by the man wearing black. I will not be trapped. The waterway is my road out, I accept this is my choice.

Grateful for any expedient travel away from the place where she had been chased, *Maria* acknowledged her fate, and accepted traveling in canoes and other small water vessels. She was afraid, yet she managed to put her anxiety behind her by mimicking those around her. She did not allow panic to control her. Freedom was sought mindfully, soulfully.

The rainforests will provide my cover if someone is looking for me. I will keep moving and stay alert. Surely the past will not survive this territory.

～〜

Among the natives, whose homeland she was adopting, *Maria* found *peaceable* faces were abundant. The apparent congeniality did not make the people or their territory any less threatening. Now the outsider with her foreign ways, *Maria* in the jungle was an unfamiliar who turned heads; there was nowhere to hide and no way for her to blend in. Some of the painted individuals would watch her for a time, at a safe distance, like rain clouds at the ready, subject to the restless winds. She counted herself fortunate "they" did not find it necessary to know where she had come from, few made verbal queries about her presence, and if someone did ask, she would say, "I am a teacher on sabbatical, I am here to learn your ways."

As it turned out, one of her early "native" lessons meant she did not have to carry disguise items to avoid being identified. As explained to her, the leaves of the "huitol" tree, when crushed and boiled, were used to heal the scalp. The mixture also effectively blackened the hair, and the skin for weeks at a time. The dyed hair and skin were less vulnerable to dandruff, lice, and other pesky bugs. The stark change in her coloring also helped her to integrate with the people, who were mostly persons with darker coloring. *Maria's* new "native" look, including shorn blackened hair and skin, loose khaki clothes, and a machete hanging from her waist belt, brought out her maleness. Living as a darkened non-binary person made the world feel different, safer.

The observant natives, knowing *s/he* was not one of them, were impressed with the light-footed bravery and unpretentious spirit. They watched *her/him* humbly respect the earth and witnessed a lack of entitlement; it seemed obvious that *s/he* did not wish to leave a "footprint." Among the close-knit tribes, the prevailing response was not to interfere with *her/him* spirit's efforts to learn from them. From the customary perspective, the stranger was a spiritual wanderer, and was not lost.

The indigenous upstanders would not make physical contact with the blackened-white-wayfarer based on local practices, but they were curious about *her/his* willingness to be away from *her/his* own kind. They tracked the stranger's movements in a prodigious manner, and surmised the stranger was interested in the ways of the rainforest. Unlike the typical flatlander, who was dependent on foreign words, and shows of power, they believed this wayfarer to be a unique anomaly, and they allowed *her/him* to move freely.

The daily progress of becoming a whole-free-person, meant there was no pressure to be female or male. Gender constructs were unnecessary, and *Maria's* daily actions became more tribal. Living among the natives, *she* listened, as if with their ears, and looked, as if with their eyes. Rapidly, *he* became adept in the ways of the Amazon. The deep immersion with nature was profoundly instructive; gone were most of the mental distractions which had come from trying to "escape" the past. Each day had new people, new animals, new ways, and new meanings to understand. When heavy rains prevented travel, *he* stayed with various tribes for weeks at a time, absorbing their language, their leisure ways, and their eco-activities.

In awe of a "she" non-native's ability to quickly grasp their way of life, one tribe began to refer to her as *alma bonita,* meaning beautiful soul, they felt blessed to have had her pass among them and they demonstrated it by sharing little gifts with her, and watching over her when she slept. The *alma bonita* spent nearly a year in the company of the hospitable Guarani tribe. Undoubtedly, the greatest impact on her being, came at the end of her time there, during an unexpected *trip* to a "magic kingdom." Her guide, she counted as one of her *angels*, the Shaman named Yaguati, meaning jaguar.

Yaguati was the medicine man for his tribe, and he was gifted at foreseeing future events. *Alma bonita* thought his name was fitting, since he wore a headdress with long orange and white feathers, accented with small black circular feathers. Having fallen in love with the tribe, *Alma bonita* found herself considering not going any further, and had shared as much to one of the women. She was immediately taken to Yaguati. He would need to give her a blessing in order for her to stay, but a two-day fast was required before she could speak to him. She complied.

Yaguati welcomed her into a clearing where a small hut was used for the traditional ayahuasca ceremony. Inside the dwelling there was a circle outlined on the ground. The two sat on the circle, cross-legged, without speaking until night fell. Yaguati began by smoking his mapachos, cigarettes made from tobacco the tribe grew. He blew the first puff of smoke into a bottle of pre-prepared ayahuasca brew. Once he had finished smoking, Yaguati shared a drink called oje, this was followed by several liters of warm water, which they drank every half hour, coupled with "power song," chanting by Yaguati. Occasionally, sobs would emit from the healer, after which his hands would hover over her head.

Ceremony dictated the shaman's every action, including removing coverings and bathing himself in huitol. The plant dye was also freshly applied to *alma bonita*. On the second night, the time had come to drink the sacred plant-based ayahuasca brew. Before allowing her to drink, Yaguati asked her to think about the purpose of his blessing, what meaning would it have for her. The answer came to her quickly.

How do I stop thinking about what I could have been, and begin living what I am or will be? The purpose of receiving this blessing is to help me know where I belong.

Once they had consumed the brew, the fire was stoked. There were moments of direct eye contact, but as time passed, she felt he was looking inside her. She felt as though Yaguati was seeing through her eyes, as if he had become omnipresent. Hours passed, and she began to feel she was seeing through his eyes, and together, they shared a vision.

During the trance-like state, different beings existed and ruled the world, although new to her, she felt like she knew them, as if she had always known them. They called to her, saying, "Ariel Black, come away." As she saw and heard the spirits, she understood them. It seemed her life had become the body of the smoke rising from the burning ashes, she knew she was not meant to stay. At that point, Yaguati stood and informed her she must wait a week before leaving to find her home. Then, he announced, "You have my blessing, Ariel Black. If ever I visit North America, you can share your home with me."

The spiritual name, and a budding sense of place and purpose was profoundly motivating for the sojourner. According to the vision, her first step in actualizing her purpose was to go to find a home in the United States; Canada was not an option. Absorbing the culture and native wisdom, the former Maria, reached Georgetown as a much stronger person than who she was when she began in São Paulo. and she recognized she had not done it alone. She counted the number of individuals, who with nothing to gain, had been willing to help her along her way; they were her ten *angels*, reminding her of human goodness, inspiring trust, and her own resilience. She would never forget them.

Three months and several precarious boat rides later, the slight bodied escapee arrived in Miami. The people she had arrived with were destined for a city in Texas, she had pretended her intention was the same. No one showed any interest when she parted ways. She had given up the blackening of her face with plant dye, but she continued changing identities with the help of disguise, including her gender presentations; it seemed prudent to do until she determined where she should live.

CHAPTER 10

ARIEL'S ANGELS

*"Tranquility, allied to loneliness,
possessed no charms.*
MARY SHELLEY

While Miami's temperatures reached winter lows, confined to neither name nor gender, the *fresh off the boat* traveler mulled about wearing layers of Cuban guayabera's, men's casual wear, also known as cigar shirts. Some layers were long sleeved, some were short, but all had the signature four-pockets on the front of the shirt. This was handy for carrying items, as well as making herself appear larger. She did not dare to rent a motel room, or go to a homeless shelter, believing it was best not to leave a record of where she had been. She did not plan to stay long, although, after the jungles of the Amazon, living on Miami's streets and beaches were not a hardship, especially when dollars were handed to her on a daily basis. The generous souls of Miami kept her pockets from being empty.

America is the land of the plenty, especially when strangers push cash into my hand, without having even been asked, those are the ones who feel sorry for me. The others think I am a famous personality trying to hide from my fans. All or nothing, I guess many suffer from being stuck with polarized thinking. I wish they could all spend a year or more in the Amazon.

~~

Ariel did not plan to stay in Miami, but she did want to buy new identification. The money she had saved was enough to put her vision name, Ariel Black, onto a social security card, a birth certificate, and an official I. D. card; it was to be a month before the documents would be ready. During the wait, she thought identifying as a transgender male was best, it required the least amount of acting. Dressing like a *female to male Tran* was simple, although somewhat gender-behaviorally complicated as an "American." Nonetheless, Ariel must have been convincing because "he" was stopped by another gender non-conformist.

"Asere que bola? Que cute! You must belong to Disney."

What does that mean? I do not belong to anyone. She must think I'm famous.

Getting more blank stares than shee was used to seeing, the friendly transwoman decided something was being lost in translation, and "shee" dropped the Spanglish.

"It's okay fella, I don't bite. You do look lost, and I know I've never seen you before, I would never have forgotten those blue eyes of yours."

"Oh meu, uh, hola. I am pretty new to this area, still trying to learn my way around."

"Hola. I am Dixy, Miss Dixy to my friends. I'm a Panromantic tg. My pronoun is shee with two e's, and hur, with a ur, if you're interested. Are you? Cuz, mmmmm, you are a heartbreaker if ever I saw one!"

"Oh, uhm, pleasure to meet you, Dixy."

Ariel's honest pleasure came from seeing and hearing the charismatic colorful being who wore a pink wig, the same shade as hur lips, and a dress fit for a princess, with cutouts for hur shoulders. Hur frolicking thick-ish hands had distinct fingernails, each one painted a different shade of pink, and hur pitch was shrill and yawn-like. Ariel was intrigued but reserved.

"Aha, is that so? Well, Mr. I'm pretty new to this area, if I were your friend, what might I call you?" The ongoing blank stare said "he" did not understand he had been asked a question. Dixy tried again with more flair. "What is your name handsome?"

Pushing a flier into the little fella's hands, Dixy was flirty and all smiles. Stooping, and leaning one hip and knee outward, Ariel wondered if shee was self-conscious of hur generous height, then, *he* noticed Dixy was wearing four-inch heels. Before *he* could decide what to say next, just as quickly as shee had appeared, shee twirled out and away, picking up hur heels as shee took off down the sidewalk.

"I gotta run, here comes el guagua, and that's bus, not baby, and I abhor sitting in the back. Come to the meeting tomorrow, it's for people like us!"

Dixy, a *male to female Tran,* was the first person in Miami to extend a welcome; it made the newbie smile and wave back. Shee had made a positive, if not colorful impression. Ariel did not look away until hur guagua had disappeared, and even then, hur perfume had stayed behind.

Too much fragrance, but likeable and she reminds me I need a name for my man identity. I am? How about Trin? Yes, I am Trin. People like us, shee said, us.

The only "us" Ariel had ever known had been with her teacher, Lily. Having walked among various people-groups living in Canada, Greece, Brazil, and the Caribbean Islands, the blue-eyed *newbie* had witnessed diversity, but Dixy was something new.

I would like to learn more about hur and more about us, I will go tomorrow.

⌇

Within the first fifteen minutes of the meeting, *Trin* had become a fan of the "people like us." They were all unique, all identified non-conformists, not related, but infinitely similar and equally support-ive of one another's differences; and their laughter was contagious.

These might be heavy-hearted souls, but they know how to make one another laugh.

As modeled by the others, when *Trin* was invited to introduce *himself* to the group, *he* announced *his* pronouns were he/his/him, then, inspired by their humor, *he* offered, "Since you all are so witty, I've made up a little ditty. I'm a Tran named Trin, no hairs on my chin. Not opposed to using whisker pasties, if the rain will let them stay on my face-es. I'm complicated, but I don't want to hurt, I have layers but I'm nobody's dessert. You can call me Trin, and you can call me sir, I am a transman, and not a Cuban chauffer."

He was an instant hit. Attending the transgender support group also gave *Trin* a sense of comradery. *His* new Tran friends were also helpful in giving advice on where to get freebies, hot showers, and they were clear on where "not to go alone."

The morning following *his* third weekly meeting, having walked around the city until dawn, *Trin*, was making a pass through a homeless alley; a "safe one," according to Dixy. *He* meandered along the row of cardboard and junk dwellings, poking *his* head in and around loose sections, and eyeing the abandoned piles of over-used, discarded things. Having become somewhat of a scavenger, *he* was hoping to find a large coat, instead, *he* found a dead body.

"Da madre, oh meu Jesus!"

The words stumbled out with horror. At *Trin's* feet, lay a woman, clothed in dirty rags, laying on papers, face up, already stiff and with bluish coloring. *He* had seen the woman before, she was a regular on a beach bench, always alone, but always with a smile on her face.

No obvious injuries if I don't count her forlorn expression. So sad, she looks so sad. What a lonely way to die, if only I had come earlier, I might have helped in some way.

Standing in the frigid temperatures, *Trin* stood and offered tears of mourning for the woman, it seemed apparent there would be no others to honor her spirit. Then, feeling chilled to the bone, *Trin* took a trench coat which *he* found draped over the deceased's cart. It wasn't until several days later that *he* found an expired driver's license, and vanilla scented car fresheners, buried deep into pockets which had been sewn shut.

The following morning, when the doors opened for the library, *Trin* was there, having decided to do some virtual investigating; *he* could not get the woman out of *his* mind. The woman found dead was Caroline Davis, born in 1959; her license had expired more than ten years prior. Some follow-up investigating on the Truckee, California, address, proved it was legitimate, the deceased woman owned a home outright, having paid off her VA loan. She had been in the military, the Navy. *Trin* searched for missing person reports, there were none that matched her description in Florida or in California. Given her status at death, and without I.D. on her body, *Trin* thought it possible that no one would know Caroline Davis had died.

Google maps offered a live satellite view, and a street view of the neighborhood.

It looks like a wonderful place to live, why would she leave it and live in squalor across the country? There is not much around the place, a bicycle, a few rusted shopping carts, and weeds. Weeds that divide her place from the neighbors, another natural A-frame, and nothing to suggest anyone is staying there.

Searching a few other addresses from the immediate area gave *Trin* the answer. Most of the houses in the neighborhood were vacation rental homes; there were links for more information about renting.

This is a beautiful country; no wonder people go there to visit. I think I would like it there. There are trees everywhere, forests, definitely more trees than people. This could be the safe house I had hoped to find, a real home for Ariel Black, like in the vision from Yaguati.

After sleeping on the idea, a decision was made to relocate to Truckee, California. *Trin* would not return for a goodbye with the new friends from the group, even though *he* imagined they might be concerned when *he* did not return.

It has been a blessing to have met so many loving supportive people. Being a part of an "us" has given me much personal happiness. The cultural knowledge has been a gift. Hearing their struggles, and the joys of being a transgender soul has helped me understand some of my own feelings. I do hope they find what they are looking for, each one, they all deserve to be loved. I know they will understand why I could not stay, especially Dixy. Miami is not my place to settle.

Before leaving the Miami district, *Trin* pushed a note under the door where the group had met for meetings. *His* words were few.

"Thank you all for sharing your truths with me, thank you for seeing me, and respecting me as a man. I am leaving to find my new place, but I will not forget you. You are all beautiful. Trin."

~~~

Caroline's home was a two bedroom, with a loft, and a four-piece bath, literally filled with storage boxes, newspapers and magazines stacked neatly from floor to ceiling.

No wonder she left, there is no room for the living, although this place smells deliciously sweet. Thank goodness there is no actual food to attract varmints or roaches, I've had enough dealings with those disgusting things to last a lifetime. If I can live in a box, I can make this work.

Stacks of mail on the porch, spoke of a lengthy absence. It also suggested that no one had come looking for the owner. By carting bundles of the hoarded papers out at night, the bathroom was emptied, and a five-foot-wide path was made through the house. The cleared bathroom was large enough to utilize as a place to nest. The microwave, and the mini refrigerator were extricated from the kitchen and put into her new room. A cot was also added to the space, giving it the look of a fully furnished studio.

Caroline apparently had no family, and no friends, and very few regular neighbors. No one came around, aside from the postman delivering junk mail. On day five, when he saw her in the yard, he called out to the rag dressed form, assuming it was Caroline.

"Oh you're alive? I was beginning to think you died in there." Adding in a lowered voice, "Now take your mail inside, you batshit crazy hoarder."
~~~

The secret lodger was convinced Caroline had mental issues involving hoarding. She knew little about such illnesses, only what she had picked up from group discussions in Florida. Even so, she could not judge Caroline's unusual behavior, knowing her own mental health was anything but normal. It was weirdly comforting to be able to hide within the over-stuffed house in case someone did have cause to peek inside the windows.

Maybe that's why she stuffed the house full, a kind of emotional wall to protect herself?

～～

Taking a shopping cart filled with paper as her prop, *Caroline* took a fifteen-minute walk to reach the nearest convenience store, which had a functioning coin operated public phone, and local phone directory book. It was a frightening call to make, as most human contact was still a test of faith, but to truly set up "home," the squatter needed the electricity turned on, and to verify the water would stay on. Wearing the "Caroline" garb, and acting the part, her dirtied hands located the number, dropped in the coins, and dialed.

"Good morning, Truckee Donner Public Utility, district office, my name is Laura, how may I direct your call?"

"Oh, Hello. I need power restored to my home, I've just returned from a lengthy time away, and I…"

"I'll need your name and account number."

"Uh, Caroline Davis, I don't remember my account number, it's been about a year."

"Well then, I'll need your date of birth, and answer to your security question, to verify you, then I'll need your address to pull up your account history."

Making a safe guess that turned out to be correct, the security question was to answer where she'd like to go on vacation; the answer was Miami, Florida. A brief search on the account revealed Caroline had left with a large credit on her bill; the same was true for the water-sewer, she had a credit on her account.

It is tragic to think about Caroline dying alone on the ground, in the cold, when she had such a nice home and a year or more of paid utilities.

When she returned to the house, Ariel thought to look in the most accessible boxes along the interior path, to see if she could find any personal information on Caroline, she still had not ruled out the possibility of family. The boxes revealed a number of unopened items, purchased in bulk; Vanilla scented, flameless candles, there were cases of them. The newly adopted 1500 square foot home might have had less than a hundred square foot for walking space, but it had the most delicious smell of vanilla, and now Ariel knew why. She also found boxes of vanilla scented car fresheners, dozens of them. Ariel took it as a positive sign.

Caroline may have been troubled, but she was a good person. Only an angel could love vanilla that much.

When out, in "Caroline" character, Ariel presented herself in layers of unmatched clothes. Her petite features remained veiled among the scarves, and disposable face mask she wore. She limited her "Caroline" outings to the local soup kitchen, the nearby convenience store, and a thrift store, as she pushed a cart filled with cardboard boxes between her hangouts.

While in character, Ariel would stand hunched, and speak in low tones. She also wore an unkept gray, shoulder-length wig, dirtied her face and clothes with charcoal dust, and pushed around a trench coat covered shopping cart. If she felt noticed, she would speak some kind of nonsense to herself; most would turn away to avoid making contact. However, one day on her *Caroline* walk, a familiar shelter volunteer appeared on the street, and stopped to speak to her while she tried to pull her cart up and over a curb.

"Pardon me, I couldn't help notice you, I saw you at the soup kitchen last week, I served you. I don't know if you remember me, my name is Beth."

"No, wrong person. I need to go, I can't be late," hoping to sound brisk, *Caroline* kept her eyes down.

"I'm sorry, I don't want to delay you. I just thought, well, I can offer you a bus pass, and information about a nearby shelter. And I have some wet wipes, if you'd like to get some of the black off your hands. Or if there is anything else I can give you?"

Oh my, another angel.

Choking back sentiment that willed her to trust the woman, Ariel decided it was still best to be thought crazy while impersonating Caroline.

"Shhh, squirrels are listening. The government is using them, it is a secret. The corruption is seeping out. They put it in the soup. Need more papers, lift your tail, they are under the sidewalk."

Beth ignored the word salad and tried once more.

"I'm not trying to bother you, I only wish to give you a pass which will allow you to travel by bus, for free. You owe me nothing. You can keep this paper, and whether you use it or not will be up to you."

Beth tucked the small card between the large stacks of newspapers on the cart, which had finally been pulled up onto the sidewalk. *Caroline* dropped her head and kept moving.

Thank you for the bus pass. Thank you for seeing me as worthy and not wretched.

The gift was generous, however, the Caroline impersonator could not risk losing her safe nest until she found her *true* home. The recognition by the woman prompted Ariel to change up her routines once more. Although she was nearly out of money, there would be no more visits to the soup kitchen. *Caroline* and *Trin* would switch more frequently in order to utilize the pass. This was helpful for Ariel, as she could see and learn about the area, without having to ask questions. In the brief span of a month's time, Ariel became familiarized with many miles of the mountainous terrain in Nevada, Sierra, Plumas, Lassen, and Washoe counties.

My true home is close, I recognize the mountains, I will find it soon.

CHAPTER 11

I WILL FIND YOU, MY PET

"No man chooses evil because it is evil; he only mistakes it for happiness, the good he seeks."

MARY SHELLEY

Deep under the ground, sitting at his desk, behind secret iron walls, watching the bank of monitors like NASA seeing a final countdown, Neffen Oliver Jones, referred to as "Jones" when providing leadership to the underground network, lifted, then relaxed his shoulders. He felt rested and fortified. He was well prepared to tackle anything that entered his vast province, not that any living person could outsmart his customized computer operations center. He alone had knowledge of, and access to the hidden door, which opened into his private soundproof office suite. The space was filled with multiple computers, touch screen monitors, and panels of controls, much like an Airbus A380's cockpit. The exceptional sound system allowed for the precise monitoring of all spaces below and above, as well as several remote locations. Most importantly to Jones, those who had been involved with designing, building, and installing his "brain station" had since expired.

Wearing a brilliant white shirt, starched heavily, showing no wrinkles, or wear, made him feel like a deity, one who never perspired. In actuality, the atmospheric temperatures in his domain were programmed to his body's needs. By wearing a flexible wire, the size of a small digit bandage, his vitals were tracked by an application on his secure phone and interfaced with the HVAC system. If his temperature went up or down, the immediate spatial zone could turn frigid or warm within seconds. This also made him feel like a god, one who controlled his environment with infallible finesse.

Seeing all was secure, he turned his attention to the camera on one of the hidden entry points. The appointed time had come. His P.I.'s had returned to the outer roost. Three sedans approached the eastmost entrance. Jones squinted with a snarl.

Right on time, but no cargo aboard. Don't think that punctuality is enough to keep you on my good side.

Thoughts blurred as a labored sigh left his chest, the pain could not be denied. He was staggered by the inconvenient sensation which called attention to a weakness in his chest cavity.

Why does it hurt? It hurts where she tried to hurt me, it's not right. You had no right to leave. Where are you my pet? Why do you not come home where you belong? I dreamed you were back in your room and you're not here.

The tender sentiment was momentary, it triggered resentment.

You belong to me. Only me. You can't possibly be living any kind of existence without me. Only I make you happy. Why are you so selfish? You have deprived me of your obedience for nearly three years.

Encouraged he would have her back soon, he tried to remember her aroma, but all he could detect was the smell of gunpowder; presently, it was heavy in the air. His thoughts naturally returned to their last day together, their last moment. The look of satisfaction on her face was unanticipated, though not as startling as when she pointed the .45 caliber and pulled the trigger. He rationalized until he could not deny her action had been intentional.

You thought you were only putting me out of unnecessary suffering, you knew I would not wish my pet to leave me. It was your mercy and your ignorance; you didn't know I was wearing a bullet-proof vest. The nick on my head produced enough blood to fool you and the force of the bullet to my chest, knocked me out. You only left me because you thought I was dead. You were not smart enough to kill me. You could never hurt me, and you are not shrewd enough to hide much longer. My little tarnished one, I will find you. Do you hear me, you fucking bitch? I will have you back. Soon.

He paused. The room became cooler as his bitterness prompted boyhood memories of his famous mother leaving him in the care of drug addicted whores, and then of his mother, dead in her pink Cinderella bathtub. He reached up with both hands, closed his eyes and rubbed against his temples with his fingertips. It was an atomic habit that reminded him he needed to focus on what he could control.

All things in the Universe work to support my dreams, my world, my monopoly. It is only a matter of time; I will find you. Your ingratitude is not acceptable. You and China-bitch have betrayed your master, you both have debts to pay. With me, you'll live, if contrite. If not, I will be your worst nightmare until your last breath.

His calm was restored, the chilled air began to climb toward normal. Jones entertained one last visualization of his Golden Girl.

My Golden Girl, my pet, I will find you and put you back where you belong.

The thought of having his desired pet back in her room had animated his spirits, it enabled Jones to perform his various management tasks with notable elation. He set the stage for the punishment of his ineffective investigators. And based on their whispered conversations, each one had already confessed he had not done enough to please their boss.

They are afraid to speak to me and well they should be. Your own words have convicted you. I've been exceedingly patient with you, I haven't even taken any fingers or toes…hmmmm, an eye might be more fitting? Perhaps, I will show some leniency. I can be benevolent knowing my pet will be back in her cage soon. It's decided then, if she's returned within the week, I will let you keep all your piggies.

Aside from personal interests, which he would address soon, the day's schedule included the master having an outside visitor. All was planned over a period of two weeks. Years of experience had honed his instincts and cultivated meticulous safety precautions. Because his current methods included thorough background and deep identity checks for all persons of interest, there were few surprises. Not that Jones depended solely on written reports. His own voyeuristic needs were often minimally met while keeping up with standard surveillance procedures. He had virtually approved of his guest, and soon, he would see her in the chamber.

Jones punched the code in, opening the first gate. The iron fence receded into the ground, allowing the cars to enter. Once inside, eerily, the gate returned to the surface. The procession continued forward until coming to a non-descript rocky embankment at the end of the dirt road. He punched another code into the console. The earth began to move, rumbling like a garage door opening, and the rocks split apart. The vehicles drove forward into the darkness, entering the cavernous space on a steep decline, as if driving straight down into a well.

When the rocks returned to their resting place, an automatic wind and sprinkler system, hidden in the artificial rock, kicked on. Within seconds, the ground preceding the opening had been transformed, manipulated to hide any sign of tire tracks. The movement inside triggered the lighting at 100 yards from within the tunnel. White brightness from every direction prevented any shadows from emerging. The black clad men wearing dark sunglasses, parked, and exited their cars. Their arms and legs moved at the same tempo, like robots, all identical, except for the one holding a briefcase in his right hand.

Each golem removed his sunglasses, emptied pockets into waiting dishes, and took turns in the x-ray booth. The security personnel were accompanied by a guard-dog on leash. After the inspection of the lock, the briefcase was handed off and placed in a nearby dumbwaiter shaft. The trained snout checked for odors on the men, while a low growl escaped its throat. The men completed the security routine without speaking, and all were careful to move slowly in the presence of the irritable hound. Satisfied with inspections, security led the dog away from the group, and located an opening in the wall. Unhooked from the tether, the dog disappeared into the wall, and the partition closed.

Jones was signaled, as per instructions, letting him know the men would be arriving at the designated stop in sixty minutes. On the other end, a driverless tram awaited the passengers. The monitors, inner and outer, blinked the countdown before departure. One by one the look-alikes boarded the underground transportation, each one a mirror of the other, each one silently fearing for his life. The counter reached zero, and the doors closed.

Jones, having completed the keyboard tasks, reflexively reached for a squirt of hand sanitizer. He rubbed the solution all over his hands. Then, hearing the delivery, Jones walked to the dumbwaiter to retrieve the briefcase. Moving the locks in place, the snaps opened to free the lid. It was a written report, updating him on the search for his pets. He skimmed the first few pages, stopping on the fourth page. It was another *Jane Doe*.

"My pet, your thin thread has finally unraveled, I now have proof that you live. It won't be long before we reunite. Your punishment will be worse for not coming home on your own, but you will take your discipline. I know how much you used to enjoy the sting of my whip."

Reading a plastic surgeon's report, he noted the relevant breadcrumbs: Blood type, O Positive. Patient's approximate age, 30 years.

She does keep a youthful appearance, thanks to me, her benefactor, she looks younger than she's lived, as do I. The new 30, my body age, not bad for a god-man over 70.

Weight, 80 pounds.

Staying thin, good girl.

The skin grafts and the reconstruction notes had nothing remarkable, he knew that she would want her scars repaired, if only to disguise herself. Fortunately, there were other ways to identify her. Reading forward, the smirk on his face, widened.

No fingerprints, the kneecaps with indelible burn marks.

"Ha-haa! Fools can't even read a sign. It's her! It must be the tricky little bitch."

Why more master's do not brand, I cannot understand? One good burn, and a pet can always be recognized and claimed. Of course, no one has my brilliance. Burning off fingerprints, replacing dental work, and if necessary, changing blue and green eyes to a muddy brown. Amazing what a little bimatoprost can do for an eyeball.

Another manic laugh erupted, then pride chided.

All reasonable precautions for the little bitches. Any serious trafficker is a fool to do any less. And one can never be too careful with untamed animals and sexual deviants.

The summary noted that the patient reported being in a structure fire. The marks on her knees and lack of prints were attributed to the injuries sustained in that fire. Follow-up appointments were scheduled, but "no show" was written on three occasions. The emergency contact information was left blank. The associated prescriptions were never picked up, and the patient's status was listed as "unknown."

What Fools, do I have to be reminded when a pet's status is unknown?

An attachment served to acknowledge the report was based on discovery of a medical file that could have been more than five years old, but her name and the date had been blacked out with ink. Jones turned the next page.

No date, but what else have we here? What? No other interviews conducted. And no photos. No photos? There must have been photos taken. No plastic surgeon will begin without a before photo.

The attending physician's name had "deceased" written over it in red ink. Also, in red, "no other medical staff available for interviews."

What is this supposed to mean? Not available? I cannot believe you idiots left so many stones unturned. Leaving a hot trail to get cold while you return with your tail between your legs? I have taught you better.

A rage rose in Jones' chest, then a fleeting pain shot behind his eyes.

You leave me no choice. Your incompetence is inexcusable. How dare you return to your master without completing the job. You were told to bring her back.

The eye pressure generated childhood memories. They were the ones he longed to forget; men, using him, treating him as if he were an animal. He heard the word he hated, above all words, "bastard."

The surge in adrenaline, and his rising blood pressure, kicked the air conditioning unit on. The sound of the fan caught his ear and stopped the descension. Jones centered himself by acknowledging his superior intelligence.

He looked at his reflection in the monitor, smiled and spoke to himself, "Neffen Oliver Jones, NOJ, God, Master, Genius. You will have her soon, time to change."

Having donned his play clothes and mask, Jones went down to observe all the in-house *animal* facilities; all was met with approval. Then, he went to check the *sub* room. When inside the soundproof room, he pulled his mask. He was alone, and he was the only one who could open the door. No one could enter without his biometrics to release the lock. The space had been cleaned and readied for play.

"Spotless, set to perfection I see, and yet, it lacks…luster."

His sly mouth pooched, smirked, and puckered, sending a kiss toward the mirror. Returning to stern business face, he turned away from his image to look around.

"No scent. Just as well I suppose." Seemingly content, he sniffed the air a second time, "There it is, gunpowder. It returned, and yet I did not bring it in with me."

~

Jones longed to smell his pet slave again, and today the need for her was visceral. *Golden Girl's* room had been stubbornly filled with her scent, despite the rigorous cleaning, week after week, month after month. During her absence he had decided that her *spirit*, indebted to him, returned to keep her body scent with him. Akin to a floral vanilla in his mind, smelling her presence allowed him to feel connected with her. The hovering scented spirit was there, in her room, until there was a shift; it was the day he realized a full year had passed since he lost her. On that visit, day 366, all traces of her redolence were gone from her room; it had been an olfactory hallucination, lasting an entire year.

In Neffen's mind, smelling her "spirit" had been a singular curiosity, one he marveled over during his weekly visits to her empty room; particularly because he was the only "ghost" he believed in. Not lacking ego, Neffen was fanatical at being the only one who was visited by her scent. He had brought a few select others into the room, to test what they could smell; nothing was always the answer. When her sweet scent left him, rather than doubting himself, his obsession with her intensified. He decided it was his use of advanced air purifying technology that ultimately completed the work of disappearing her scent. She was a thing he refused to lose, and he was determined to own her, body, and spirit, once again.

Impressed with her natural golden hair, Neffen had named her "Golden Girl." Twisted as he was, he found her at age three, made her an orphan, then trained her, and groomed her to be his perfect pet. Golden Girl had never failed him, until the day the plan failed. Jones had accompanied her delivery to a first-time destination in Vancouver. His "perfect" plan was piffled by the client who turned out to be a liar and a fool. Gun in hand, threats were made. His pet was loosened. There was gunfire, multiple shots and the client went down. Neffen was also grazed, it knocked him down, giving his pet opportunity. She took it. When he awoke, the client was dead, and the golden one was gone.

Her two-room chamber had been vacant until recent months. When confidence of her return, re-activated his fantasies; a new "smoking-gun" phantosmia came with them. Jones, however, found the gunpowder smell could be temporarily diminished with fresh, "wanton bitch sweat."

～〜～

Jones eyed the lock pad to open the door and replaced his mask. He had timed the opening perfectly. Two henchmen, one on each side of his "golden girl" stood at the ready, gripping her at the elbows. A Sack had been put over her head, but the master could see she was wearing the wig he had sent her.

"Remove her covering and put her on the wheel."

~~~

Playing "Sub" games with substitutes was rarely satisfying, although it did sooth his need for her, if the bitch was her body size, willing, and one who enjoyed heavy bondage and humiliation. Unlike his pet, the sub-women he played with, were not his slaves. They were "customers" who responded to "Dom" advertisements; they paid to be treated like his bitches. Neffen did not need their money, and smuggling the hooded women, in and out required extra dedicated personnel, however, it was a practice which allowed him a measure of bolstering fantasy-time with his *Golden Girl*, even if he had not found any who were pure enough to equal her caliber.

~~~

Much to his dismay, the day's bitch, now painfully exposed, was not special, she was alike the *Golden Girl*, but not enough to be satisfying. Nevertheless, he decided to grant himself a brief break before seeing the cloned P.I.'s, who would soon be paying for their negligent efforts.

Jones found his playful voice, "I am thinking about adding an electrical saddle with four vibrating parts, each with variable speeds. What do you think?"

"I'm not deserving Master, I'm so bad, please, please punish me."

"If I suspended it next to the wall of shackles, I could bind ankles or wrists while you ride it, and you would have no control over the speed. You could be the rodeo queen for hours."

"Master, I am yours, do what you will."

He gave the wheel a spin, two times around and he stopped her.

"You know you need to pay your debt; you know you deserve to be hurt."

"Slap me, I am a bad girl."

He slapped her with his gloved hand, leaving handprints as he went. She cried out a few times, but she was acting. The abuse would stop if she spoke the safe word, "gunpowder." Her face was left alone, he stopped the smacking when the redness covered most of her body.

"Thank you, Master."

He gave the wheel another spin and retrieved his favorite whip. At the appropriate distance, he flicked the leather cord severely, bringing it close, but not touching the sub.

"I doubt you have learned your lesson, you're one stupid bitch."

His wrist flicked the whip, landing the end of it across the front of her thighs.

"Yes, Master, whip me, whip me until I learn my lesson."

Two more stinging flicks were delivered, the second drew an honest shriek.

"Once you've shown enough remorse, I will let you heal, hanging in your gill net. You know how much I enjoy your spider-monkey moves, so helpless, yet so resolute."

He was not speaking to the woman in front of him, she was in effect, a mirage.

"I can be your bad spider-monkey, yes, I'm begging you, whip me and then punish me in your net. I can be very bad."

Behind the tiger mask, Jones eyes were glassed over, his breathing shallowed. He sniffed the room. The gunpowder had intensified. The woman was talking too much. He did not like talking, but he ignored it in favor of letting his delusion play out.

"You will be muzzled like a dog, and your paws will be tied together. Yes, that should sufficiently remind you of your dependence on me."

The woman groaned, expressing her pleasure in the role play. The unfamiliar sounds dashed the imaginary away, stoking Jones' temper.

"Open your eyes, you will get no favors. If you think I enjoyed any of your groans, you would be wrong. You are clumsy, ugly, and fat, aren't you?"

"Yes, Master, I'm not worthy, punish me."

He placed the muzzle gag over her mouth, leaving it loose enough for her to be able to speak her safe word. He spun her in the other direction, stopping to use a short bat on the bottom of her feet. The stinging slaps were cursory.

"Look how you drool. Do you deserve to be treated like an animal? I have dogs that behave better than you."

Standing in the duplicate room next to her chamber suddenly felt like an off-putting activity. The woman was a poor imitation for what he wanted. He looked around. There were whips, wooden bats, masks, collars, gags, spreader bars, bondage appliances, a rack of S&M outfits, all things that once excited him. He felt nothing. The woman was strapped to the Catherine Wheel, hanging sideways, the way he liked to pose his pet, but the scene suddenly felt like a cruel disappointment. The sub's muffled moans had grown more lustful, even with the bindings digging deep into her wrists and ankles. Another musky grunt came from the woman, indicating she wanted more. The master exhaled, not quite a sigh.

"Time for a break. I shall right you for the sake of your circulation, give you a few moments to collect yourself, and then I will return to complete your punishment."

Jones was done playing make-believe. It took more than a little amount of self-discipline to keep from bleeding her out with his whip, but he had a rule not to kill the customers unless he was prepared to kill all her personal connections, and Jones had another plan for the day. One of his clones would be sent in to wrap up the play session, then the woman would be returned, alive, to her boring life. His mask was moist with perspiration, which further annoyed him. After trading places with his clone, and entering his secure lift, he pulled it off purposefully; he was headed for a shower, then he would resume the day's business.

~~

The whirring hiss of the incoming tram, sounded from a speaker, alerting Neffen to the arrival of his droids. He tasted bitterness. He drank from a water bottle and then tossed it into his trash shoot. Next to the hatch, he lingered, collecting a goodly amount of hand sanitizer, then he rolled the cool substance all over the tops and bottoms of his hands.

The incompetent ones have arrived. What feeble words will be offered to convince me they are worth keeping?

In play were two key aspects of Jones' dominance, eliminate all individuality, and demonstrate the fungibility of all. The security team were disposable, without consequence, and they knew it. Prior to coming to *work* for Jones, each one had chosen to commit one or more horrific crimes, and had been condemned to death row. Having the right people in his *net*, meant Jones was able to arrange freedom for death-row-inmates, with the "right stuff." They would all accept his employment contract, unaware their *job* satisfaction would be, at best, brief. There was no brotherhood, no connection, no empathy for the other. At the start, the underlings were made to understand, what happened to one, happened to all. With his business mind fully engaged, Jones left his secure nest to meet the men on the arrival platform. The assembly were a solemn bunch, their fate had been sealed before they had begun to work for Jones. All were in their places, numerically lined up.

Determined to play his cards close, and to keep them uncertain of what was coming, Jones began pleasantly, "Good afternoon, men, it has been a fruitful journey, yes?"

No one spoke up, and only one dared to lift his eyes to meet Jones' gaze.

"It's 27, right? You followed the Canadian leads, am I right?"

"Yes, Sir."

"Ahhh, why so serious? You must have known I'd be pleased by the report, yes?"

"I, wasn't sure, but I did think the progress would be agreeable to you."

"We will need to discuss a few details, and I do have some outstanding questions, but agreeable is possible. And since you are the only one to speak up, you may answer my next question, as well. What do you think of the support your fellow P-eyes have given you?"

"Uh, they did their part, they were able to put an end to the false leads, Sir."

"Ahh yes, like you, right? And do you think they should enjoy the reward you have earned?"

There was no doubt among the men, Jones had posed a trick question.

"If it pleases you Sir, we serve you as one, one force, all for one," the bot man tried to lighten the moment, his tension needing some relief.

"Ah yes, all for one. That one would be me, yes? Let me hear it from all of you, answer the question, now."

The men instantly found their voices, responding with "yes Sir" in unison. Each made confident eye contact, except for one, and the boss did not miss a blink.

"Hmmm, 23, you do not appear as self-assured as your cohort. Perhaps, you have a different opinion?"

"Sir, yes. Uh, I mean no, Sir."

"Well, which is it 23, yes or no?"

"I am not thinking anything different, Sir. I was hoping, like the rest, to please you by bringing you good news."

Hoping? Hmph, only the weak, hope. News? Eehh! News is not synonymous with cargo, which is what you were expected to bring me.

Jones' words did not match his narcissistic thoughts, "Oh, of course you are hopeful, very thoughtful of you, and we do have some good news, do we not?"

No one dared to respond. The change in their employer's tone and his ambivalent manner felt like thin ice to his men. They had been warned of his reputation at the start, knowing his displeasure could manifest his malevolence, along with violent penalties. Regardless of Jones' gentlemanly manners, all were fearful.

"25? Good news, or bad news?"

"Sir, we strive to serve you only good. You have the last word, and we await your direction."

"I can certainly offer you some direction 25. For example, you are looking lighter than your mates, two to three pounds I'd say. It is not acceptable to be different, and that is a last word. As for direction, be sure and manage your caloric intake to correct the issue by day's end. Are we clear?"

"Sir, yes sir."

"Now then, I recognize you have all toiled, striving to return to me with good results. Let me assure you, there is no doubt that something good will come from your performance. You have demonstrated your worth, and you all shall be recognized for your efforts."

"Yes Sir, thank you Sir," sputtered out, but there was no tension relief for the men. They knew their taskmaster was a harsh one when he did not get what he wanted; all remained unsettled and stiff.

"Relax. At ease, men. Please note how reasonable I am. You have all had arduous journeys. The layovers for Tokyo and New Zealand were brutal, I'm sure. You must be parched, if not famished. Before we formally meet, why don't you enjoy some well-earned refreshments? And 25 can fill up, as he should. I have had catering set you up in the employee lounge. And I will call for you individually once you've had a chance to decompress."

Their response was more relaxed, "Yes Sir, thank you Sir."

Their words were accompanied with shivers. The room temperature had been dropping since the moment Jones arrived. Angered at the ease in which they took his generosity, but maintaining a calm tone, Neffen continued with his game.

"That is all. You are dismissed, you know how to get to the lounge from here?"

In unison, "Yes Sir."

Turning on their heels simultaneously, the men stepped away from the arrival platform to follow the ostensibly pleasant orders of their boss. Before they were fully out of sight, Jones gave a snap-clap. Knowing the sound was a call for attention, the men stopped and looked back.

"Oh, just one question that cannot wait. Pardon my curiosity. 27? How confident are you that your work has put us on the right trail?"

Number 27 turned to fully face Jones, "Very confident, Sir. I'm about 90 percent certain your slave remains in Canada. We'll have her back soon."

"Very well. Thank you."

Unable to play the game a moment longer, Jones shook his head disappointedly after the men left his sight.

Here I thought they all had a little more substance, but no, they are all worthless, selfish, and weak. A total waste of my oxygen on these fellows, I don't know why I should even be cordial to them. I truly am a reasonable man. Look what they offer, 90 percent? What good is that? Who gets the other 10 percent? Am I the only one here who understands there are consequences to inefficient work? Buffoons, every one of them. They should be groveling and begging my forgiveness; that would at least have been entertaining. Ahh well, I can be generous with a man who gives me 100 percent every time. Yes, number 14 will enjoy applying the recognition. He doesn't get enough torture time since he started in the kennels. He will be thrilled to know that he will be extracting the left eye from each of these buffoons.

Then chuckling to himself, "Private one-eyes, now that's funny."

CHAPTER 12

FROM BASTARD TO MEGALOMANIAC

*"Will people ever be wise enough to refuse to follow bad
leaders or to take away the freedom of other people?"*

ELEANOR ROOSEVELT

Embracing the ever-dominant Alpha-Master role, Jones saw himself as a type of *Oz-Wizard*, only he believed himself to be more powerful than the iconic character. Humility was a mask he wore, when necessary, an act for those he wanted to manipulate, to create a pretense of transparency and ease. To be "approachable," Jones shared an office suite with resort staff. The large group office was a multi-purpose space that included a glass conference table for *team talks* on one end, and an open bank of wall mounted, touch screen computers, at the other end. The artwork, mostly nature-based photographs, provided an outdoor open-space design. The design features also served to distract the curious from discovering the two-way speakers and recording features of the electronic art frames. In the center of the space, Jones' desk sat on an elevated island, with an adjustable glass tabletop, allowing for stand-up or sitting work. The island could also be lowered into the floor and out of sight, to allow more room for *team* events.

Equipped with high-tech essentials and ergonomic furnishings, the "group office" was considered state-of-the-art, and *team member* friendly. As was typical, he was prepared to be the ever-gracious host, courteous, with the utmost respect for diversity, and judgement free interactions. He frequently praised himself with personalized affirmations.

I am a gentle, and generous Tarzan among animals, Neffen Oliver Jones, a man beyond reproach.

As far as he believed, no living person could prove *the* Neffen Oliver Jones was anything other than what he presented himself to be, "an exceptional animal whisperer and trainer." The business professional supremacy Jones exuded, announced his opulence, and his successful status. It was something his mother had modeled. His mother, a famous animal trainer known only as Olga, was a toughened swede, who also modeled egosyntonic aggression, and antisocial paranoid traits.

In 1938, there was no status to be gained from a single mother, having a fatherless child in a hotel room. Rather than name him legally, she kept her baby off the grid, and called him "Tiger," since he was born in the Year of the Tiger. Initially, she had no use for a baby, having just reached a professional pinnacle; one of her trained leopards had been in a Hollywood movie. The success of the movie made her sentimental enough to keep the infant, although her first thought was to drown him in the bathtub.

The work training large animals kept Olga too busy to care for a baby. Off-the-clock whores were used to care for him, never using the same harlot more than a few times, so as not to foster attachments. Olga would not take care of a baby, but once the diapers and toddler ways were behind him, her self-importance as a parent budded. Rather than showing love, which she believed taught weakness, Olga used her skills as an animal trainer to teach her fatherless son; she expected him to value her affectionless affluence.

Rarely, did Olga admit to having a son, as she liked being the center of any attention she received; and seldom did she even speak to her spawn. During his early years, when she wanted his attention, she would use her famous training snap-clap motion, while popping her lips apart, which meant, "I'm in charge, pay attention and do what I tell you, now."

Olga thought of herself more as an animal trainer, than a parent; training and instruction came easier than nurturing ever would. Accordingly, she began using her animal whip to "exercise him properly." The whip only landed on flesh when she intended it, when the child chose the wrong path or if he slowed before she said, "Enough." It happened seven times: three times, the whips landed during exercise, four times, they landed when the child mistakenly left something unclean. Olga could not tolerate mess, of any kind, particularly "children's germs." She made certain her son had the highest standards of cleanliness, even if it meant having a few scars. By age four, *Tiger* could climb, run, hop, and skip with excellent agility.

Rather than judging the child by age, his mother continued to make decisions based on his size. She knew most kids were sent to school by five, but she believed he had not become tall enough; homeschool was the alternative. By the time he was six, she put the whip in his hand, to learn, and to assist his mother with the newest pets. Within six months, his abilities were commendable. He was good at delivering the correct amount of whip snap for training the smaller animals, and the pupil understood which ones needed more or less and why.

When Tiger turned seven, his extraordinary intelligence stoked Olga's paranoia that someone would try and take her place. She had purposely fostered distrust of all women, as was her bias, therefore, it was not surprising she decided her "genius boy-tiger" would do better with a male-only influence to provide the additional education he required. The Horace Mann School for Boys seemed to be the right choice for her. The institution had an established reputation for an unsympathetic educational environment, delivered by men, with no female instructors.

To convince the faculty to take her illegitimate son and make him legitimate, she paid his eight years of education all at once, in cash; paying extra for the legal fees to have him named, and to have her son in a private room, rather than the shared rooms or the dormitory bunk rooms. Olga did not want her child sharing a room with another boy, as if he was from the lower class. She further assumed that having his own room would keep him from illness exposure, as well as preventing him from becoming a homosexual. With funds paid in advance, and her position crystal clear to the boy, and the faculty, she felt freed from any further responsibility.

Having an absent mother, together with the pervasive educational methods used by some of the teachers, would serve to misshape the character of the boy, who was not to be treated like the other students. Blind to their abuses, Olga was not aware the faculty would not permit him to be addressed as *Tiger*, nor given a legal name; they called him "Bastard." While the fathered students enjoyed family time on weekends, and in the evenings, the bastard-boy was made to do chores; he was forbidden to call his mother in private and had little free time to himself.

Because the boy was exceptionally clean and organized, he was made responsible for spit shining all the instructor's shoes, in fact, his private room had been used as a shoe station prior to his arrival. Some of the men preferred to be wearing their shoes during the spit shine, and several demanded their cock in the bastard's mouth before the spit shining was over. He reviled them for their disgusting requests, and he hated being cornered in his own room, but there was no one who would advocate for a bastard. Being segregated from the other children, also made him different in the eyes of the students; the unjust punishment was accepted as normal. There were other more aggressive abuses, and humiliations, performed in the name of "discipline," by the school's athletic coach, and by some of his minions. Until he hit his own growth spurt, the victimized child with no defender, suffered greatly.

His tormentors had no misgivings about handing out immoral consequences to a bastard, who had a "working mother." She was single, wealthy, and Hollywood-famous. The faculty assumed her status meant she was secretly, a highly paid whore, and this bought her son no favors. Besides being chauvinistic, many of the school's faculty were adamantly against women's rights. These misogynists discoursed about women having less intelligence and being the weaker sex. This further ensured the "bastard" would have a twisted view of women, sexuality, and a soul void of empathy.

In defiance of the lack of emotional support, or perhaps because of it, *Tiger,* at age eleven, developed Megalomania, a psychopathological condition, characterized by delusional fantasies of wealth and omnipotence; or so thought the school's contracted medical doctor. Arguably, his mother was wealthy, and his obsession with being the best was hardly a delusion. And because he wanted to impress her, he was driven. As a lad, he would win fairly, or he would manipulate the situation in order to win; either way, he thrived on his accomplishments. His sense of self was so haughty, he saw himself as being above the natural laws.

Tiger was proud to demonstrate his lack of fear, and his high tolerance for pain; multiple times in chemistry class, he held a burning ember longer than any other student dared. Moreover, his skills at dart throwing, knot tying, and dissecting animals, gave him hero status among students, and some of the faculty, which stimulated his belief that he was more intelligent than anyone. In truth, Tiger was a genius, having the highest IQ in school, 168, by age fifteen.

A self-given name, "Neffen Oliver Jones," otherwise known as NOJ, was acknowledged by the end of his sophomore year, and then, respectfully used after his I.Q. score proved his superiority. Armed with his supremacy, Neffen turned the tables on his abusers by his junior year, using deadly blackmail to achieve all manners of revenge. He perpetrated many evils to prove himself, including murdering their precious pets, and killing a few of the molester's family members. His kills were staged as accidents and suicides to teach fear and awe for their new master, the one and only, NOJ.

Although a fatherless bastard, most saw Neffen as a brilliant, talented, radiantly good-looking, and exceptionally clever student. Those who had taken advantage of him, also knew his dark side; the ruthless narcissistic monster, who insisted they behave according to his wishes, while keeping the truth about his power over them, unreported. His power reigned absolutely, and without resistance for the remainder of his school days.

Even without a single family member in the audience, NOJ, as some of the boys called him, gained the loudest, and longest applause at graduation. Undecided about college, but accepted at all the top universities, Neffen decided it was best to visit his mother, before making a final decision. It had been six years since he had seen her, and he was confident she would be impressed by his "manly" growth, he was now over six feet in height. However, the "hero's" welcome he had imagined, did not manifest, and there was not as much as a "dinner party" planned for his accomplishments. Instead, upon his arrival, Neffen found his mother passed out on her bed, inebriated.

Seeing her laying among empty gin bottles, and a dirty ashtray, sent him into a quiet rage. She had promised that she had quit her vices, and he had believed her. In addition to lying, he found her guilty of weakness, gluttony, and filth. Three strikes by the rule of NOJ, and *a slut* had earned severe punishment; a fourth, and she deserved to die. His rules had become the law, he would not bend or neglect them, his mother would have to die. Neffen filled the pink tub with all the alcohol in the house and put his drunken mother into it; it was half filled. Then, he waited for her to wake up. As soon as she was conscious enough to recognize him, and realize where she was, he turned her over and held her head under the liquid, until she drowned.

After the *accidental suicide* and burial, Neffen liquidated much of what his mother had acquired as far as her personal belongings. He was silently impressed with her assets, but he rationalized she must have had the help of a good lawyer and agent. After some time inspecting the properties she owned, he decided to keep a few random land parcels, the animal refuge land, and some of the larger breed animals. The cages, and related training tools were also kept. Neffen skipped college and assumed his mother's professional life effortlessly, with poise and confidence. He worked with feral and undomesticated animals as his mother had done. It was not long for him to earn the admiration, and trust of hundreds of wealthy, famous people from the film industry, as well as other elitists with wild pets.

Even with his newfound fame as a wild animal tamer, Neffen did not limit himself to large animals. At age twenty, he began to grow his own brand using his special gift, training canines. His early work won him recognition at the Brussels World Fair as a "dog whisperer." The accolades increased his grandiosity, and after successfully murdering a total of forty women, sixteen men, and four children, without consequence, his psyche took on a fixed delusion of grandeur. He embraced what he had already proven, he had reached Godhood.

Socially, like his mother, Neffen was always cautious not to reveal too much about himself. He preferred appearing as a lifelong bachelor. And he was indeed everybody's favorite bachelor, invited to all the parties, even if he did not stay long. He did in fact find it useful to rub elbows with famous personalities, having an instinct for finding and exploiting the perverted among the wealthy.

Although he did not express his feelings openly, Neffen had crystal clear thoughts about women, and how they should be treated, privately. On his 25th birthday, speaking in the mirror, his favorite audience, he had decided on the *beast* he would give to himself.

"Bitches (women) are dogs who have learned to walk on two legs, in order to fuck the superior human male, and bear the seed of the male. Besides whoring, bitches do little to deserve the food they eat, and the booze they drink. They are weak and selfish. They need the kind of discipline that only I can provide. They need to be trained as beasts, and learn to live as beasts, not always, just long enough to understand their place. My birthday gift will be a new pet, one that I create. She will be young and innocent, so that I may participate in her brain development, but old enough to have teeth, I won't keep a snaggletooth. She must come from good stock; preferably European descent, married hetero couple, smitten with parenting, and enamored with their first-born girl. She must have doll-like features, I want to enjoy looking at her face. She will learn to be a perfect princess, who when *kissed*, will turn into a bitch, walking on all fours, on demand, without fail. I will keep her as my special house pet. I will teach her to embrace her animal status, and she will be grateful when she is permitted to be an upright bitch. She will love, honor, and obey me, unconditionally."

When he had six well-trained bitches, he wanted to show them off, believing he could market them with "zoo-ish sex charms." He gathered known minions, and his highest regarded "clients," to celebrate his milestone with a circus themed dinner party. The masked guests, unknowingly, were being tested by their host; he would evaluate them based on their level of participation. He was, after all, giving them an opportunity to join in on humiliating his bitches, and they were encouraged to give into their sadistic pleasures.

His circus event was more successful than he had dreamed, the guests were indeed awestruck by the new "animals." Pleased with the success of the event, Jones decided to continue exploiting and expanding his unique brand, and he decided to make the circus party a quinquennial event. His underworld reputation as the "Green Ghost" was becoming greater than Hitler's had been. His net worth, along with his propensity to stay on the cutting edge of technology, earned the attention of elitist men, particularly those who were attracted to power and control.

~~~

Neffen prided himself on having more than one plan of action, alternate *eyes,* his additional *tools* in the field. He took a moment to think through his earlier field reports.

She will not stay in one place, she doesn't know where home is, but her instinct will keep her in cooler locations. She is a smart one.

To catch his favorite pet, Neffen knew he needed a trap, and since the lure had been found alive, he felt surer of his own reasoning.

I know my girl had a thing for her little china-dawl teacher, how could she not, I fostered their relationship, I allowed it. Too bad that ungrateful bitch had to grow a conscious and go catatonic on me. But she is a come-back bitch after all. It will be sweet justice to use her to help bring
~~~

Golden Girl home. Of course, she won't want to help me, but I know how she thinks, and if she doesn't know I'm using her, she will make an excellent jig. In the end, a win-win for me.

Several calls were made. Jones put two new henchmen on the chase.

It must be my China-dog has reinvented herself as a human. I wasn't sure she would go that way; she made a stronger animal. She's a smart one, smart enough to be useful once again, after all, there is no better lure for my pet.

Returning the phone to his pocket, he rubbed his eyes, and then located and added eye drops. He pictured having his two best pets back under his control, to mitigate the irritation of their defiance. To encourage himself further, he spoke in his most charming tone.

"Your bitches will be thrilled to see your handsome face, perhaps they will recognize you look even younger."

Imagining Golden Girl could hear his voice, he sweetened his tone.

"I have your room prepared for you, the view from the hanging gill net will be divine. All your favorite devices are displayed quite expertly. When your gag is back in place, you will be able to drool all over your toys."

~⁓~

Reaching the age of 30, the entrepreneur NOJ, had already developed a set of skills that enabled him to identify and make the most of opportunities. After the 1971 Budapest Expo, he decided to linger in that part of the world, choosing to visit China. His plan was to increase his collection of wild animals, and more, if the opportunity presented itself.

"There are many children, and adults too, who fall into the hands of human traffickers, who then, sell them for a one-time fee; they do not appreciate their value. By contrast, the children I will take, I will raise, and make them useful, and they will make me very rich. The world has seen fit to acknowledge my work with canines, why should the underworld do any different. I will bring home a souvenir, and name her China-Dawl, and this Dawl will make me famous.

When he found her in China, the slight bodied seven-year-old, his China-Dawl was sinewy, sturdy enough to endure his tests, and intense enough to learn absolute obedience. The care, training, and marketing strategies used for Dawl's career became the foundation for the full-time sex-trained children that came after her. By age ten, she was the most sought-after child sex slave in the underworld. She worked harder and longer than any other, and always with the same amount of enthusiasm.

Whether she had been with five or fifty men, Dawl was dazzling and breathtaking. Dawl became the master's strongest commodity. Early on, her earnings kept her master's other sex slaves, fed, and housed, and her reputation, made him infamous. Known as the Green Ghost, he became one of the wealthiest in the sex-trade within the first three years of marketing her.

Regarding the public "Neffen Oliver Jones," the media and socials all agreed, "the man keeps getting younger!" Well supported by a top-level PR team, a publicist, and a team of "legitimate" private investigators, the NOJ brand was designed to manage and protect Jones' prestigious animal training businesses, manage his properties in Nevada, California, and Utah, as well as to allow him personal privacy, in the U.S. and abroad, in order to enjoy his wealth. NOJ's significant net worth, along with his propensity to stay on the cutting edge of technology from the 80's to present day, had earned the attention of elitist men, particularly those who were attracted to high standards, power, and control. His absolute business standards, and reputation for intolerance of complacency, at any cost, coupled with his "70 going on 30 GQ-image," was enviable; his staying power showed no signs of decline. Adding in the testimony from A-list clients, proud to have bragging rights on the success of his private training sessions, coupled with their wealth and influence, and you had one extraordinary man, with unmatched mastery in the business of animal training.

CHAPTER 13

A NEW TRANSGENDER GROUP

"We've got to have a dream if we are going to make a dream come true."

WALT DISNEY

Ariel convinced herself it was wise to stay connected to a "people like us" support group, and she found one in Reno. The group was intended for people with various gender identity and relational issues, and it was free. *Trin's* story mirrored others in the group. Ariel's apparent dysphoria was from living as a sex slave for most of her life, but she did not believe it was safe to tell the whole truth.

Using the clinical language she learned in Miami, *he* said, "I have been struggling with gender incongruence since early childhood. I often suffer from social dysphoria, which makes me feel depressed and anxious, sometimes at the same time. My first therapist told me it stems from the early childhood sexual traumas I experienced. I am not able to talk about those things, but I have decided I do not want to be a slave to my past. I want to focus on who I am today, and I do want to understand my gender."

Troy, the leader, was a licensed MFT - Marriage and Family Therapist, who had acquired a federal grant affording him to provide his clinical expertise pro bono. The group met two times a week, giving attendees the option of participating once or twice a week. In addition to education and clinical training, Troy had a remarkable life story, and was brave enough to share it as part of the therapeutic group process.

Troy's was an uncommon tale of courage, having been born an "Intersex," having reproductive anatomy that was not distinctly male or female. The parents and doctors decided on surgery, to assign a female gender, and the infant was named Helen.

As the *girl*-child grew, it was clear, the gender assignment was not the right fit. Sadly, the parents would not entertain a conversation about the "sex" of their child, even though they had been warned it could become something of an issue as the child grew. Instead, they force-fed Helen, all things feminine. They insisted their child dress like *Jonbenet Ramsey* and forbid her from playing with boys, lest they give her unsanctioned social ideas.

In the first grade, the school officials had stood up for the right of the child to behave naturally. The teachers and the school counselor sympathetically reported they were seeing, "a boy being forced to act like a girl." The parents rejected the district's "progressive" views, in favor of their own religious rights, and Helen was homeschooled for her remaining school years.

Helen's parents held hard-right-anti-LGBTQ-religious sentiments and prohibited their *daughter* from doing anything athletic. She was in every way discouraged and humiliated for non-feminine gestures or sounds. They went so far as to starve their *daughter* of protein, to prevent muscle development. The situation escalated on Helen's 14th birthday, when her father lost all civility, raping his *daughter*, while his mother sat nearby, knitting a pink scarf, pretending nothing was happening.

Rather than reporting the abuse, Helen decided to run away from home. Having the courage to journey alone, the runaway made it out of the country without help. *She* was a rare fortunate child who found sanctuary in Mexico with Jesuit Nuns. During the stay with the godly sisters, Helen was permitted to be whatever felt natural, no right or wrong, and no judgement. It was healing. Four years later, Helen legally became "Troy Of Helen."

Thirty years later, Troy, the 48-year-old therapist, felt most comfortable dressing as male and identifying as a Pan-sexual-non-binary. Instead of- he/she/they, or his/hers/him, Troy's chosen pronoun was "of." Troy's story made a strong impression on Ariel. The comparison of Troy's physical imprisonment in a woman's body, and her own experience of not having a choice over how her body was used, and other *similar differences* in life experiences, provided fascinating new insights.

There are many kinds of masters in the world, many ways to be a victim, even in the free world, and for all our differences, we suffer much the same. We also heal. We all face experiences which require us to make complicated choices. If, and when, we get to make our own choice, our differences become more evident. I'm not the only person who didn't have a choice on how I grew up, we are many. Now, I do have choices. Troy chose nobly, not from a selfish agenda, and in the face of real and threatened consequences, of found the strength to be true and kind. I need to be more like of.

Ariel's "nearly" honest relationship with Troy, and the group members, were a testament to her growing development. Outside of a few experiences in the Amazon, she had not practiced honesty with others. The time in Troy's group was teaching Ariel about being "safely genuine."

No one is an island. We all need human connectedness, but we can choose who and when, and how much to put out there. I can't be so honest that I put myself in danger, but I can be genuine with those who make up my support system.

Following a day of thinking about her own "new" thinking, Ariel decided to test her resolve to be more genuine during group.

"I have much to learn about who I am and what I am, but I realize it is important to be real with all of you, since this is a safe place. Okay, so, here it goes. I have been looking for work. I found something I think I could be good at, actually, it is special event mannequin modeling, and it pays very well. The position is for a "femme woman." So, I went to the interview as a woman, and it felt better than I imagined. Since then, I have been struggling some with worries about how this might make me look to you. Part of me is still trans man, here I am today, still Trin, still he. I don't want to be wishy-washy, and I don't want to be fake, but I think I might still be she too, and maybe there is more she in me than he? I can't know if I don't try again, but I'm worried I will lose your respect. Anyway, I do want your honest feedback, and if you don't think I belong in this group as a femme, I hope you will say so."

To her surprise, the group's feedback was positive. She was praised for taking a leap of faith and embracing a cisgender experience. No one used the term "detransitioner," and most shared how they too have presented gender differently, depending on the context in their lives.

In response to the sharing, Troy offered, "Identity is deeply personal. Often, we are not given encouragement to explore femininity or masculinity, which is independent from gender, while still being adjacent. We may indeed experience our individual narratives as being outside the norms for a specific identity, regardless of the identity, but, being authentic to yourself is critical to mental and spiritual health. Whether identifying as transgender, cisgender, genderqueer, drag queen, non-binary, agender, or any identity that is not constant, we all need to respect every individual as the authority of their own gender story."

Responding to Troy's words, *Trin* wanted to acknowledge the learning.

"I hear you, Troy. I get to decide what I am. I am queer and clearly, I am not the only one with a non-linear gender story."

Troy affirmed *Trin*, then asked, "I wonder if anyone else will share about choosing to be true to self, despite how it might impact a close relationship?"

Another member in the group spoke up, sharing about her conflictual relationship to her mother. Her chosen trans identity had been a problem for their relationship. She shared about how she had been coping since being a part of this group. Each of the other members took turns acknowledging their fellow member, until *Trin* was the only one who had not re-joined the conversation.

"Trin? Do you have a verbal joining to offer Jo-anna?"

Troy's eyes were gentle and supportive.

"I, yes, I do want to join. I heard you say you planned your self-soothing before you went to see your mother, to prepare for any anxiety the visit might trigger for you. You have recognized how your mother's disappointment is a trigger, that's important. I agree with you, it is not your responsibility to make your mother happy with who you are, and I'm glad you had a fun time at the pet store," laughing with tears now, "...and glad you went home feeling proud of yourself for not buying all the bunnies in the store. I'm proud of you too."

The trans woman wiped her own tear away before responding to the therapeutic joining, "Thank you Trin. I feel heard and seen and accepted."

Troy thanked and encouraged each group member by name. Restating the group goals and the concepts of togetherness and separateness, and empathy. Troy then renewed the no-self-harm contracts, with those who needed them, and closed the session with a relaxation exercise, using a singing bowl.

～～

Waking the next morning from a positive-sensory laden dream, the optimistic woman pinched herself. The joy of the dream spread throughout her body and lifted her spirits.

Yesterday was my best day of freedom, the best day ever. Troy and the group have given me hope. I will have a baby, someday, I will have my own family. I will find my home, and it will be everything we need. We, my partner, and my baby. If it's a boy, I will name him Troy, and if it is a girl, I'll name her Lily.

CHAPTER 14

SEARCHING FOR PREY

"I have had what others call crosses, but I don't look at them that way-what's the use?"

CATHERINE M. SEDGWICK

I don't look too bad for a fifty-something, passing for forties. I can count myself lucky. No, not lucky, resilient. Breathe.

Debbi, in the bathroom, was seeing herself in the floor to ceiling mirror. Holding a perfect plank position, she lifted her chin enough to catch her reflection; she was six minutes into her pose. All of her muscles engaged and worked together. Noticeable burning, and twitching began at nine minutes, and she checked her form. Dropping her gaze, keeping her arms, back, and hips straight, she pushed with all her might, driving her toes and hands to hold her weight.

Okay, it's Lily-time. Focus up.

She spotted a grayish mark in the marbled tile, the way it twisted was a natural attraction for her. She pushed thoughts away to meditate on the spot.

Focus…see the color. See the size. See the shape. See the edges. See the temperature. See the contours. See the…

A tiny but audible timer began to sound, bringing her out of the meditation, it had been fifteen minutes. She stopped. Her body rested flat on the cool flooring, first pressing one side of her face down, and then turning her head to press the other side. She returned to the shower, turned the water to cold, and began her mental lists. As her mind worked, Debbi lost touch with the cold. Her sense of gratitude for the clean water pouring from the artfully crafted faucet rose to her awareness. Her mind retrieved the childhood memories of living in a rural village mud-walled hut.

⌒⌒

A sickly kid in her early months of life, Lily garnered only disdain from her mother. It made no difference to her mother that she herself was under-nourished during pregnancy. Barely nursing the baby-burden, Lily was given only the minimum to survive. Weakness in 1960's China was costly, and resources were few. As far as the mother was concerned, Lily's needs should not take from those more valued, namely, her husband and her two sons. When the breast milk dried up, Lily was kept in isolation away from the males in the family. Her mother knew the baby-girl-burden would likely be suffocated or drowned, if any of the males found her sleeping.

At three, Lily was no bigger than most twelve-month-old babies, but she passed for a boy, and that kept her alive. Renamed Li, and re-introduced as a nephew, *he* became a scrapper. Surprisingly quick, and smart enough to do house chores, *he* helped to fill the water buckets, a task most families gave to slaves or the lowest in the family. In their village, clean water was scarce, and there was a hierarchy to consume it; children were in line behind any profitable livestock, to get their share. When Li proved *he* could walk the two miles to the river and return with water, the father agreed to allow him to be fed daily. *He* had to steal, forage for wild food, and beg, in order to tame hunger most days, but *he* eventually grew strong enough to retrieve water twice a day. Running back and forth, dragging a little over ten pounds at a time, *his* physical strength continued to support the boy act, which was proudly, and carefully perpetuated, even though the older boys bullied the *boy* who carried water with the servant girls.

Walking near the main road one day, Li found a role of heavy-duty plastic. *He* surmised it had fallen off a military supply vehicle. Li wisely hid it, knowing *he* risked losing a hand or being killed for stealing from the government. The resourceful little lad created teardrop shaped bags to contain the water, also slicing the plastic to make ties, which prevented the water from splashing out. A fraction of the weight of a water bucket, the water bags allowed Li to bring more water to the family. Li smartly used discarded painter's canvas to cover the plastic. Following the example of some older women, *he* eventually found a pole, wide and strong enough to support the water weight. With a canvas bag hung on each end to hide the water bags, Li carried the pole triumphantly. The bullying continued, and Li endured beatings for being "like a girl," but *he* kept her food portions growing.

The young pretender's encumbered life became disturbingly worse at age seven, when the bullies pulled *his* pants down and learned *he* was a "she." When her father found out, he refused to keep or feed the girl, even one that carried water. He sold her, along with a sterile goat, to a larger family in another village. When the buyers of Lily discovered the goat was sterile, they took it as a sign that she was cursed. After a severe beating, she was left for dead at the place where the unwanted babies were abandoned. Lily made her way to another village by floating down the river, holding on to logs to keep her head above the water.

Begging kept her alive for another two days, until she was found by a young man traveling through the area. He picked her up out of the mud, wiped her face, and showed her compassion. She had never experienced kindness from a man. The foreigner turned out to be an animal trainer, and a collector of sorts. When he picked her up out of the rice field, he had already formed a plan for her.

"You can call me Master, and I will take care of you. You will be mine and will obey me just as my other pets do. I will give you a better home."

Lily had no idea what he was saying, as she had not heard English spoken before, but she understood his name to be "Master." His round eyes were pleased to know she had *she parts,* which made her feel special. Her paradigm shifted. He smuggled her into the United States, along with a few captured animals; Lily, newly named China-Dawl, began a new life in a boarding house which had water piped in.

～ ～

Drying off after the shower, Debbi stood in front of the vanity, recognizing her present-day strength, health, and vitality; it gave her courage to trust herself. The responsibility of protecting the innocent, taken on in secret, compelled her to be smarter, and more prepared than any enemy. She tapped into her wise self for a pep talk, as she put on her robe.

I may be small, but I am strong. Always remember Lily still lives inside, and she is fierce, and formidable. This is my home, and I am able to keep the innocents of Loyalville safe.

The hair dryer sounded. Debbi was in the final stages of cleaning the vanity counter, which she did simultaneously while styling her short silky hair. Hearing her, Donald felt cautious.

It's best for me to stay out of Smurf's way. The more I'm idly lingering, the greater the chance she will hand off some honey-do's or quiz me about how I will spend the morning.

Watching, but keeping a safe distance, Donald stayed near the picture window. He knew Debbi would soon come out to get dressed. Donald's bird's eye focus went back to the place where he, and a dog, first discovered the opening to the tunnels. As he stared out the window, he traveled back to a day he was hiking on the mountain…

The sounds of a barking dog came out of nowhere, and there were whining sounds too. Donald followed his ear to an old mining shaft.

"Oh, oh my God. How in the heck? It's okay, it's okay girl. I have no idea how you ended up way down there, it musta been twenty feet before you hit ground, and I can hear your pain, it's alright, good girl, I'm gonna get you out. Lay down, it's okay."

The dog stopped trying to dig her way out, a futile effort with broken bones. She laid down, licking her injuries to pass the time until the man would come to her. Donald recognized the dog from his neighborhood. He imagined the dog had become loose and then got carried away by chasing a rabbit or some other wild critter, he had seen her go up the hill chasing a deer once before. Donald was empty handed, no phone, no rope, his only choice was to climb down into the hole and climb back up with the dog. Dirt and rocks came loose with every hand and foot hold, although he managed to keep from falling until the last six feet or so.

"Ouch, oh, umph! Lucky, I didn't break my ankle."

Sitting at eye level, Donald waited until the crumbling dirt had quieted. He looked around the cavernous space, he had never seen this kind of a *mine shaft* before, it was larger and wider than he had seen from above. The dog did not attempt to get up.

"Oh, you're a big girl, aren't you? No offense now, but I'm guessing you to be about 60 pounds, maybe a few pounds heavier than when I last saw you. But hey, no judgement, I eat meat too. Looks like I'm going to have to carry you out of here."

Bending down, tenderly patting and holding her in place, Donald checked all over for signs of injury. The dog yipped when he located the breaks, there were two.

"Okay, you're a big girl, and I'm going to need my hands to climb, so this is what we're gonna do, I'm going to wrap my jacket around you, and this won't be easy, but you can't fight me, you need to stay. Stay. That's a good girl. I know, I've never done this before either, but we can't wait until someone finds us, no one ever comes around this part of the mountain."

He wrapped the dog inside his jacket and pulled his belt free from his jeans. He wrapped the belt around her and then slipped his arm through the strap, it barely went around them both, but it helped to hold her in place. The dog's face, just under his chin, tickled him with her whiskers, as she looked to see how he was going to get them both out.

"I know, doesn't look like we have a chance to climb up, but hey the good news is we have each other, and between the two of us, we will figure this out."

The two did figure it out, though it was not an easy task. They found their way out of the *shaft* and discovered something much more; something they would be keeping to themselves. Hours later, when Donald and the dog made it back up to the surface, he carried her all the way back home, and to the worried arms of her owner, who had been standing in the yard calling her name. A brief explanation was given, then the dog was placed in the car and taken to the animal hospital. The details about how they emerged from the hole, were never mentioned, everyone assumed Donald had climbed out through the shaft.

~~~

As the memories faded, Donald's eye caught movement on the mountain. It was a large moving truck. Astounded, Donald called out.

"Hey Smurf, come look! Well, I'll be. Is someone actually moving into that haunted ol' eye-sore back here? I can't believe what I'm seeing. Do you see this?"

Donald and Debbi had a house with two levels that sat on an elevated foundation. The upstairs windows gave the Harrison's unblocked views of the neighboring single level homes and the vast range behind their lot. Enveloped in the mountains that shadowed their community, and surrounded the carved-out lake valley, there stood an abandoned dwelling, built in the previous era. More than one homeless encampment had been forced to move off the private property; what was left behind, no one had bothered to clean up. There were trees and brush to block the mess from most of the homeowner's views, but the Harrison's range of view was greater. Their street, the part that continued past the manicured neighborhood, formed a "Q" shape roadway that crossed a leveled area, and then continued, ascending into a spiraling incline, all the way to the old grand lodge.
~~~

The pint-sized woman quickly responded to her husband's beckoning, scuffling along in her bath slippers. The large window provided a bird's eye view of the mountainous terrain behind their home, her eyes widened as she inspected the scene, "Oh Donald, there can't possibly be someone moving in, it's been condemned, I'm sure I heard you say it?"

Donald's eye was fixed to the opening of the secret tunnel. His worst worry surfaced.

What will happen to this community if people find out about the underground?

He nodded to Debbi, who stared at the moving truck in disbelief. The two were both surprised to be witnessing the unannounced activity. As the president of the homeowner's association, Donald had been the one whom the locals came to regarding that particular property, as he was the one person who cared enough to keep a close eye on the place. He felt affronted for being out of the loop and his bruised ego gave way to a self-indulgent pity party.

After all I've done? And no one bothered to call or email me? I'm the one recognized by town council for rooting out the indigents, I established the neighborhood watch program, heck I married into one of the founding families of this community, and I'm the President of the home-owner's association. This ain't right!

Debbi stood beside her husband with similar exasperation.

My honorable husband, a man that stands head and shoulders over everyone, a trusted leader, a local hero, how could he not have known about this?

Feeling confused, Debbi's sense of control, and her sense of order, went out of balance. Her PTSD began to narrow her airways. She noticed her pulse quickening, and her nose detected the fragrance of a floral bouquet, even though there were no flowers in the room. Her limbs tensed without effort, and she felt a boost of adrenaline. Her eyes went instinctively to the open window. The silky drapery testified of a breeze entering the room. Her eyes knowingly closed to allow an inner knowing to speak up. It was slight, but she felt a premonition of something sinister. It caused her to shudder, even though the drapes had stilled, and there was no air movement in the room.

Sensing her stiffening, Donald noticed her mood shift, and he saw her quiver. He watched her close her eyes and take a long slow breath. The trembling was not from a chill, but a shudder that came from a *knowing*. When she opened her eyes, he discerned that she had formed a dark worry on her mind.

Mrs. Harrison kept few secrets, or so Donald believed, but he was immediately nervous to ask what she was thinking. Regardless of his verbal disbelief in what he referred to as "Woo-woo," he knew his wife was skilled in spiritual and transpersonal kinds of practices. He was convinced, unlike most of the hole-in-the-wall palm readers, she had the true gift of divination. Debbi humbly called it a gift of paying attention. Donald believed there was more to it. He had seen for himself, her ability to know things, things no one could possibly guess, and she was especially sensitive to premonitions about misfortune, bad luck, accidents, and the like. He attributed some of her knowing ability to her Chinese heritage, the wise ancient intuition her family had passed on. He also knew she was born special.

She knows something bad is going to happen.

Without saying a word, Debbi announced the impending doom, her countenance made it clear to Donald. What he saw in her eyes gave him a fearful start, but humor was his reflex. Reaching out and catching her hand, he easily intertwined their fingers and pulled her close. Next to him, she was petite, her shoulders barely reaching his waistline.

I want, no, need, I need to put some joy back on Smurfette's little face.

Lifting her easily, and holding her in the air at eye level, he began, "Now, now, don't you go taking a trip to smurf worryland. You know little one, you are not the only one gifted in face reading! I can see you brewing a storm on that pretty little face of yours before you have even brewed the tea leaves. How about I do some investigating with some phone calls, while you go catch up on stories about parking tickets, and kids out past curfew, new babies, and someone's arthritis; in no particular order."

Laughing heartily and giving her another boost above his head, before she could find her words, Donald continued, "Don't forget, your job is to save the Loyalville-residents, one postage stamp at a time."

He chuckled as he did his strong funny man routine, but Debbi discerned it was not a natural laugh; it was a mask for fear. To hide his feelings, he lifted her higher than was typical, over his head as if to flex his muscles.

Debbi gave her husband the smile he was looking for, but with a stern tone, added, "Oh you feel it too, don't deny it. A spirit came as a sign, it's a warning. An evil shadow passing near, he's searching for prey."

She looked away until he lowered her to his eye level.

"He who? Don't worry," he eased, "whatever it is, it's nothing compared to my little feng shui smurf. With her hands, there are no stains unsurrendered, no wrinkles left unsmoothed."

"Now, how can I be worried when I'm depending on your strong legs to support us."

"Is it my legs you trust, not my brilliant mind?"

Debbi was comfortable being held in his arms, until her lingering glance saw his fear. He would object if pinned down, but she knew Donald was picking up on the threatening energy that stopped the air. The unspoken exchange brought her protective instincts forward.

I will not let anyone hurt my Donald.

To answer him, Debbi kissed Donald, a smoldering kiss that would serve to help them both relax. His macho facade melted, and he bent to set her back to her own feet. Before releasing her, he kissed her back, much harder, and then softer, to thank her for lifting him out of his prideful self-talk. She gave him another look, this one said she trusted him. Her confidence in him increased his attraction toward her, more than he realized.

What does a woman like you see in me?

His lightheartedness produced a grounding effect. She knew he loved her. He was sincere in his respect for his wife, and she recognized he was a man worthy of love.

You, Donald Harrison are a man I can trust.

"Don't you worry, and don't think you will be the only one looking to find some answers about those strangers on our mountain. I have a feeling everyone that comes in the shop today will be talking about these happenings," her eyebrows lifted, "and I will be paying attention."

Donald loved how his wife cared for all the unfortunates, including himself, for that is how he saw himself. After two failed marriages, and a heart condition that forced him into early retirement, he did not see himself as a winning prize. He gave her his best smile, thinking how she could bring him to his knees with a kiss.

Standing high on her toes, Debbi reached up, and Donald leaned down. She squeezed his face between her hands and gave him a quick smooch on the chin, which was as high as she could reach. She quietly called upon her strength, believing he could not bear to know how she came to be so attentive to dangers. Her mission was to keep the past in the past, and she intended to do everything in her power to protect her man, and the place she called home.

I will not be naive in thinking that the lodge re-awakening is a random event. A premonition came, that means evil is not far behind. Strangers coming out of nowhere, taking over an abandoned property without notifying the layers of leadership in our little city, spells some kind of trickery. Whatever it is, it is likely connected to the people moving into the lodge, whoever they are. Besides this new development, I know Donald and I were followed the other day, it was too far away from here to have been a coincidence.

The sound of a load bearing engine rumbled them out of their brief intimacy, taking their full attention to the happenings beyond their window. A large moving truck in front of the abandoned lodge, and other vehicular hustle going in and out of the long driveway, was not welcomed. Already, a few of the neighbors were gathering near the end of the street. Pointing as they talked, the inexplicable activity would not be ignored.

"Those people, whoever they are, cannot move in, I don't know anything about them." Debbi stated matter of factly, as she dropped her hands to her hips.

Before Donald could respond, his wife was spinning on her heels. Without missing a beat, Deb grabbed the comforter which had been kicked off the bed in the night. She swung it with just enough umph that it laid over the bed in place. Smiling at her own evident skill, and then finding approval in his eyes, brought a lighter energy to the room.

"No wrinkle left unsmoothed," she winked and then returned to pick up the decorative pillows and set them in place.

"I guess the idea to demolish the building to build a parking area is off the table," he said this as he turned in search of his binoculars for more detailed viewing.

"You left them on the bookcase in the living room, on the left side," she called out after him, knowing his goal. Adding, "Oh Donald, you had me excited for the new parking lot, now what?"

The lack of public parking was not a true problem. Debbi was uneasy with strange cars parked near their home. She developed a knack for memorizing license plates, as well as having a thorough knowledge of the Loyalville DMV records. When an unknown car was parked near their home, she made it her business to find out why the driver had parked there. Her answers came, often by deduction, although it was not unusual for Debbi to sneak out, pretending to have an errand, just to figure out who belonged to the vehicle in question.

Donald called back, "I guess there must be free parking at Smurf Worryland."

She laughed. The fact that Donald could make her laugh, a true laugh, even in a serious moment, amazed Debbi. She felt the pride for him swell in her chest. He was everything she wanted in a partner, and she counted herself fortunate to share her life with a man like him.

My Donald, not like some spineless men, and women for that matter; the kind who can stand by to see an innocent being harmed by a non-innocent, and not give one thought to try and make a difference. Do the next right thing, you should not waste a moment, whoever means harm will return.

～

Retrieving his binoculars from downstairs, Donald found them exactly where Debbi said they would be. Once in hand, he had to steady his breathing before climbing the stairs. The surprise activity triggered thoughts, memories, and forgotten frustrations; a past scene, from more than ten years ago, clouded Donald's mind…

The mountain was a place of refuge, a place where Donald could be quiet in nature, to think, and clear his head. Because he was not one to talk about problems in his life, he kept his mountain expositions to himself, letting friends and other associations believe he was blowing off steam in the casinos in Reno. Instead, he was on the mountain, alone, anguished that his unhappy wife was in the house they shared. They shared little else. Feeling irrelevant, Donald had hiked into the untamed areas. Distracted with his personal situation, he missed the signs of a big storm rolling in. Before he knew it, rain was falling, and lightning was landing all around him. To create some cover for himself, while pulling at heavy overgrown foliage between large rocks, he discovered what turned out to be the roof of a hidden hut. More rooting, and he found foot holds, steps made of rock. It took some effort with the flashing lightning, rain, and slick mud, but he managed to locate and free the door to gain entry. Donald explored the space. Guessing it to be built pre-war, the interior of the hut, approximately 100 square feet, had six feet for headspace at its high point, too low for Donald to stand straight.

Within the small space, an earth wall with a crawl through squared hole, created a dividing wall in the middle of the cell. An old military cot stood on one side, and a miniature pot belly wood stove on the other. Noticing the other elements, he found a three-inch porthole, drilled through the rock. It gave the exhaust pipe an exit to the sky, but the screen had become knotted with plant roots and plugged. Another porthole, this one horizontal, and five inches in diameter, housed a foot long metal tube; inside, he found a sleeve of steel wool, presumably to keep rodents out. It was sealed with metal fasteners on the inside, which were easily removed to provide a peephole window and additional air exchange.

Built so efficiently, even without a fire, the hut kept Donald dry and warm, and it gave him time to think about his discovery, while riding out the storm. He considered the hut might be related to the underground cavern he had found, but then dismissed the idea due to the distance between the two places. Soon after the hut discovery, his second wife had hit him with, "I need my own space, I want you to leave." His efforts to keep his wife had been ineffective, and his obsession with the mysterious property had pulled him away from the people who mattered. Being a practical man, he had decided to leave the secrets buried.

～

Ah Debbi, you are my best friend, and one of these days, I will tell you about this ancient secret, just not today.

Donald returned to the bedroom in time to see his wife's expression, it had shifted. He doubted she had ever been late for anything, nevertheless, she worried about punctuality like it was a curse she could not shake.

I know that look, she's afraid she'll be late for work.

CHAPTER 15

THE BATH HOUSE

*"This arbitress of fashion, this dictatress to society, was a woman
of no particular face, no particular figure, no particular
dress, and no particular conversation. But she was well
aware of her position, and made use of it accordingly."*

ELIZA LESLIE

Upon arrival to the designated location, the small crowd of women, including Ms. Black, were escorted to a dressing room, where they were asked to remove all clothing and jewelry. They were given a sheet-like dress as covering and were told to sit and wait. To manage her own fidgets, Ariel let her imagination play, creating make-believe biographies for the other women. Her thoughts were inspired by a gossip magazine she had read.

Hmmmm, that 20-something blond has just come from getting her nails and hair done. Her southern born aunty works at the salon, and believes every woman needs "big" hair, especially if she's poor. Thus, the look. I will call her Penny. Penny works as a grocery cashier-bagger but needs a second job in order to get her own apartment. Living with her mother is getting old. The squeaking bed on the other side of the wall is keeping her up at night, which is why poor Penny has bags under her eyes. But right now, she's dreaming of meeting a rich Mr. Right, once she can call herself a model. Good luck Penny.

Okay, hmmm. Oh, yes, the one holding onto her shoes. She is a high maintenance type, who must come from money. Surely daddy paid for her breast implants, and she's got trust money to float her wardrobe and upkeep, but she wants more. I'll call her Fergie. She has a shoe closet which has more square footage than most bedrooms. She keeps a video camera pointed at the shelves with her Manolo Blahnik, and the other Jimmy Choo shoes, so she can look in on them if she is having a bad day. And there she goes now, seeing to it that no one has touched them. The more common Louis Vuitton, and Gucci are as safe as anything else in the home, with high-tech security protection 24/7, not to mention every shoe is insured. She is sitting there thinking she should have increased the Botox in her monthly injections, still she is not particularly worried. If she decides she wants the position, Fergie won't pull her shoe from the door until she has it.

Interrupting her wandering imagination, a staff person entered the waiting room.

"They are ready for you to gather in the main room, please follow me, um Miss, you'll need to leave your shoes in the locker."

A few guided steps later, and each of the candidates stood on a riser next to their assigned tub. White gloved staff, wearing black and white uniforms, and microphone headsets were already in their places. Ariel looked at as many faces as she could without being obvious.

So far, so good, everyone looks professional.

"Greeting's candidates. Welcome to the Bath House and your action-interview. Today you have an opportunity to prove yourself worthy of becoming one of our full-time models. As with your initial interview experience, you are expected to maintain your composure without questioning directives. You will hold and maintain any position you are placed in, as well as presenting any facial expressions you are instructed to demonstrate. Understood? Those who are successful will be offered a position by end of day. So, please do make sure we have the correct phone number to reach you this evening. I also have a little surprise. All who accept our offer will be paid $500 for your time today. Those who do not hear from us, or those we cannot reach, will not be getting an offer. For this occasion, we have assigned a handler for each of you. Handlers will support communication between us. They are here to help you be successful. You will be given a few minutes to become acquainted. If you agree to these terms, please step forward."

Ariel took a deep breath and stepped forward. She was determined and her confidence was rising. The familiar sounds of running water in the tubs calmed her senses; still, her lips trembled. Controlling every aching muscle or twitching nerve was tough, not impossible. She had made it this far, and the anticipation of being paid today was a great bonus. Ariel's handler had soft eyes, and a firm handshake, conveying an easy professionalism. She gave Ariel the wireless earbuds, and a brief sound test was conducted to be sure the handler's velvety voice could be heard.

Time to get my breathing in check.

Ariel breathed slowly, and deeply without allowing her chest to rise, just as she had practiced the past couple of days. The candidates moved in unison to the individual tub platforms, and then blindfolds were placed over their eyes. This put Ariel at ease.

I see more with my ears and nose when my eyes are covered, I can do this.

Standing in the breezy space, Ariel could not help but relish the way cool air was blowing against her form. Her breasts swelled despite her willpower to remain motionless, and then the light covering billowed into the grip of her handler. Ariel did her best to control the shiver running from her shoulders to her ankles when the gown was removed. She felt her nipples stand, and her areolas tighten as if in defiance of the coming stillness. Again, she checked her breathing, until her handler spoke up.

"Congratulations Ariel. You look relaxed, and that is essential. Concentrate on my voice, newbies do better with a little chatter, and I am told my voice has a calming effect. I may pose a question here and there, consider them rhetorical, and don't overthink anything I say. Did you know that twenty-two young ladies have already been turned down because of obvious nerves? Only five will be offered a position. Your physical attributes, especially your skin and teeth, are excellent. I do hope your weight is stable."

Ariel continued the shallow breathing from her nose.

"Today you'll need absolute focus, and keep in mind, today's work is a cakewalk compared to some of the more specialized work given to our models. Only the best will get the high paying gigs, and if today seems hard, you're probably not going to want the job, just saying."

A pregnant pause, and the need to swallow. Ariel prayed for minimal movement.

"This setting is occasionally requested by our clients, and some of our best clients will be joining us today, not that you will see them. At the appointed time, the blindfolds will be removed. You must demonstrate perfect eye control, so I strongly caution you now, before I leave your ear, do not look away from the direction you are faced. And if you are instructed to close your eyes, you will keep them closed, even if you are touched. If at any time you are unable to continue, you may forfeit your application simply by saying stop in full voice. All you really must do is trust and be still. If you do the first, the second will be easier."

All she had to do was *trust*. Ariel could not see a thing with the eye mask, but she felt hands, moving everywhere, assisting. A small damp hand pulled her upward, her feet followed. The three steps up were followed by two steps down into the water. Pressure from hands on her shoulders, pushed her into a sitting position. A soft neck pillow greeted and supported her head. Hands, hesitated, lingering on Ariel's flat stomach, and then pulling back at her shoulders, to force her chest forward.

"Give us a little more arch to your back, that's it, now lift your chin, not too high. There."

An audible sigh followed the instructions.

Don't lose focus, they are here to help me be successful.

Senses informed Ariel it was a male pair of hands accompanying her handler's sigh; perhaps, it was the size. Before she could fully settle on the pillowed seat under water, one ankle and both wrists were gathered and positioned on the side of the tub. She did not resist, but a shudder from the abrupt change of warm water to cold air, on her leg and arms, caused her to move. Immediately, her handler spoke up.

"You are in a vulnerable position for a reason. Your trust is being tested. If you fail to maintain your composure, you could very well be eliminated. Modesty will only help you to fail. I will not deduct points for that move, but any additional movement will surely end this session. You can expect to be viewed for 30 minutes, easy peasy. Soft smile please, yes, that's it. Your time begins now."

Carefully, Ariel maintained a pleasant and unchanging facial expression. A deeper breath came up, and she relaxed into the position she had been placed in. She did not allow herself to feel relief for the pass. Instead, she began the breath-counting she had learned to measure time. Nine sluggish minutes ticked off.

Her mental count was unexpectedly interrupted by another sound in her ears, a distorted voice, "Her, that one, did you scout her?" Suddenly, crackling sounds and a feedback pitch torted through the main system. Her handler's sigh reached in through the ear buds, and then went silent.

"Candidates, we've experienced some technical difficulties. Please disregard the interruptions, you have twenty minutes remaining in this session."

A rush of humid air hit her face, Ariel inhaled slowly, feeling its heaviness. Her senses sharpened, she counted the remaining minutes, fighting back the questions.

Were they talking about me? Did someone recognize me?
Her breath and count focus kept the panic from seizing her.
No, don't think, keep counting.

～

"Thank you all, well done handlers. Candidates, we need to make equipment changes. You will have a few minutes to relax and prepare for your next directives but stay in the bath, and leave blindfolds in place unless otherwise instructed. This will continue to be a no-talking set."

Ear buds removed, Ariel drew in her hands and feet, and sunk in the tub up to her neck. At any moment, her dreams could come crashing down, but she held tight to her courage. She breathed deeply, filling her lungs slowly and deliberately, then she exhaled and made a pleasant-happy expression. Her eyes, though behind a mask, were deliberately soft and easy. She allowed her body to slacken in the warm water. Her arms floated in the shallow water. Her stress lightened, until her intuition told her she was being watched, closely. She breathed in all the muffled sounds and breaths, while pretending not to notice them.

They don't matter. This is paid work, my choice. I will never let myself be used again.

The blindfold kept her from seeing, but she could hear them, smell them, and feel how they changed the air flow.

Ghosts or living persons?

Her demeanor did not give away her senses. The two watchers did not speak or touch her, yet she could feel them as they moved around her tub. One motioned to the other.

Oh, they want a little more show.

Ariel feigned a tight muscle, and lifted her leg up and out, stretching like a ballerina to massage the fake cramp. She felt as if she was born to act, she knew how to draw complete attention, and was well skilled at maintaining a detached attitude. She reached up, then crossed her arms lightly over her breasts. She leaned forward to give herself a hug, then back again as her hands lazily returned to the water.

Her movement caused the *watchers* to step back, enabling her to hear there had been three of them. Tingles skipped up her spine and out to her shoulders. The shiver went down to her groin and caused her to pull her kegel muscles tightly. Her sexual excitement had been triggered, a flush colored her neck and face. She felt her pulse quicken; her breath sounded through her mouth, but she did not want to come across as over-confident for the job.

Warm water was being added into several tubs, Ariel thought they sounded near full. She heard the others moving in their tubs. No words, just a pattering of wet hands on the sides of the tubs, and water dripping from sleek bodies. Soft footsteps pulled at Ariel's attention, announcing a group entering the room. She listened closely as they found seating. Men and women. Some had strong scents, and one male aftershave was oddly familiar.

Water nearby became a trickle, and then a few drops. Ariel's animal instincts were sharpened. Her ears followed the sounds in search of the dimensions of the room. She could perceive the various sounds echoing from the stained-glass windows, the brick walls, and the metal doors. The heavy air being released from those present reverberated from their forms. The damp human arousal was familiar to her. The practiced use of sense, sound, and smell helped Ariel to anticipate changes. It also helped to pass the time. The well mastered mind game kept her sane and still.

When break time was over, there was another proclamation from the facilitator. Models were asked to stand in their tubs facing the faucet, arms at side, to receive a set of headphones. As she stood, Ariel remembered to swallow, and to breathe deeply in preparation for the shallow breaths to follow. The darkness of the blindfold was interrupted by the sound-canceling instrument placed over the ear buds; it was uncomfortable. Ariel's head was lifted, and her hair was patted and stroked back into place, then her shoulders were pressed down by hands, guiding her deeper into the water.

Headphones, darn. I prefer to have use of my ears, I know more when I can hear, eyes are much better at deceiving thoughts, but I know what they want, they want to see if I can follow directions, and they don't want us to hear things. Oh. Now I can see. Breathe.

Suddenly, the darkened areas of the room were lit up. Before her, were six column statues, caryatids, replicas of those which stood at the Acropolis in Athens. Ariel held her gaze, willing her eyes to stay relaxed.

See, you're not alone. You can do this, focus on breathing. Listen to your heartbeat. One, two. Three, four. Five, six…six ladies, all six? Not here, but I have met these great divas of ancient Greece. How did they come to be here? Maybe the owners here are Greek? What a gift to see them again.

The caryatids stood over a water feature that fed into the main bath house pool. The pink and yellow spotlights, pointed upward at their base, made it appear they were wearing the apricot-tinted patina of the original marble. Ariel had been to Athens and had stood with five of the originals.

How easy this is compared to the agonizing cargo plane ride, I remember my two days in Athens, it was the last flight leg taking me to Brazil. It is muggy here, but nothing like the temperatures on the plane, I had to get out or I would have died from heat exhaustion. Thankful I was not afraid, or I would never have discovered the Parthenon.

The place and the history of the temple had been all new to Ariel. She remembered the sound of the Acropolis Museum guide, a woman who spoke with a thick Greek accent, as she told stories from her people's history. Passionately, the guide reported the original artifacts were replaced with reproductions in 1979, "to keep the five weeping maidens safe."

Ariel's gaze lingered on the column represented by the one maiden who was torn from her sisters, kidnapped from Greece in the 19th century. Her form was not present at the museum in Athens. The guide explained the original sixth maiden, installed at the British Museum in London, was separated from her marble sisters, despite pleas from Greece for her return. The story of the caryatids had resonated with Ariel, and she felt sentimental being in the presence of all six.

See how beautiful you are. See how your reflections dance in the pool water. Just as the spirit of the maidens gave me hope then, they will keep me strong now.

The nameless ladies were easy on her eyes, and the distraction kept Ariel from blinking.

The air moves, someone is nearing, I must pretend I am one of the statues. I am like them, something to be seen and not touched, I wonder if I brought their spirit with me? It seems like a miracle to have you here with me, I shall name you, now…

"Ariel, Ariel, snap out of it. Are you asleep with eyes open or what? Did you not hear or understand? You can relax now."

The sound of her handler's voice woke her from her thoughts.

Steady yourself! See how eyes can keep you from being focused? Did I move? I pray I did not move. The time went by so fast, how did I lose track?

"Okay, there you are, boy you are good, I thought you had frozen. Next time, just be careful you don't get lost in that pretty little head of yours and miss a directive."

What? I can relax? Yes, she said next time. I must have passed their test.

"You're really good. I probably shouldn't say it, but everyone was mesmerized by you. Don't tell anyone I said so, but I can tell they want you. The weaker ones must stay for another thirty minutes, but you, you get to go. Just don't look around, and don't speak to anyone. Okay? Time to go, here's your towel, dry off, and head to the dressing room, you're done."

───── ∽ ─────

Two hours later, resting on her cot at Caroline's, Ariel's cell phone rang.

Oh, it is the agency, so soon? I thought they weren't calling until the evening.

Ariel inhaled deeply and then answered the phone.

"Hello, this is Ariel speaking."

"Hello Ariel, this is Anne, calling with good news."

"Hello, Anne, do tell, I'm holding my breath."

"Good, that is a great practice for a mannequin, keep up the good work. We are offering you the job."

"You are? Thank you, I accept!"

"Wonderful. And we think you're ready for your first assignment, if you're available, this Sunday?"

"Oh? An assignment already? On such short notice? I guess, I thought there would be some training."

"Come now, don't be modest. Clearly, you are skilled at meditating, and you are comfortable with yourself. Besides, this is a g-rated gig, two hours, and the client will have a jazz group playing, as part of the package entertainment. An easy five grand, if you can hold your pose, and we believe you can."

"Thank you. Actually, it could not come at a better time. What's next?"

"Wonderful, congratulations. We are having a small reception on Friday evening, for you and the others. You can pick up your earnings from today when you come. It's the same office where our first interview took place. You will get to meet some of our seasoned models too, I'm sure they can share insights, which can be helpful. Seven o'clock, see you then. Ciao!"

What great news! Congratulations, Ariel Black, you did it. Okay, Trin? What about you? Oh, I don't know, I still don't know who I want to be. Why is this confusing? I've just had true success as Ariel, so, why is my first thought about being Trin? Hmmmm. I guess Trin has become my safety net, it definitely suits me when among the mountainfolk and that's where I'd like to go. But today, I've earned a job, and my own money, and I deserve to celebrate, and it is good to act out of my comfort zone. So, no Trin, and no Caroline, and I guess Ariel needs more time to be real out in the world. As Troy likes to say, imagine your best self, then be it. I can do this. Ready or not, today, I'm a highly resourced powerful woman, mysterious, and famous, and rich, and I'm looking for an obscure property to buy.

CHAPTER 16

NEW CURSES

*"Accursed be he who willingly saddens an immortal spirit—
doomed to infamy in later, wiser ages, doomed in future stages
of his own being to deadly penance, only short of death."*

MARGARET FULLER

*L*ook at him. *My dear man thinks I'm concerned about being late, he worries over me like a hen. And I know he'd rather do all the providing, not to keep me in, only because he believes it's his responsibility. But I do not work for the need of income, I go for our security; I must. I am more equipped, despite his bravado, he is an innocent. Thankfully, he doesn't feel the dangers nearing. I do. Those people, whoever they are, whatever trouble they are bringing, I intend to find out.*

Renewing her mind, away from the dread of evil, Debbi left her man standing and returned to her strict morning routine. Cleanliness, order, and strict habit ordained her moves as she prepared for the day, and it supported her sanity. The ample bathroom cabinetry allowed all personal products to have their set place, and after use, all things were put away, out of sight. It was her habit to check every cabinet and drawer, for a second time, ensuring nothing had been jostled out of place. As she did so, she thought of keeping her secrets "out of sight." It was critical. Under her breath she reminded herself of an important truth, pronouncing it as Papa Yan sounded, *Tŏu tóu shì daò.* Then her own version. *You must think carefully about the way to proceed.*

Self-discipline, strong-will, and practiced self-preservation, dictated Debbi's thinking. Her offensive strategies, and actions were determined based on worst case scenarios. The dual lifestyle she secretly lived gave her a sense of control, and provided safety for the people she cared about, her Donald and the other *innocents.*

I will identify the enemies, and destroy them, and still safeguard my relationship with my husband, and our home, I cannot fail. I will use any means to destroy this evil lurking in the shadows of Loyalville, I will. Come out come out wherever you are, ready or not, here I come.

A surge of clarity consumed Debbi. Applying the lessons life had taught her, like a double agent, she planned how she would use her skills of deception, along with her animal intelligence, to unravel the mysterious happenings in her community.

"If this is the splitting of an overachiever with traumatic issues," it was something a hospital social worker said of her from the other side of a curtain, "then I resolve to split wisely. I'm a resilient, resourceful, overcomer, Lily is my truth, together we are strong."

Debbi was confident of resources and clear on her safety plans, including places for her and Donald to retreat, if necessary. A few seconds of fired determination helped her push the cold and the trivial, out of mind. Agenda fixed, compartmentalizing complete, like Batman and Bruce Wayne, Lily and Debbi were now in stealth mode.

Anything seeking to commit nefarious activities, had better beware, I am not about to let anyone take advantage, this is my home territory.

～✦～

The community demands of the day kept both Debbi and Donald from learning anything substantial about the lodge or those responsible for all the activity on the mountain. Their lunch date was spent in the emergency room with Bud and Nan. Unbeknownst to Bud, Nan's child-mind disposed of her medicine in a tall glass of milk, then forgetting sometime later, proceeded to drink it. Bud was near her all the while, not noticing until she passed out. Then he saw the empty pill bottle, assumed she had taken the pills, and immediately called 911. He had no idea she was capable of opening the child-safe bottles, until then, he had never seen her try. He was sure it was an accident, his wife was forgetful, and had not displayed any suicidal tendencies.

The medical team pumped Nan's stomach and provided the physical care she needed as gently as they could, and given her agitation and distress, it was challenging. Bud, defeated with guilt, hardly knew what to say. Nan was transported to the hospital and would be required to stay 24-hours, at minimum, for observation, blood analysis, and follow-up blood tests in the morning. She wanted none of it. Every new thing terrified her; her mind unable to comprehend any of the noise. Even Bud's presence was no consolation to Nan, who believed the medical team should be "rescuing the people in the fire," a fire she was convinced was happening in the present. She pleaded with Bud to explain it to them.

Nan's mental state made it necessary to restrain her, chemically and physically, which broke Bud's heart, and forced him to reach out to the Harrison's for their assistance. Once Debbi was aware of the situation, her priorities changed in a heartbeat, as did Donald's. She and Donald rushed to Nan and stayed by her side, along with Bud, until she became compliant, and they prayed, lucid. The cloth bands around her wrists and ankles could be removed, if she could understand she was the one who needed medical help, and no others. Fortunately, with Debbi's assurances, Nan stabilized. The medication restraint was neutralized, and her mind became more reasonable having those she trusted around her, though nothing would change her request to go home.

Fortunately, Nan showed no sign of wanting to harm herself, or others, and her blood tests proved she was rescued before her body absorbed much of the accidental dose. The doctor would not require her to stay after the 24-hour period, her condition was assessed safe to leave when she woke in the morning. With a solid exit plan in place, and with Nan sound asleep, Donald and Debbi found their way back home, arriving around midnight.

The stress of Nan's health emergency sparked a much-needed release, by way of passionate lovemaking, for Debbi and Donald. Their sleep time had been short-lived, but they rested fitfully, dreamless, in one another's arms until the morning alarm sounded. Feeling urgent the moment she awoke; Debbi did not linger next to her man. She shot out of bed, going into her routine without hesitation, and Donald drifted back to sleep.

He's asleep, good he needs the rest. Time to get dressed.

Debbi glanced at her wardrobe, then pulled her choices from their hangers; a shapeless broad long hanging skirt, and a woman's high collared button up blouse. The colors she wore to work were all dull, often khaki, tan or light brown skirts. On top, a cream or off-white blouse, and always with her brown cardigan sweater, and brown Naturalizer pumps.

Donald woke to the sight of his wife flitting from the closet to the window, it gave his manhood a rush. The surge went to his lustful mind.

Regardless of her public appearance, there is nothing prudish or vanilla about my wife. Her moralistic manners in the workplace would never give away her genius for finding ways to pleasure me.

Donald did not especially like the way his wife dressed herself so plainly. He thought her "work" clothes made her look less attractive. He didn't know much about fashion, but he thought the style and colors made for a frumpy look. Even so, he respected her choices, and he kept his opinions on her wardrobe to himself. When he saw his wife, who he likened to a monochromatic smurf, he thought about the obvious contrast, her Yin and Yang.

She has a proper-practical-lady-smurf side, and a fearless-sexpot-smurf side, contradictory opposites, existing in one package, inseparable, and one of a kind. My better half if I only count one leg. Heck, who am I kidding, I am one lucky devil. No one in this community could ever imagine the naughty side of my smurf, she saves it all for me.

The thought of her mouth on him sent direct heat to his extremity, forcing a frustrated "arrgg" from his chest and throat.

"Donald? Are you okay? That groan sounded like you're in pain?"

Debbi turned from the window and rushed over to check on Donald's wellbeing.

"My sweet worried smurf, if you want to help relieve me of my current pain, call in sick, take off those clothes and let's climb back into bed."

His wanton smile made her redden.

Encouraged by her color change, Donald continued, "Oh, I love when you blush. Look," pointing to the dresser mirror, "...you are blushing. If you will let me, I can make that color spread all the way down to your little pink toes. Or, if you prefer, you can make me blush, and tell me what to do."

His voice had just the right amount of husky for Debbi. It caused sparks to shoot from and between, her sensitive parts. The playful words, spoken with breathy emphasis, and dripping with desire gave her a lustful pause. Debbi's panties, moistened by his pillow talk, suggested he would get lucky, later. The knowing of *later*, made her smile mischievously, but she turned her face away. If he saw her *smirk*, he might not give up until he changed her mind.

Managing her tone, "How can you be frisky with these strangers on our mountain? Who knows what trouble or new curses they'll bring?"

Playing dumb, to instigate a spirited reply from his wife, he shrugged his large shoulders as he answered, "New curses? I don't even know about the old ones?"

"Come now Donald, you can't have forgotten the terrible things that happened at that place, I know you know the history. You can't deny it." Lingering over the jewelry box to choose a broach, and then looking in the mirror to get the right position, Debbi continued matter of factly, "Everyone knows the old place is cursed. They should have known better than to build anything at that elevation, four thousand, then to add further insult, the address number, 44, didn't they know fours are a bad sign? Triple death as Mama would say."

Donald rolled his eyes at his wife's superstitions, but knew she was not totally off.

"Well, a whole bunch of people and horses burning up in a barn fire is not exactly what you'd call getting lucky, but jeeze Smurf, it doesn't mean that place is cursed. Besides, think about the land donation, that alone should have given them good-enough karma to keep the ghosts away."

As if chiming in disagreement, the downstairs clock sounded off, ending the sparring match between the couple. Debbi was at her core, still a little shaken from her evil premonition. She had a strong desire to be at work, where she could investigate. Reaching for her lip gloss and her bag, and using her best take-charge voice, she declared, "Please walk with me, honorable husband," Debbi motioned for Donald to follow her down the stairs.

He obeyed, and mechanically, she reminded him of the day's schedule as they went.

"You will need to be prompt for your appointment with Hia, you're scheduled for a shave, and haircut at 12:45 p.m., or did you forget?"

Donald feigned remembering the commitment, and underscored how much he liked Hia's scalp massage, to see if his wife was listening. She did not blink, it was too late, his fate was set.

Ahh, at work before she even gets there, so much for getting lucky again.

Debbi turned, as if she heard his thoughts, "Are you listening? Or has your fantasy with Hia taken over your mind."

"I, uh, what fantasy? You keep making my appointments with her, and besides, what else can a guy do when his head is resting in her bountiful bosom?"

"Yes, her naturally endowed breasts do make for a soft place to land your head, and you are the one who preaches support local businesses."

Donald's all-American smile, shined, causing Debbi to continue her chide, "For the record, if you get lucky, and she does give you her 90-minute special, you had better tip well."

Neither were totally serious, and neither immune to the charms of the voluptuous Vietnamese stylist. Donald was not aware Debbi generously compensated the woman for her extras, always giving her gratuity over and above the fee. Debbi wanted her man to have a good experience, and she was fond of the woman.

Debbi added, "I'd like to try again for lunch in the diner today, after the rush. It's the best place, after the lunch crowd leaves. The early girls always pass on the rumors to the dinner girls, and those dinner ladies love to play one-up, with their own gathered gossip tidbits."

Donald agreed, "Sounds good Smurf, I will meet you there at 1:30-ish, clean cut, shaven, and ready for some of Betty's meringue pie."

"In that case, you might want to call ahead and have them save you a piece, you pouted for a week the last time she ran out before we got there."

"Ya, see how you are, you always think of everything, what would I do without you? And you're right, I am behind on my allotment of Betty's pie. I will have them girls save a half for us; I'll want to be sure my Smurf gets her fair share too."

They both laughed then kissed distractedly as they reached the inner door to the garage, then parted ways; him back up to the bedroom window to spy on the mountain, her, to the vehicle with the dark tinted windows.

~～～

Mr. Harrison made a late-lunch reservation for two, even though Betty's didn't require advance booking, and the dessert order was placed. Betty tried to sell him a whole pie, but he knew better and stuck with the half order. After the call, Donald lingered, looking past the bedroom window, recalling the mountain's history. The expansive property behind the Harrison's subdivision, the land, and the mountain that bridged their city to Independence Lake, was a place designated for a *Disney* ski village. The ecological studies were commenced as early as 1965, in anticipation of the project. Unfortunately, in 1966 Walt Disney passed away. Perhaps few believed it would or could be a viable project, without Walt's direct influence. Walt was the avid skier, and it was his vision to build a winter-wonderland on the mountain.

"Yup, on top, the place that was almost something if Walt Disney had lived. But below, that definitely started before ol' Walt was born. Huh? I wonder if Walt had any idea what was under foot?"

Up on the mountain, in the area behind and above the old lodge, ski lifts were planned, but never completed. Steele cords hung in the air like the threads of a sticky spider, a reminder of what could have been. The area was a wonderland of trails for cross-country skiers and hikers, but with no main highway giving direct access, relatively few outsiders came around. The locals, willing to ignore the ghost tales of the valley, and the curses of the lodge, could cross over and travel up the dramatic winding driveway. From there, off the split in the drive, the trails would take them over the top on the far side, and down to Independence Lake.

Presently, the refuse and rubbish from the past homeless encampments stood as a deterrent to block foot traffic at the split in the drive. Using his binoculars, Donald watched the crowd who supervised the trucks which were hauling away the old mess.

It's inevitable more local looky-loos would come check out the haps. Wish they would all go away, no one should be congregating in the area, unless they live on this street. If this keeps up, our neighborhood will become an excavation site, and once this place is dug up, it won't be the same; the hometown lifestyle we cherish, will go poof, and Loyalville will be cursed forever.

THE SPORT CENTER

"The devil's most devilish when respectable."

ELIZABETH BARRETT BROWNING

Jones liked thinking of himself as the Green Ghost, the "green" represented his wealth, the "ghost" represented his godly omnipresence, and the lack of any record of his birth. His one-of-a-kind, *Sport Center,* gave him a secure stage, something he needed to be able to receive the green ghost accolades, he knew he deserved.

To date, Jones had provided *opportunities* for most of the big money players in the world. His established security practices weeded out those who had nothing to offer; while those same stipulations brought adoration from those who could afford the products, and the unique services he rendered. His business, esteemed by these singular men, offered the rarest menu of *"pet services,"* as well as other *"non-gentlemen games."*

In this hidden world, created and controlled by something akin to both genius-man, and vicious monster, he liked to say, "Here at the Sport Center, there are boundaries to be tested, and xxx-rated secrets to be made, and there is a year's waiting list, poor slugs get to the back of the line."

If patient, those wealthy and immoral enough, those who sold their souls, for surely that was the cost, could petition for access to his *kingdom*. Clients had much to lose, and the bullet-proof contracts with the Ghost were not in their favor. Still, the Ghost guaranteed safety and anonymity, sufficient for the big film jet set, heads of states, pharmaceutical CEOs, and oil barons; to name a few.

Even with an invitation, all were subjected to a minimum of a half day's "blind journey" to get to the Ghost's lair. His muscle, known as the *Sport Team,* were all highly trained armed guards, providing security, and transportation, to and from the secure locations for clients, guests, and a small number of *qualified* employees. They understood, the Ghost's rules did not vary, and if they wanted to live, they carried out their duties with zero failure. Nonetheless, it was easy to surmise the *Sport Center* was in a remote location. Those who had been inside, would surreptitiously guess the place to be among western states. Utah, California, Arizona, and Nevada were all possibilities, given authorized visitors began their road trip at the Salt Lake City Airport.

Picked up by ground transportation, the Ghost sent his security team to attend to the visitors in limos with blacked-out windows. Unless the window was down, there was no seeing out for the passengers. All were frisked and inspected for wearable recording and GPS or tracking devices before they entered the limousines. Cell phones were collected, batteries removed, and placed in a Faraday holding bag, to be returned when they were delivered back to the airport for departure. Newer phones, without removable batteries were among items, not permitted. The routes driven were designed to confuse and mislead the passengers.

The armed guards who accompanied them, were prepared with scripts, and pregnant whispers, adding disinformation to conversations, to prevent visitors from knowing their precise location at any given time. Jones had uncompromising rules for men "sporting" with his animals, and ironclad security measures to protect his surreptitious practices.

The sport clients were handpicked, although some came by a *special customer* referral. In either case, unbeknownst to his customers, the Ghost learned everything about them, public and private, before any services would be offered. Skilled at increasing his power over individuals by first feeding their lust, and then absorbing their resources, Ghost always prospered, money, power, and souls, he would always take it all, and hunger for more.

A large contingent of men arriving in limousines, appeared on the monitor, motivating the boss to leave the control seat, and walk to the mirror. Jones intended to give his reflection a cursory glance, but he was enamored. He stopped to enjoy the whole package. He saw God, it pleased him. He ran a hand over his neat course brown hair, checked his posture, and washed his hands thoroughly. He kept an eye on his reflection, prepared for the part he would soon play; Jones intended to project a pleasant and positive persona. He consciously contracted his face muscles, to lift his cheeks, enough to pass for warmth.

The seventy-seven or rather fifty-three years that I have graced the planet, after my rebirthing, are my gift to the world. Just look at me, flawless.

Mr. Jones had many physicians, and surgeons in his grip, experts in maintaining his angelic face and his Zeus-like body, among other assignments. He had optimum healthcare throughout his adult life, and he wore it well. Those following his public career would say he was ageless, swearing he had not changed in the past forty years. His image made him giddy; he checked his profile one last time, before moving on. In a rare moment of lightheartedness, entertained by the exceptional beauty of his own image, he began to walk with rhythmic swagger.

Time for some fresh air. (Humming first, then changing dog to God, in his mind.) *Who let the God out, huh, huh, huh, huh, huh! Who let the God out.*

Jones took his personal elevator. He only had to round a dividing wall to reach a tram platform. The tram took him to the first security area, the place where sport clients began their descent. The agenda was prompted by the decision to take a few *pups* to the next level in their *zoomorphic training*. The day's participating clients were businessmen from North Korea. They had the resources, the right appetites, and their props tended to be small enough, and safe for the little ones. Jones believed his *bitches* were no better than animals, still, animals had value, and should not be wasted. His was an incongruent standard, used for the purpose of keeping his "stock" *salable*, it was also the way his mother taught him.

～～

The security man in the "greeter" position, stood six foot, eight inches tall, and weighed in at 300 pounds, he was an intimidating figure. The buzz he had been waiting for tickled his ear. He spoke up with authority to the men who had just arrived.

"Gentlemen, please step forward in a single file line. Have your picture certification and reservation ready to show at the window. Empty all pockets and place possessions in the baskets on the table. Once inside the gate, find the printed footprints and step into a set. Wait there."

The Korean *clients* were vetted over a two-year period, and this was their second visit. A group of ten, all with little to no moral virtue, except when it came to matters of business. They, like other clients, took the associated risks to fulfill their extreme hedonistic desires. The scene, much like an airport, had various security fulfilling their expected roles. Welcomes were offered, and identification was checked against the list of authorized guests. A tight knit group because of their professional affiliations, and their overseas financial status, the Korean's were a stoic bunch, except when it came to their sexual proclivities. Like sheep, the men followed instructions without looking around. They entered the sterile security center, where the walls were dull painted cement, the lights were harsh, and acoustically, it echoed like a prison.

The Ghost had invited the *Chon* to send their untamed stock ahead to complete his "zoomorphization" training. The instigator, Mr. Gyeong, had declared this to be a rare opportunity, and he prodded until he raised the interest, and the funds for the return visit. Gyeong had promised the others, "It will be worth the costs, particularly for those who can return home, with their own trained *pets.*"

Three bitches had been entrusted to the Green Ghost, their owners believing they would return from their training as "ideal" pets. Once on U.S. soil, the feral bitches were transported via Ghost's private trucks. The men would be transported separately and were told not to speak of their inventory until they reached the secure play space. The experience these men sought, would not be condoned elsewhere, and they paid a huge price for the security provided by their host, which supported patience through the convoluted *welcoming* process.

Visitors were gradually stripped of all personal effects, and then herded onto a slow-moving tram. The driverless tram used by visitors, had room for twelve seated riders and was highly sophisticated and comfortable. Shaped like a bullet and fully enclosed, it had no windows. In contrast, Jones' personal bus was appropriately outfitted for a king, including windows. It had all the automated driving mechanisms in place, plus two rows of bench seats, a kitchenette, and a custom bedchamber.

The ride was swift for Jones. He stepped from the platform, and took the short walk to the security area, from within, unseen. Observing and listening from behind the two-way mirror, staff were aware of the possible surveillance. Visitors, on the other hand, had little knowledge of the number of ways they would be monitored. Jones spoke twelve languages, and was fluent in nine, and yet, he rarely let on. Beyond common greetings, he only spoke English to his foreign visitors. He preferred them not knowing his language abilities. Jones knew enough Korean to track the men's private exchanges, but today they were all tightlipped. Watching from behind the mirror, Jones viewed each man as he stepped into the body scanner.

Timing his entrance to avoid lengthy conversations, but also to appease the Korean male ego. Jones believed in keeping customers of this caliber happy, and the day's quarry were ripe for crushing. Lighting overhead flickered, a signal to security that Jones would soon appear; their changing demeanors signaled to the visitors that someone important was approaching. Walking into the cold space, causing the temperatures to rise, gave Jones an ego boost, which he feigned as humility upon joining the visitors.

Bowing deeply, Mr. Gyeong offered his respectful greeting. His cohort followed the example, and Jones returned the token.

"Welcome. I see you arrived safe and sound. I shall pass on the news. Carry on men, thank you."

No need to make unnecessary conversation, they all had met before. The security team were working in a proficient manner, seemingly without error. Following the fleeting pleasantries, Jones returned to the security of his private office, where he could be omniscient. He believed it quite necessary to watch and record his staff, and his guests. Visible and hidden cameras were strategically placed at every level between ceiling and floor. These were his omnipresent god-eyes. Jones could see a person's sweat droplets collecting on their forehead, which could help him determine deception, among other "dirty" things. "Liars are not tolerable. They can be caught quicker when at first, they know they are being watched, and then watched when they do not know." Jones also knew some could grow a guilty conscience, and if they did, termination was immediate. A few rare others, similar to himself, were not what they appeared to be, he knew the type. They were to be observed more than any since they were the least predictable.

Jones considered his god-eyes a mighty weapon, as well as a tool to conduct basic staff inspections. Proper presentation, including foot to head grooming was required for anyone to be able to work for Jones; keeping oneself clean and neat also earned face-value respect. Beyond face-value, people were either useful, or they were not. And even if Jones found a person useful, he trusted no one. To assuage his paranoia, he used the most advanced technology to manage his many interests. *Big Brother* surveillance systems were in all his professional and secret facilities, as well as in his vehicles; his smartwatch allowed him to watch two live feeds simultaneously, from anywhere under the roof. A customized bluetooth device, which also served as a hidden hearing aid, allowed him to listen in on live or recorded conversations, without having to move to his private space, unless he chose to.

CHAPTER 18

THE LOYALVILLE PLAYOFFS

"So disguise shall, by the disguised, pay with falsehood
false exacting, and perform an old contracting."

WILLIAM SHAKESPEARE

Mrs. Debbi Harrison, the one everyone knew to be a "good teacher's pet" and "mind-reading-smart," was privately guilty of federal crimes, such as opening other's mail, periodicals, and brown papered packages, among other things, with the aim of staying free and alive. She could respond as if she were the intended recipient, if it served her purposes, as it occasionally did. At the same time, she was a devoted employee at the Loyalville postal store, punctual, the type who always went the extra mile. The model of efficiency as assistant manager, Mrs. Harrison knew all the box holders by first and last name, as well as their children's and pet's names. She was pleasant, friendly, with a mind like a trap.

Among other duties, she was responsible for mail dispersal, which she completed well before the front door was unlocked for business.

Unlike Debbi, Tom, the owner, would never be accused of catching the worm. Box distribution was not completed until noon on her days off, making her the most popular among the early-bird customers. Success was key to keeping anyone from questioning her cover. Remaining elusive to her past equaled survival, and punctuality served more than one purpose.

Arriving before the store owner, meant Debbi had time to do her brand of investigating, and for her, it was not difficult opening and resealing envelopes and packages in ways no one could detect. It was a talent she had perfected over the seven years on the job. She had no substantial interest in the dirty magazines, sex toys, and other such things she occasionally found, but she preferred knowing about the things her neighbors ordered and sent in secret. People were easier to read when they thought no one would see their doings.

~~~

The early customers who patronize the Loyalville Postal for their "social" needs, were surprisingly absent that morning. The bulk mail distribution was also light, giving Debbi much time to examine all the mail, and make her notes. There was no relevant information on the mountain lodge, and not many other items of interest to be checked out, which moved the time slowly. On her morning break, Debbi took ten minutes to move her car, just for drill; it gave her a chance to squeeze in an eight-minute fast-walk. The jog felt quicker than normal, as Debbi noted the sidewalks were mostly vacant. She wound her way back to main street on the alley road and slipped back into the postal store. She had not been missed.

The late morning hour finally brought in a regular patron. The woman shared about people gathering around a nearby subdivision, not realizing it was Debbi's own street.

"Something like a local mob is loitering at the end of the long grand driveway, the one leading to the haunted lodge, and it's not even Halloween. Everyone is simply baffled at all the activity. I swear it's better than watching morning game shows, and everyone's thinking
~~~

we are going to have our own local reality TV show. Next, we'll see limos and other dark windowed sedans bringing in famous talk show hosts, right? Sorry, I'm just going on and on, and I haven't even given you a chance to say a word. What do you know about it, Debbi? Any gossip come your way?"

"No, can't say I've heard a thing. You're the first in the shop today, you've seen more than I have."

Knowing the source, Debbi expected the speculation; she did not prod for more. Soon it would be midday rush, the working locals on lunch break would flood the store, and she would be held captive in the front, until her own meal break at 1:30 pm. Standing at the upright desk behind the counter, Debbi was checking in the packages an express mail service had dropped, however, her immediate thoughts were on a new box holder.

Only bulk mail for the new box, and no names addressed, so far. I wonder if the box is connected to the lodge owner; the timing seems right.

As soon as the words "lodge owner" were formed, Debbi felt hair rising on her arms. It was a sign. Ambiguous curiosity that was simultaneously petrified and eager, stood poised to see what would happen next.

"Jingling, ling," the door announced a customer, startling Debbi, she dropped the pen in her hand. "Oh!" She caught herself.

Oh, it is just a startle reflex, you're fine. Tom is here, go help your customer.

She bent down to pick up the fallen pen, and took a deep breath, letting it out as she stood. By the time Debbi had eye contact with the lobby, the door opened again, and the incoming voice was a familiar one.

"Hello, good afternoon Mrs. Harrison! Nice as always to see your smiling fortune telling face!"

Chuckling as she entered, a jolly woman, known as, *Sage-the-crossing-guard,* found her way into the postal store. Boxes filled her arms. Maneuvering around the stationary stand, and backing up to the counter, doing a stiffened waltz, the crossing guard swept in with her usual convivial spirit. All the while, she kept her rather plump chin on top of the stacked packages, holding them in place.

"Sage, good afternoon to you too! Please call me Debbi," pointing to her name tag, "that's Debbi with an i," an infectious smile spread across her angelic face. "There is no need for formalities here."

She said it loud enough for the other customer to hear. Eyeing the packages, Debbi continued, "My goodness, you have been a busy lady, haven't you?"

"I have Mrs. Debbi, and no surprise to you, it's all that magic Chinese mind reading you do. Tss-tss, now don't try to deny what the evidence proves. Okay, let's have it now, I know you can tell me what I have here, and I bet you can also tell me where I plan to send them?"

Before a comeback could be uttered, Sage continued with her notions. Seizing the attention of the older customer in the shop, by way of stepping in her path, the exuberant cross-guard spoke without hesitation.

"Oh hello, do I know you? Oh my, thought you were someone else! I'm Sage! I've probably crossed you safely on the street before, yes? I've surely crossed all of Loyalville, have we met before?"

The unknown woman's face was shrouded in a bulky neck scarf. Her way blocked, she held the mail guiltily, and looked up and around, checking to see who else might be watching. Debbi noted the box number printed on the mail in her grip.

Must be the new box owner. Eyes appear dark, possibly bruised, or perhaps her make-up has been smeared, she does not look real, something not right about this woman or is this a girl trying to look older?

The woman turned toward the counter, needing to get past the generously sized pleasanton to break free. Speaking softly but using deeper tones, the aloof customer spoke, "I, I, uh, have to meet someone, excuse me," her voice faltered.

Ariel's head was spinning, she was seeing a ghost from the past, and she was standing just behind the counter.

Lily? It can't be. I need to get out, now.

Not able to accept the loss of her audience, and assuming all would benefit from a little show of magic, Sage stepped back. Using her best cross walk arm signals, she held a no pass to the exit. With the warmth and grace of a manatee, soft-pedaling her will, the round face had impressive smile lines reaching from her mouth to her out-stretched hands. Not aggressive, just over the top with charisma, Sage was a commanding presence.

"Now watch and see for yourself! Mrs. Debbi with an I can do it quick! Listen, her prediction will be right on spot! I'm not exaggerating!"

Sage's eyes widening as she gestured, looking at her captive, then offering another crossing signal, successfully directing the unnamed woman to the counter.

"I need to go."

The darkened eyes plead for understanding then she dropped her face deeper into her scarf, dismissing the recognition.

It can't be her, she's dead.

Ariel held her panic back with directed self-talk.

Hold it together. Wait, your chance to leave will come any second, they think you're old, you're slow, just pretend to go along.

Making an ill-timed entry, Tom, the owner, appeared from the rear of the shop. Eyes down, he did not know he was interrupting. The stranger dropped her head lower and spun out of the shop; her exit shocking everyone speechless.

Debbi was first to find her voice, calling out as the door was closing, "Please, wait, I didn't get your name?"

It was too late, the stranger stepped out of the doorway, and disappeared down the block without turning back.

It was Tom's turn to be confounded.

"Never thought you would miss a name Debbi; I think that's a first."

Sage was not concerned about the visitor leaving, she was intent on hearing some magic from Debbi.

"I guess she was in a hurry, oh well, Mr. Gridley, at least you're here. It really is remarkable how Mrs. Harrison knows what I'm mailing, seriously, now let's have your prediction, tell me what I've got here?"

Another day, Debbi would have been thrilled to play the game, but the mysterious woman who picked up mail from the new box, then ran, had her full attention. The new account, *A.B. and T.A. Enterprises*, gave no clues, the woman's body language gave volumes. Debbi thoughtfully assessed.

Her posture and stance indicated she did not want to speak or be noticed. She never gave a name. Her voice sounded forced, an unnatural tone, but polite. Odd. Sage's warmth and mirth almost brought down the facade, if Tom had not interrupted, she might have given more away. She fought from smiling, no show of teeth. Her eyes definitely smudged and smeared, intentional, and something familiar about her movements.

As was her nature, Sage talked to everyone with her persuasive crossing-guard speak. She had waited for Debbi to respond, but she was not a patient woman. Holding a finger in the air, formulating her next words, then, interrupted by the door's bell, a high-pitched voice burst in; it was Cookie, Tom's wife.

"Hello, hello, all! Oh, my goodness, I see my besties are hard at work! Surprised to see you both in the front at the same time!"

A hideous laugh erupted, like a squeal, along with sow snorts, and a riff of hyena type cackles. Tom Gridley rarely came out of his den when Debbi was working. He understood that most preferred to see and talk to her, and he was rarely social. As for Debbi's other talents, Tom had also been impressed with her predictions, and he credited her with saving his business numerous times over the years. Tom waited for his wife's cackle to reach a stopping point.

"Cookie, what a surprise. I didn't expect you until this evening. Is everything okay? What on earth are you wearing?"

All eyes were on Cookie, who was wearing a bedangled pant suit, white with sparkles and colored beads, something an Elvis impersonator would wear for a show. Full bags in each raised hand, showed off the store tags still attached at the wrist of the garment. Sage became distracted from her Debbi-game, turning her focus onto Cookie, and her outfit.

Basking in the attention, Cookie turned around slowly, to allow everyone to see all sides, "Tell me what you think? I've just come from Truckee, where I found a divine clothing store. I left the tags on in case you didn't like it Tommy, but isn't it perfect?"

"Perfect for what, trick or treat?" said with slight displeasure, partly for the spending, partly for calling him Tommy.

Sage could not contain herself any longer. Mesmerized by the flashy young woman, she eyed her camel toe, and the roundness of her other parts.

Belting out her own brand of laughter, "Hahaha, your name's Cookie? Honey, you look good enough to be Birthday Cake!" Looking back at the lone man, she added, "Your Cookie looks good enough to eat. You are one lucky man!"

Tom was on his third wife; her name fit her superficial mentality. In addition to fashion trends, Cookie was completely devoted to romance authors. When she learned Debbi never read anything else on her days off, she declared Debbi was her "bestie." Debbi's intuitiveness and acting skills, along with her knowledge of common storylines, and her ability to read the back cover, were convincing enough to make everyone believe she, like Cookie, was a devoted page turner; when in reality, she dreaded having to act the part.

As soon as she heard "bestie" Debbi's stomach did a flip flop, and her focus turned to getting the packages weighed and the shipping labels ready for Sage. Thankful for the diversion, she quietly went about her tasks while the ladies schmoozed. Sage, loving the prospect of squelching the tension between husband and *goddess*, to win favor with the lady, jumped to exclaim her revelation.

"Look, look, our little fortune teller has struck again! I never said where I was sending these, but look," pointing to the completed address label with enthusiasm, and taking hold of the tagged arm of Cookie, pulling her closer, "...can you believe it? It's exactly right! This little mind reader took it right out of my thoughts!"

Raucous laughter ensued, except for Tom, who shook his head and turned to go back to the quiet back office. Debbi calmly waited, adding a fake laugh of her own. Sage laughed the loudest, before returning to the attractive Cookie.

"I see you have a heavy bag or two, let me help you," Sage's persona had become decidedly butch.

Fully infatuated with the blond, Sage took the largest bag out of Cookie's hands, and set it in front of her.

"Books? Why there is a whole bag of books! Wow, beautiful and studious, what a combination! And I see Nora! One of my favorite authors, yours too?"

With that lead in, Cookie went into full chatter mode, discussing the authors represented in the bags, and admitting she had read all of Nora's stories several times. She stopped short of disclosing she had brought the books for Debbi, saying instead, "If you haven't read any of these, I brought them to share. Tommy says I've got too many books in the house."

It was a solid ten minutes before Debbi could speak; she was thrilled to skip the romance novel chatter. Sage reluctantly finished her business and left with three of Cookie's books. Cookie, all smiles, and hyena cackles, went in the back to talk to her husband, returning after five minutes with a pouty face.

Debbi offered an empathetic tone, "Tom wants you to return the outfit?"

Cookie, near tears, "Yes, how did you know?"

Having seen the price tag, Debbi pretended not to know.

"Something tells me he is worried about money. How much did you pay?"

Cookie's face peevish as she replied, "Two hundred, seventy-three dollars, half off the original price. Not that it matters. Tommy said it looked too snug, not that he has any idea about fashion. None. He's making me drive back to Truckee. Made me promise to get a full credit back on the card today. Now I've got to git; talk about a good reason for a pity party, right? I left books for you, on your desk. I know you don't like reading at work, but I swear you'll love the new series. And lucky for you, I have the whole set when you're ready for them!"

CHAPTER 19

HIA'S FANS

*"Genuine learning has ever been said to give polish to man;
why then should it not bestow added charm on women?"*

EMMA WILLARD

Donald and his wife were honest admirers of Hia, Debbi because of her past, and Donald because of his experience in her skilled hands. In truth, Debbi's research into her dark past had not been shared with Donald. He was only aware of Hia's expert services and sound practices; she was always prepared, efficient, and faithfully on time from beginning to end. Donald also knew Hia had purchased her place in Loyalville, a salon with upstairs living quarters, rejecting the standard lease option, and was in good standing with the bank. Based on Debbi's insider knowledge, he understood the services Hia provided in the salon scarcely kept her afloat, while the monies she earned by selling catalog makeup products allowed her a meager amount of spending money. Contrary to town gossip, he knew for certain, Hia did not sell her body in order to keep her shop open.

Hia, pronounced high, came to America, escaping the fate of a fixed marriage, at the hands of a dirty village bride-broker. Hia's sister was not as fortunate. Their village law did little to protect women. A man could prove his unwanted wife was "unfaithful," by simply gathering the local beggars to get them drunk and riled up. When the booze was all consumed, he would throw his wife out to them, naked, and lock the doors. The woman would be humiliated, beaten, and gang raped, while the "reputable" men of the village stood by as "legal" witnesses. If she survived a week or more, a legal proceeding would allow the husband to divorce the "whore." If she died, as was the case with Hia's sister, the religion of the man would determine the burial and mourning practices. Debbi was thankful Hia escaped that life.

Debbi understood that some misfortunes could produce positive outcomes, and such was the case of Hia. Tainted by a relative at a tender age, she could not qualify to be a virgin-bride. Scorned and unwanted by age eleven, she found her way out of Vietnam on a refugee boat. Hia also made her way out of prostitution. She had been forced into the work by the welcoming immigrant family, her second cousins who ran nail salons. Hia eventually attained her green card. She found a job as a live-in nanny for a wealthy Caucasian family, and eventually became a naturalized U.S. citizen. She was honored to be American and took pride in being a Loyalville resident.

~~~

Donald barely got off the phone in time to complete his honey-do tasks and make it to the salon on time. An uneventful morning, as far as he was concerned, especially after waiting on hold for the title company, only to have the line disconnected. He called back, but the phone had switched to the auto message that played during the lunch hour. Accepting the delay, he let all his questions go once he was in the wash sink, in Hia's hands, and under the spell of her spicy fragrance, he felt blissful. Today, he had an hour of her time, and the shop was empty.

Hearing his sigh, and seeing Donald's smile, Hia offered her friendly wink, adding, "Someday you will get lucky and have Hia's Full Treatment, the 90-minute special."
~~~

Skilled at making others look their best, Hia also made every effort to beautify her own appearance, always highlighting her best body features. It was true her work apparel could have been worn to a nightclub, her dress skirts were slit up high, and her necklines, all cut low, and she was a flirt, but she was always professional. And being a seller of beauty products, made her feel obligated to present herself as fashionable as possible.

Hia offered, "Mr. Donald, sir, let's give you a little stress relief with a head massage, yes? I can feel tension in your hair follicles. I hope the folks around here are not giving you hard time about the lodge?"

"Thank you Hia, a little massage wouldn't hurt, but only if you let me pay you for it?"

"No extra, this is just a taste of the 90-minute special. You important man in town, I am happy to do my part to keep you looking well. You retired, but you do so much volunteer work. I know Mrs. Debbi takes care of you, but she working. I do this for her."

The soothing hands of Hia, did not distract him from something she said. "What have you heard about the lodge, what do you know of it Hia?"

"I know people say that place is haunted. Some say, you go there, you die there. Silly. I hear you wanted parking lot, cleaner than homeless campers, and you make it safer for neighborhood. I hear other people talk yesterday; they say you failed to keep your promises. They say you broke your promise and made another deal."

"Who?"

"I cannot say names, you understand?" A nod from Donald and she continued proudly, "I hear the place was bought by a company. Green Mountain, Incorporated, now own it. I know. I have friend who works at title company. New owner plant all new landscape, all nice, fix it real good. How's that temperature, good? Not too hot?"

Donald was doing his best to keep his mind on her words. "It's great, feels perfect Hia, thanks, I've been looking forward to this all morning. Go on, what else did your friend say?"

Hia's hands worked as she chattered on, "My friend say corporation will use place for a retreat center, employee only, not for public. They have long dollar, lots of money. They have security starting tonight to watch place. Ok? Sit up, let me help, there you go Mr. Donald, Hia take care of you, real good. Up, now, to my chair."

Donald was both surprised, and worried. He imagined security walking all over the grounds and finding *his* secrets. A strange feeling began to rise in his chest. He took a deep breath through his nose and tried to release all the bad air through his mouth, the way Debbi showed him. He had to know more. Donald took a moment to look at Hia. She was dressed in a bright turquoise blue top, with a deep cut in front. A skirt hugged her shapely hips and showed off her toned legs. When she saw him looking, she reached down to the bottom drawer in her station to get a *dry* cape. Her move was not lost on Donald. His attention to her body, converted his stress, endorphins rushed to both heads. After his hair was towel dried, and Hia began to gently comb his hair, he continued with questions.

"Security at the lodge, you say? How do you know about the security Hia? Oh, and short on the sides, but leave it longer on top."

Hia began snipping on the top section, forcing Donald to close his eyes. Hia always started with less, often saying, "You can always take more, but you can't put it back on." He liked that about her, but it meant he had to close his eyes during the cuts in front, when he least wanted to close his eyes.

Donald opened to a squint, enough to see decolletage dancing dangerously close to his face. He saw pieces of his hair land on Hia and were now falling deeper between her breasts. He imagined her pulling her low-cut top well beneath her breasts, leaning forward, and releasing the snippets of hair from her breasts. Hia turned, her firm breasts made slight contact with Donald's jaw; enough to stimulate an erection twinge. She stepped back, reached out, and took a hold of his scruffy chin. Turning his face from left to right, she looked at his hair and then met his eyes.

"Hia give you a smooth shave after your cut."

"Thank you, my face is yours to do as you wish."

Hia was beaming. She enjoyed having interesting conversation with one of her favorite customers.

"I know, customer told me. I can't say names, you understand. He say, owner very picky. He say, salary paid for next three years, in advance. Chin up. Yes good. Hia make you handsome. You get lucky tonight Mr. Donald, so good looking. That good for Mr. Donald, security, less work for you, yes? Mrs. Debbi will be happy to see you all cleaned up. There. Good? Hair not too short."

When Hia pulled out her trimmers, she was all business, carefully shaving his neckline, and around his ears. She used the attachment to trim eyebrows, ears, and nose too. Once she was done and blowing off cut hairs from around Donald's neck and face, she retrieved a steaming hot towel and wrapped Donald's face, expertly. She waited, replaced it when it cooled, then went about arranging her shaving tools, in preparation of the chore. While Donald was under the towel, she chatted on.

"My cousin works for big landscaping company in Reno. They got contract to come and make place nice again. Ok, how that feel Mr. Donald, good? Ok, relax, Hia shave you now, make you nice, and soft for your lucky wife. You be still, I won't cut you."

Hia's skill with a straight razor was far superior to the barber in town, but most local women sent their husbands to the barber instead of the salon. For Donald, the shave was like a dream; the razor, held like a feather, and sharp enough to remove every stubborn hair follicle. Before she was done, she rubbed the back of her hand against Donald's freshly shaven face and jaw. Taking his hand in hers, she wanted him to check her work the same way.

"Mrs. Debbi will like, yes?"

"Ahh, very nice Hia. Soft as a baby's bottom."

His comment caused Hia to laugh. It took her a moment to regain her professional composure. She checked her eye make-up in the mirror, and then continued with her treatment with after shave lotion and a face massage. Donald was ready with additional questions about the lodge, but the sound of the shop doorbell announced someone's arrival. A small-framed man, dressed in casual clothes, and smiling like a Cheshire cat, waltzed in like he owed the place.

"Surprise, cousin Hia, your biggest fan has come to visit you! Well,

well, look at you in your fancy salon! You are doing very well I see," spoken with a sardonic tone.

Hia's hands finished toweling off Donald's neck and ears. Switching language to Vietnamese, with emphasis, she talked to her cousin directly. Donald understood most words, having spent a year in the country, and having a knack for picking up languages. He knew she was scolding him for his rude interruption. The man continued smiling, and said she looked like a streetwalker. He asked if she was ready to bend over and get lucky. Hia did not respond to his crude remarks. She managed to add a brief temple massage for Donald, before returning to her English tongue.

"All done now, Mr. Donald, sir. Sooo handsome! Mrs. Debbi a lucky lady. Ok, all done. Please meet my cousin from Reno, Dien Nguyen. He works with the land."

It was a subtle dig, but it gave Hia a little swagger to bolster her dignity. The men exchanged a polite handshake, then Donald stood to his feet, towering over the tanned man. Donald wasted no time in getting to his question for the obnoxious individual.

"Nice to meet you, Dien. You'd be a landscaper then? Tell me what you think of the job out at the lodge, did you get to meet the new owners? Can you tell me anything about them?"

Hia's cousin was put off by the white-man's lack of subtlety. Dien's culture would have had the two strangers exchanging superficial small talk upon first meeting. An open-ended statement about the work site, allowing Dien to decide what to share, would have been the culturally appropriate way to talk, as far as Dien was concerned; he promptly scowled. Hia delivered a look that was meant to convey Donald's guilelessness, but her cousin gave her a "pfff" in return, followed by a barrage of Vietnamese.

Donald got the message, even if his Vietnamese vocabulary was limited. To catch the assuming man, unawares, Donald interrupted, using his best Viet-tongue to thank Hia for the hairs cut and the face polished. Seeing Dien's face slightly redden was priceless.

Laughing at the man heartily, Donald parted with, "Ah, time to meet my wife for lunch, best not to keep her waiting, a happy wife is a happy life, isn't that right Dien? Or perhaps you have not yet saved enough to buy a wife?"

The tall man's words did what his hands wanted to do, shocked the breath right out of Dien. A gulping cough choked him the truth was too much for him to swallow. So shocked by Donald's audacity, Dien could barely keep himself from striking back. His frustrated blush triggered another laugh from Donald, which gave Hia the giggles, briefly. Dien feigned a laugh to go along and keep from revealing his own wicked thoughts.

"Mr. Donald, you so funny, you make jokes to everyone. He is joking, Dien."

"Ah yes, occasionally, but as they say, not enough to quit my day job. All in good fun, isn't that right Dien?"

"Sure mister, sure."

Gracious, in manner, Hia gathered her cape and towels and deposited them in her laundry cupboard. She wanted to thank her customer for not making a fuss about her cousin's vulgar behavior, but she did not wish to stoke her cousin's temper. "Thank you for your business, Mr. Donald. Please give Mrs. Debbi my best for sending you; you look much refreshed for your date. I am happy when my customers are happy. Maybe next time let Hia give you a mani-pedi special."

"Thanks Hia, you can be sure I will give her the message." He knew the answer, but asked it anyway, "What do I owe you for today."

"Not a thing, Mrs. Debbi take care of it in advance."

Donald winked at Hia, then hard-eyed the compact man.

"Ah, well then, I'll be on my way, oh and Dien, good luck with your work up at the lodge, and don't worry about the curse, the ghosts there are mostly friendly, and I hope your day is as nice as your personality."

Hia picked up her broom and went right to work cleaning the station, even as her cousin stood there watching. When Donald was out of sight, Dien twisted his face, then spit out his bitterness without filtering. He accused Hia of letting her customer go without paying, just to offend him. He was filled with hostility at the entitlement and rudeness of the "white man."

Hia knew not to argue with her spiteful cousin, it was best not to correct his notions. Gratifying him with an approving nod, she set her broom aside, leaving the hair cuttings piled up, and pointed to the chair, "I have few minutes until next customer, cousin, sit down, let me give you a shoulder and neck massage."

Dien sidestepped her artificial agreement, with his own fake smile. He moved toward the chair, then responded to Hia with a stinging slap across her face. The façade was gone.

"Liar! I saw the way you flirted, such a slut. I should bring my crew here and have you service them, I'm sure you secretly long for a gangbang, like the old days. Once a whore always a whore, no matter how white you pretend to be."

Hia stepped out of his reach after the hit, but fearfully stayed her attention on him. She had turned her back on his type before, and painfully regretted it. She knew a customer was due any moment, but she dared not indicate she was looking for help, she managed to say, "Tôi xin lỗi vì đã ích kỷ."

Dien translated it in English to exhibit his dominance, "Yes, you are a sorry selfish bitch," adding, "living alone when you could be helping your family."

Dien wanted to smack her again but stopped when the door sounded. He gestured as if he needed to smooth his hair, then turned directly to see who was keeping him from acting out his wrath. Dien did not turn back to address Hia, who was now holding a moist towel to her tender face. Smugly, he went past the woman customer, and with his hand on the door, called out, "I'll be back, soon, my dear cousin."

Another rich white woman. You're both lucky I have no time for trouble. I will be back little miss Hia, back when you are all alone; then you can pay for your selfishness.

CHAPTER 20

ASHEESH IS PROMOTED

"He knows nothing; and he thinks he knows everything. That points clearly to a political career."

GEORGE BERNARD SHAW

Systematically, Jones reviewed all camera feeds, roving his realm, scrupulously searching for imperfections, and verifying absolute obedience. Expectations, satisfied, he stopped to watch Number 10, a model NOJ-45 *graduate*. Ten was highly skilled at impersonating NOJ, and could emulate the training techniques, well enough to stand in as the "Master." The signature "tiger" mask hid his slightly younger face, otherwise, he was a mirrored image of the Ghost. Jones was pleased to see 10 deep into his role.

Ten was thrilled to be out of lock-down, it had been four months. The isolation, part of Ghost's brainwashing system, had him expectant for *social* interactions, and needy to have his own lusts fulfilled. He also believed pleasing his mentor was key to getting what he needed. He had been trained to demonstrate excellence, *tutored* by the Master *himself*.

Feeling mollified, Ghost changed feeds to see how the processing was going with the incoming group. Immediately nettled to hear pitched voices, he reacted to the scene on his monitor.

Uncivilized vulgar tones. Let me see what is happening? Oh, I see. That man, a guest under my roof, thinks he's got the right to assert himself, there is no reason for any disagreement to occur. Who does he think he is? Oh no, this is not acceptable.

A professional tone was always expected, and the Ghost did not forget to punish mistakes. His judgement was prompt, even if the application of retribution was an unhurried process.

Hmmm. Leo reacted in an unseemly manner. He is no longer worthy to be my first man here, not acceptable Leo. Sloppy. I deserve better than you, even before this outburst. I have felt a change was needful, look how you keep your nails, shoddy at best. And let's face it, you are a stale middle-aged man, and your balls have shrunk. I suspect your end is nearing.

Mr. Jones had two *recruits*, staff from his dog resort team, *willing* to shift their employment to "higher levels of trust" with their employer. The *"acceptance"* into the Sport Staff was individualized. The process, insidious and ultimately pernicious, necessitated a timeline dictated by specific criteria. As Jones stood from the chair, a calendar reminder sounded.

Ahh yes, another perfectly timed plan. Today I have a promotion for the Indian, Asheesh. He knows how to present himself.

In addition to his manicured style, Jones admired the younger man's use of subtle cruelty. Some of his other attributes were also agreeable. Knowing what was ahead of him today, Jones could not help but root for the man.

It's do or die, Asheesh. Choose your options wisely, I'd like you to reach your potential.

Making certain no one was in the area, Jones stepped out from the wall passageway. He pulled up the relevant view on his watch, as he walked.

And where is Asheesh? Hmmm, his shift begins in two minutes. Ahh, there, I see he's cleaning lint from his jacket. Nice to see a man who takes pleasure in keeping up his appearance.

Whenever it was feasible, Jones believed in growing his team from within. Asheesh was one of two, being brought *down* to the inner circle. Asheesh was a Pakistani man, not yet thirty years old. He had the smile and charm of a saint. Jones had also privately witnessed how he delighted in the misery of others. Asheesh knew nothing beyond the public Jones, who he had worked for just over a year. He was hired because Jones liked his black and white thinking, and saw how his wicked charm worked on both men and women. Asheesh also proved to be intolerant of weakness and excuses. His promotion was in order if he could prove himself. Asheesh was told only that he would have an opportunity for additional responsibility in another area. Little else had been explained, still, his eagerness was apparent.

The other "sport" recruit was an educated thirty-something, Caucasian man, named Ron. He was found to be vastly superior on paper and lacking in the flesh. He was on a different trajectory, and Jones decided it was time to accelerate his future.

～～

Asheesh stepped from the employee lounge, out into the wide corridor, finding Mr. Jones just beyond the doorway. They held one another's respectful gaze. Jones could sense the man's tension, forcing him to curb a sadistic grin.

"Greetings Asheesh, and right on time. Come. I will brief you as we walk. I will escort you to your new work area."

Walking through a rising wall, did not appear to surprise Asheesh, even as it receded back into the floor behind him. Speaking in soft tones, to avoid being overheard, Jones gave Asheesh enough information to understand his new role, which called for immediate leadership action. Asheesh nodded with confidence, as he listened intently to his boss. Just before reaching the designated area, where Asheesh would meet staff and visitors, Jones stopped short.

"You will go on without me. I will observe from here." Jones reached down and gave his employee's manhood a full hand squeeze.

"Be yourself, and prove to me, I chose the right man for the job. Any questions?"

"No Sir. I will take it from here," Asheesh spoke emphatically, while still submitting to his boss.

～～

From his vantage point, Jones checked to see that his staff had freshly polished shoes, and crisp uniforms. Satisfied, he watched as Asheesh proceeded to meet the security team. Jones wanted to know how Asheesh would perform under pressure. He was given accurate information, but only enough to guess what came next. Without so much as an introduction, the *new supervisor* was expected to convince the staff to listen and follow his leadership as well as maintain ultimate professionalism in front of the visiting clients.

Asheesh presented himself, and spoke to each one, apparently wasting no words. In the presence of paying "company," he went quickly to his points, knowing he would be judged for what he did and did not do. He offered his managerial appreciation, and then went straight to task delegation. Asheesh handed out few instructions, those he gave, he qualified by saying, "Have no fears, I will be reporting your good results directly to Mr. Jones."

Following the staff *briefings*, Asheesh turned to one of the Koreans, a Mr. Woo, and continued with unblemished poise. Mr. Woo appeared cordial, also discombobulated. He wore an expensive suit, but the soles of his shoes were worn down on the outside of each shoe. An odd thing to note, but for NOJ, it was a simple benchmark that spoke volumes about a man's status and values. Jones sensed that Woo was not a typical client, even for a Korean; his manner smelled vanilla. Jones stayed quiet and brooded.

I'm insulted that any would dare to enter my domain in worn out shoes, strike one Woo.

The jacketed Asheesh continued to establish his dominance in the situation, stepping aside to speak to the uniforms assigned to watch the x-ray monitors. Soundlessly, they exchanged information.

The security team had been privately asked to stall Woo's processing. Jones could see Asheesh had the staff's immediate respect. Woo submitted when asked to step into the body scan for a second time, without insolence. Once Woo was in the scanner, Asheesh met with the handlers, individually.

After speaking together, one of the men departed. Asheesh did not respect the co-worker named Ron, but it seemed his boss wanted him used. When Ron's name was mentioned during his brief *on-boarding* with Jones, Asheesh took it to mean he was favored. Seeing Ron among the other men, changed his mind. Asheesh felt confident the weak-eyed man would not win any kudos from the boss. Putting him on an important task, might result in a little celebratory humiliation when he failed; Asheesh was certain Ron would be found deficient.

Having completed what he thought he should do, Asheesh turned and gestured to his boss. Jones nodded him forward, and Asheesh returned like a *good sport*.

"I'm ready to hear your report, Asheesh."

Jones spoke with a disinterested tone, despite his curiosity.

"Yes Sir. Mr. Woo was detained in the security area. The staff could not verify his fingerprints as the returning client he professed to be. When the others were being escorted away, Woo had words with Leo, who ultimately lost his cool, that is to say, Leo, did not maintain a professional manner. Leo also displayed some resistance to receiving instructions from me, I will address his attitude in private. The guest, Mr. Gyeong requested Mr. Woo, his secretary, be permitted to join them. Leo appeased him by saying you would be summoned for a decision. I perceive it was his attempt to display his own management status. Mr. Gyeong and the others are awaiting next steps. In accordance with the protocols on dealing with obstreperous guests, I have requested sentry prepare to remove Mr. Woo, if that meets with your approval. They will arrive shortly."

"Thank you for the precaution with sentry, very clever of you. We will talk to Leo together, yes, I believe that will be best. He has been in your place, and he will need to teach you what he knows. You will be fully looped in on Sport business, once I'm persuaded you are the best man for the job. I like what I see so far. Back to Woo. Am I to understand he has not yet met the entry criteria?"

"Yes Sir. I was told this is his first visit. Reportedly, he took the place of another man named Woo, who frankly, looks the same. Once security learned he did not match the previous fingerprint file, he admitted he was not Jae-Hwa Woo. He then produced his own identification, as well as submitting an affidavit given to him by Gyeong, stating he had been internally approved."

"Where are we with our own verification?"

"My understanding Sir, we are currently working to complete the background checks and his funds were previously verified along with the rest."

"Have you made Mr. Gyeong aware?"

"Sir, I sent Ron to provide an update."

As if on cue, the flushed team member returned. He stopped several feet away, clearly unsure of himself. He waited for an approach signal. Jones motioned him forward, and he moved closer, still standing a step apart. He was close enough for Neffen to notice the man had a dirty ring on the inside of his neck collar; he was not pleased. Ron sensed his vexation, unaware of the source. Looking at the ground, it took a moment for him to find the courage to make eye contact with Asheesh.

There was no kindness in the new supervisor's voice, "Speak up Ron, Mr. Jones does not have all day."

Stuttering and still unable to meet eyes with Jones, Ron began, "Yes Sir, I, uh, he, uh, the man in charge of the group, he stated it was not his problem."

Asheesh did not hesitate to add to Ron's distress.

"It? Be specific, and don't waste Mr. Jones' time." The tone was professional, even if touched with impatience.

"The guy, I don't know his name, Mr. G-something, he didn't want to be blamed for Mr. Woo's missing documentation. He said that all the men with him had passed extensive background checks, before they could accompany him."

Asheesh looked to see if Jones had anything to add, before

addressing Ron again. The boss was a blank slate. Having not been in this kind of situation before, Asheesh had to predict the expectations of his employer. He did not feel they were difficult to measure.

Speaking with firmness, "Was there anything else, of importance, Ron?"

Ron stepped back, and pulled his arm over his forehead, wiping his growing perspiration. His voice tentative. His gut rolling the morning coffee, forcing a suppressed burp downward.

"Uh. Yes. Mr. Woo has something waiting for him, he wanted to pick it up as soon as possible. He said he was not at liberty to speak further about it, but he wants an update."

Jones did not withhold his judgement, although he kept it to himself.

Woo, I'm confident you've already signed a form agreeing not to speak of your bitch-property until in the play area. Strike two.

Sensing increased displeasure, Ron took another small step backwards and returned his gaze to the ground. Jones had tired of the unpolished reporter, and his mind was definite on the man's future. He stepped back, locking eyes with Asheesh. Asheesh read the look, and calmly continued.

"Thank you, anything else, Ron?"

"Well, yes, uh, they started speaking in Korean," the man looked at his cell phone to read, "uhh, the G-man said he expected the delay, said he would not have brought him, but they needed his share of costs to cover the minimum, then said he expected that everything would be resolved soon."

While the young man stammered his words, Jones looked at his own watch, navigating to the device that would allow him to eavesdrop on current conversations. He was not disappointed, the group had grown talkative, thinking they were alone. Before leaving the men to tend to other tasks, Jones looked over at Ron to ask a final question.

"Ron, may I ask, did you learn your Hangul in Korea or in state education?"

"Actually Sir, I used the translator app. Uh, I don't know much about their language," Ron's voice faltered.

Jones' tone did not hide his displeasure, "You also do not know much about our uniform standards. You are dismissed to the employee lounge, until you have made the necessary corrections."

Responding barely above a whisper, Ron whimpered, "Yes, I'm sorry Sir, it won't happen again. Thank you, Sir."

Waiting until the sniveling man with the soiled shirt had walked away, Jones leaned close to Asheesh, "I must say, I'm disappointed you did not catch the error before allowing him to represent me."

Asheesh pulled at his own shirt collar, and shook his head, indicating he had noticed the grime, "I'm sorry to dissatisfy, Sir. He passed my initial inspection. He evidently has problems with perspiration and hygiene. I will follow up with him accordingly."

"Thank you Asheesh. His manners are atrocious. We will keep him for the rest of his shift, assuming he can find a clean shirt, but this will be his last day. I will meet with you later to prepare his dismissal. In the interim, please have sentry take Woo to the tram platform. Tell Woo they will be escorting him back to his group. Then I would like you to go to meet with my newly hired chef. See to her comprehension of your role. Reinforce my standards, in particular, the uniform and appearance standards. Your intelligence and utmost professional charm are required to establish positive rapport with her. She is useful to me, but make no mistake, she is on a need-to-know basis. I will judge what she needs to know and when. Let there be no rogue overtones or otherwise. Like you, she remains on a thirty-day probation period. I've read her resume and heard her practiced answers. I've not learned enough to form my final opinion about her. You are to elicit personal background information, I know you are skilled at making females speak, put her at ease, and get her talking about herself."

Jones reached out greedily. His firm grip took hold of the new supervisor. Asheesh submitted in his familiar manner; he no longer minded acting sub for his boss; his response was favorable to Jones.

CHAPTER 21

CAROLINE'S BROTHER?

*"Whenever A annoys or injures B on the pretense
of saving or improving X, A is a scoundrel."*

H. L. MENCKEN

Returning from a bus ride, Ariel pondered the possibility of seeing a ghost from her past.

I know I wanted to think it was Lily, but she can't be alive, no, that woman, Debbi, she is a local who grew up here, she just looked like her. And see another day in Loyalville, a good day, and no sign of trouble.

Relaxing once she reached Caroline's Street, there was a sense of ease coming over Ariel, it felt like a warm-hearted hug as she reached the yard gate. The feeling did an about-face when she saw the large yellow sticky note stuck on the front door of Caroline's house. A panic took hold of her instantly. She scanned the area, looking for who might have left the note, also checking to see if anything else was different. The area was quiet, no people or cars to be seen, no other changes since she left earlier that morning. Still, she approached cautiously, reading it when she was close enough, without touching it.

Hey Linny, It's me, your brother Gary. I know I have not been a good brother to you, I know we have been strangers, but I am doing very well as a real estate investor, and I want to reconnect with you, for old time's sake. I promise I am not wanting to borrow money. I just want to try to make-up for the years gone by. If you will meet me in town at the Mellow Fellow Pub, I will buy you a beer, like old times, 9pm. I'll likely be the only man in Gucci shoes, and oh by the way, I changed my name, just flipped it around actually, I now go by the name Davis Gary Goodman. If you have internet, you can google me. See how well your little brother is doing. See you soon. Davis.

Ariel's heart stopped, and the porch began to spin. She stopped herself from a full panic attack by quickly going inside the house to do as the note suggested. Unfortunately, it did not take long to find information about Davis Goodman, but which one; there were 68 listings. She scanned as many as she could, there were no obvious ties that could prove any were Caroline's brother. The note itself offered the best clue, Caroline's nickname. Some weeks back, *Trin* came across two Truckee locals who remembered Caroline, only they knew her as "Linny." Related or not, Ariel's instinct told her trouble had just popped her happy bubble.

How can a brother just show up after years, and not even know his sister needed help? If she had a brother, she would have something, a picture at least, something to prove he was telling the truth. Unless, as his note said, he had not been a good brother, and in fact was a very bad brother. Maybe Caroline didn't want him around? I must know!

What followed was a manic-madwoman-like reaction. All her energy went into searching for some evidence that Caroline had a brother. The boxes in the spare room, untouched until now, because of how tightly everything was packed, would have to be examined. Ariel charged the room like a person on meth, absolutely crazed with need. She used her slight frame as leverage and climbed halfway up onto one stack of boxes. She swung herself and kicked with all her might. The stack gave way. The weight of the boxes pulled her down and forced some of the smaller boxes to hit the floor and bust open. Ariel was dizzy from her fall, luckily no pain.

Once she regained her senses, Ariel realized the contents around her included cash, and a lot of it. She also found Caroline's dog tags, and some military related paraphernalia, including a photograph. The photo depicted a thirty-ish butch-woman, dressed in a navel uniform. At her side, stood an angry looking teen boy. A banner hung above them, reading, Welcome Home Linney!

The family resemblance is evident, if not her little brother, maybe her son? Hmmm?

Collecting herself, Ariel looked at the mess she had created. She found what she had hoped not to find. To her amazement, she also found money, a lot of it. In fact, every spilled box, and every container that had smashed open in her fall, had money mixed among its contents. She could not immediately decide how she felt about the money, although now she felt compelled to do a full audit on the storage in the house. After several more hours of digging among boxes filled with papers, shoes, and other random items, she organized and counted the bounty, it astounded her; she had $75,000.

Besides being kept in bundles, the hoarded money was concealed in a variety of ways. Ariel found rolls of cash, mostly hundreds, tucked into glassware, plastic containers, and rolled socks. A goodly amount of the money had been placed in the bottom of the collected used shoes, all ladies, mostly boots. When the room was completely sifted, Ariel felt exhausted, but also hopeful. She lay back on the floor, giving herself a physical break.

There are other closets with items like these, maybe she hid even more money? Maybe it's a gift left for a woman to find, and keep, otherwise why would she hide it in the woman's shoes? Or maybe she would want her brother to have it. No way to know without checking closer. So, now what do I do? Where do I put it? I'll need to hide it, until I decide if the brother is deserving, if he is the real brother?

Ariel, fatigued from her treasure hunt, took a bath. As she soaked, she allowed herself to imagine buying a small cabin in the mountains. Loyalville felt like the safest choice, it was prime in her mind. Brother or no brother, she assumed it would not be wise to continue living in Caroline's home. By the time water drained from the tub, her thoughts had settled on meeting the man, as *Trin*.

~~~

Ariel walked briskly to the meeting place, hanging out in the shadows before the scheduled time. She watched for Goodman to arrive, a man with Gucci shoes would not be difficult to identify. Ten minutes passed the meeting time, she saw a bright red convertible approaching. Eyeing the driver, Ariel judged it could be the man she was to meet. Watching from across the street, she saw him ogle a well-dressed woman while passing the entrance to reach the parking area. As he pulled into the congested lot, a couple, presumably lesbian, were crossing on the sidewalk. He braked fast, just short of running into the women, screeching his corvette tires, awarding the startled pedestrians with a long horn and his middle finger. Seeing him park, taking up two spaces, one, a spot for the disabled, gave Ariel a glimpse into the man's character. Whoever this guy was, he was not considerate of others, and definitely a man out for his own interests.

The man looked in his rearview mirror, checked his teeth, then, practiced his smile. He brushed light wrinkles from his slacks as he got out, then strode away from his car. Reaching the front door of the pub, he clicked his key fob over his shoulder, setting the alarm for his vehicle. It was then Ariel spotted his shoes; he was real. He gallantly entered the venue as if all the patrons were waiting for him. Ariel followed him inside but held back. She would eavesdrop on his conversations, before presenting herself as *Caroline's caregiver*. She sat down among those waiting for a table, and he went directly to the bar and ordered a drink. A wait staff with a tray of glasses filled with water offered the drinks to those waiting to be seated. Trin accepted the glass and kept her eye on the man calling himself Caroline's brother. He did not look around for his sister. Instead, Davis began trying to flirt with the busty female bartender.

"Hey, are you Australian? Because you meet all my koala-fications. By the way, what did your hot-mother name her mini-me?"
~~~

"Name's Kate. Let me know when you're ready for another drink."

"Better make the next one a double, Kate, it's getting so hot in here, I think my zipper is falling for you."

She was busy, and aside from a perfunctory smile, and serving his drink, she was untouched by his cheesy pick-up attempts. Ariel watched as he reached into his pocket, then threw down some cash, making a thud sound on the bar.

Kate spun away from her glass washing when she heard the thump. She leaned toward him, "Whatcha need?" Her eye spotted a fifty-dollar bill.

As soon as she saw it, Davis picked it back up, adding, "I thought you might be the curious type, now, now, if you want to know how much I'm willing to tip you, you will have to earn it by taking the time to talk to me. Come on, it's not like this place has anyone who will treat you better than Davis Goodman, thee Davis Goodman."

"Excuse me, Mr. Davis Goodman, I've got glasses to wash and limes and celery to cut, before the shift change, unless you want to order something you will have to wait until I'm finished."

"I'd like to order you right out of your shirt, but you don't seem the type to do it just because you were told," chuckling in absence of the admonishment, he added, "just kidding ya. I'm in no hurry. You still have time to get to know me."

The bartender apparently was not looking to get-to-know the obnoxious customer, she was aware that his type was not worth it. She straightened and returned to her sink duties.

"Okay, no how-to get-rich tips for Kate. Why would a minimum wage earner ever think thee Davis Goodman would take the time or go out of his way to try to help-ya out with some free advice?"

"Be with you in just a minute, Mr. Cheddar."

"Ahh, you're melting my heart, I just might have to tell you my whole-life story."

Without looking back up, the bartender rolled her eyes. Watching every nuance, Ariel perceived the bartender to be turned off by his efforts.

He prefers to talk about himself, now, isn't that a surprise. Oh, I think

I might be sick. He's too important to even look for his sister, and I guess she is supposed to identify him by his fancy shoes which are tucked under his stool. How thoughtful. Has he already forgotten he invited her to meet him here? Smart girl behind the bar, although I would like to hear him say more about himself. Maybe I could motivate her. I could learn more with her asking the questions. And if she plays her hand right, she could still get that tip he alluded to giving.

Trin pulled a pen from *his* pocket and scribbled the bartender a note on the cocktail napkin. A moment later, *he* stood and walked to the far end of the bar, out of earshot from Davis. Tapping the bar to gain the bartenders attention, *Trin* waved her over when she looked up from her tasks. The napkin was discreetly handed over, along with a fresh Benjamin tucked inside. The bartender read the note and offered a guileful smile. After the exchange, *Trin* retreated to *his* seat with the sparkling water. The note asked the bartender to help a friend "avoid a blind-date blunder."

By way of explaining, *Trin* wrote, "He's pretended to be a family guy, and a fan of large families. I'm here to gather intel, any talk on topic would be appreciated! $100 for your trouble."

It didn't take much effort by Kate. Davis was all too pleased to answer her questions, which began with, "I hope you're not the kind of guy who wants to take a girl home to meet your mother and start a family of your own, you wouldn't do that to a bad girl like me, would you?"

Goodman was keen to express he was not a fan of monogamy. When she inquired, he said the only family he had was an older, troubled sister. The rest of his story, a portrait of a baller, a generous one, or so he wanted Kate to believe. *Trin* gave a wink and a nod when *he* had heard enough, also noting the shift change was about to take place. When Kate left, a heavy-set man, her replacement, begrudgingly washed the remaining unclean glasses. With the pretty distraction gone, Davis turned to look over the crowd. He peered casually from end to end. *Trin* had second thoughts.

All things considered, he might still have a hidden soft spot for his sister, I should at least speak to him.

Trin was not planning to disclose much, only that Caroline had health issues, and that *he* was employed as her caregiver. *Trin* returned to the bar, taking the stool, two away from Goodman. As *he* pulled up the stool, Goodman's cell phone rang.

Seeing he now had company, Davis turned to look *Trin* over, allowing his phone to keep ringing. He shrugged, evidently uninterested, then answered his phone. After a rowdy greeting, he lowered his voice, and turned his stool to face the front door.

"No, not yet, still waiting. My gut says she will be a no-show. The note I left her is still where I left it. No one knows who she is, I went to all her old places, and no sign of her. I looked in her place and around. She is living there, from what I could see, there was fresh garbage, and a whole lot of mess waiting to be hauled off. I'm thinking my big sister's a head case for sure. Yeah. Trippy. Maybe? Naw, haven't thought about her brand of crazy being a disability, but I guess so. All I know, she was never that smart. Hey this is me, listen, it won't be hard to get her to sign the house over to me. She can't possibly understand credit or equity; she probably doesn't even know what the place is worth. No, it won't take long, I'll have the title in my hands by the end of the month. Yeah, yeah, I know. Hey, who are you talking to here, this is the powerful Oz, Davis Goodman, I can handle it, trust me!"

Ariel had heard all she could stand to hear. She decided it best not to engage with him after all. She left, going past Goodman without looking back.

What a bastard. His type doesn't deserve a single penny, let alone the remainder of his sister's savings, which he would steal from her if given the chance.

On the walk back to *Caroline's*, she decided she wanted no part of the brother's power play. The sooner she could disappear, the better. More than ever, Ariel needed the modeling job to keep her mind from being driven to panic with anxiety and paranoia. She knew moving and establishing all new safe zones, would be both unsettling and triggering for her; it was a lot to consider. Needing to look rested for the next day, she warmed some almond milk, drank it down, and went to her cot.

CHAPTER 22

SURPRISES FOR DEBBI

*"Once the feet are put right,
all the rest of him will follow."*

C.S. LEWIS

The postal customers of the day had come and gone, and the diligent Debbi Harrison began her closing tasks, which included cleaning every possible surface with bleach-wipes. Tom, her boss, had been in-shop since pre-light hours, and still was hard at it. He was preparing to be out of town for the next two days. Debbi said the man lived in a rut. His habit was to work seven days a week, two from home, and every day he had a list of must-do's for his business. He was fastidious to a fault, with a propensity toward tunnel vision. On this evening, he had stayed even later than she expected. Finally, he approached Debbi to offer his parting words. She knew what he was about to say, and she appreciated his gratitude more than most, certainly more than she could ever express.

"I guess that will be it for me today, Deb, so, goodbye for the next couple days. I couldn't leave if it were not for you, I swear you keep this place together, and sanitized better than a hospital surgery room. Thanks for all you do, but hey, don't stay too long, your husband will be wanting you home. I know you could've done it tomorrow, but I went ahead and did banking, and the deposit bag is ready. I took care of the loading area too and emptied the lobby box. Everything is ready for pick up in the morning."

She was not surprised by his efficiency, only that he had done a task normally left to her.

"Thank you, Tom."

"You are welcome, don't mention it."

"You are the boss, still, you didn't have to do the deposit early, but I'm sure you'll rest easy knowing your bank balance."

"It's true."

"I won't be long, just sanitizing until it's time to lock the doors."

"I didn't want you to think I was shirking my responsibilities. I do appreciate you closing tonight. You'll have Cookie *working* the next two days, not that she's productive, but you can keep her in line better than me, so, thanks for that too. Okay, I've got a plane to catch, and all that security to get through at the airport with my crossbow. You best tell Donald I said thanks for this; he's a good man for letting you work the extra time tonight. Alrighty then, I'm off to hunt me a wild hog."

Tom left for his hunting excursion, leaving Debbi alone in the shop. The evening brought clouds rolling in from the north; they gave beautiful texture to the colors of the sunset. The mellow lighting eased Debbi's thoughts, as she considered how excited her boss was to meet up with his hunting buddies for their annual male bonding retreat. She half laughed, thinking again how many times he packed and unpacked his crossbow. Puttering as she did, she would double check to be sure nothing had been left in the lobby mailbox, before giving it a once over with her bleach wipe.

"What's this, trash? Uh, no. This is definitely not trash, but how did Tom miss it?"

A handwritten note had been scrunched in a ball and dropped into the outgoing mailbox. The sight of it made her question what she already knew.

Tom emptied the box just before he left, he said as much, right? No one could sneak in without me knowing, so how did it get in there?

Her mind searched for any clues she might have missed. She did indeed see many locals walking along the main avenues, enjoying the weather before the expected cooler temps arrived, but as was typical, there were no customers since Tom's earlier departure. Debbi had kept busy with cleaning tasks away from the front counter for a time, she would have heard the bell announcing a visitor, had there been one. The mystery triggered a shiver, and hair rose on her arms. Her gut said the balled-up paper had been intended for her. The feeling made her look up to the bell's location.

Huh? It's gone?

It was hard to fathom how the door's bell could have been removed without her noticing. Debbi noticed everything. Thinking back to when she arrived, and Tom left.

I know the bells were in place when I came in, that's how Tom heard me. He left out the door too, but no, I guess I can't remember hearing the bells when he left. He wouldn't have removed them without telling me, so who is responsible?

She carefully opened the paper ball, flattening it out on the counter. Having no clues did not help her disposition; still, she would not allow herself to feel afraid. Promptly, she recognized the author of the note had poor spelling, and grammar ability. Reading the cryptic note, the message had indeed been meant for her, even if her name were not on it.

"You think you no evereethin about this plase, but you donnt You donnt no whut I'm planing on doin. If your so smart, why donnt you reed my mind? Sum say you can but you cannt! But I can reed yours. You dum bitch, who marrys white, you desurvs to be teeched a leson to. Donnt you worre your prity litll fase, your tern will cum, when I fined you alone."

The writing was unfamiliar, telling Debbi the author was not a local. She briefly considered it could be someone writing badly on purpose, or a prank, then the thought was dismissed. It was a threat, and Debbi not knowing "the who," had made it a dangerous one. The uncertainty brought Lily out of her quiet.

That's man talk, an uneducated prick, you know the type, you need to stay alert. Customers know the hours for closing, they can easily guess when you are leaving, when you will be alone. Whoever took the bells is watching at a safe distance!

Debbi hung the closed sign in the window ten minutes early. Once everything was off, she stayed out of sight, strategically waiting until the last minutes of daylight to leave the shop. The ringing of the shop phone startled her. She had no intention of answering at this point, she preferred hearing the message on the machine. After seven loud rings, the phone rolled over to voicemail. A loud beep followed the "sorry we missed your call" message. On the line, there was the faint sound of breathing. No one spoke up. Then, the phone went silent.

Debbi found her cell phone in her sweater pocket. Donald had texted a heart and a kissing emoji, but there were no missed calls. Debbi's hands felt cold. She managed to reply to her husband, "Love you too, see you soon."

Her eyesight blurred for a moment, causing her eyes to close. Lily was still at the edge of her game.

Leaving sooner is better than later.

Scanning the well positioned mirrors above the entry, Debbi searched both sides of the sidewalk.

No one out there. Wait. Don't leave yet, you need to wait for cover.

A trance-like state might describe Debbi, as she prepared for worst case scenarios. Lily was taking over. It took a few seconds, then Lily felt centered. She looked outside, thinking she would know more once she stepped onto the sidewalk, as if the ground would direct her feet.

The walls that protect us, also divide us. Unlike you, I need no protection, and out there, my senses are at their best.

Lily knew to connect with her *animal instincts*, she first needed to listen to a body's truth. The body would have its limits, and those could not be ignored. Fully in the moment, Lily checked herself. Starting with her toes, she felt and listened to each part of her body, scanning for anything important, registering abilities and weaknesses. It was like an internal lift, taking on information, instead of passengers, then moving slowly up to the next floor, until reaching the top. When the elevator reached her hands, she recognized that her right palm was sweating on the doorknob, and the left hand was in a fist. Lily's wisdom looked to the remaining body parts.

Your brows are moist too...and your neck is tight. All indications of weakness. This would not be a good time for a panic attack.

Loosening her grip, Lily shook both hands out, and began shifting her weight from foot to foot. She lifted her shoulders and then dropped them. She did a slow head circle in both directions.

Relax. Breathe normally, even if someone is watching from a close position, he'll never be able to keep up with you. What he doesn't know, can't hurt you, remember that.

A small backpack, which could be worn on the front or back, hung low over Lily's stomach, giving her something to hug. Over her shoulders, a plastic makeshift cape hid her shape. She did not attempt to disguise her height, although the thought of rigging something fleeted in her mind.

Taller is not necessary, you have a good plan, you are prepared to kill, if necessary, and you will be home before Donald worries.

Debbi shook Lily out of her head. The sense of being in attack mode brought her back to her own mind. She often carried a gun with her, hidden in her bag, only this day it had been left in her car.

It will do me no good to allow myself to believe I need the gun. It's my home, I don't need a gun-show to take the upper hand. My instincts will tell me what I need to do to keep this quiet.

Breathing to calm and ground herself, Debbi drew air in through the nose, then exhaled out through the mouth. Reaching up, she tapped the bones around her eyes, and then tapped from center brow wrinkles to her temples. Then, concentrating on her pulse, she eased back the throttle by doing little karate chops, landing the side of the hand, lightly, on the underside of the opposite wrist. Having done it many times, she could go through the motions without counting. The natural weight of the hand made a thumping clap, but the form of the hand remained unchanged. The sound of it was soothing until it released a memory; the assassination of a particular evil man.

Lily was remembering the murder of an American actor, one who had unpopular morals, along with untouchability. His looks and charm had seduced many powerful women, all of them with young daughters, or other young female relatives, who also became victimized. One such victim, a supermodel, would not play his game and was willing to pay to save herself and her daughter. She did not wish to lose her status, nor taint her daughter's reputation, which he threatened to do.

Lily, aka L, had overheard the two talking and stayed with the couple until the woman was alone. Signing her name as "L," Lily did not write much in the note she dropped in the woman's bag, only enough to reveal her willingness to help the Parisian model by removing her problem. Responding according to instructions, the woman readily agreed and promised to compensate the mysterious L, if she could make it look like an accidental overdose. L's work was flawless. As a result, the man's death was not questioned, and L was paid a sizable amount of money.

In the moment, with dusk's shadows encouraging her to pay attention, Debbi "tapped" until she felt focused and poised. She found the ritualistic tapping, taught by Mama Yan, helpful in reducing stress. It was a form of energy healing that produced prompt, although impermanent results.

After both hands were treated, Debbi exhaled her remaining stress. She was feeling grounded, though it did not prevent Lily from speaking up again.

Your chance has come, three figures approaching from the north end. Perfect, a mother and two kids, good you can hide right next to the girl. Even if a lurker is watching, you will blend in. You can do this, go now.

Timing and movement had to be furtive. Debbi knew to avoid being a singular figure in the distance; it would be too noticeable against the setting sun. Her ability to blend into the shadows of others, allowed her to exit safely. Intuitively, she matched the stride, pace, and the attitude of her cover. The joining was effortless, the cover did not notice. Her self-confidence grew as they walked together. Lily encouraged Debbi with another quote from Mrs. Yan.

A fox will have the power of a tiger! Hŭ jihŭ wēiă as the mama liked to say.

The trio and their silhouette walked past several shops. They were headed straight toward a restaurant. Debbi sensed their destination.

This is where I leave you innocent ones.

Stepping around the family, Debbi turned down a residential street. She spotted and joined the shadows of a couple of younger teen boys. Like a chameleon, she became one of them. Her pack went to the back, like the boys, and the cape disappeared. They were walking in the direction of her car; it was just inside the parking garage. Her coupling undetected, her exit, like a light gust of wind; she felt calmer.

Always leave a little room for error, baba's favorite proverb. I'm here now, I made it.

Lily spoke up.

Look behind, look around, see everything, you can't afford to make a mistake.

Debbi looked to her right and then to the left and saw no movement. She pressed the unlock button on her car and stealthily opened the door. Reaching the inside of her car safely did not cause her to drop her guard.

Am I alone? Alone? No, wait, there's a figure stooping, over in the corner, there. Wait, no, it's a trash can, breathe, it's just a can.

Debbi's eyes closed briefly as she reached for the start button, then she felt the hair on her arm raising.

A knowing, in preparation of...what? There! Who? Too late to run.

Abruptly, the glass in the passenger rear window warned her with a knocking. Three fast knocks. Debbi felt her chest rising, her pulse racing.

Has someone come to kill me? No, keep calm.

Debbi turned to see a face pressed into her rear car window. The lips were forming words, but a loud tone was vibrating in her ears, deafening her, confusing her.

"Mrs. Debbi! Mrs. Debbi! Mrs. Debbi? Hellooo, hello? Hey, hi! Oh, I can't believe I was parked right next to you!"

The ringing in her ears had to be stopped. Debbi plugged her nose and blew. Popping in her ears resulted in dizziness. She could hear sounds that did not make sense. *Lily?*

Lily did not like the ringing either.

Someone was waiting for you, you were followed. You are not safe, kill or be killed.

Debbi's hand reached below her seat, where a weapon had been hidden, the other hand reached for the ignition. The eager visitant continued tapping on the glass, as she approached the front passenger window. Debbi started the car's engine.

"Oh noooo, don't leave. Please Mrs. Debbi, it's fate we parked next to one another. I need your help. Please don't leave. I need to know if the person I'm dating is the right person for me. I know you can tell me something, if this is right or if I'm making a mistake? I'm just desperate to know something before this goes too far, please?"

Shaken, but alert, Debbi finally made the connection with the words, and she remembered what they meant. Recognizing the voice outside her car, came next, then the blurred vision lifted. Debbi's hand found the button to lower the window.

"Hello Sage. Where did you come from?" A breathy laugh escaped. "You know you shouldn't sneak up on people like this, I might have used my self-defense moves, before I recognized you."

Seeing her serious expression, Sage's voice wavered, "I'm so sorry, I thought you saw me? Oh, look at your face! You didn't know it was me? I'm sorry, it looked like you were going to leave, I thought you were teasing me. I'm sorry I scared you. Are you alright?"

"I'm fine, just thought you were someone else," she said as she released the gun from her hidden hand, back under the seat. "I do need to be on my way, perhaps we can talk another time?"

Disappointed, the woman's face dropped, but she persisted, "I guess this isn't the best place or time for this kind of conversation, maybe we can talk tomorrow?"

"Uh, yes, I suppose, although I cannot predict what is best for your love life, especially when I don't really know much about you. I hope you understand?"

"Oh, I understand alright, you don't want to help me, you don't care to make predictions without an audience, I wasn't born yesterday, I know when I'm being brushed off."

"No, please, I'm not brushing you off, it's been a long day, I'm just anxious to be home with my husband."

With that, the oversized woman turned, made an about face, unlocked her own car, and opened the door. Her smile had turned sour, and Debbi thought her tone was forced.

"Yes, I'm sure your husband will be happy to see you, it is getting late."

Debbi detected unnatural, if not contrived geniality. The behavior poked at Lily's pessimistic tendencies. The situational explanation, and the woman's body language were not in sync. It was undeniable, the *"crossing guard pleasanton,"* had become *"a person of interest."*

CHAPTER 23

SNAKE IN THE GRASS

"The snake stood up for evil in the Garden."

ROBERT FROST

Ariel arose early and recognized the lack of nightmare dread.

A new day, what a precious thing.

Flooded with gratitude, her peaceful mind guided her morning routine. She grinned as her new K-cup coffee maker created dark magic, the smallest cup portion was all she wanted.

This is perfect, so delicious, and I'm feeling like Trin this morning.

Dressing as Trin was the easiest, it required no make-up or fuss, just the typical catholic schoolboy's uniform, penny loafers, and a newsboy cap. It would be several hours before Ariel's first modeling gig, and *Trin* decided the best thing to do was take a morning hike. The sun would be up in a couple of hours, and *he* intended to welcome it.

The buoyancy of *his* mood had energized *his* stride during the hike. Relishing the scent of the air, *he* stopped downstream from a place called Prosser Creek, near where the Boca Reservoir flowed into the Truckee River. A couple of brown sparrows were singing their songs.

The endless duet held *Trin's* attention. The light wind lifted the fragrance from the riverbank and joined *his* reverie.

Breathe normally, I will control breaths later. Here, now, I'm alive.

The water buttercups spread its splashes of yellow and white all along the edge of the water, determined to outlive the season. *Trin* sat among the bloomed wildflowers willing them to nod and smile back at *him*. Another breeze lofted by, accompanied by a flurry from the birds.

Agitation, what is it?

Trin's eyes automatically widened for the bigger picture. The birds' movement was a warning saying, *beware below*. Instinctively, *he* searched the place beneath the birds.

Oh my, a snake.

An unwelcomed visitor, a garter snake, slithered past the birds' bush. The serpent did not linger, it pushed off a stone and wiggled away, but the disappearance into the grass changed the atmosphere. *Trin's* mind shifted away from the sweet sense of appreciation for nature, to more intense contemplations.

I must leave Caroline's, I had hoped to be able to stay longer, another year would have been nice, but it is too dangerous to stay. That piece-of-shit hustler is bent on getting his sister's house, and I doubt he's the type to give up easily. On the flip side, I'm at least as smart as he is, no sense doubting myself at this point. I've got my backstory cover if he shows up and finds me. I'm her caregiver, period. I'd tell him she's left the house, as she was known to do, and she would be told of his visit when she returned, period. As Troy says, we cannot control others, and if we put the energy into ourselves instead, we make ourselves stronger for the things we cannot control. I will give more thought to my new job. If I do well in the G-rated setting, I can attain the higher paying jobs. At least the models at the agency were good enough to warn me about today's client, Mr. 404. I'm not about to get tricked into moving before the time limit. His reputation for getting new girls to fail doesn't scare me. This girl plans to be the best.

The sound of human footsteps interrupted the self-pep-talk. *Trin* jumped to *his* feet and spun around to see who was approaching. Stoic eyes spotted a fishing pole advancing along, above and behind the heavier brush. A few feet away, a camo-dressed male figure, carrying the pole, emerged into the clearing; his other hand gripped a tackle box, and he wore waders up to his chest. Their eyes met.

"Aha, good morning there, eh, uh, fella? I didn't expect to see anyone here at my fishing hole, don't tell me word has got out?"

Laughing at his own joke, the man took a moment to look past the slight bodied man, over to the river. He appeared to be more interested in the water, than in the surprise of seeing a stranger.

Trin stepped toward the man looking him straight in the eye, and replied, "Naw, I didn't expect to see anyone here either. Nice place you got here; too bad I haven't picked up a California fishing license yet." Turning to look back at the river, *Trin* made *his* voice sound sincere, "I just saw a Rainbow Trout as long as my arm, and probably a good bit heavier."

My cue to leave. Why did I stay so long? Wait, no panic, if I did need to run, he could not keep up in those rubber pants.

The man paused from his evident fish-quest, to speak again.

"Heya, I'm going to guess you've exhausted that excuse, that is if you are one of them Nevada residents that has no woods of your own to hike. Am I right?"

His manner is relaxed, as if he doesn't care, then why are his eyes searching every part of me? Because that's what men do.

Trin returned the scrutiny as another male would do.

Look at that, he forgot to pull the transparent sizing tape from his new waders. The tackle box looks clean enough to eat on. No doubt he is misrepresenting himself. Why?

"No not Nevada, I'm from Utah, just visiting family here, and they will be out of bed by now, and wondering where I've gone off too. I snuck off on my brother-in-law's KTM, good thing it's quick."

"Oh yeah? You don't look like the type that rides motorcycles."

You're right, I actually road Caroline's old bicycle to get out here for a hike, but a motor bike would be impossible for you to try to follow on foot.

Stepping away as *he* spoke in man-tone, "Ha! Yeah, that's what my brother-in-law said when he dared me to jump on the first time. So hey, your secret fishing hole is still your secret and I'll leave you to it."

"Come to think of it, I didn't hear any moto-bikes this morning, where did you leave it?"

The mysterious fisherman got no answer. *Trin* moved quickly, careful to avoid leaving any trail to follow.

I'm not afraid, I'm just being careful. Surely that's what a normal person would do.

~

The initial apprehension Ariel felt from meeting the man on the riverbank had subsided. The fresh air in her lungs and the beauty of the sunrise and the riverbank had staying power. It kept her mind calm, despite the precautionary routing back to the A-frame. As she changed into the public version of Ariel, her mental shift was decidedly self-assured.

That guy earlier was just some random wannabe fisherman, that's all, a harmless garter, like the one that disturbed the birds. No bother. I am ready for legitimate work, the gig today specified a fresh girl-next-door look, minimal make-up. Check. I don't need to do anything with my hair. The client provides the wig and the event clothing, and I can be relaxed in the casual wear I've got on. Healthy amount of breakfast to prevent tummy growls, check. I've got the bus pass and my route plan is solid. Okay, time to go. The lights off, check, my timer, check, my nerve, check. Congratulations Ariel Black. Go show Client 404 what you're made of!

~

The model reached her destination with ten minutes before her two-hour shift was to begin, as per company recommendations. Like a deer in the headlights, she was stunned when she arrived and saw a life-sized photo of Client-404. It was none other than Davis Goodman. She might not have believed her own eyes if his name had not been printed in bold lettering on a banner above the entrance.

Okay, didn't expect this, but for the sake of Caroline's memory, and for the sake of the job, I will not let this keep me from doing what I planned to do, if anything, I'm more resolute to be a success.

The infamous client and his *snake* reputation had become a worn-out discussion at the new model's welcoming gathering. The seasoned models who had fallen for his tricks, did not hold back their venom, nor did they ever actually mention his name. The fact that she had been an arm's length away from the man, only the night before, was somewhat unnerving, still, the parameters of the contract were designed to protect everyone's privacy. The client was not permitted to ask any personal questions, and she would leave no time for talking once the job was done. In the bathroom stall, Ariel added the event clothing over her own, donned the blond wig, and started her personal timer. She went out and took her position on the provided pedestal with only seconds to spare. Davis checked the model out from across the room and waved, just after the time started. She did not fall for the ploy.

I can't think about him now. He won't be able to place me, I'm not his type, he likes the stupid big-titted types, he barely noticed me last night. Now breathe, and count. Another 7080 seconds and this will all be over.

〜〜〜

From what Ariel could hear and see peripherally, the *investment* opportunity presented by none other than the slickster trying to steal his sister's house, Davis Goodman, and his fancy reception, were quite the sensation; the attendees were thoroughly enjoying the excess. The musical entertainment, the live mannequin, the free high-budget food, and top-shelf liquor were all part of Goodman's seduction. The crowd had begun interfacing with one another, and less with their exceptionally handsome host, though he maintained a position on the riser in plain sight.

Davis was bathed in a warm golden light, giving him an angelic appearance, and he felt optimistic. Experience told him that some of his audience would leave disgruntled if not permitted to express whatever obtuse notions they came with. Providing a segment for Q&A allowed time and place for their brief verbal soiree, which he deemed needful after a morning of brainwashing. Encouraging his hungry guests to speak, made him more human in their feeble eyes or so Goodman supposed. When it was time to demonstrate that he had listened to the "want-to-get-rich-crowd," he would have *their* words to use. A manipulative twist here and there, and Goodman believed they would convince themselves to *invest* their money into his scheme.

Utilizing their words, along with a few other tricks he had learned as a grifter, made for a winning formula. The ease of it threatened to take the excitement away. To deal with the potential monotony, the man of the hour stopped to imagine the attendees in various stages of undress, blushing and thanking him for allowing them to give him their money. The time alert on his watch, caused Goodman to shift his gears.

Microphones on stands were positioned around the reception area, they were hot. A skinny man from the crowd stood when Davis offered him an affirmative nod from his perch.

Loud enough to be heard without the microphone, the speaker blurted, "I'd say strong sales is like physical strength, it's really more about know-how and leverage, than actual muscle mass, uh, I mean it's not like you need muscle mass to be strong, uh, hopefully that makes sense."

Davis replied in his mind.

Seriously? Do you even hear yourself, no, that doesn't make sense, you should seriously think about giving me all your money, and then going home to hang yourself for being such a fucking idiot.

Smiling and nodding, Davis redirected his non-verbal invitation a few feet away, it was another's turn; this one was a self-proclaimed pessimist. The doubting-Thomas stood and spoke, "I gotta ask, in terms of selling, what gives you, the know-how?"

Davis was almost beside himself having to work at not rolling his eyes.

Anyone going to answer this plump imbecile?

Then, with no encouragement, a big-voiced attendee, a butchy gal, stood up to speak.

"With all due respect, I believe it's not about what you know, but who you know. We come to seminars like this one," pausing to look at her table, and then taking a faster look around the room, "and we network. There is strength in networking."

Her friends, a pair of non-partnered, white-pickup driving lesbians, both with flat-top haircuts, and squarish-styled clothes, audibly agreed. Their echoed words, "networking," and "who-you-know" set off similar sentiments like a stadium wave in the crowd.

Ready for the tedium to end, and needing to control the after-lunch crowd, before they strayed, Davis restrained himself knowing their words would abate on their own. He waited, smiling, and gave manipulative subliminal messages with charming eye contact and practiced body language. His thoughts hid behind his cloying sweet facial expressions.

Look at you. Like sheep, and most of you as poor as you are stupid. All followers, all lacking, and you don't even know it. You hunger for meaning. You wouldn't know meaning if it bit you on your lame-ass noses. OMG lady, leggings should be the only thing you wear. Anyone tell you your camel toe is hot? Yes, I'm looking at you sweetheart. Later, I will rub against your fat tits again, and you will blush and masturbate for the next two years to the memory of it. And jeeze, yes, bend and stick it out. Oh, that is one incredible ass. When was the last time anyone fucked you while looking at your face? Average, but baby, with an ass like that it doesn't matter what you look like.

Davis raked his eyes through the crowd. Then, finding some less pleasing to look at, he widened his gleaming smile.

Wow, they let any douchebag come to these things. Dude, the only way I'd ever let you suck my cock is in a glory hole. You desperate fucking man-whore. Fuck dude, you are butt ugly, did your mama hit you in the face with a frying pan too many times? And what the fuck, did someone send out a memo to the dykes are us? Those must have been free haircuts with the purchase of your tent shirts. And what's with those idiots who can't step away from free food, fuck, this is a seminar, not an all you can fucking eat buffet. Look at them, if they only knew what I honestly think of them, alright then, almost time to pull out those checkbooks.

Tapping his lapel mic, it was time to shift into his own script.

Davis authoritatively interrupted the crowd's mumblings, "Okay, great participation, great energy, thank you all for sharing."

His tone was commanding, and friendly. Ariel's count on pause, she reacted to the speaker's practiced niceties.

You almost sound human, you didn't even hiss.

Goodman waited for their full attention, then continued with the air of an eager schoolboy, "Now then, let's see if I can offer you feedback from the comment cards you submitted earlier. I understand many of you are concerned about being judged based solely on your appearance?"

It was not true, but they would never know it.

With manufactured joviality, he quipped, "Okay, this is an easy one. I'll give it to you straight. Strong real estate sales are not about your age, or your body weight. Are we agreed?"

Half of the crowd, overweight, undernourished and racing to their middle age, began moving their heads with the speaker; they were unconsciously under Goodman's influence.

The *investment guru* had a gift with those who lacked confidence, he had been giving them strong subliminal messages to hook them all morning. He had effectively worked the crowd one-to-one, charming them as they arrived and during the breaks, speaking as if they were already his business partners; their egos were engorged. The confident leader subtly searched the room until he found a specific pair of eyes; eyes he had earlier bewitched.

Let's see, oh yes, cameltoe's name is Bianca.

Pulling the girl forward with his hypnotic gaze, Goodman's eyes had encouraged Bianca. In her innocent mind, she owed him a kindness, and that was something he knew how to use.

Girl, you make it too easy, you have victim written all over your pretty face. I'll enjoy taking advantage of you later.

Bianca pushed herself to show her appreciation for having been noticed. Hoping for the courage to match her anticipation, it was her moment to become memorable.

He remembers me, he wants my opinion. He said I made an excellent first impression. He said I was meant to do more than housekeeping and dog sitting. He likes me. He wants me to ask the ice breaker questions.

Bianca stepped away from her table, and up to the lonely microphone directly in front of her new hero. He smiled and wordlessly directed her by lifting his eyebrows, forming a larger smile, and then with his hand, motioning her to speak. It was as if Bianca's questions, the ones planted by Goodman, burned to get out. The feeling she was returning a favor, blocked out her natural self-consciousness. Her eyes glistened.

He signaled, and Bianca blurted, "What about first impressions? How do looks impact earnings? Is there credible research, or is it just public opinion?"

"Good questions young lady, I'm impressed, thank you. I am aware of a few thoughtworthy research findings regarding appearances and pay rate, if you are interested? Yes?"

He waited until he had a wave of "yes" nods.

"Okay, according to a recent study from George Washington University, obese workers are paid less than the normal-weight workers at a rate of $8,666 a year for obese women, and $4772 a year for obese men. Even not wearing makeup can bring about bias in competence and trustworthiness, according to a study by Harvard Medical School. Women wearing makeup earned 30% higher than the non-makeup wearing women."

Watching for the self-minded to show their uneasiness, Goodman paused, then said, "Does this mean a woman must wear make-up to make sales? Ridiculous, I think so, but it would seem we cannot change the unconscious mind from ruling from this bias. Well, to reach our goal of growing a strong property investment team, I must decide who is worthy of the opportunities I have worked so hard to produce and offer. Who among you? I don't judge a person because of his or her ability to be like Christie Brinkley, but aren't we all guilty of making money decisions based on a perception of success?"

Davis winked at Bianca, to trigger the next part of her script.

"Mr. Davis, if I may? Earlier, I heard someone ask if you could be successful based on someone else's efforts and leadership? Maybe it's not necessary for every woman to be a good-looking cover-girl type, maybe guys don't need to be tall, handsome, gym-junkies to enjoy earning high dividends from their investments?"

Bianca was poised, the perfect stooge for this group of gullibles.

"Hmmm, Bianca has a great point." He held her eyes with his innocuous smile, sending his furtive messaging with a hand motion. "Bianca, my dear, let's talk about your investment interests when we're done here, I can see you have potential."

A well-executed wink directed at Bianca, made her blush. She nodded affirmatively, to reply, and returned to her seat.

I did it, he winked. He's pleased. Weird I feel like I have just woken from a dream.

Davis looked at his subjects inquisitively, "Well? Does your success depend on your looks, on your ability to stay in shape? Can your money make you money, even if you don't possess an expertise in investing?"

His deliberate pause struck the target. He could see it in their faces.

"You came here today to learn the answers to these questions. Did you learn them?"

Davis waited, then slowly nodded his head. He made eye contact with his new puppets.

"Alright, we're in the stretch now, and with so many well-read and educated thinkers in our midst, I can't help but wonder, is there anything else you need to hear to make your decision?"

Having found his stooges ahead of time, all Davis had to do was meet their gaze and blink, and smile, two times; the hypnotic work done earlier was triggered. The food, the free booze, the three-piece jazz band, and the too-skinny doll model, all spoke volumes about the success of the celebrity investment speaker. What followed was a group of sheep all walking off the money cliff together. In the end, all were satisfied, especially Davis Goodman, who collected the money.

An easy $475,000,00, gross, with a tab of just $10,000.00, that makes me warm and fuzzy after a day's work.

Davis, the paradigmatic investment guru of the hour, decided he could be even better off, if he could pay his "party" debt, minus the $6500.00 fee for the model.

I'm no cheapskate, but they practically make it a challenge to get a free model by playing up how their freeze girls are better at staying in character than the guards who protect the Queen's palace.

Davis lightly chided himself, knowing his sadistic ideas were not in keeping with the image he had presented all day.

An easy puppet that sax player turned out to be, and he's not costing a dime, just a little bad weed.

～

The sated crowd had no idea they were there to fund Davis Goodman's "expert" lifestyle. Not that he could fool Ariel, she had seen his kind before. Ariel noted movement approaching her as she stood frozen on her pedestal.

What is that musician up to? I see you coming my way.

"Hey yoooo there, I know you're a live model, never fooled me for a minute!"

The sax player reached for one of her hands, barely missing. She did not move. His stance wobbly, and glassy eyed from the drinks, and the weed. Davis secretly watched from a safe distance. Some of the crowd began to draw closer, seeing a musician poised for a different kind of show.

"Hey, did y'all know thiss ith a rreal ice princesssss?"

Waving his arms toward the model, and turning with his best Vanna impression, the inebriated man slurred, with spittle flying from his mouth as he carried on.

"The last blond I dated chatted on and on, as if her thoughts were interesting, but I like this set of peaches," reaching up and pretending to cup her breasts, just barely keeping from touching her.

Clinging to the business of counting, she would not budge. To the left of the platform, two drunk heavyset women, noticed the antics. They begin to gush with oohhs and aahhs, laughing and pointing to encourage the teasing.

One said to the other, "I think a cats got her tongue!"

The other replied more boisterously, "The poor cat didn't get much from this skinny thing!"

Laughing, then stepping aside, the fat ladies grabbed some crab cakes, dropped them in their purses, then strolled over to the diminished pile of shrimp. The sax player was having a hard time staying upright, he swayed as he laughed with the ladies. Then, seeing he had the attention of the crowd, he continued.

"Hey that reminds me, what do you call a skeleton in the closet with blonde hair?" No one answered, waiting for his punchline. "Last year's hide-Nnnn-ssseek winner!"

Much laughter ensued. Ariel breathed and blinked carefully as the distractions permitted; no one noticed. The outspoken attendee who talked about networking, stepped up to the jokester, and the model. Having had her fill of liquid courage, she had her own insult to hurl.

"I know you are here for our entertainment, and you're not supposed to be real, by the way, well done!"

Clapping her hands high in the air, the small crowd followed her lead and applauded enthusiastically. She went by the name Robby, and she had an entourage to increase her daring. They approached behind her, chanting, "Go Robby, go Robby."

Loving the attention, Robby pulled out her most manly tone for full effect, "And now, entertain us by giving us your opinion. A privileged white tart like you must hate to be objectified. You do realize you are being objectified? While these people taunt you, don't you think you ought to speak up for yourself, if not for yourself, on behalf of all victimized women? Or are you one of those poor excuses for a human being, one who needs to be humiliated to be turned on?"

Robby's words had no other competing conversation in the room. All were trained on the two women, even Davis Goodman had given up the pretense of ignoring the sideshow, knowing Ariel could break her contract at any moment. Ariel remained steadfast, not even a blink.

Eight minutes left, and I'm not about to lose a dime on your sorry asses.

Robby was relentless, "Oh come now, don't be a shy one, we have given you positive recognition for a job well done. Don't be stingy with us, we might decide to stop going so easy on you. Just answer the question *Barbie* and then we will leave you alone," said with a sickly-bittered curiosity, "or do you enjoy being humiliated?"

Most of the attendees, well stuffed, left after writing their checks. The remaining crowd closed in on the model. The antics did not bother Ariel, she had another well-timed blink. Davis had one more trick up his sleeve, he had changed the clock, it was about to appear her shift was over. He counted the seconds, gleefully expectant. His Armani loafers were soft heeled, but Ariel heard him approaching and would soon have him in her sights.

"Gentlemen, ladies, please, please, what have we going on here? Some early celebrating for the big dividends to come, yes, and look what money can buy."

He touched the hem of her sport pants, then positioned himself to look into Ariel's eyes.

"Isn't this a smart, flirty color? Did I mention your outfit is free with any investment of 500 dollars or more? You would not have to change, you could wear it home, go home just as you are, what do you think Miss? Interested?"

Davis inflated his stature as he spoke, until the last word, spoken demurely, with just the briefest indication that he expected her to move or at least speak. Knowing better, she held on.

Last stretch here, you know you can hold your breath if needed, this really has been an easy gig, oh but he is a snake and a predictable one at that.

Ariel was not fooled with the time trick, or the casual conversation. She tuned everything out waiting for the preset timer to release her from her employer. When it went off, she dropped down folding herself up in a ball, hugging herself around her knees. The buzzing stopped and she unfolded herself, pushing her legs in front of her and sat on the pedestal until she felt her breath had evened and her calf muscles had stopped burning.

The not-so-clever Mr. Goodman had lost. She said nothing. A few of the remaining looky-loos twittered with some laughter and then offered more applause. Goodman bowed deeply, as if the clapping had been for him. As he retracted, his hands flew into the air, signaling the event was over. Ariel was out of sight in a flash, moving behind his back while Goodman was taking in his fans. She practically ran directly into the restroom.

Davis was disappointed the model left before he could corner her in the small crowd. Assuming she would need to change her clothes, he staged himself at the door to stop her as she exited the lavatory. His business card, one with his neat penmanship having written the words "call me," remained in his pocket. After waiting about ten minutes, he asked the house-dog-keeper, who had been hovering, to check the lady's restroom for the model.

Bianca carried out Davis's request without hesitation, she had been hoping for another conversation with him, and this had given her another chance.

I'm so glad Davis asked me to do him a favor. I think he really likes me; he sure did pour on the charm. Oh no! Where is she, I don't want to let him down.

Opening all of the stall doors, tentatively, Bianca saw the room was empty.

Darn, and I wanted to ask her if she remembered me from the group interview, not that that was my best moment, but she seemed kind. Oh well, I need to tell him she's not here.

Bianca rejoined the man standing patiently for her return, her chin lifted with confidence, "Bad news, she's not in there, I checked all the stalls."

The model had left unnoticed, Davis was surprised she had dodged him.

I might have to make an exception. There is something about losing to such an etiolated wisp which makes her infinitely intriguing. I must hire her again. My reputation depends on it.

CHAPTER 24

NOT A TYPICAL ROMANCE

"We are all a little weird, and life's a little weird, and when we find someone whose weirdness is compatible with ours, we join up with them and fall in mutual weirdness and call it love."

DR. SEUSS

Exhausted by the events of the day, events which he would not be discussing with his wife, Donald turned on the television. When she finally joined him in the living room, she flopped onto the couch and stared straight ahead.

"What no romance stories tonight?"

Donald teased hoping to break-up her dry mood.

Laughing artificially, Debbi replied, "I will watch what you like, I doubt either of us will be up much longer."

"Okay, if you say so Smurf, I'm happy to be your cuddle bear, anytime. You sure you're, okay?"

"I'm good, nothing a good night's sleep won't fix."

Donald gave her a wink, then began channel surfing, he stopped on a commercial he had not seen before.

"Here at the Green Mountain Dog Resort and Training Center, we aim to keep our facility welcoming, and one of the ways we do that is to maintain high standards of cleanliness. From basic brushing and baths to oral hygiene and paw care, we will customize a program that will have your dog looking great and smelling fresh. Regular bathing and grooming results in less shedding and gives your pet a healthier coat. We use only the highest quality grooming products, and with our highly skilled groomers, we make your pet's hygiene experience positive and fun. Whether here for overnight lodging or day care, you have the option of a basic or a premium bath and grooming service prior to departure. No more struggling at home getting your dog into the bathtub. We are here to keep your pet smelling fresh and looking their best between visits too. Your dog can be pampered every few months with our premium service, and then enjoy the simple maintenance bath as needed."

Happy not to be hearing yet another pharmacy commercial, and thinking the dog resort was unique, Donald turned to see if his wife was watching.

Yes, but is she mesmerized or is that fright on her face?

"Smurf? You okay? Deb?"

Getting no response, he turned the television off, and lowered his recliner, pushing hard; it made a thud. Debbi jumped, then froze, eyes wide, still under a spell.

A fearful reaction to an ordinary sound, what the heck?

"Debbi?"

Finally hearing her husband, Debbi snapped to the present. Seeing his dismay, she felt exposed, then, she composed herself by relaxing her facial muscles, and taking a deep breath.

That was not just a strong impression. There was something about the way the man signaled for the dog, I know that motion. It was one of the monster's techniques.

Fearing she might break down, she swallowed, cleared her throat, and forced a smile.

"Smurf, are you okay? What is it? You're pale."

There was compassion in his voice, and confusion in his eyes.

She evaded, "I am fine now, a passing ghostly visitor, that's all, no worries."

"Are you sure? You looked scared. I wondered if it was the dogs in the commercial. I know you don't like dogs. Although, if you would let me get one, I'm sure we could change your mind about them. I could build a dog run along the wall, so you wouldn't need to worry about a dog in your garden."

Her fake smile had vanished. "No. And no dog! It's ridiculous to allow an animal to dictate our lives, and it would. It was a passing ghost, that's all."

Debbi's go-to excuse had worked in the past, but she knew he was seeing through her. She didn't want to lie to him. Then, Lily spoke up.

You were followed, your instincts are true. No such thing as coincidences. Sage is not an innocent.

"Okay, okay, it was a ghost. I won't push, well, I guess I just did, I'm sorry, I was just surprised to see you so disturbed."

Debbi's mind had already shifted.

There was something about Sage that was not authentic.

"Smurf, what's really on your mind?"

His sincerity touched her tender part, and Debbi knew she could not bold face lie to those caring eyes; she contrived instead.

"Probably just being silly. Sage Vaughn keeps coming to my mind. She comes around the postal shop at odd times. I saw her earlier. She's a volunteer, a crossing guard, hiding behind an imposing personality, the kind that tries too hard to impress. She tells people I'm psychic, she has become a pest about it."

"Oh, her?" Donald was relieved she was not still mad about his dog comments. "She is annoying with her dramatic arm signals. Don't let her talk bother you Smurf, you're a bigger person than she." Laughing at his own words, "Well, not literally of course, she's more like a 55-gallon drum, and you're just a pint size dixie cup, but you know what I mean."

The desired smile finally found its way to Debbi's face. Donald's cloud was gone.

"Go ahead and watch your program, I think I will read a little, I could use some light distraction."

~~~

In the evening, per doctor's instructions, Debbi insisted her man put his feet up. Donald did not mind, he felt spoiled. Debbi would remind him that his brain needed exercise too. She was kind that way, not saying the truth that would make her man feel less manly. She was not a fan of television, but her fondness for seeing him relax was evident. The normalcy of their quiet evenings, him with his TV, her with light reading, worked to support Debbi's minimal need for relaxation. Their romance might not have been typical, but it was authentic.

~~~

"How about Criminal Minds? If it bothers you, just say it."

"Watching programs like *America's Most Wanted, NCIS,* and *Bones,* feeds your Sherlock Holmes alter ego, and the forensic science keeps your brain in shape, but don't get any ideas on becoming a detective."

"Ahh, but what about the bad guys? You know, with you as my smurfy-sidekick, we could kick some ass, intellectually, of course."

Quick to reply with her own brand of wit, Debbi played along, "Have you never heard of Mighty Mouse? We'd do more than out-think the bad guys, we could put their dicks in the dirt."

He had laughed heartily at hearing his wife use such a phrase, then continued, playfully and with a gleam in his eye.

"Now, you know I don't touch no dirty dicks, and I damn well don't want you to, either. But if it's a clean dick you're looking for, got a good one for you right here."

"Yes, my Dick Tracy, you're the Dick for me."

~~~

Donald had enjoyed getting out on his own a couple of nights a month, more so before his heart had troubles. He had a kink-hunger, developed in his wilder days. He enjoyed the company of Tranny-girls for discreet paid-sexual experiences. When they first met, Donald considered telling Debbi about his fetish; it turned out, there was no
~~~

need to say it. They were becoming *re-acquainted* at the time, and she had surprised him with the actuality.

"Mr. Donald Harrison, I know what you hesitate to tell me. If I may? I know you have just come from Reno, and have spent money on a prostitute, with lipstick and a penis. I do hope you are in the habit of using condoms with the pros. It is your health safety I'm thinking of."

"What? Uh, yes, but how did you know?"

"You, sir, cannot hide anything from me."

At first, Donald thought that she might judge him negatively for his queer fascination, but it was quite the opposite. She told him she appreciated his discretion, and she accepted that he might need to have this type of sexual *itch*, scratched from time to time. The next time he ventured an "itch," and to avoid the white-lie part, he tried telling her in advance. But then, thinking of Debbi thinking of him, had resulted in his junk not getting hard, even though the Tranny was beautifully attractive. The next time they talked about their sexual proclivities, they had already begun to couple up. Debbi said she preferred not knowing about the details of his other dates, and she did not want him to be self-conscious.

Instead of full disclosure, the two agreed to an arrangement. On Debbi's nights *helping Nan and Bud*, if his desire arose, Donald went into Reno for his *Tranny date*, and to ease his conscience, he would match the money he spent, depositing it into a joint account. In this way, he told her without talking about it. The extra money was intended for her to use as she wanted. Debbi being extraordinarily generous, always used it to help others; it caused him to cherish her, even more.

Amplifying Debbi and Donald's non-typical romance was their uncommon love for their community. Demonstrated in different ways, his through local leadership, and other neighborhood service efforts, and hers, by caring for those who had genuine need; they both gave unconditionally. Debbi provided respite care, and some meals or grocery shopping for families dealing with serious illnesses, including Bud and Nan Barlowe. In addition to keeping the Barlowe's cupboards and refrigerator stocked, every month, Debbi took a couple of overnight shifts to stay with Nan.

In Nan's case, the early-onset dementia, thought to be Alzheimer's disease, began at age thirty. It had been overwhelming for her husband of only five years. Bud, a self-employed mechanic had saved little, and given the medical expenses, his bank account was lean, if it stayed in the black at all. His wife's care and the associated costs, emotionally and financially, put them in Debbi's special category of vulnerable people, deserving of support.

Bud, rarely spoke of it, but he was honest with his friend Donald, sharing how grateful he was for the *food program* his wife had found for them. Not only did Debbi pick up their food portions, she delivered and stored it all away. The Barlowe's always had fresh healthy food, which they both needed, since Nan's dementia was too advanced for her to shop or cook.

Bud was like many others in their established community, part of the older working blue-collar middle-class, and not yet old enough for social security. The expensive medical insurance covered less than half the cost of Nan's pharmaceutical needs. And, due to the limited "network" of physicians, Nan had to see out-of-network doctors, which was also quite costly. After paying their mortgage, garage rent, and utilities with a mechanic's salary, Bud barely had enough to get by, and yet, they always seemed to have what they needed; Debbi made sure of it.

The support of the Harrison's was abundant, still Bud had the responsibility of keeping his wife from wandering away and getting lost, which she was prone to do in the middle of the night. Neither Bud nor Donald knew that Debbi's monthly sleepovers had a twofold purpose. Keeping watch over Nan in the night hours, meant she could do her *secret research,* without having to look over her shoulder, and it allowed Bud to have a little time with his buddies, to share a beer, and catch up on his own need for sleep. Her secret spying notwithstanding, the friendships were meaningful for both couples.

CHAPTER 25

THE DINNER PARTY

A watch tone reminded Jones when the time had come for his sport team dinner party, and he salivated at the prospect of his anticipated finale. The evening's entertainment would change his staff roster, and Jones was ready for a savory meal; he had not eaten since his investigator's faxed report. Jones informed his minions of their responsibilities, then walked with added vigor to his tram car. His *hunger* would soon be sated.

The person with the least awareness, the Chef, was a new resort hire; a 32-year-old woman, named Carla. She was a certified nutritionist, the new chef for the kennels, and she would be preparing the event menu. Hired by the master "dog trainer," Mr. Jones, himself, Carla was asked to demonstrate her culinary skills for a group of Jones' associates, before she began cooking for the dog resort. Jones intended to study her every move as she worked in his kennel kitchen, she had proven to meet his standard thus far, the event would be another test. Carla was instructed to create a healthy blend of food items, a signature "dog food," tasty enough for people to eat, and was given specifics for the presentation. The prepared foods were to be mashed together in the Cuisinart and poured into molds. Jones had ordered various mold shapes for each *guest*, ranging from a simple dog bone to whole fish and other small game shapes. His plate would be the exception. He requested that each of the fresh ingredients be prepared appropriately and plated in five-star style. The gathering would serve several purposes, and NOJ was at his best when he could kill multiple birds with one stone. The chef placed name cards upon each plate cover, to be certain Mr. Jones' requests were met without error.

Jones, the ever-gracious host, pulled the names as he set the hot covered plates at each setting, according to his prearranged seating chart; the two newbies, Asheesh and Ron, were served last.

When he pulled off the cover to reveal his meal, Ron gasped, "How disgusting, I get a rat shape, when everyone else gets a fish or a hen?"

A few seats apart, Neffen had gained the response he desired, the twinkle in his eye attested to this fact. His private gesture had achieved his objective. The brief elation was followed by bitter thoughts.

The rat deserves to eat his own kind. No gratitude. No surprise. He should feel lucky to be getting such nutritious food at my table. Hmph, what a waste.

Standing with glass and butter knife in hand, Jones drew attention as he tapped the glass.

"I am pleased to have you all join me for a meal. Thank you all for accepting my dinner invitation, I recognize many of you have not dined together. I do hope you have introduced yourselves and have at least become acquainted. To support your familiarity with one another, I would like to propose a team building opportunity, but before we do anything else, I would like us all to recognize our new chef, the immensely talented Chef Carla!"

Jones' applause was exuberant, and his guests followed his example without reservation.

"I expect that you will enjoy the special shapes, the themed molds add that little something extra, don't you agree?" More applause erupted. "You may show your pleasure by leaving your plate clean, and please do take time to complete the meal survey once you are done; your feedback will mean so much to the Chef. A link to the survey has been sent to your personal emails."

Feeling the creator side of his God-ness, Jones was proud of the artistic ambiance he had calculated and accomplished. He beheld Ron, Asheesh at his side, and then his menagerie of captive clones, stopping once he reached Carla, who received Jones' standard "good dog" signal. Those sitting around the table did the standard smile and nod response, then began digging in. A few awkward bites, and then a cascade of positive comments resounded in the room. The meal flavors and the fun animal shapes had a unifying impact, the plates were emptied, with one exception; Ron had scarcely touched the food.

The atmosphere was light when Jones announced it was time for a team building event. He asked that everyone share a "fun fact," one which was not common knowledge to the group. Carla was the first to speak up.

"Hello everyone, Mr. Jones, sir. I do appreciate your positive feedback. You all know I am an experienced nutritionist and a chef, but fun fact, when I am off the clock, and having some excess stress to release, my go-to fix is comfort food, McDonald's Big Mac and fries, with a chocolate shake. It takes me to my happy place."

The sharing went on around the table. The men in the room offered something blithe, tales about winning card games, driving fast cars, losing drinking games, and so on. The mood of the room shifted when Ron's turn came. Ron began by blowing his nose into a hanky. Jones barely kept his face from showing his disgust.

Ron's voice waivered as he began, "I, I ha, ha, have been allergic to animals all my life, but I, I have always loved dogs, the small non-shedding ones. Now that there are improved twelve-hour allergy medications, I am doing better, and I can tolerate being around all breeds, not just the non-allergenic ones. My share is my personal goal. One day, I hope to be a dog trainer, and I believe the time here working for Mr. Jones will make me a good one."

An awkward silence resulted, until Asheesh stood and garnered everyone's humor with a "fish" tale about his name. He did, of course, begin by acknowledging the host and complimenting the chef, adding, "Chef Carla can come to my home and cook for me any time she wants to try out a new meatless recipe." He then, rolled into his fun fact, "…and when the family gathered around to hear what my name would be, my mother sneezed, and my grandfather declared, that's it, the boy's name is Asheesh!" It wasn't true, but it made for a good laugh to end the team activity.

When the sharing was complete, Jones stood, repeated thanks to the team, and to the chef, then collected his dishware, and excused himself. Chef Carla followed his lead. Asheesh, wanting to demonstrate leadership, suggested everyone take their own plates to the employee lounge and avoid leaving any mess in the boss's office. All complied. Everyone present was sensitized to Jones' standards on cleanliness; spotless was the only acceptable way to leave the offices.

Ron and Asheesh found Jones waiting for them outside the employee lounge. Eager to see how his men would respond to their "promotion," he swiftly walked them down the long corridor, toward the lift. When they arrived at the elevator control panel, Jones pushed the button indicating they were about to travel downward. Pausing as they waited for the doors to open, Asheesh made a low whistle, then spoke in his signature syllabic rhythm.

"Sir, this place is much larger than I realized. It is truly a thrill to see what you have built, and what an honor to be in your presence, and to participate in these special events."

Unlike Asheesh, each step away from the recognizable spaces, had Ron's anxiety intensifying, and his empty stomach made it obvious with a loud gurgling sound.

"Excuse me, I am having a little gas, but Mr. Jones, sir, I do think the chef will make a great addition to your team. In fact, I think very highly of her, she is creative, and I have to say it, she has a lovely smile. I hope you don't mind me saying, but I noticed she did not wear a ring, does that mean she is single?"

Jones surmised where Ron's simple mind was going and responded without filtering.

"Our chef was not asked to attend the next segment, Ron. This will be a male-only bonding exercise. But if she were here, I doubt she would have accepted your flattery, you did not have the courtesy to eat the meal she prepared."

Ron's disappointment showed on his face. He had hoped to be able to ask the pretty woman out on a date. However, he was relieved he had not been fired, and thought being included in the male-only event meant he had somehow pleased the boss. He decided whatever came next would be better than going home alone.

Four brawny men met them at the elevator. Jones had brought the muscle, in case Ron was smart enough to figure out, he had just eaten his last meal. Another three men stepped into the elevator with the group, as the doors were closing. Both Asheesh and Ron were astonished at learning that Jones had additional staff, which they had not seen before. Asheesh was better at hiding his thoughts, but he was beginning to feel a surge of adrenaline as the movement began. The ride in the lift was slow, giving both Asheesh and Ron a chance to note they were riding with a set of identical triplets, and a set of quadruplets. Ron thought it strange the large men were dressed exactly alike, down to their shoes, Asheesh speculated whether he would be asked to wear the same uniforms. The set of triplets each had a patch over their left eyes, which Ron pretended not to notice. The Indian, on the other hand, wondered what they had done to deserve losing an eye.

When they exited the elevator, they had only a few steps to reach a spacious room with no windows. The team building was going to be messy, or so it appeared to Ron; there was a wall-to-wall plastic tarp in place over the flooring. Jones introduced the two *newbies* to his men, declining to divulge the men's "numbers," then declared the reason for the event.

"Asheesh is being promoted to Supervisor for the Sport Center, and he will have his first-kill performance, here and now, in a circle of trust."

All but the two newbies were smiling. Jones was the picture of relaxation and ease, as he stepped back and lifted his arms to his sides, indicating it was time to form a circle around the newbies. The security team followed his lead, and all eyes were on Asheesh.

"Let the kill be a messy one," Jones jubilance was almost comical.

In that instant, Asheesh recognized the setting had been prepared, and a simple deduction identified Ron, the ill-mannered, defenseless man standing next to him, as his "first kill." Naively falling for the boss's apparent humor, Ron was kind enough to throw his head back as he laughed with the men who had encircled him. Knowing Jones was not joking, and feeling the peer pressure, Asheesh bent forward, taking his knife from the hidden ankle sheath. In one swift move, he straightened, turned, and neatly pulled his blade across Ron's neck, severing the trachea, and the carotid artery. Startled, and gasping for breaths, Ron's gargling and coughing took center stage. Jones began clapping his hands. His team of droids and muscled outcasts followed his lead, until their cheering drowned out the last moments of Ron's consciousness.

As was his practice, Neffen filmed the entire evening, it would be his pleasure to review later, during alone time. His team enjoyed some non-alcoholic refreshments while Ron bled out, it was a celebratory atmosphere. Asheesh was handed some disinfectant towels to clean his knife, and Jones keeping to his schedule, nodded to the men who were assigned to clean up. The two retrieved the chainsaws they had been asked to bring. They did not hesitate to begin cutting Ron's body into smaller pieces. Jones felt jubilant as he watched Asheesh working with them without being asked.

Now that is team building at its best.

CHAPTER 26

THE DUTIFUL DOG MAID

*"An adventure is only an inconvenience rightly considered.
An inconvenience is only an adventure wrongly considered."*

G.K. CHESTERTON

Not far from where the Harrisons lived, in the most expensive house in Fair Oaks, a listing barely under seven million, lived the famous daytime soap opera star, Sandy Silver, along with her husband, Arnold, and her Dalmatian, Chip.

Feeling poutier than she wanted to admit, the famed Sandy whined to her husband, "Oh Arnie, are you sure our sweet boy, Chip, will be okay?"

The woman held her pet more like a lover, and since no one was around, she opened her mouth and allowed the dog's tongue inside. The dog eagerly explored her mouth. Her husband watched with a petulant face, knowing better than to speak his mind. His wife rarely kissed her pet outside their bedroom. If anyone learned of her special closeness with the dog, they would be likely to jump to the wrong conclusions. In Sandy Silver's mind, it was not bestiality, only a little friendly tonguing. As an actress, Sandy had to kiss actors all the time, and at times, she found their breath was worse than most dogs. She rationalized her affection with her pet.

At least I know exactly what has been in my pet's mouth, and we have spared no expense to keep his teeth healthy and clean.

Privately, Sandy knew the upcoming separation from their pet would be as hard for her husband, as it would be for her. Her husband would miss his evening feet lickings, which helped him to relax. Generally, the dog's licking served both her and her husband, as a type of foreplay. Their taboo fetish was once shared during a marriage counseling session. The overreaction of the counselor caused them to quit attending. Their strange fetish became more frequent after their first disclosure, but they never spoke of it to anyone else again. Arnold instantly worried his wife would change all their plans at the last moment, as she had done in the past, when their pet was not going to be accompanying them. When he responded to her, he was careful to use his most positive tone.

"Of course, Sandy, only the best for Chip! I have thoroughly checked out this place, and I can say with 100% assurance, this place is top shelf. Totally legit! These people know how to care for dogs, and I'm telling you they know how to do it, tastefully."

Another licking session started, but Sandy pulled back, and gave Chip the look that sent him back to his dog world. Chip turned, presenting his rear end to her. The dutiful mistress gave the expected scratch to his back, just above his tail, the way he liked it.

Still childishly sulking, Sandy continued, "Well, I know you are right, but I can't help feeling guilty for not taking him with us to the Bahamas. Shouldn't we keep him close to where we are staying?"

"Sandy, dear, he's not going to know the difference. I promise you he will be in the best hands. You know Bianca has planned everything for our dear boy. She would not let us send him to a place unworthy of our standards."

The couple leaned toward one another, sharing a peck on the lips, then moved closer to the large picture window in their spacious living room. Arnold spotted the van with the resort logo, and his relief was evident in his voice.

"Look! Here they are now."

The super van pulled up, the side door opened, and a ramp unfolded until it lay open on the ground. Seeing the mechanism complete its movement impressed Sandy.

"Wow, that was so James Bond for a pet van."

Arnold was quick to agree, "Yes, that is some fancy dog transportation."

The vehicle shined like a new dime with many chrome features. The windows, blackened with tint, made it impossible to see inside, but the signature on the side door announced- *The Green Mountain Dog Resort, where we treat your companions like our own!* Within seconds of pulling into the large circular driveway, two handlers representing the dog resort were at the door. Chip, the overzealous Dalmatian, began barking and jumping as soon as he saw the van through the window. Bianca, the dog nanny, aka the housemaid, appeared in the doorway when the barking began.

Sandy tried to sound cheerful, "Now-now, Chip. It's okay boy, these nice men are going to take you to a special place, you're going on your own vacation."

The dog, picking up on the woman's nervous energy, was more restless than normal. He continued to jump and bark out of control.

"Now, now Chip, come here. Here. Don't worry, this van is air conditioned, isn't it Arnie?"

"Yes, of course, dear, Chip, sit, no, come here, come."

The couple tried in vain to catch the dog; he avoided their every attempt.

"Chip, down," a command given by Bianca, after the owners failed efforts.

The dog jumped off the couch as ordered, but as soon as the housemaid turned away, he returned to his game. The couple, assuming their favored *good-guy* roles, followed Bianca toward the front door. They stopped short at the threshold of the roomy entryway, making no effort to tame their pet.

Before opening the front door, Bianca turned around and gave a stern look at the dog. The uniformed housemaid had ample tresses on the top of her head. She had wrapped the shiny dark locks into a neat bun, but there were enough loose ringlets to show that she had long curly hair. She was a beauty who did not know it. The dog paused, sat down on his hind quarters, and allowed Sandy to pet his head. Bianca opened the door and used her most professional-grown-up tone to greet the resort staff. Chip, seeing new uniformed people, and seeing upset on Sandy's face, resumed his jumping and barking. He stayed out of reach from the strange humans.

Extending the open door fully, the housemaid turned toward her employers to make an introduction, "This is Mr. and Mrs. Silver, and their dog Chip. Sorry, he gets a little excitable around visitors."

Looking to Mr. Silver for help, and getting none, Bianca recognized he was focused on brushing the dog hairs from his slacks. Taking charge again, the attractive brunette called over the barking.

"Chip! Come!"

Bianca's authoritarian effort resulted in the dog finding a safe zone, next to Mrs. Silver, who in turn looked at her husband. Arnold's tattooed eyeliner, coiffure, jeweled fingers, along with the custom fitted pastel leisure suit, might lead one to think he was a fashion-conscious gay man, but Arnold was decidedly a straight metrosexual. He also happened to be wedded to a famous daytime television star. Arnold considered their marriage fate, since he enjoyed the finer things, big money could buy. Additionally, he liked worrying the Paparazzi might show up at any moment, and he didn't want to get caught looking bad at the checkout lines. Bianca could not help but think that Mr. Silver would have fit right in with the modeling agency she had visited. In the moment, it occurred to her that it might not have been so bad working as a mannequin model, especially after seeing one in action, however, the normally shy housemaid could never see herself naked in front of strangers. Getting the nod from his wife, Arnold spoke to the resort staff directly.

"He's quite a handful, especially around new people. Perhaps, his time with you might help him to learn some manners, like how to take instructions better."

Arnold regretted his words when he noted his wife's soured

expression, although Sandy had stifled her rebuttal. She would not dishonor her husband in front of the "help." Hoping to dissuade her typical remarks about the dog's "self-esteem," Arnold changed emotional gears and began gushing.

"We'll miss you boy! But we have spared no expense to make your vacation as nice as ours."

The insincere words from Arnold made no impact on the dog's barking, and Sandy was having second thoughts on the plan for Chip, as evidenced by the whine in her voice.

"Oh Arnie, look at him, he knows he's being taken away from home by strangers. He thinks we don't want him!"

The tall man with a name tag reading, Tim, Green Mountain Dog Resort - 11 years, stepped in, past the threshold. He was familiar with wealthy pet owners and knew better than to make any contrary comments. Instead, he pulled two items out of his pocket, a high frequency whistle, and a bacon flavored dog treat. His sidekick, a two-year employee named Ted, held a short leash. Ted kneeled, effectively blocking the dog's exit, and waited for Tim's lead.

Speaking with polished flattery, Tim began, "Mrs. and Mr. Silver, Ted and I can take it from here. Trust me, we know how to help dogs calm down and feel safe. And may I say it is an honor to meet you in person, I've seen your faces on so many magazine covers, the pictures do not do you justice."

Tim raised the silent whistle to his lips and blew. Hearing the high frequency, the sound caused Chip to stop his headstrong antics, for a moment. Chip looked first at the housemaid, and then at the stranger offering his hand. When his nose picked up on the scent of the bacon, his rear feet launched him toward the treat. Chip was quick, grabbed the treat, and then bounded away from the uniforms. He began his barking again, careful to stay away from those trying to corral him. Another whistle brought Chip looking for another tasty treat. The dog, focused on the bacon treat, missed Ted's movement, and suddenly he was captured in a noose. The handlers were gentle, and praised the dog, giving him their full attention, which kept the dog from jumping, but the barking persisted.

The maid wanted to assist the good-looking men, who had both shared flirtatious stares with her. She stepped over to the entryway table and picked up the dog's bark-shock collar. She held it in the air, toward the dog, and locked eyes with him. Out of necessity, for lack of any other given discipline with the privileged pet, she had used the shock collar enough for Chip to know what it meant. The dog, watching the human antics and seeing the collar, stopped barking, and sat down. Suddenly, the dog was a willing participant of the agenda, namely, him having everyone's attention.

Tim promptly gave him another treat, adding "Good boy."

The well-to-do soap opera star took immediate offence to the dangling shock collar.

"I won't have you threatening my Baby Boy Chip! Arnie, I told you to get rid of that thing! Oh my gawd! Chip, my poor baby, Mommy is not going to let that mean maid hurt you."

Before she could continue, Bianca, who had reached the end of her patience with her employer, stopped hiding her disgust, "Have it your way Mrs. Silver."

Dropping the collar back on the table, Bianca picked up a Louis Vuitton overnight case. She had put in many hours of overtime to ready Chip's belongings for his two-week "vacation," and after two failed attempts at finding other employment in weeks prior, she was done with the pretense.

"This is the dog's bag," drawing her eyes up and down in dramatic fashion. "His vitamins and supplements are separated for each day. All his special toys are marked with a black dot, and blankets are labeled with sewn in tags. The emergency contact information for Vet and Dog Dentist, and his vaccination record are in the binder in the front pocket of the case. His food and water are packed in dry ice. The coolers are just out to the right of his carrier. The instructions for preparation, serving temperatures, and his feeding schedule are also in this envelope."

Thinking her job was done, Bianca handed the information to Tim, and went through the door, past the dog and onto the porch. Her flared temper needed space, and she was looking forward to her brief freedom from Chip, and the Silver's. She dared a brief fantasy of the handsome Davis Goodman, as she had developed a crush on the successful man. She was hopeful that he would grow her meager $3000 investment into much more, and ultimately, free her from being a doggy housemaid.

Tim, the employee from the dog resort, picked up on the tension between the dog's owners, and their personal assistant. He wanted to ease it for her. He thought she had a pretty face, and presently, it looked stressed. For a moment, he felt like a decent guy.

Sandy sent her stern eyes to Arnold. The soon-to-be browbeaten husband, responded by calling out to their dog-maid, rather indignantly, "That's it? You're leaving before the dog has even been loaded in the van? What if he needs you? What if they have questions?"

Sandy added more insult, "Do I need to get another dog-nanny?"

Stopping and turning in her tracks, Bianca smiled pleasantly, calling out, "Please Mrs. and Mr. Silver, there is no need to worry. I've taken care of every detail, and I assure you Chip will have everything he needs."

The dog handlers took Chip out on to the porch, and the couple followed to the threshold, all eyes were on Bianca. The working woman could not be prideful, she needed the job. She was a glorified dog nanny, despite her daydreams.

Pointing to her watch, "It's already ten after the hour, I thought you only needed me today until two? That was the plan, and I'm sorry, but I do need to go pick up my sister's children from summer school. I should leave. I hope you all have a great vacation."

Bianca waited, hoping her confident reply had been enough to please her employers. She could see they were preparing to say something to her.

Oh no, please don't fire me. That's it, they're going to fire me. Damn, why was I in such a hurry and in front of these cute guys.

The couple stepped toward one another, clasping hands, and took two more steps to reach their precious pet. The dog, held calmly by the resort staff, whimpered toward his *maid.*

Oh god, even Chip knows I'm going to get fired. Poor Chip.

Regardless of losing her job, and getting to her next commitment, Bianca had to give her last goodbye to Chip. She retreated, knelt down, and gave the dog's muzzle a firm kiss, and a scratch behind the ears.

Still quiet. Awkward, but they have not fired me yet, maybe they won't?

After a few tortuous moments, getting to her feet, and looking directly at her employers, Bianca found her voice, "Look, Chip is good. He's going to have fun and do great. Okay, see you in two weeks then?"

The couple produced an envelope of their own. Mr. Silver pulled it from his inner jacket pocket. He handed it to his wife, who took it, and offered it to Bianca.

Sandy started meekly, "Please wait. We have something for you. Thank you for taking care of all the arrangements for our boy Chip. You're like a third mother to him."

Genuinely surprised by their gesture, Bianca accepted the white packet, "Thank you."

"Please, open it, Bianca. Open it." Arnie Silver smiled with his pearly white teeth. He felt pleased that Bianca was surprised, "I should have given it to you earlier."

Bianca opened the envelope to find a pile of *C-notes*, and a travel document. She pulled out the paper, "What? I, uh, I don't understand?"

Arnold appealed, "We didn't know if you could get free from babysitting your, ah, cousins, is it? Anyway, we thought you deserved a vacation of your own. We've got you booked in one of the nicest suites in Reno, an all-inclusive stay, including open reservations in the spa, and the dinner club. All you must do is call a day ahead to confirm services, and the number in your party, in case you need take the children with you or have a friend. Everything will be charged to the room. We have also included a generous account in the casino if you care to gamble. All meals and gratuities on us, of course."

Before the speechless woman could find her words, Mrs. Silver added, "If you can't go for the whole two weeks, we understand, but we want you to take some time off, ten days, a week?"

Bianca nodded as if to say yes to a paid vacation but wondered if there was a catch. She held her breath when Mr. Silver moved to kneel, putting his face next to Chip's perky ears, while holding her gaze.

"And, it turns out, you won't be far from where Chip is staying. We thought you'd go and see him once or twice? At least mid-way into his stay, to assure him we will be bringing him home. Of course, we'll have a private driver available to take you, and provide all your driving needs. The money is yours no matter what you decide. We wanted you to have some pocket money, while we were away."

"Wow. This is astonishing, and very-very generous of you both. No one has ever given me this kind of bonus. I would have to make a number of arrangements to be able to go." Bianca looked again at her watch, then back to the couple. Fanning the bills in the envelope, her fingertips counted at least a thousand dollars. "I will definitely go and visit Chip. The place looked amazing online, and it would be great to see him having fun with other dogs."

Mr. Silver stood, using his employer's tone, "Good, good, then it's decided. You will go and have face time with Chip on two separate days."

Clearly this was the soap diva's idea, but Arnold would pay anything to avoid losing another maid; they had four women in the past year, and Bianca was the first to genuinely like their dog. Bianca reached out to Chip, petting his head tenderly, and tugging on his ear, the way he liked it.

"Yes, Mr. and Mrs. Silver, I do accept your terms, and thank you again, thank you so much,"

Bianca nearly teared up. She thought the full expectations were not unreasonable, in fact, it was like a dream come true. The beneficiary boldly looked at the resort staff.

Wow, this must be my lucky day, both handsome, without wedding bands, both look interested, and I didn't get fired. This has certainly worked out for good; my first paid vacation.

Tim shifted his feet, as if waiting to speak, and the Silver's took that as their cue to leave *the help* to work out any remaining details. Tim used the dog to hold the girl's attention. Leaning over Chip, he offered whispered praises. Chip stayed quiet and calm.

Tim took his chance, "Sounds like we will be seeing you at the resort, Miss...?"

Tim's left hand began petting Chip in the manner Bianca had. He could see it was soothing for the anxious dog. His right hand reached out, as if preparing to make their name exchange an official introduction. He touched Bianca's hand; however, she missed the cue to shake hands.

"Miss Bianca Verde, and yes. Uh, Tim, do I need to call ahead to arrange the visits?"

She asked her question as she stepped backward lightheartedly, trying to tactfully check the time. Nieces would be waiting to be picked up, and now, she had many additional arrangements to make. She did not wish to appear rude to the friendly man named Tim. She had been feeling depressed after her shocking experience with the modeling agency, but today's surprise events had lifted her spirits. In the moment, Bianca felt as though the world was not as bad as she had been thinking. Tim was all teeth, as he grinned in response to the fact that Bianca was a "Miss."

"No, Miss Verde, it is not necessary to announce yourself. We're caring for the pets in our kennels 24/7, and pet visiting is unlimited, even if our main center is closed to the public for private events. If you do want to make reservations for your visit, calling ahead will save you any waiting at the entry booths; the welcome staff will pre-arrange for a greeter to bring you in. If you show up without a reservation, they will just call a kennel staff member to take you to Chip. A minimal wait to get to see this big guy," he stopped to scratch Chip's ears the way he liked, "unless you are coming during his scheduled training camp. Uhh, but we don't have Chip signed up for training camp, do we?"

Tim was asking the other handler, Ted, as if he didn't know, then he called toward the couple, who had stood and stepped backwards, adding, "Mr. and Mrs. Silver, did you want Chip to have some special TLC training? The TLC program comes with an evaluation of your needs. We would need you to complete the survey before he can be enrolled. We have one in the van, if you are interested?"

Bianca knew it was coming, the couple's plea for her to complete the dog survey on their behalf; she knew she would accommodate them. The Silver's put their heads together and lowered their voices as soon as the question was posed.

Nodding to Tim in the affirmative, Arnold extended his request as he turned to follow his wife, "Bianca, we're surprised you missed this detail, but we won't hold it against you. Sandy and I have other matters needing attention, Chip will need you to complete the necessary paperwork. Thank you one and all. We'll trust you to see to Chip's needs, and we will be in touch as necessary."

The couple retreated to their home to escape debate. Bianca nearly winced at the suggestion she had made a mistake; her calendar notification kept her self-confidence from taking a dive. The reminder was her attempt to avoid the late fee she would have to pay if she lingered any longer; her nervous fingertip finally ending the alarm sound.

The skilled veteran signaled to expedite the loading of Chip and his belongings.

"No worries, Miss Verde, you can complete the survey online, over the weekend some time, I doubt you will have any trouble locating the form, our website is user friendly. His training camp will not begin until Tuesday, and I'm happy to alert the TLC training team once we get Chip checked into the resort."

"Please, call me Bianca, and thank you, Tim. Thanks so much! Bye Chip, be a good boy and see you soon. I've got to run now, or I'll have to pay late fees. Thanks again!"

CHAPTER 27

MR. WOO

"I can resist anything except temptation."

OSCAR WILDE

I am the man everyone wants to be, as if they could, an innovator, a genius, the creator of a heavenly operation that reflects my glory. The Green Mountain Dog Resort, and Sport Center are far above any like-businesses. I am the powerful and benevolent Neffen Oliver Jones, a man of impeccable taste. Only I am wise enough to decide who is worthy to see the light of day.

Jones would present *himself* to the Korean group on the platform, and then decide how to best yield his power. With each step, his footsteps announced his greatness, or so he thought. In fact, he believed he had been exceedingly gracious with the visitors, and in the moment, his estimation of himself was nothing short of glorious.

The sport business model, as designed by the Green Ghost, had self-cleansing and self-sustaining elements, including utilizing "certified" customers to *assist* with the new slaves' training. The *assistant's* portion of the training required him to copulate with the slaves, per the demands of the director, and be filmed doing it. According to Jones' standards, any who did not cooperate with the masked *Director*, or any who had second thoughts or regrets with the filming, would be permanently deleted.

Jones' system had proven to be highly profitable. Not only did the Ghost's *customer* pay for the initial experience, but the recording was also made available for an additional fee, on a time-limited basis. If purchased, the video would be attached in an email. The customer would download it to a highly secure server at their own risk. All videos clearly showed the customer's face and other identifiable characteristics, making the copy a personal liability, should it ever be handled indiscreetly. These videos were remarkably expensive. Even so, most were willing to pay the price to preserve the memory of an extraordinary one-time experience, which also elevated their status to "client."

In addition to the scripted *training*, a sport menu was created for every *client* group visit. These groups, all men, had particular tastes for the rare, the unusual, but mostly for the forbidden. They chose from an array of taboo role plays and/or lewd sexual acts with the "bitches" in training, as well as the *ordinary* slaves. Each man would choose from the *experiences* available, and if multiple men chose the same experience, they would draw straws to determine their order.

Furthermore, a client would be expected to sign a document verifying he understood the rules, and the consequences, should any missteps occur. Breaking established protocol would void their contract and increase costs for any future visit. With fees that started at $75k, one could not be frivolous. Plus, they would have to recertify, effectively delaying any future requests, and considering the limited supply, and high black-market demand, one did not want to forfeit a client status. The Korean group knew and understood how the system functioned and they were militant in taking and following orders. Gyeong's sanction of Woo changing places with another approved customer was the exception.

Jones had arrived at the tram waiting area, and by pushing a button on his watch, an overhead spotlight became activated. He cleared his throat to gather their attention, then stepped into the center of the light. The temperature in the room grew cooler. The Korean men, enthusiastic for the games to begin, and entertained by Jones' entrance, offered their applause.

"Ahem." His steel gaze was intimidating and reassuring. "Honored Guests, welcome again. Thank you for your graciousness. My team are completing their duties, and our internal transportation system will arrive momentarily. It will take you to your next stop. I expect you have found our hospitality to your liking. Unfortunately, as you know, we have an unexpected guest among your party today. There will of course be fines, associated with this omission, assuming he gains authorization."

Instinctively, everyone looked to Mr. Gyeong, who was guilty of bringing Mr. Woo, his secretary, without the necessary clearance. To be considered for access to lower levels, where *stock* were held, one had to be a proven heteroclite, friendly to perversion, and male, and pre-approved by Jones. The additional criteria, known to only Jones, would be another hurdle to jump. Gyeong felt obliged to explain.

"Woo came in place of the approved contingent, who, at the last minute, could not afford to participate. I trust he will meet with your approval."

Bowing when his words were met with silence, Gyeong could only hope all was not lost. Before further words could be spoken, two sentry officers arrived with Mr. Woo. All attention shifted to Jones, and then to the guarded man. Woo's face grew white, and he could not stop a full body shiver, even with his eyes focused on the floor. Feeling the pressure, he stepped toward Jones to offer a closer look, as if being seen would be enough to gain his acceptance. Neffen gave his nod to the sentry, they turned on their heels and left the group. The movements jarred Woo's thoughts.

I knew Gyeong was underestimating this man. He doesn't appear too bothered by the surprise. I doubt he is the Ghost; the ghost would never show himself to a man without certification, he's too careful. Jones is a hard-ball player, just not our guy. I hope Katie's okay, I hope she's alive, no, of course she's alive, she's a smart agent, she knew the risks, she doesn't need me jinxing her by doubting her; I'm sure she's fine.

Pushing his dread away, Woo offered another deep bow. He waited, flat backed, long enough to show humility. When he arose, he spoke directly, with seasoned confidence.

"I will fully cooperate, Mr. Jones, Sir. Believe me when I say, your reputation precedes you. I have no issue with you completing your required security checks. My money is good, and I have trusted you with my personal goods, and I am eager for our visit to proceed, but I will be a patient man."

"I assure you, we will resolve this matter shortly," Jones' voice was authoritative and friendly. Seemingly unruffled, Jones addressed the group, looking each man in the eye. "If there are no other surprises, I expect Woo here, will pass our security checks, and will be joining you as soon as my staff complete their work."

Some of the men spoke only a little English. Jones paused to give Gyeong time to translate his words. He listened carefully to their tone; he was talented at discerning sour or rebellious attitudes. He noted only their eagerness for what was ahead.

"As previously outlined, your journey is nearly complete, only two steps remain. My staff will escort you to your individual changing rooms. You will leave your personal clothing in the lockers provided, and if you prefer covering, there is an assortment of protective disposable clothing and foot covers available for your use. When Woo is cleared, and everyone has reassembled here, I will reunite you with your caged stock. We appreciate you entrusting us with their secure transportation. I assure you they have received excellent handling these past three days in our care and have learned a great deal from our training methods."

Waiting again for translation to be completed, Jones looked at his watch fleetingly, and then back to the men who stood before him. The tram arrived, and the doors opened. Lifting his hand toward the entrance, Jones offered parting words, "Here we are, please do not hesitate to let my team know if you have additional needs. You can expect the master of these ceremonies to join you within the hour."

Woo and Jones watched the men board. The tram disappeared down the tracks, and the spotlight went out. Jones stepped awkwardly close to Woo and landed a hand on his shoulder, leading him away from the platform in a brotherly fashion. As he did so, Jones briefly touched a few buttons on his watch, then winked at Woo. Jones reached to adjust his ear wire, as if he were listening to instructions or so Woo judged.

He moves with the ease of someone who is well practiced at taking orders. He puts on airs, but he's just a yes-man like me.

The next second had Jones' hand back on the shoulder of Woo, still friendly, but adding a few firm pats to move him along. Woo barely warded off his panic, moving as if he were an excited teenager, taking in every detail of the building as they walked. Working as an undercover agent meant putting himself at risk, and Woo was proud to be working for the FBI, even while fearing this assignment might be the greatest risk he had ever taken.

Woo could feel Jones watching his every move, and he could ill afford to fail. Watching for risks, and being aware of treacherous surroundings, while staying in the clandestine role, were common for an undercover agent; this, however, was anything but a typical assignment for Woo. He felt less prepared than ever before. The pressure of his own life, and that of another agent, one in which he had developed unprofessional feelings toward, weighed heavily on his mind. The two agents were cut off from any support, and they had no idea where they had been taken.

Speculating he was in a western state, Woo could guess little else in terms of his location. His last communication with headquarters was close to two days past. Given the deep undercover situation, his supervisor would not expect to hear any updates for several more days. Woo and his partner, both having career ambitions, had to be ready to do whatever was necessary, their lives depended on it. Woo picked up on Jones' activity.

He continually switches his attention to me, to his ear, to his smart watch. Smooth operator when everything is systematized, and it appears it is, even the temperatures. The man is acting upon directives given to him through the ear wire and by text. He is only a lacky, not the primary decision maker.

Allowing room for cultural misunderstandings, and if Woo cleared, Jones decided not to be punitive to the group, at least not in any way they would not ultimately enjoy. Their business was too lucrative to turn away, even if Woo did not make the cut. Perceiving Woo's doubts about his position of authority, Neffen decided it was best to control his ego, and play it up.

"My apologies, Mr. Woo. It seems another unexpected situation has just occurred. I do need to excuse myself, briefly, I've been asked to deal with this firsthand. I'm going to have to ask you to wait here, you may use the bench here to sit. You will not have to wait long."

Fool, filthy too, ear wax, disgusting. Exceptionally foul to be near you, smelling you, listening to you. My flesh says I should feed you to the dogs. It is only nature; it is only right that the strong should devour the weak. My mind cautions me to wait until I know more. As foul as you are, you may be useful. I will wait.

The intensity of Jones was unmistakable to all, as was his dignified, fluid management style, however, Woo was assigned to find the Kingpin. Given the intelligence passed on from headquarters, the monster he sought was a narcissistic egomaniac, not a man who would humbly, if not patiently, carry out these types of menial tasks. Woo measured up Jones.

The man is highly regarded, as are most high-level doers, and he certainly has a virtual connection to the Green Ghost, possibly the right-hand man. His insight into these operations will serve us well, although his kind don't believe in snitching. No. Mr. Jones is not the type to be easily flipped, he's a stickler for keeping the status quo, I'm sure of that. I will have to play it his way and watch him carefully.

CHAPTER 28

A SHOT IN THE DARK

"Nobody knocks here, and the unexpected sounds ominous."

D.H. LAWRENCE

The evening was passing without many words, as both Mr. and Mrs. Harrison were in their heads, thinking about things they were not willing to speak about. The television interrupted Donald's thoughts when it began to spew out the negative side-effects of a *wonderful* new drug. Donald thought it should be illegal to market drugs on commercials, and almost said as much, until he noticed his *smurf* was now deep in her romance novel.

If Deb was doing one of her overnights, think I'd find a good porn to watch. Maybe I should tell her I am feeling frisky? I could go sneak a blue pill, if her book is a good one, she'll be wanting the attention sooner than later.

He lowered the recliner quietly, hoping she would not notice.

"Donald, where are you going? May I get you something? You know the doctor wants your feet up at night?"

"No, thank you little one, unless you have a bedpan on hand?"

She smiled, then resumed her reading.

It must be some good stuff, that was too easy, then, mumbling as he walked away, "Jeeze, can't a guy even go take a piss?"

"I heard that dear husband, I'm only thinking of your heart condition, and I enjoy caring for you."

"Thanks Smurf, I can handle this one on my own." Donald blushed a bit as he lied, but once on his feet, he really did have to rush to the bathroom to make it in time.

After Donald returned to his recliner, he was careful not to provide any distracting interruptions for his wife's reading; she was glued to her story. He was delighted she was not busy. Cleaning was often her way of dealing with anxiety, seeing her sit still was a good sign.

She always puts herself last, good to see her relax. Nice you can take a break, instead of your tireless tidying, and worrying over me. I don't get the romance paperback choice, you're so much more intelligent than that, but the books are always worn out by the time you finish, so you must enjoy them.

⌒‿⌒

Debbi's time at home was always centered first around her man's needs, then keeping their home, and their belongings, in pristine condition. She often said attending to him was her greatest honor. Donald attributed her fixation with serving him, and neurotic-like cleanliness to her upbringing. Her parents, both proud of their Chinese culture and belief systems, had always insisted she keep her hands and feet busy while there was something for hands and feet to do. Her parents also seemed to have an aversion to books. Debbi had explained that in her parent's language, the word book sounded like the word lose. They believed if "book" time conflicted with something of value, she would lose something of value.

⌒‿⌒

Seeing his glance at her book. Debbi's antennae were out, as were Donald's, and both were suffering a little private frustration. Donald's blue pill was beginning to take effect. He hoped his wife would finish her book, and soon. Debbi noticed her husband was restless, she rightly guessed he was more interested in sex, than beginning a discussion about the people moving into the lodge. She held her book carefully, making certain he could not see beyond the cover.

There was no doubt, Mrs. Harrison hated romance novels as much as her husband, and as it turned out, so did Tom, her boss. Romance novels were yawn at best, with big doses of predictable contriteness, as far as Debbi was concerned. However, based on the need to hide information at home and at work, the books made the perfect decoy.

The outside of her paperback appeared to be a normal used book, even though Debbi had carefully hollowed out a section. The hole was exactly right for a spiral pocket notebook and a pencil, which she hid inside; careful to leave some pages before and after the cut-out ones, to keep it hidden. She added an inner cardboard border, giving the inner box space more stability. The notebook, or other small, papered *intel* was for Debbi's eyes only, not meant to be known or seen by others. She switched covers regularly to make it appear as if she were reading different books.

Debbi could see a blush rising on Donald's cheeks.

Time to take care of my man.

"Donald, would you mind closing the blinds? I am going to put a little sexy something on, then I'm going to put my lips on you."

The rest of the evening was exhilarating and fulfilling, for both. Donald was not the only one who needed his sex itches scratched, and with a little help from the blue pill, he loved pleasuring his woman. His regular doctor prescribed Viagra, once a week, but it was not sufficient for their more regular practices, and it did little to help him with the urinary problems that came with an enlarged prostate. Donald found he could buy Cialis from Canada, and secretly supplement his sex drive, as well as relieve frequent urination in the night. He had taken both doses.

〜〜

Worn out after their exertion, and sated by the sex, the Harrison's closed their eyes for sleep. As they rested, their bedroom darkness was disrupted by a soundless light, coming from behind their home. The light traveled up and down, in the windows, until it landed on the security system box. Having located the power line, the light followed the path of the wire leading from the box to the house. A pair of wire cutters were retrieved from a pocket, and the line was cut.

Debbi sat upright, and Donald met her with a protective arm.

"I hear something."

"I hear it too. You sit still. Wait here, understand?"

"Donald, you're out of breath as it is, what? You're getting your gun?"

"Debbi, I'm serious, tell me you will not move from our bed?"

"Okay, yes, I'll wait here, but please don't leave the house without me!"

Donald silently made his way out of the bedroom, careful to avoid the squeaky floorboards along the way. Debbi strained to hear him, barely able to follow him with her mind's eye. Reaching for the house phone, a wireless handset, she dialed 911, then crawled under the blankets and pillows on the bed. Her instincts told her to get help. She found herself holding her breath as the number rang. Before the operator answered, the handset went dead. She and Donald had unknowingly knocked it off the stand, during their earlier activities. The battery light was blinking. She eased the phone back to the charger, let the air out of her mouth and began counting. She would count, up to five minutes, hoping it would not take that long for Donald to return to explain it had been something silly, like a neighborhood pet.

Donald made it downstairs in the dark. He passed through the dining room to make his way to the security system box, which was installed immediately next to the back door. There was a sound emitting from the security alarm box, alerting them that the power had been cut off. A shadow outside, passing in the window, caused Donald to duck down before he could hit the reset switch. He cursed his reflex, fearing he missed his chance to see who was sneaking past their back door. Donald focused on staying low, maneuvering around the streetlight that shone in from a nearby window. He misjudged the distance between himself and a table, sending a vase filled with top heavy flowers, crashing across the floor.

The crashing sound brought Debbi to her feet, and reaching for her own weapon, a fifteen-inch club flashlight, which was kept in the bedside drawer. She skillfully floated over the floor, to the top of the stairs, and pointed her light down the stairs. Finding no forms, she continued down the steps to the first landing. Next to their home, the neighbor's dog began yipping. The animal sounds caused Debbi to contract her muscles and her grip hit the power button and turned off her flashlight. The darkness was not as startling, as the sudden sounds of screeching car tires outside. Debbi could tell they were going away from their house. As she released her breath, her body swayed, and the floorboards beneath her feet made a squeaking sound. The flash from Debbi's flashlight, startled Donald, and the sounds outside further disoriented him. Dizzy, he spun around trying to orient himself, pointing his gun in the direction of the sound.

"Donald, it's me…"

Chest pain that was traveling down his right arm, suddenly caused his trigger finger to involuntarily contract. The explosion of gunfire lit the darkened house.

～～

As if on cue, the neighborhood lit up with flashing red and blue light. A nearby police cruiser was called to do a drive-by after the silent 911 call came from the Harrison's landline. The officer, more of a desk jockey, knew the couple, and fully expected to be alerted of a false alarm. Instead, just as he was approaching the address, he heard gunfire. He drove past to report the situation. He made a neat U-turn a few houses down, just as the dispatcher came on the line. He sparsely relayed the situation, saying there had been one shot fired, only he was not sure where it came from. From his vantage point, he could see the lights were off inside the Harrison's house, but their landscaping lights, and a porch light outside the house were lighting up the scene; nothing appeared unusual.

"Affirmative. There are several houses on the street with lighting. No cars, presently, no, wait, there is movement in the distance. Car lights coming toward me from the other end of the street, uhh, might have been a parked car, I didn't see it coming from the far end of the road, uhh, now it's turning toward Main. Should I follow the car?"

The officer waited for the dispatcher to relay his question to the senior officer on station duty. The Chief, although on medical desk duty, upon hearing the address, was moving to get to a patrol car. He was a personal friend of the Harrisons, lived in the neighborhood, and was not about to wait around to find out what was going down. He reached the vehicle, and struggled to get his left leg, great with cast from foot to thigh, into the vehicle. The dispatcher came on the car radio.

"Chief, are you sure you're supposed to be driving? Are you there, Chief?"

"I'm here, I'm here, and jeeze, it seems like the front end of this thing has shrunk, hehe."

Speaking fast, taking few breaths, Cheryl blurted her whole mind, "Chief, seriously, I don't think you should try to drive. Hal called in a parked car leaving the area, likely heading to the highway, he wants to know if he should follow it? Aahh, hold on, Chief, another call coming in. 911 here, what's your emergency?"

Except for some static, the radio went silent once the dispatcher put the Chief's line on hold. He was still struggling to get fully into the car, when the reality of his status finely sunk in.

"Eye-yi-yi, who am I kidding."

Recognizing his failings, the chief changed his mind. He began to work his large casted appendage back out of the car, when the dispatcher returned to the radio.

"Chief? Chief are you there?" there was a lengthy pause, "I'm patching you into Hal's cruiser," spoken breathily, as if the dispatcher was exasperated.

The chief maneuvered himself to reach the console, to answer, bumping his head and leg in the process, "Aargh! Ow! Shit! Damn it! Sorry Cheryl. Can you find someone to fill in for you? I need a ride over to the Harrison's asap. Tell Hal to sit tight and keep an eye out for any other unusual movement, and tell him, I'll get over there as soon as you can get me there."

"Heya Chief? It's Hal here, not Cheryl. Uhh, the house lights have come on, and now Mrs. Harrison is on the porch madly waving her arms for me to come inside, I will go and see what she says."

～

Crickets sang unremitting as evening temps dropped; the stars above replied by stunning any who dared to gaze upward. Standing within the yellow tape boundaries, Bob Ropier, Chief of the Nevada County Sheriff department, and an active member of Donald's Neighborhood Watch, was briefed by Officer Hal. Bob had spoken to Debbi, but he wanted his officer's take on the incident.

Hal spoke matter of factly, "This was not a 10-16, just a medical emergency, although it began when the Harrison's heard an intruder. Donald got up with a gun for protection. Mrs. Harrison called us, but their phone battery died before she could talk. In the dark, Donald knocked over a glass vase, the smashing sound likely scared off whoever cut their security power line. Mrs. Harrison thinks Donald's heart condition became an issue; he became confused. He thought an intruder had found his way inside, he heard sounds in the dark and turned toward them. Mrs. Harrison went partly down the stairs to see if she could help, she dropped to the ground when she heard Donald's gun mechanism engage. She was confident it was an accident, since

Donald also fell to the ground following the shot. He was unconscious when I walked in, though still breathing. She barely missed getting hit by the .45 caliber bullet sent from Donald's gun. The medical first responders arrived right behind me and were able to stabilize Donald with oxygen."

"Okay. Thanks Hal. You know how close I am to the family, and this is my neighborhood too. This is personal. I want to be kept up to date on every detail with this case."

The two parted, Hal back into the house, and Ropier, limping along in his walking cast toward the street. He made it around the other emergency vehicles to reach Donald's side.

"Donald, Hi, sorry it took so long, but I'm here, and I promise you, I am going to keep additional patrols in the area."

His words could not restore peace of mind, but his obvious concern, despite his own physical status, inspired tearful gratitude from both Donald and Debbi. The Chief, seeing their emotion, responded with his most reassuring tone, "Listen, you two, it looks like it was a close call for Donald's health, you don't need to worry about anything else."

"Thank you Chief."

The chief pulled Debbi a few feet away from Donald's stretcher.

"Debbi, please let me know if you need anything, anything at all. I have no doubt my Mrs. will come by to see you at the hospital, tomorrow is her auxiliary day. Now listen, I made a few calls."

Donald's hand shifted from his lap to the gurney rail. Debbi moved back to his side, laying her hand on top of his, so small in comparison. Her expression begged the chief to continue.

"There have been no other attempted break-ins or other residential property crimes in our county, if that is what was intended? You two don't have any enemies you haven't told me about do you?"

The chief laughed at his own question, hoping it would take the sting out of his insinuation. Donald was struggling to keep up with the conversation. He thought his friend's laughs were contrived, and he did not see any humor in their situation.

"Naw, everybody loves you two. Chances are this was random.

You know you do have the biggest, or at least the highest house on the block. If I were a burglar, I'd find a big house with no dog, not counting you ol' salty dog, Donald."

Donald tried to laugh, for Debbi's sake, he hated to see her face upset; he could only cough. The paramedic held her hand up in front of the patients face, then brought her forefinger to her lips, saying do not talk. Debbi's mind raced through the long list of her mortal enemies. If any knew she was alive, this was just the beginning. Debbi cut off her spinning thoughts to focus on her husband.

A quivering lip offered consolation, "Donald, shhh. Please rest while this efficient, uhh, I'm sorry, Liz, are you an EMT or a Paramedic?"

"Paramedic Ma'am. Thanks. It's time for us to get Donald here, to the hospital."

The driver, who had been talking to the other officer, came around to help load the gurney. He offered reassurance, "Liz is the most experienced on our unit, he's in good hands."

Chief Ropier, standing at the foot of the gurney, put a light hand on Donald's foot.

"Man, you need to relax, I've got this. Just do what these good medics tell you. You need to get better. The home association meetings will be as dry as stale toast without you. You know who with a stick up his butt, will step up to cover for you, but you're the only one who can keep everyone to the agenda. Alrighty now, get better, got it?"

Lifting a weak thumbs up, Donald was perturbed with himself, but he was happy his friend was on the job.

Debbi spoke for both, kindly, "Thank you Bob, I know Donald trusts you."

CHAPTER 29

THE INTERN'S THESIS

*"Any fool can know.
The point is to understand."*

ALBERT EINSTEIN

Good to see that Agent Stanovich is progressing with tracking the slave from Canada. Something good could materialize from this, keep on top of it, and make sure he has what he needs. Any word from Packton or Park?"

"Nothing in the last 48 hours, Sir. Based on their last message, we projected up to four days of silence, with the expected return travel to Korea. We received a signal from the dog collar near Sparks, Nevada, and we are looking into a reported caravan traveling north of Sun Valley. Our satellites lost images when the storm clouds became too thick, the weather is a factor in us being in the dark right now, but not for much longer. Our intelligence has our *ghost* working from Canada. We are looking at land and air routes between Reno and Montreal.

"And the caves under Montreal? What's our status on getting into the ancient tunnels to see if some not so ancient digging has been done?"

"With all due respect, Sir, it's going to take much more than a hunch that the Ghost has an underground city there, but we are working every lead for hard facts."

"Well, I don't know about you, but I won't sleep until I know that Packton is safe, of all our agents, I fear the worst for her."

Saying the words, unleashed the supervisor's imagination and doubts about the ambitious manhunt.

"Yes, Sir, I agree. I'd hate to see this one played out on late-night TV."

"There is no turning back now, let's hope this dog-slave show doesn't end with our agents permanently damaged, there have been too many so-called eulogies already.

The FBI chief thought back to the chance beginning of their official chase, and the intern, Erin Mendez, who as luck would have it, had been a fan of late-night television.

Beckoning gallows humor, a satirical *late-night show* contrived a comedy skit highlighting the multiple evening prime-time programs featuring bio-memorials for men of high status, who had recently committed suicide or had some type of fatal accident. Their "eulogy" high points had become a stochastic occurrence on several prime news shows. The necessity to recognize the passing of numerous "notable persons," ordained several of the big news outlets to present three memorial stories, in one; one station made it a regular segment. The comic play actors poked fun at the casual-if not irreverent way the string of "accidental deaths," were regarded.

The dead had all been *stand out men*, all expert professionals, living vibrant careers, and they met their demise, before any sign of physical or mental decline, and it appeared, no one was questioning the trend. In the skit, each man was told their "number" had come up, and like fat cows sent to slaughter, the death sentence was given because "their heads were too big." The satire's content reflected the loss of life and talent, as being noteworthy in multiple industries.

The late-night show caught the attention of Ms. Mendez, a female master's student, studying Forensic Sciences, also interning with the FBI. She was inspired to look further into the insinuation that Al-Qaeda was killing the "smart" Americans, three at a time. Erin devoted her thesis to the idea, and as she worked on the criteria for making "the list," it became clear how statistically significant it was for all the deceased to be male. While there were more males to females in similar positions, the ratio was still remarkable. Erin's completed thesis was read and taken seriously by the FBI, after her supervisor offered support for her work.

Based on the intern's findings, many of the incidents were triggered by an initial personal disappearance. Further, the fatal incidents were incongruent with the men's professional, and private reputations; these were not depressed individuals, nor were any of the personalities insecure. Their deaths, deemed suicides, had no precipitating events; often, the deceased were at the pinnacle of their career. Another significant factor, as Erin pointed out, there were no suicide notes. Additionally, the fatal "accidents," were directly connected with some unreputable element, such that one might say "he deserved what he got," even though there was no supporting evidence that any such involvements had occurred, prior to the deadly one.

The list of those who had died was staggering, while still not considered an exhaustive account. There were some others, loosely connected to the list, who were currently listed as "missing." Those deemed most suspicious included engineers of biomedical, solar, hydro energy, aqueducts, mining and geological, satellite and telecommunications; and scientists of astrophysics, molecular cloning, homology, geothermal energy, and actuary.

Among the medical professionals, there were faculty of doctoral-research programs from Stanford Medical, Harvard Medical, Duke, and John Hopkins, and at government research laboratories. There were also numerous surgeons, some with expertise in plastic reconstructive work, facial and genital. Military figures were also heavily represented.

Several experts analyzed the collected data, and all agreed there was a sinister pattern. However, with no clear motive, and no identified suspects, they could not come to any productive conclusions.

Those in high level positions within the investigative agency, formulated various theories suggesting they could be dealing with a highly organized group, likely terrorists, subtly working to undermine American leadership.

The *late-night hosts* did not miss the irony on the FBI's public remarks, creating additional triviality on the issue based on official quotes. The agency's embarrassment over the event was evident when they made an immediate official announcement regarding the case.

"Due to a total lack of evidence, the agency has ceased their interest related to the impolitic, if not foolhardy, suspicious suicide theory."

The FBI stopped making any further related comments, and there was a media blackout on the story. In addition to the sudden *censorship*, the related "suspicious-missing" trend receded, and the "death rate" abruptly stopped. The inconclusive casework was forgotten by most, until one dubious witness for a human trafficking case, came forward. The witness, a woman, who allegedly hid herself when her boyfriend was visited by "tattooed men in black," had heard things. Sadly, her boyfriend was escorted away and there had not been any contact since. The witness was not able to see anything from her hiding place, all she could do was share how she made sense of what she heard.

"They were cleaners, like for the mob, serious shit! But they were worried about someone called the Ghost, the man they worked for, they were sure he was not going to be happy about them returning empty handed. I'm not sure what or who they were looking for, all I know is if they had found me, they would have killed me, I'm sure of it."

The other bits of "random" information she overheard, made for some curious ties to the old case, and connected the Ghost to another ongoing case. The FBI were already aware of the illusive man-ghost, but connecting him to the suspicious suicide list, meant he was possibly more dangerous than they imagined. Despite the witness hearing his name, little was known about the Ghost, for example, there was no biometric evidence to identify him. The working premise was that he was Caucasian, quite possibly a Canadian, and he had taken his vast trafficking operations deep underground, literally. It had been speculated to be somewhere in Canada, but the upper western states in North America were also strong possibilities. Strengthening their hypothesis on the connection between professionals going missing and the creation of an underground lair for human trafficking, was the astounding work being done by a billionaire who was working with a truly indistinguishable group of engineers and scientists.

The billionaire's legitimate project, a tunnel forty feet under the city of Los Angeles, was intended to become an underground high-speed highway. Minus those professions related to the medical and esoteric fields, the project's team had many similarities with those from the "suspicious suicide list." Whilst the billionaire's drilling project had nothing to do with the case, the futuristic high-tech quality of his work, made the James Bond-like conjectures of the suspected underground Ghost hideout, more conceivable.

$$\sim\!\sim$$

A year into the FBI's "sex-trafficking" investigation, two of the agents, Katherine Packton, and William Park (undercover names Katie and Ji-Woo) had managed to gain an invitation to one of the Ghost's special sport events. They were forced to travel separately, but both were tracked to Seoul, to Los Angeles, and then to Salt Lake City. The agency believed their undercover team were close to coming into direct contact with the Ghost himself and could possibly identify him when the time came. In support of the case, there were additional agents following other threads of the investigation. One targeted an alleged sex slave survivor, who had putatively escaped the "Green Ghost," and was hiding under a different identity, currently in Nevada. Their intelligent sources guessed the Ghost was looking for this same slave, finding her could be the key to locating the kingpin himself.

CHAPTER 30

THE GAME IS AFOOT

"The truth must dazzle gradually."

EMILY DICKINSON

I need self-care, a shower, and a change of clothes. Perhaps some music too, I am on the edge of a headache, and if I feel pain, heads will roll.

Jones, not inclined to watch television, had no idea the comedy parody had been created, but even if he had, it would not have changed his high opinion of his security practices and his ordained systems. His cogs turned like flawlessly timed clockwork handling the business at hand. Neffen felt some amount of ease, and needing a shower and change of clothes, he left the player on a whim, entrusting him and the others to his securities. With the push of a button, a wall disappeared and a closet and ensuite were revealed. Neffen spoke to Tiger, his customized AI system.

"Tiger, set the showers for 103, twenty minutes, and play Purple Rain, extended version, followed by Dream On, and tell me some related music trivia I haven't heard before."

"Here are some trivia facts found on the internet. The ballad, "Dream

On," by Aerosmith was first released as a single in 1973. It reached number 59 on Billboard Top 100. It was re-released in 1976, and it went to number six, earning the band their first of eight top-ten hits. Steven Tyler felt insecure about the way his voice sounded on tape. He changed his voice to a more authentic raspy vocal sound, which became his trademark style. The song is about dreaming until your dreams come true, and hunger, and desire, and ambition. Enjoy your shower, Mr. Jones."

Neffen had not heard the minutiae on the singer, it pleased him enough to in fact, enjoy his shower. Afterward, he continued to ready himself, occasionally giving directions, and receiving alerts from Tiger. He heard the printer warming up, to print an incoming report. When he heard the printing sounds, he picked up his smartwatch, and fastened it to his wrist. In front of the mirror, he stroked his freshly shaven chin. His steel eyes noted the light of an incoming cell call on the watch; he assumed it had to do with the incoming report. Jones let the call go to voicemail as he completed buttoning up his shirt. It was rare for him to call ahead of reading the written reports. His gut, however, said return the call.

He moved from his personal quarters to the main computer station, the wall returned to its place as he dialed the number. His voice held back any emotion, although giddiness threatened to sound when his man answered. Jones kept his words few, "Tell me some good news."

"Yes Sir. I'm on route to Henderson, Nevada, another thirty minutes, and my feet will be on the ground. Our facial recognition software had two hits in the area, one was at the bus station, and the other near, one of the regular bus stops, I faxed the shots."

Jones navigated to his satellite view and zoomed in to see the Henderson, street view. To his left, the printer completed its job. He reached for the printed photos, his heart pounding in his chest. Neffen's eyes widened, he recognized the figure. He stopped short of an audible exclamation.

The faultless chin, perfect nose, and the most superb arch to the forehead, I styled that profile, she belongs to me.

His business tone was unwavering, "We do indeed have a match. Do you have what you need to locate her?"

"Yes Sir, I have her file."

"You have 48 hours, I want addresses, and names and phones of primaries, and she cannot know you've made her. Is that clear?"

Jones' hunger for his special pet could not be sated, despite his progress. The feeling irritated his nasty side. He indulged his feelings of bitterness toward the men who had failed him. He imagined a total slaughter of his senior investigators. He had new, malleable staff coming up in the ranks, and one, acting alone, had found his mark. Ultimately, Neffen felt the investigative team's performance was not acceptable, and their gratitude for living was lacking. He mentally went through his entire team, numerically, giving each one a pass or a fail, or needing more testing. His thoughts turned to the young man named *Asheesh*. Jones spoke out loud to himself.

"True, Asheesh is new, and so far, deserving of a test, but the effort to manage the peon makes me feel used."

A whiff of self-pity sounded. Jones had to restrain himself. He had a strong inclination to commit mass murder with his unwanted staff. His pride and grandiosity ultimately kept him in check.

Bringing things to life, and taking life, this is the work of the gods. God is the only authorized murderer, and this is so fortunate for me since it gives me such pleasure. And being God, should that not allow me to indulge in pleasures, I Am, after all the only one who cannot make a mistake, I Am, after all the most generous of living gods.

Jones' watch informed him of a new phone message waiting, it came from the *sport* hotline.

Everyone needs to speak to God at some point. Everyone needs something from me, I get it, but why is everyone so needy today? What is it the weak ones need now?

The sport hotline was shared with a chosen few, and they were entrusted to keep the number to themselves, with one exception. If they were willing to risk their own status for another like-minded man, they could refer services, using the code name *"regular guy."* The exceptional were expected to use a coded script when contacting the Ghost. Jones played the caller's message expecting to hear it.

"Hello. Do not worry, I'm no ghostbuster, just a regular guy who's not good with rules. I'm thinking about buying a dog, or a she-pet. Actually, I visited a regular dog resort yesterday morning, The Green Mountain Dog Resort. Impressive program, it got me thinking. I will need a proper cage, and training program for the she-pet, so I can keep her safe in my home. I'm told it takes months for you to clear a customer, but that will not be necessary with me. I'm an open book, just not so much on a recorded phone line. I will tell you, I have a big checkbook, and I do like games, so let's play one. A man of your reputation should not have any difficulty finding me, and when you do, you'll have learned what you need to know about me. Talk soon. Chow."

Flooded with rage, Jones demanded, "What? Who the fuck gave this punk my number?"

Most of his coded script was missing in the message, and it was the first time anyone had ever named the dog resort in connection with the Green Ghost. Suddenly, there was absolutely nothing more important to Jones than playing this game.

～

Jones stepped from his secret office to return to Woo. He felt fresh, alert, and ready for his next ploy. Placidly, Jones arrived at the bench where he had left Woo to wait. Woo stood and bowed, hoping to hear he had been accepted.

"I had hoped everything would have been cleared by now, but I'm afraid that is not the case. In keeping with our Sport contracts, Mr. Woo, we will need to have you wait until all formalities have been completed. I do appreciate your patience. The personnel who will clear you, had duties in other areas, they'll be wrapped up soon.

While you wait a little longer, please be my guest. I want you to feel comfortable. The waiting area has a patio, where you can enjoy some *fresh* air, it appears you could use some."

Reaching their destination, Woo was surprised by seeing a female badged staff, he found it difficult to believe any woman would choose to work for this outfit. Jones stopped, bringing his hands together for a double clap, like a child preparing to open a gift.

"May I introduce Mary, one of our most delightful guest experience staff."

Noticing Jones' rate of speech had deliberately slowed, Woo looked the woman over, just as purposefully.

I know the Ghost wouldn't trust a man who would ignore an opportunity to demoralize a woman, and certainly this lovely vape was sent as a test, they want to be sure I'm as disgusting as these other pigs.

In keeping with his cover role, Woo's thoughts were lusty.

Nice figure, too bad she's special ed, probably as dense as she is cute, but an improvement compared to the last two goons.

"Mary...this...is Mr. Woo."

Jones stepped back and turned to present Mary with a gentlemanly bow. When he had straightened himself, he carefully reached for a dose of antibacterial gel; the dispensers were placed at every juncture. Those who were with him felt his silent directive to follow his example. They thoroughly rubbed all sides of their hands, as Jones demonstrated, then he continued with measured verbal instructions.

"Mary, please show Mr. Woo our best hospitality, while he waits to join his group. Besides looking after him, I would like you to do two things. First, give him a personal monitor. Do you remember where those are found?"

Mary nodded yes, then to clarify, she began with a slow roll of her long eyelashes, "Pardon me, Sir? Do you mean the little black tablet-thingies in the public lounge? The ones on those fetching stone tables?"

Oh, Mary is not special, she's just southern with dimples. I had the dense part right, and that cleavage, no doubt part of her uniform.

"Yes, Mary. Once you have put it in his hand, you will do the second task. Instant message me with the monitor ID number. I will need that before I can send Mr. Woo a private video link to watch, while he is waiting for clearance. Do you understand?"

Mary winked and gushed, "Yes Sir, Mr. Jones, I'd be happy to take care of those little ol' things."

Receiving a brief nod from her boss, before he left them, Mary was primed to give her attention to Woo. Her counterpart thought the young, voluptuous woman, with the irresistible southern accent, was no doubt sent as a distraction or a test. Mindful of the danger, Woo was hopeful the video link would give him the assurance that Katie was alive and well.

Smiling deep into her dimples, Mary continued, "I will be pleased to take you to the waiting area, and I do recommend sitting on the adjacent patio. The trees are dripping with moss. It's such a divine day, and it should be enjoyed under the shaded arbors, the natural light is truly flattering for all skin types."

As Mr. Woo was led away by Mary, he turned to look back at Jones, who had a polite smirk on his face. Instantaneously, Woo felt a prick on his neck, "Ouch! Wah, what was?" He reached back, coming away with the tiniest droplet of blood on his fingertip.

"Oh my! Did a little ol' mosquito bite you? I knew you was sweet sugar when I laid eyes on you. They are apt to bite us, instead of the dogs ya know, what with the insect protection, they have, no flea, tick, or mosquito has a chance on one of them. Not safe for humans I hear, but they spray every four-footed critter in the place, suppose they are hoping no bugs gonna have the gumption to hang around long. I can fetch you some human bug spray if you would like? And how about a nice cold glass of sweet tea?"

"No bug spray needed sweet Mary; your perfume is beautifully odiferous. I would love to see that figure of yours with less clothes on. I think it's only fair, since we have been buddied up and sent off to, uh, now where are you taking me?"

It was not sudden, still, the undercover agent felt eager to act out the creepy womanizer-type he was pretending to be. He felt his pants tighten, then found himself thinking about his southern fla-vored keeper, and not in a G-rated way.

She is attractive, wow, guess her type turns me on more than I'd like to admit, I'm getting hard, and might as well use it.

Mr. Woo felt a sort of dizzy confusion wash his mind, but he attributed it to his growing erection, and the perfume Mary was wearing. She smelled like something out of a fantasy. For Woo, certain fragrances, the subtle kind, could trigger a hard-on, and the one he sported was getting firmer. The idea of gripping himself was forgotten when Mary leaned her bountiful cleavage into his space.

Mary pressed her breasts into his arm, and pointed across the way, to give more boost to her decolletage, "I think we should stroll over and look closer at those flowering vines."

Woo stepped back, not to escape, but to better take in her breasts. Reaching around her form, he pulled her close, and pressed her lower half into his boner. Getting no resistance, he began squeezing her ass, both cheeks, firmly holding her against himself.

"Hold on there, little Mary, you can't tempt a guy with all your sugar and then only offer sweet tea?"

Mary giggled demurely, and threw her arms around his neck, "Oh Mr. Woo, you are wooing this gal right off her feet, and Sweetie, you are a bonafide catch if ever I saw one, only I am on the job, and I can't afford to lose this one."

With that comment, she rolled off his chest and spun gracefully out of reach. Careful to stay a few steps ahead, she led her charge to a nice outdoor table, and gave her finest curtsy when they reached their assigned stop, saying, "Now isn't this a dandy place to sit a spell? Do go ahead and wait here, my precious."

Mary shook her shoulders, unabashedly giving her breasts the freedom to quiver. "I will be right back with your monitor."

Woo squeezed his own junk; he could not help himself. It left him feeling flush. Returning with a plate of scones, and a small tablet-sized monitor in hand, Mary was all smiles. Seeing her hands full, Woo did not hesitate. He reached up her skirt, finding her rump as smooth and luscious as he imagined. Mary gracefully set the items on the table, then reached back to grab his wrists, taking them away from her bottom.

"Here you go Mr. Woo. Mr. Jones wanted you to have this, now will you kindly use your hands to help me find the ID number?"

Mary had her cleavage full in his face, briefly, then she separated herself, stepping back gingerly. Woo could not focus. He wanted more of Mary.

Mmmm. I could take her right here on my lap, but no, wait, think Katie.

"You're a tease, aren't you Mary? You come here and sit on my lap. We will find the ID number together."

In a dominant manner, Woo reached out and grabbed a hold of Mary's waist, pulling her to his knee. Anxious to avoid a scene, she pretended to be comfortable. She picked up the monitor, turned it in her hands, and showed Woo the underside. Covered with clear tape, the ID number was in large font.

"There it is sugar, clear as day." Mary laughed coyly, "Read it to me while I enter it into my smartwatch."

Woo took the item from her. He pressed her free hand into his crotch. "Look how excited I am to assist you Sweet Mary."

Blushing wistfully, Mary gave him the recognition he desired. Running her hand outside the fabric of his pants. She found his lovestick firm and thick, triggering a momentary fantasy, which she had to shake from her mind. The last thing she wanted was to anger Jones, he would anger easily if she did not stay on task.

Mary bit her lip, adding "Another place, another time, and I'd let you be a hooligan, but Sugar, I can't lose my job."

Mary pulled her hand back, stood and smoothed her skirt, and pointed to her watch, "I'm ready for that number."

Woo continued his act, longing for his manhood to settle down. He read the number and decided it might be more expedient to pivot his thoughts to Katie.

I'm not going to see her until I get through this game, gawd I hope I pass all his tests. I feel like I'm drugged, but no, I'm just tired. Katie, hang in there, just a little longer.

Once the brief task was complete, Mary was elated, "Well I declare, I think it is finally time for some sweet tea. I'll be right back."

Alone, Woo focused on the monitor. The virtual wallpaper was a live dog, jumping through a hoop to catch a frisbee as water sprayed from a ground sprinkler. Woo entered himself as a guest.

"Hmmmm." Nothing yet, but hopefully a video link to connect with Katie, who knows? It seems a bit too easy, it could be another test.

Mary came from behind him, she was careful to stay out of his reach, "Are you looking for your video link? I'm certain Mr. Jones will send it, and it will pop up in the next few minutes. Now, here's a nice cool beverage, drink up, maybe it will cool you off?"

She set the tray with fresh sprigs of mint in a bowl and topped the glass of iced tea.

"By the way Sugar, I also found your personal phone in the bag with the others. Since you isn't downstairs, yet, I figured you might want it, especially if your droll video does not pop up soon. But Sugar, ya just gotta shhh about this, and leave it in the seat cushion when you're done. I will see that it gets back to the secure bag. Is that okay with you Mr. Woo?"

Mary pulled the cell phone out of her pocket, and discreetly dropped it on his lap.

"Thanks, for both Sweet Mary. I'd love to have a scotch on the rocks right about now, and a roll in the sack with you, uuuhhh, but sweet tea will have to do."

Woo was surprised by his admission. He attributed his loose tongue to the relief he felt when he saw his cell phone. Also, he felt giddy given his success in stealing Mary's watch, without her noticing. He realized his emotions and words were not being properly filtered, he would need to be more careful. The watch was slipped into his socks securely, while taking up the phone from his lap with the other hand.

Who knows, maybe the watch will help Katie and I find the Ghost. Oh Katie. Maybe I can reach her, if she still has her collar on, if they didn't cut it off, if she's okay? Yes, you're okay Katie, I can feel you, you're close, hold tight, you are not alone. Don't lose hope.

A video link finally appeared on the screen, as if it were a sobering cup of coffee. Woo clicked the link; he had received a direct live feed to Katie.

She's in her cage wearing the collar, gawd only knows what you're going through, still you're, "Alive."

Seeing Katie alive continued to sober him.

Wait, don't look too excited, they're probably watching, maybe listening too.

Woo moved to angle himself away from the obvious overhead camera. He had to angle his face to allow for an iris scan to open his phone.

There, I'm in. I've reached the collar google number, okay, look cool.

Moving discreetly, he sent what he thought was a safe message.

Seeing you on live link if receiving, turn around and lie down. Good girl. Now, behave. Seeya soon.

Woo set the monitor down. He had to close his eyes for a few minutes.

Following the flight from Seoul, the drive was thirteen hours. He had slept for a brief time in the car, then he had pretended to be asleep for another two hours. At one point, he perceived the car not moving, although the thug-escorts acted as if they were. It worried him enough to keep his other senses activated. When he faked snoring, one of the thugs whispered, "How long do we sit, do you know?"

"Hey, tight lip, not my concern, you know how this works, stick to the script."

If Woo had been sleeping, he might not have learned they were putting on a scripted show. As they went forward, he filtered out the apparent fake news, and attended to body language and innuendos to gain information. He was grateful for his instinct to pretend to drink the offered champagne, judging by the others, it had sleep drugs added.

Given the ambiance of his current location, and lack of sleep, Woo's eyes became too heavy to focus. He and his fellow agent were alive, and that was all he could think about.

Watching the monitors, Jones saw the phone hand off, noting the iris security on Woo's phone, which was no surprise to him. He felt pleased to see the man doing what he had predicted. At the same time, Jones felt insulted by Woo's poise.

How dare you come into my domain and think you can make up your own rules. You do not even look the least bit worthy.

One of the other monitors blinked. It was the deeper background information on Woo, and Jones knew if the man had any record in the past, it would be on the incoming report. Jones stopped watching Woo and turned to the intelligence. He did not get far down the page before laughing to himself.

Ha! Woo you are a buffoon, who obviously thinks more highly of yourself than you deserve. You are a flasher, can't keep your dick in your pants.

Jones' laugh had an evil ring to it, he heard himself and added a few purposeful "ha" syllables to entertain himself.

It's a wonder you could land a job at all. You are a dirty man, but here, it works in your favor. What about the money? You're a mere secretary, and not smart enough to have saved this much money. Where did your money come from? Heh, you're a fucking thief, aren't you? It speaks to the worn shoes. No self-respecting man would wear those shoes. You have no self-respect. It does not add up. I will pay your bitch a visit and see if 10 missed anything. I do not like thieves, as a rule, and you have already earned two strikes. If there is more to this creep's story, I will soon know.

Speaking in a leisurely fashion, Jones phoned Woo's keeper.

"Mary, congratulations, you have exceeded my expectations. Even I believed he had been stung by a bug. Perfect dose too. Only one more thing, please wake Mr. Woo, and escort him back to the platform. The tram will take him off your hands, and you can return to your regular duties. I will reward you during our next scheduled playtime. Be sure to wear the leathers I gave you; and bring your lipstick, the long-lasting kind. That is all."

CHAPTER 31

CIGAR TO HER RESCUE

"The better part of valor is discretion, in the which better part I have saved my life."

WILLIAM SHAKESPEARE

Ariel left a bag near the building, to retrieve after her event. Finding it on the run, she continued moving away as fast as she could. She slowed enough to pull out a hooded reversible sweatshirt and managed to get it on without stopping. She also had glasses and a gray wig in her bag, but presently, all her senses told her to keep moving away. Anxiety was setting her pace, and she urged herself to be invisible. Davis had tried several tricks, expecting to force her to move; she had been smarter. Slipping out the men's bathroom window was pure instinct; it was a good decision. It allowed her to leave on the opposite side of the building, furthest from the entrance, where Goodman had posted a fellow. Ariel suspected Goodman might have deduced her exit route, and she was not about to get cornered by him. Now, less than a hundred yards away from the venue, her mind clouded.

My dignity is in place, but at what cost? Boy did I make him look bad, though it was his own fault for trying to set me up. His game was exposed. He's a bad egg, a hoser if ever there was one. Hope he won't try to make trouble for me at the agency, I don't think it would be good for me. Damn that guy gave me the major creeps, and I don't believe it had anything to do with him being Caroline's brother, there is something about him that makes my skin crawl. I need to walk this off, and think, what should I do, maybe nothing? Maybe my hand will be forced?

The trepidation was not spinning her out, she would not allow it. She ran through a quick mental scenario, where she explained her actions to the supervisor, she had done nothing unprofessional.

His clocks were off by minutes. I had my own timer set, and I exited as per the contract. I left the clothing he had provided. And don't you think he would have synchronized them in real time unless he wanted to win my fee by cheating?

⌣⌣

Ariel's feelings of dread persisted. Before long, it occurred to her, the source of consternation in her gut was something different than defending herself from Goodman. It took a moment for her to understand where her feeling was coming from. She found a shadowed entryway to linger and took a slow breath. Straight away, the hair on Ariel's neck raised. Her inner voice spoke.

You're in trouble. Disappear, now.

There were goosebumps on Ariel's forearms which popped up when her reactive nose detected a male aftershave in the air. She stepped into the next public doorway along her path when the door opened.

It's a bookstore, a good place to change.

Ariel made no eye contact with the person exiting the shop. She slipped in behind, avoiding the door, and steered clear of the clerk behind the desk. It was luck he had turned to look at his cell phone, right as she passed the counter. Moving calmly but urgently, she went between the isles, then bent down, as if looking at the bottom shelf.

I cannot make a mistake.

Ariel's mind went back to the street she had come in on, she was trying to remember the nearby businesses she had seen earlier. Hearing the shop door open, she stayed low.

There's that aftershave again, but that doesn't mean he saw me come in.

"Hey dare, how ya doin'? You know, I'm tryin' to catch up with my teenage daughter, she's sposed to be studying for her SATs, huh-huh, shoulda worn my gym shoes. Didja see her come in da last few minutes?"

He's lying. That accent says he's not from around here.

The person behind the counter answered the man, "No one's come in, had a few teens go out the last couple of minutes though."

The stranger, not satisfied, asked, "Do ya have a washroom or a rear exit?"

"Yes, both are back that way, but the exit only leads to the dumpster alley, and my parking spot. No one ever goes back there."

Ariel froze.

No. You're not trapped, find your options.

Staying in her squatted position, Ariel swiftly turned her gray jacket inside out, showing a Walmart-blue underside. In the pocket was a short gray-haired wig, and large thick-glassed prescription eyeglasses. She pulled the wig onto her head as fast as possible. If seen, at least she would not appear to be young. Pulling a book from the shelf, she buried her face in it. She rose some, but stayed hunched, and waited.

Breathe, breathe, stay calm.

There were footsteps moving toward the rear of the store, sounds of doors opening, and falling shut. Ariel tuned into the breathing that went with the footsteps.

Definitely a man, he's pissed, and he's determined. I want to see him but can't take the chance. Gotta keep eyes down.

A few moments later, the steps and the aftershave returned, then grew closer. The man looked right past Ariel, as he looked down the aisles. Being crouched, helped her to look old, and bent.

It worked, he missed me, but I saw his shoes and pants. Big guy. Saw him standing around the entrance for Goodman's show.

The stranger went back out the front entrance, and on down to the south end of the street. Ariel waited in place, until the door opened with a small group of customers entering the bookstore. Her agile moves allowed her to get out unnoticed as they were coming in. Instinct told her to head north, even though it was the opposite direction she needed to go to get home. She did not have too far to get to a place where she might have caught a cab, but it did not feel safe.

Cab drivers will talk for very little money, can't chance it.

An outdoor cafe was steps away. She eyed a woman's floral sweater hanging on the back of the chair, and a large sunhat sitting on another chair.

Thanks this will help, and this.

Gathering the items easily, and unseen, Ariel added the hat to her wardrobe immediately, and walked another two blocks. Finding an electrical box to duck behind, she switched the sweater for her hoody, and stuffed the hoody into her pants. The sweater hung low, so she had sort of a bubble-butt look. There was a bus coming, and she could see the next stop ahead; she would have loved to jump on, her feet and back were killing her after the two-hour shift. It occurred to her that buses had cameras, and knowing she was being chased, she decided it was best not to be recorded.

If the man looking for me is reasonably convinced I am still in the area, and if he's a resourceful type, he could be able to check any recording devices.

Another block further north, Ariel dropped the stolen sunhat in some bushes and moved on, reasoning the hat might draw attention. Not feeling safe yet, and needing some rest, Ariel looked around for another place to hide until darkness could provide her with better cover.

That car is unlocked and looks like no one around.

The runner made her way into the backseat, making herself as small as possible. She clung to the floorboard of the car for support. The sun was on the horizon, and the shadows in the car would help to hide her form.

Why, why now, why here? I'll just rest a few minutes; I must catch my breath and think.

The car was warm, and she was sweating from the running, but she felt a shiver that started at the back of her neck.

Am I overreacting? Surely the guy has given up on catching me by now. Just in case my senses are giving a valid warning, I do need to lock the doors.

Carefully without lifting herself, she turned and reached for the button to lock the door. She pulled the hoodie out of her pants, turned it the gray side out, and hid herself under it, as much as she could. Within a minute of her actions, she heard some crashing sounds close by. Then, the sound of someone kicking a metal object, she heard it scraping on the pavement, then bounce off a larger metal object, then, more scraping sounds. Her breath, barely calmed for a few seconds, now began rushing out of her mouth. Running footsteps and the sounds of voices were approaching, and although she hid under her sweatshirt, she could see a flashing light bouncing in and then out of the car. Her heart was beating so fast, she was beginning to get dizzy.

You must get a hold of yourself, now. Breathe. Kids? A gang? They're nearing. Gangster wannabes by the sound of it.

A car alarm began sounding, followed by another, and then the sound of breaking glass made her jump.

That was close!

The youth gang had just moved past her hiding place.

Thank God they didn't break the glass on this car! Sounds like they have moved on.

～∽～

A police siren sounded from afar, but it was getting louder. Taking her chances, she adjusted her body to be able to peer out the windows. Doing a slow sweep of the area, she saw people standing around just yards away.

Okay, concerned citizens, they fit in. They came out to see what caused the car alarms. Oh my God, I hope the owner of this car does not find me.

Continuing her visual sweep all around, it did not take long for her eyes to spot a figure standing back in the shadows. The figure's face was obscured, but the form looked familiar.

It's him.

Pulse racing now, Ariel's mind was torn between freeze or flee. It was clear the figure was waiting, looking. Ariel lowered herself and stayed in place. What felt like an hour, was only another few minutes, and then there were blue and red lights, flashing. Police were finally on the street, collecting reports on damages caused by the young hoodlums. The added lights in the area allowed for better seeing in the dark car. Looking around revealed a man's overcoat, and hat on the front seat. Ariel felt the need for a different perspective. She kept her head down and managed to do a body hurdle over the seat, neatly rolling onto the floor in the front. She found items in the pockets of the coat and thought they could be added to her disguise tricks. Then, without hesitation, she pulled all the contents out of the middle console.

Gloves, compact umbrella, dark sunglasses, some bills and change, a cigar, and a lighter.

Ariel did not want the money but thought it best that the car appeared as if a thief had cleaned it out. As an afterthought, she reached under the driver's seat. Her hand recognized the cold metal she found; it was a gun. She had not held a weapon since she shot her captor; and was not pleased to have found it, still, it would leave with her.

It's a Glock, and how do I know that? I hope my waistband is snug enough to hold it.

Putting the other items into the front of her tucked shirt, Ariel wanted to give her mid-area more fullness. She knew the interior light might give her away when she opened the door; she told herself it was better than getting found in the car. Ariel concealed her face with a gloved hand, as the door opened. The nearby police presence provided a good enough distraction for the looky-loos' and likely steered the thug-type who had followed her, away. Like a stealth cat, she made her getaway from all the lights and activity.

<center>~~~</center>

Caroline's house was still several miles away, and although she felt the adrenaline slowly draining away her energy, she kept walking.

Completely exhausted, she did not mind walking slow and old-manly-like. She resolved to match the masculine outerwear as much as possible. If seen, her feet could give her gender away, but the overcoat was long, and stooping helped keep her shoes undercover. The streets had few people, which did not help her apprehension.

A car moving slower than the speed limit was coming up on her left. Reaching into the pockets, she pulled out the cigar and lighter. Stopping to light the cigar, she prayed she would not cough. By the time the car passed, she exhaled a large plume of smoke. Her vision was impaired by the dark glasses, but she thought she saw a man behind the wheel. After it passed, a nondescript van went by, then made a U-turn in the intersection ahead.

There's more than one looking for me? Maybe Davis figured out I've been impersonating his sister? No doubt he wants revenge for failing to make me fail, and he's got a couple of low life friends to do his dirty work.

The van returned, this time on the far side of the street; it slowed. A blurred face looked right at her. Her gloved hands at the ready, one holding the cigar in front of her face, the other, reached up to tip the hat at the passerby, in a neighborly manner. The driver ducked back into the dark of the vehicle, satisfied by the illusion, and ready to look elsewhere.

~~

Another hour had passed before Ariel arrived at Caroline's house. Bone tired, once inside, her first thought was to pull the gun from her pants. Instincts she did not realize she possessed, helped her to look to see if the gun was loaded; it was. Needing a hug after her ordeal, she reached around to hug herself gently.

It is time to move on. Caroline, I have no idea what kind of game your brother is playing, and I will not stay to find out. If your spirit needs a new place to live, you are more than welcome to come with me. Loyalville, I hope you are as safe as you seem to be. I'd rather not ever have to use this gun.

CHAPTER 32

PULLING FOR DONALD

"Whatever you are, be a good one."

ABRAHAM LINCOLN

Standing in the cool night temperatures, under the expansive blanket of stars, anxious for her husband, and his heart, Debbi Harrison was fighting the urge to begin her own search for clues on the 10:15 pm intruders. Their neighborhood was safe, still, someone had cut the wires on their security system. Based on Debbi's experience, the local police were not polished enough to investigate what they refused to admit; a bad element had come to Loyalville. Local and county officials were numbered among the 346 residents in the small town, where everyone knew everyone, and people watched one another's back. Debbi watched too. Working at the local postal store gave her superior *perspective* into the lives of her neighbors.

The chief was wrong in assuming that this was a random happening. I know it is much more ominous, my gut says this was no false alarm, in fact, it screams trouble. But my man is in more trouble, and right now, he comes first.

When the patient was settled in, Debbi climbed into the back of the ambulance, and landed a kiss on his forehead. Choking back her mixed emotions, Debbi swallowed hard before speaking to her husband, "I will drive my car over to the hospital. I won't be far behind. I'll grab a few things you'll need and lock up the house. You. You need to listen to what they say. You are not in charge. Don't go trying to take over, I mean it, and don't you dare let that heart of yours behave badly." Calmer after the admonition, she added, "My honorable partner for life, we have many travels yet to make together."

The last words Debbi offered, meant more to Donald, because he had written them to her in their marriage vows, seven years earlier. He smiled, softening his eyes, and managed a wink, showing he understood her underlying sentiment. He did not try to speak; the oxygen mask would have garbled his words. His hand found his forehead, touching the place where she had kissed him. She took hold of his hand to assist him, sensing his need to touch her lips. The paramedic, Liz, watched the tender display. As a first responder, it gave her pause.

They have a special bond, don't see that very often, especially with a man who has so much grit and a woman who absolutely reeks of tenacity. What an oddly inspiring couple, sure do hope I can find a partner like that someday.

The petite Mrs. Harrison maneuvered around the gurney without disturbing her man. Before stepping out of the vehicle, she took one hand and gently pressed it upon Liz's shoulder, "Thank you Liz, and to quote Emerson, 'to know even one life has breathed easier because you have lived, this is to have succeeded,' keep up the good work. I'm proud of you."

"Thank you, Mrs. Harrison. It's my honor to serve, and our duty to get this man to his doctor, safe and sound. You drive safe too, we've got this."

～⌣～

The local "investigative" team were police who doubled as crime investigators, with little experience in local crime scenes; there had been no local crimes. Consequently, they were always up for "practice" if a situation called for it. Chief Ropier decided the interrupted *job* merited extra eyes, especially given he was limited by his casted leg for another week, and he was technically on desk duty. The fact that this incident transpired on his own street, at his long-time friend's house, who was now on his way to the emergency room, in critical condition, unable to conduct his own Sherlock-probing, meant this very personal offence was up to him to resolve.

The fading sound of the ambulance sirens left Bob Ropier queasy. He was upset about his friend's condition, and he was in pain after skipping his prescription dose, choosing to be more alert while away from his desk, even if he was not driving. The forensic players were gathered on site, Chief Ropier passed authority to the Crime Scene Leader, as per the protocol, and he stayed until a permanent record of the event was conducted. Donald was a man of integrity, and he would want to know all evidence had been collected and documented properly. Pictures of the scene, including the bullet hole left by Donald's accidental gunshot, and video of the footprints in the mud, were taken. They also dusted for fingerprints at the box where the wire was severed, and there was an immediate effort to canvass the neighborhood for possible witnesses.

With the i's dotted and the t's crossed, and dawn, only a couple of hours away, Ropier said his good-byes to the team. Ten houses down the street felt like ten miles to Ropier, it made him thankful for his cane.

Thank God Cheryl made me hold onto this dang walking stick, I must insist they give that gal a bonus, she's a saint for puttin' up with the likes of me.

The chief had just found his walking rhythm when his phone ringer sounded. Fumbling with the phone, Bob did not see the caller identification and assumed it was Cheryl checking to see if he needed a ride home; it was like her to worry that way.

"Ah Cheryl, I've only got another eight houses to go before I hit my front step, Whatcha got?"

"Chief Ropier? This is special agent Stanovich with the Federal Bureau of Investigation. Do you have a few minutes to speak privately?"

"Whoa, what? Someone's got jokes, not that I…"

"No Sir, this is not a joke. On the contrary, I think you'll want to hear what I know."

Cut off before he finished his thought, the caller made it clear he was not jesting. Moments later, two dark-windowed SUVs pulled up alongside the weary Chief of police.

Mrs. Harrison spent the rest of the night in the hospital. Her sleuthing put on hold until her man's condition improved. The night was not an easy one for Donald, it took a considerable amount of effort to keep him calm. Several times, he woke confused, and called out for his wife; he needed to see she had not been hurt. Each time his agitation was eased by seeing her reassuring eyes, and feeling her hands take hold of his own. By late morning, his vitals were steady, the staff had stopped coming in and out, and Donald was in a deep sleep. Debbi closed her own eyes for a quiet minute, not that her mind could rest.

The situation was far from peaceful. The mysterious intruders left few clues. The Police found some footprints in the mud outside their home, which led back to the pavement where they began; indicating the feet likely had a waiting vehicle. The shoe prints were larger than Debbi's, and too small to be Donald's, otherwise they were not distinct. The cut wire on the home security system was clean, no fingerprints and there were no other damages. If the gun had not been discharged inside, Debbi believed the police would not have become involved.

It was somewhat comforting that someone beside herself cared, and Bob Ropier's sincere interest caused Debbi to wonder if he had perhaps found anything new. Given her husband's deep sleep, Debbi moved to the CCU waiting room. She would be a few doors down from the central nursing station, and still in sight of her husband's room door; close enough to see any movement in or out. She decided to use Donald's phone, dialing Ropier's private cell number. It took a few rings more than she expected, then the police chief's steady voice came on the line.

"Donald?"

"Hello Chief, no, this is Debbi Harrison, I hope you don't mind I called you on your personal phone."

"Of Course not, you know you can call me anytime Debbi. How's he doing?"

"The staff have worked diligently to keep him stable; he is resting now. But his heart is tired. So, right now, it is wait and see."

"Everyone's pulling for Donald. And our prayers are with you too."

"I'd prefer prayers all go for his heart; he is not a man who is ready to slow down. Bob, I don't mean to be rudely direct, but tell me, have you found and arrested the guilty party."

I don't think she's going to like my answer, guess this is not the best time to ask her why she is growing deadly poison in her garden.

"I wish that I could say we had, ya know I'd have called if we found anything. I'm sorry, got nothing new, except the folks in the neighborhood watch program activated their phone tree for y'all. It's a proud day to be a Loyalvillian. Darn near every resident in Loyalville has been called or visited by a neighbor and made aware of what happened last night. My team and I have also reached out to other blues, Truckee, Susanville Police, and Plumas County Sheriff. As far as home burglaries, none reported lately."

How about cutting the Mr. Roger's act and doing your job, and I can hear something in your tone that says you've got another agenda on your mind...I wonder what you're up to Ropier?

Debbi barely kept her thoughts to herself, "No burglaries, hmmm, have you considered that this was not intended to be a burglary?"

"Uh, we have no suspects, and no certain motive, unless there is something you're not telling me? Naw, I know you and Donald don't have any secrets. And no enemies, so yep, all we can do is keep our eyes and ears open and remain alert. Believe me little lady, we have your back."

In his mind, Bob was doing his best *Columbo* impression. *Can't say the FBI will trust you, but if my buddy trusts you, I gotta hold his place in line.*

It was 2 p.m., when the attending physician made it to Donald's bedside for *morning* rounds. Debbi had been vigilant in watching for changes in his condition, putting off other agendas until it was clear they would be keeping him. She thought he looked gray and expected he would not be released before his normal color returned. Donald lay resting as the doctor spoke.

"As you can hear, he is still struggling for breath. The wheezing is not good, his edema has not improved much, but I'm confident in saying he'll be as ornery as ever in no time. His confusion and dizziness during the incident, likely due to a lack of oxygen, a symptom of his CHF. Donald was likely pushing himself too hard."

"I agree there was a bit of excitement, including before the incident. Doctor, I must confess he and I were having rather vigorous sex."

"Oh. I see. Yes, that could have triggered his uneven breathing. I suggest you plan less active, uhh, everything, until Donald's heart starts keeping up. When the edema fully improves, he will begin to feel much better. Right now, it's best to skip bed activity; bed rest is a priority."

Donald stirred upon hearing the doctor's words, "Huh? What? Let's not be too hasty Doc, a guy must have something to live for."

Donald's waking up alert was a good sign, but the doctor immediately became serious. She checked his IV and asked him questions as she did so. He coughed more than he spoke, until she gave up and stopped him.

"Slow down big fella, we'll talk later. You are improving, just not fast enough to get a pass. It looks like you will be here another day. I will be back to check on you tomorrow."

The doctor left the room.

Debbi, saddened by her worry, fought emotion back, then declared with a mischievous grin, "I'm happy to stick to *oral*, when you're ready, you won't have to lift a finger."

"My little smurf, when my time finally comes, I'm hoping you'll take me out while riding on my joystick." Donald held back another coughing fit, and managed to add, "You can write that down as my end-of-life method; if it comes to that."

Donald quieted after seeing he had cheered his girl. Her smile hid itself in the shadow of her caring eyes, then found its way to her mouth.

"We may not have a typical romance, but you, my honorable husband, are the man of my dreams. And now, you need to rest. In case of miraculous recovery, I'm your Smurfette, only yours and utterly ready for riding your joystick."

Fully grinning, Debbi's face was all Donald could think of when he closed his eyes. Seeing her big smile eased his nervousness, he accepted his need for sleep, and drifted off. Debbi, appreciative for their exchange, decided to check her own phone. She had two missed calls during the morning hours. One was from Hia, and one from her boss. Hia's message was brief, and Debbi could tell something was wrong; all she said was, "Can you talk?" Before responding to Hia's message, Debbi listened to Tom's message.

"Hey Debbi, I hate to bother you, but your hairdresser friend, Hia, she just came in looking for you. She wasn't herself. I hate to say it, I think she was trying to hide bruises behind makeup, it didn't hide much. She didn't look good. I said she might like to wait to get you on the phone, but she ran off like a scared cat. Anyway, thought you'd want to know. Hope Donald is going to be okay; you take any time off you need, Cookie said she'd help until you are ready to come back. Uh, okay, bye."

Intuition told Debbi to make a visit to Hia, in person, rather than calling. She reasoned the CCU staff had Donald's best interest at heart, in addition to being skilled in cardiac care. They assured her he would sleep and would not be moved from the floor, where he was under their close monitoring. Several nurses encouraged her to go home for a break and to get her own rest, so, Debbi decided to trust the staff with Donald's care. Alerting the nurses at the desk, she said, "I'll be back, but please call me if anything changes or if he wakes asking for me."

CHAPTER 33

WARRIOR ENCUMBRANCES

"God turns you from one feeling to another and teaches by means of opposites so that you will have two wings to fly, not one."

RUMI

Stunned to see the "closed" sign in the window of the salon, instead of parking on the street in front, Debbi opted to pull around to the little alley, where Hia parked in the back.

Hia's car is gone? It's her busy day at the salon and she isn't here? Maybe she called to tell me she had to leave, but where would she go and what about the bruises?

Deciding to call the shop before leaving, Debbi thought she could leave a message for Hia. It rang through to her cheery message but was picked up before reaching the end. The voice answering was unfamiliar to Debbi.

A sharp male greeting, "Hello, who's this?"

"Hello? I must have the wrong number; I was calling for Hia? Who have I reached?"

Debbi instinctively knew she did not want to identify herself, and she was thankful for the blocked caller I.D. function.

"Hia's sick. What you want?"

"Oh, I just wanted to make a hair appointment, I hope it's not too serious, is she there? I'd like to wish her well."

"I make Hia's appointments now. She'll open on Friday. Name?"

There was no denying, something was very wrong. Debbi knew Hia did not have anyone making her appointments; she did it all herself. If she did hire, it would have been a woman, Hia did not want men working in her shop.

Keeping her tone light, Debbi said, "Oh that's okay, I will wait until Hia's feeling better and talk to her."

"I make all appointments now, gimme name and what you want done."

"Oh, sorry, I, uh," Debbi tried to think of what to say, "I'll need my hair done today, I can't wait…"

The phone line went dead before she finished her sentence. She was certain that Hia was in some kind of trouble. Debbi knew that Hia had some rough relatives, and based on the accent, she assumed she had just spoken to one. Lily spoke up right away.

Small man's complex. Thinks he can bully Hia and get away with it. He's bad. He doesn't belong here. He needs to go.

Before deciding what to do next, Hia's car, a red Hyundai, pulled into the alley. Two young men, both Vietnamese descents, exited the car. Lily saw it first, a gun tucked into the back pants of one of the men. He had reached into the backseat to pull out a keg of beer. The other looked around, before looking up toward the windows of Hia's residence. Lily whispered.

That's beer and a gun, and a guilty look.

The man produced a key, unlocking the building's private stairwell gate, and the man with the beer ascended the stairs ahead of him. It was light, but clouds and the afternoon shadows of the buildings offered some shady cover. The remaining man peered through the gate, not seeing Debbi, but looking toward her car. Debbi had already slumped down into her seat, and given her height, she could not be seen behind the wheel. The man squinted, squaring his face with the driver side window. He was not satisfied with the view from his distance. He moved toward her. Debbi slumped further down, losing her sight of him. She held her breath, knowing he would be at her car in ten to twelve steps.

You'll need to go on the defense, in ten, nine, eight, seven, six…

The gun's safety was clicked off, Debbi braced herself for the inevitable encounter until interrupted by the thunderous sounds of an approaching waste disposal vehicle. She stayed in place as she listened to the familiar sounds of steel on steel, the garbage dumpster was lifted and dumped into the truck and returned to the ground. Waiting for the busy sounds to recede, Debbi sensed the brief interruption altered the course. Gradually, she looked above the shadows only to find the man had turned and followed the other up the stairs. She saw him enter Hia's residence and close the door behind him. Hesitating a few additional seconds to see that no one was standing at Hia's window, the self-appointed defender, backed out of the spot and driveway, then turned her mind to the many deadly assault weapons in her arsenal. Lily's voice was in her head now.

Just use the Glock 43 with its six-round magazine.

Debbi resisted the voice by choosing to trust herself, and she continued to the graveyard, parking in the obscure tree-lined lot near the mortuary building. During the brief visit to the Yan tomb, Debbi organized a to-go bag, and added a bullet proof vest and two body holsters to her wardrobe. She left her car, and taking the path less traveled, she would walk the few blocks back to Hia's. To avoid running into people, she kept to the alley street. Given daylight and the buzzing foot traffic in Loyalville, Debbi questioned herself.

You know you could be overreacting. If she is sick, it is possible that she closed early and was forced to ask for help. Maybe your visit will have to be postponed until there are fewer witnesses?

Lily did not hold back her opinion.

If Hia needed help, she would call you, and she did. Her cousins, if that's who those men were, would be the last people on earth she would trust with her keys. She does not ask men to her residence and doesn't drink. You know she is being forced against her will. We need to rescue her.

Not far from Hia's building, Debbi was preparing to scale the back of the adjacent building. Her plan was to gain access to Hia's bedroom window, without being seen. A row of Ponderosa Pines along the sidewall, provided good cover above the first five feet off the ground. Ordinarily, Debbi could climb like a squirrel, but her pack was heavy. Lily advised her to toss the bag ahead. Eying the best branches from below, Debbi was preparing to fling the pack above her head. As she released the bag, the unexpected sound of a car horn that came from the front of the building made her jerk. The bag bounced off a branch and landed back on the ground. Picking it back up, Debbi checked herself and looked around. She thought she saw the familiar face of Sage, in a passing car; the pesky crossing guard who had become a person of interest. Standing behind the trunk of the tree as much as possible, Debbi constructed an alibi for her actions, in case Sage should suddenly present herself, as she had recently done in the parking garage. Debbi felt perspiration beading up on her forehead, her pulse increased. A few seconds passed, then Lily surged again.

Don't doubt yourself, nor your abilities and do not be afraid of Sage. She is too heavy and slow to follow you. Hia needs your help. If Sage becomes collateral damage, so be it.

Debbi's gloved hands reached into the pack and produced two throwing stars, then swung the bag to her back. Clutching the stars, reaching up, and sinking them into the tree trunk, the slight figure pulled herself up the tree, until she could stand on branches. The remaining climb was quick to the roof, where she could easily walk to the end of the building.

Next, she had an eight-foot gap to jump, with an additional foot to reach a solid landing spot. Nine feet had looked easier in her mind's eye. Debbi looked and listened. Presently, there were few people on the street below, most were in their cars, and Sage's car was no longer in sight. Timing was important, Debbi would run and leap the distance. Debbi unpacked her shozoku and holsters, putting all into her pack. She needed to toss the bag ahead.

You cannot afford a miss; you must fly like a bird.

The noise of the weighted bag could not be avoided, and it had to be landed flat to prevent it from bouncing off the angle of the roof. Debbi could visualize her success but hesitated. A *knowing* was taking her attention. She felt a tingling in her feet and hands, as if they were going numb. Debbi closed her eyes. She saw Hia, who could not move or make a sound. The dim premonition included a larger, darker image approaching, a powerful being, one with evil motives, and it was nearing. She snapped out of her mind, and back into her body, hearing herself say aloud, "There is no time to lose."

Debbi would need to part with her *warrior encumbrances*. Like a practiced field and track athlete, with limited space, she turned in a tight circle to gain momentum. Holding her backpack like a discus thrower aiming for the moon, she passed it next to her body twice before releasing it. It landed with a thump, several feet from the edge. No bounce. It was her turn, and she was fully committed. Starting as far back as she could, she ran with all her might, landing three solid steps before the big leap. A gazelle flight in mid-air, with a gymnast somersault, ending the suspense, and Debbi was back on her feet.

I made it!

Lily spoke up.

Why play around with the gas, I say shoot first and kill them before they hurt you.

Repacking her weapons and subsonic ammunition, Debbi added her Sig to her right shoulder holster, her short Maxim 9 mm, to the inside waistband holster, and a dagger to her left ankle sheath. Her inner pockets held other tools; guitar strings, should strangling become necessary, and two copper vaporizer bottles, containing Fluothane. Reaching inside her backpack, she pulled out a gas mask, the kind with a canister cartridge. It had been customized for her petite features; she owned two of them. Before donning it, she took hold of her cell phone. She pulled up Hia's number, to be called when ready, then slipped it into the small chest pocket. Since it was daylight, the mask would help protect her identity, in case anyone came into view during the job. When the mask was on, she adjusted the straps, then pulled her hoody over her head.

Ready, set, go kill the bad guys.

Her 9 mm mankiller led the way, ducking where necessary, the nimble figure made her way to Hia's eyebrow dormer, the one above her bedroom window. Once steady alongside the eves, arms dropped to her side, Debbi peered into the space. Her sight was limited, due to the mask, and the drapery, but she saw Hia tied, face down, naked and spread eagle, in the middle of her bed. It appeared that she had been gagged and blindfolded as well.

Good that she's alive and better she cannot see what is about to happen. She and countless others will not be bothered by them ever again.

Looking past Hia's bed, into the living space, Debbi saw a man. He sat on a dining room chair a few feet away from Hia's doorway. Across from him, sat three other men. Debbi could see their shadows moving. They had gathered on Hia's couch, hunched around a coffee table. The smoke plumes said most, if not all were smoking. The shadows lifted their glasses of beer with ease. Debbi reached into her pocket, and hit the call button, and the speaker phone option. She dropped the phone back in the pocket, knowing the necessary sounds would still be heard. The ringing phone was not answered immediately. The casual greeting was followed by a gasp, when the eerie sound effects of Lily's raspy words caught the man's attention, "Prepare to die."

The call ended abruptly, and two of the three men were now on their feet, agitated by the disturbance. Debbi pulled the phone out, and hit the call button a second time, again dropping it back in the pocket to get the right sound effects. She breathed steadily. The call was answered, and passed around, each of the men listened to the sounds of the respirator, before hanging up. Debbi once again pulled the phone from her pocket and laid it on the sill, then soundlessly pulled herself up to perch on top of the dormer. One of her copper vaporizer cans was readied, and her gloved finger was placed on the dispenser trigger.

As Lily predicted, one of the men returned the call to the *unknown number*. The ring tone resonated through the glass. The men followed the sound. Seeing the phone on the outside windowsill, caused the one-armed man to ready his gun toward the phone. The men's faces said they were in disbelief. The gun moved to direct another to open the window. It was a French window. Slowly the framed glass opened inwardly. Looking down, Debbi saw the nose of the handgun emerge. She reached her arm over, and liberally sprayed her gas, catching the gunman directly in the face. He fell backward within seconds gasping for air. The gun dropped, and now sat half-in, and half-out of the window. The other men, caught unaware, moved stiffly, unsure of how to respond. After the fallen quieted, another man conservatively advanced. Before he had his hand fully on the weapon, another spray of sleeping gas was dispensed.

Two bad men down, but not dead, move swiftly now, there is more to do.

Debbi did not hesitate. She moved to grab the loose gun, as she launched herself through the window. The sighting of the black clad, masked Ninja caused the last man, evidently unarmed, to run for the front door. There were several locks to disengage, and he was not able to complete the task before another plume of gas was released. He choked and fell over. All the men, unconscious before any words could be formed.

Wasting no time, Debbi dragged each of the men into the ensuite bathroom. She was grateful they were all of small stature. After catching her breath, she turned the men, exposing their faces. Debbi sprayed a lethal amount of deadly gas and left them to die. She carefully stuffed a towel in the gap at the bottom of the door, before rushing to consider Hia's immediate needs.

There was bruising around Hia's neck, and both eyes were dark and swollen. Her wrists, ankles, and genitals, all red, and blue with swelling. She had been crying, her face was streaked with black eye makeup. Debbi was relieved not to see blood, but she was unconscious. In a matter of ten minutes, Debbi had Hia freed from the ties, dressed in loose activewear, and wrapped in a clean blanket. She dragged the unconscious woman with the blanket, holding her under her arms, off the bed, and over onto the couch. Debbi wanted Hia far from the lingering gasses in the bedroom, knowing the side effects could be severe. The windows were pulled wide open, to allow fresh air into the room, and Debbi retrieved her backpack from the rooftop hiding place. Hia's pulse was strong, and she was moving on her own, as if having a nightmare. Debbi administered an intravenous sedative, then fitted Hia with a gas mask.

Just sleep dear Hia. You are safe now.

Debbi knew Hia would sleep through the next few hours, while she set to begin disappearing the bodies. Down in the hair salon, Debbi found several gallons of sodium hydroxide, which would serve a different purpose than straightening hair. She also pulled the three high-heat hair dryers up the stairs, then, Lily took over.

Returning to the bathroom with the items she needed, Lily pulled off all personal items, and lumped the naked bodies into the over-sized freestanding bathtub. The lye was prepared and poured over the dead. She had done this work before; it was laborious, but very satisfying. She worked quietly, and efficiently.

At least you all had the courtesy of fitting in the tub.

The wallets, phones, jewelry, and other identifying items were all packed in Debbi's bag and Lily relinquished control over Debbi, retreating back to the shadows of her mind. The rest of the men's belongings, all the trash, cigarette buttes, and bottles were bagged; later, Debbi would incinerate them. Debbi stripped down to her own sweat suit and packed her gear and weapons into Hia's closet. She put them into a laundry basket, and then covered the items with the soiled laundry. Debbi would finish the *clean up* later. Now her thoughts switched to Hia and getting her away from the scene. She grabbed Hia's car keys, disinfectant wipes, a garbage bag, and made her way downstairs. As she walked, Debbi wiped all the surfaces, particularly doorknobs and the hand-railings.

Once outside, she breathed deeply for the first time in several hours. The job was not nearly done, and Debbi felt briefly lightheaded. Her mind adjusted itself with a reframe. Telling herself to feel relief; there was no blood, and there were no witnesses. She calmed herself with some hand tapping, as she went down to Hia's car. The cleaning also helped. The wiping of surfaces was a *normal*, and *healthy* behavior, which reimposed her conscious. Debbi gave it her full attention, beginning with the exterior. When every inch had been wiped, she entered the vehicle. A scrap of paper on the floorboard, caught her immediate attention, along with a few chunks of mud on the mats. Debbi picked up the discarded wad and examined it. It gave her pause. Her name, Loyalville Post, and her home address were handwritten on it, and it was not the first time she had seen the scrawl.

The mystery is solved. Now the wire cutters on Hia's coffee table make sense. Those creeps were the ones responsible for our late-night scare, and they were the ones to leave me the warning note. I wonder how I got in their crosshairs; too late to ask them now.

With the interior wiped clean, Debbi could think about how to transport Hia. Debbi hoped Hia would be able to walk down the stairs. Before returning for her, Debbi phoned the hospital from the car, to check on her husband. She did not ask to speak to him, knowing she was still too overwhelmed to hide her feelings. The staff reported Donald would be ready for discharge by 4 o'clock the following day, and there was no need to visit in the interim, since he was currently sleeping soundly. Debbi was pleased she would have more time.

~~

In and out of consciousness, but aware she was with Debbi, Hia did her best, willing her body to cooperate. Wanting to thank her savior who was taking her down the stairs, and helping her into her car, all she could do was weep. Her confused mind was working desperately to erase the past 24 hours. She saw the men were gone, and was grateful Debbi was not asking questions about them. Her head pounded, and that was the least of her pain. Not only did she want the peace of sleep, Hia was also having difficulty keeping her eyes open. The comforting smell of chicken broth brought her back into the present, after hours of sleep.

Waking with a startled breath, Hia saw her friend, "Debbi? Where am I? Where are they?"

"Hia, you're safe. You are in my home. This is our guest room. Donald keeps his outdoor clothes in the closet, and you'll have to live with the antlers on the wall, but otherwise, this room and ensuite is all yours as long as you need. The kitchen is out and to the left. Just through the kitchen, the back door opens into our garden. Next to the back door is the garage. Your car is parked in there, not that you'll be ready to drive for a few days at least."

The eyes looking back were still dulled. Sitting next to her on the bed, Debbi soothed, "You need your rest. It is no trouble for you to stay, no problem at all. Here now, how about a little broth, I'm sure your body needs it."

"Thank you, thank you. Thank goodness you found me. You get my message, and you come help me. Oh, what about Mr. Donald? Isn't he in hospital?"

Hia's trauma now finding her awareness, she reached to her own neck, and then noticed her wrists. Fear that felt like shame, made it hard to find her words. Seeing Debbi's kind eyes, she ventured, "What about Dien, and the others, did they come back?"

Holding the bowl, to allow the woman to drink from it directly, Debbi spoke softly, "Here, now drink. After hearing your message, I called you, and someone else answered, I think it was Dien. He said you were sick and would not let me speak to you. I knew his story was fishy, so I threatened to involve the police. He hung up. I called again, before arriving, no one answered, so I didn't bother with the police. Your door was locked, so I came in through the roof, through your bedroom window, actually."

More humbly after reading the emotion on Hia's shamed face, Debbi continued, "I found you on your bed. I untied and dressed you, and brought you here, in your car. You probably should be seen by a doctor. We can go together. Donald is doing better, but he will not be released until later today. There is plenty of time to have you checked at the hospital or the Urgent Care, whatever is best for you?"

"Oh Debbi, I so embarrassed, and so so sorry, please no police, and no doctors. I was bullied up a bit, but I'm okay, I'll be okay," choking back tears as her last words were spoken.

The dirty condoms found all around her body on the bed, told a different story. It appeared the men had gone at Hia repeatedly for many hours. Still, Debbi would honor Hia's wishes; if it helped to pretend, she was not raped, Debbi wouldn't say otherwise.

"I'm not sure what you have been through Hia, but I do have a "morning after pill" if you want to take it, just in case?"

"I'll take it. Thank you again. Thank you for letting me stay here. I don't want to be work for you, but if they come back, at least I won't be there."

Touching her forehead gently, Debbi added, "We can talk more later, after you have more rest. I have crackers and juice on the dresser over there if you would like? I will leave them for you. There, good girl for drinking all your broth. Now, here's water, and the pill. Good, now rest. I'm guessing you may feel better after more sleep."

"Thank you, thank you good lady."

Debbi tucked her snuggly under the covers, and added an extra soft pillow to the bed, as she stood up.

"Here's a good pillow to hug, it always makes me feel better to have something to hold onto."

Hia hugged as was suggested, her eyelids heavy with sleep. Debbi did not want to cause her more pain, but she had to ask one question,

"Hia, can you say how many, how many, bullied you?"

Her lip quivered, as if the telling were on herself, "My cousin, Dien. It was my cousin, and two of his crew, it was just the three, they work together."

"No worries then, they left, and they were probably guilty of other crimes too, just the mention of the authorities, and off they ran. I doubt they will be coming back."

CHAPTER 34

NOT MYSELF TODAY

"Be yourself; everyone else is already taken."

OSCAR WILDE

Urgent to find a new home, with a pile of money temporarily stashed in the Diamond Ski Hill seasonal lockers, Ariel left the Tahoe area and set off to Loyalville, dressed as Trin. She had been following her intuition closely, she took bus rides in the wrong direction and then, doubled back to her destination. She believed it was telling her to stay away from Reno. She decided to return to Loyalville's downtown Main Street. Her first stop was Betty's, the local diner, she had worked up an appetite while riding on the buses. She looked in the window before entering.

Pretty crowded, good, they won't notice one more.

As she walked in, there was a lighthearted energy among the diners, tapping their toes to *Thibodeaux's* song, *My Baby Don't Wear No Drawers*. Ariel had never heard the song before and could not refrain from laughing at the lyrics. As she did, Betty, the apparent owner, greeted her, adding, "Don't tell me, with those tiny feet, you must be a friend of Waylon's."

Laughing despite her nerves, or maybe because of them, *Trin* offered, "Yup, just thought I'd wear clothes today, to throw everyone off the trail."

With that, Betty laughed herself, heartily, then announced, "Welcome to Betty's, I'm Betty, and how would ya like to be addressed, we are a friendly bunch around these parts."

Remembering her persona, Ariel lowered her voice, speaking cautiously, "You can call me mister, if that is what you're asking, Trin is my first name."

"Alrighty then, Mr. Trin, you can sit anywhere that's open, but if you sit at the counter, you'll likely get quicker service, and it's Jambalaya Day, Nawlins style. If you want some then tell Nadine as soon as you hit the stool, the pot's getting low," reported Betty, while looking over her shoulder.

There were three empty stools at the counter, *Trin* chose the one in the center, lifting her leg as she had seen men do, essentially trying not to be *graceful.* Then, as practiced in group therapy, *Trin*, eyes wide, made eye-contact with the men around, to demonstrate male-ish confidence. The counter waitress plopped a cup of coffee, and a glass of ice water in front of *Trin*, while talking to the cook through the serving window. *Trin* took it as a sign that *he* was being treated like everyone else.

This place is neat, seems like good people.

Addressing her new patron, Nadine had stopped her multi-tasking and noticed the person at her counter was not a regular.

"Oh, hi there, sorry, did you want coffee?"

"Yes, thank you, coffee's fine, and I'd like to try the Jambalaya."

"Woooo-hooooo! Listen up everyone, last bowl going out on the counter!"

The lively announcement was made for the whole staff to hear, then to *Trin*, Nadine added, "Sorry, it's the way here, I hope we don't put you off, ya seem like a sorta shy fella?"

"Thanks, I'm not really comfortable in a spotlight, and I don't need special treatment either. You all just do what you always do, I can go with the flow," *Trin* mustered a self-assured tone.

Following the last bowl declaration, the Cajun music was switched, and the melodic sounds of *James Taylor, You've Got a Friend*, filled the diner. *Trin* enjoyed the meal, and the atmosphere, and found *himself* at ease enough to search all the faces in the room. The conversations were ongoing, and expressive, as if the speakers had nothing to hide. Laughter, teasing, and bits of lightweight gossip were being exchanged along with the hot sauce, and the salt and pepper. *Trin* caught one feisty parley between two men, who seemed to be disagreeing on the ingredients for the Jambalaya, but both stayed in good spirits. Another table of seated locals were discussing a "haunted lodge," located nearby; their descriptions of the place made her curious enough to interrupt.

"Hi, sorry to intrude on your conversation, I couldn't help hearing you talk about a haunted lodge. Mind if I ask where it is located?"

The couple were happy to have the chance to speak to the new guy, they had been wondering who he was.

"Hello, that's okay, no intrusion here, we were wondering about you since we had not seen you here before. I'm Kealy, this here is Johnna."

"Hi, I'm Trin. Nice to meet you both. Yeah, my first time here and I was lucky enough to get the last bowl of jambalaya."

"Yes indeed, it goes fast, it is one of our favorites, for sure, although Kealy likes to add a ton of hot sauce to it, I like it just the way it is served."

"Guess everyone is talking about the Loyalville Lodge, strange how a place like that should be sold to an investment company. So you are a ghost buster disguised as a guy or what?"

"What? No, wait, what do you mean?"

"Kealy? Jeeze, that's nothing to be joking about. Sorry, Trin, don't mind my husband, he's a politically incorrect sub-human sometimes." Johnna, embarrassed by her husband's lack of tact, had blushed from her cheeks to her neck.

"Uhh, yeah, sorry, I didn't mean to offend. Guess I wasn't sure if you were a guy or a girl, and Johnna is right, I'm a dope and it is none of my business."

"No offence taken, and I'm the one who busted in on your conversation in the first place. I prefer he, as far as pronouns go, but I really am interested in the place everyone is talking about.

"Oh, okay, and thanks for being a good sport. Well, we don't know much about the lodge, it is rumored to be a house full of ghosts, just know it's got some bad history, and folks around here like to spin stories about the place."

"Oh, yes, I've picked up on that bit of talk, already."

Trin wasn't offended, and the couple's honesty was refreshing, but *he* was hoping to learn more about the property.

"Yeah, everyone is talking about it, but can't imagine who would want to live there, it was glorious in its heyday, but the place is dilapidated now."

"Yes, I was just about to tell Kealy I heard it was the Green Mountain Corporation, some kind of an investment company. They are supposedly restoring the old place, for company use. Like a retreat center, for their employees, I think."

"Huh! All well and good if their retreat is around the end of October, they'd be in good company, ghostly company!"

Johnna pulled out her phone and looked up the property address, to show *Trin* the pictures. *Trin's* face displayed a fascinated recognition.

"Oh, so, you know the place?"

Trin denied seeing the property before, but *he* had in fact been driven up to the place.

Oh, this is probably crazy, but how can it be anything other than a sign? I dreamt it, then driving around looking for property, I see it, and then, these folks are talking about it. Synchronicity at work here or what?

With the lunch hour past, the place was emptying rapidly. The last words shared before Johnna and Kealy left, caught, and stuck in *Trin's* heart. They hoped *he* would be back. A few others even called out to *Trin*, inviting *him* to come back for Clam Chowder in bread bowls, on Fridays.

I can't help but imagine myself living here, making a home, and raising a child. Is it too much to hope for? If I don't decide, there is always the chance that the decision will be made for me. I can't let that happen. It is time to be a rich entitled actress who knows how to get what she wants. It's back to Incline Village, I will need to buy a set of travel bags, and I know just the place. Oh, wait, a call? It's the agency.

"Hello?"

"Hello, Ariel, it's Bea from A to Z Models. Congratulations on your first successful gig. Would you like your fee deposited in a *Venmo* account? Or do you use *Paypal?*"

"Oh, I don't have either, I thought I was being paid with cash?"

"Oh, I see. Well, yes, cash payment is an option, but there will be a seven to ten day waiting period before you can pick up your cash."

"Thank you. I do not have a problem with the wait."

"Good. Okay then, we will have a schedule for you to pick up when you come in to get paid. Have a great day."

Relieved for the call and for the payment arrangement, Ariel began mapping out her transportation plan.

~

Little did the people of Loyalville know they had given Ariel the boldness she needed to make her next move. Living in Caroline's house would not be an option much longer, as she was sure to have a run in with Goodman, and now that he knew she worked for the modeling agency, she could not depend on him believing she was a caregiver.

~

"Nice to see you, David. Today, you may call me Miss A," she turned toward the bulky luggage piled on the curb, "I'll wait until you have it loaded in the trunk."

"Yes, Miss A, my pleasure."

The chauffeur, energetic, and was exhilarated by having a "famous" person use his car services for a second time. He had guessed "daytime soap star" the first time he drove her, and she smiled, before adding, "Just Miss, will be fine." Not wanting to be rude, he accepted her wish to be anonymous, and loaded the bags.

I may not have enough to buy the haunted lodge outright, but perhaps they would consider a cash-heavy lease to own? I could act as a reluctant buyer. I could play up the town gossip, and the haunted house rumors.

It will be like Frankenstein meets The Shining, with the locals gathering at the foot of the driveway, ready to storm the place as soon as the occupants arrive. Their fear is that the old curse will be released, as soon as it has fresh blood living in the house, and the neighbors don't want that sort of trouble, but it is just the kind of place I happen to be looking for.

Ariel lowered the dividing window between herself, and the chauffeur, "David, please locate the address for Green Mountain, Inc., their offices are in Sparks, Nevada."

David drove smoothly. He knew the area, still, he scanned the road for hazards to avoid staring at her. He found her captivating. Her smile was reluctant, but when she was not trying to hold it back, or hide it under the shadow of her hat, it made him feel desired. His eyes traveled to his rear-view mirror when they could. She caught him staring and looked pleased. David marveled.

I think she might like me, if those aren't bedroom eyes, then they haven't been invented yet. She's got kind of a Dua Lipa vibe, I'm sure I've seen her before, she's absolutely stunning, maybe an actress and a singer? Definitely bewitching.

During the ride, Ariel had time to consider her situation. The scare of being followed, kept her from relaxing, although the nice folks at the Loyalville diner gave her a healthy distraction, on several levels.

The people there, I like them. It seemed as if they liked me too, well, Trin. There were several lingering smiles, down to earth people wanting to know me, wanting to welcome me. Besides their offer of fellowship, they showed me where to find the house from my dream. The house haunting my sweet dreams, dreams daring me to believe I could have a beautiful life there.

Ariel smiled broadly at the remembering of her mission.

I must find a way to buy it, it is even more perfect than I could have ever imagined. A home remote enough to be private, and at the same time, neighborly enough to make friends. Friends who help each other. They hug and touch with ease, even with a stranger. Still hard to believe so many kindhearted hands reached for mine, just to welcome me.

Ariel looked away from her hands, peered out the window, then back to the driver's rearview mirror. The twenty-something kid looked at her with the dazed eyes of a mystified fan. Her body, stimulated by all the attention she had been receiving from the Loyalville clan, though none of it sexualized, was reacting to the driver's pubescent energy. Her arousal, becoming evident through her sheer blouse, also caught the driver's eye. Her mind gave way to her body's longing. At first, unconscious of her hands, until one found and exposed a nipple. Her other hand went below his line of vision, under her own skirt. Enraptured by the endorphins, Ariel unbuckled her seat belt and leaned forward. Her lips nearly touching his right earlobe, she murmured, "I am not myself today. I hope I haven't made you uncomfortable."

David swerved in his lane, just slightly, as his eyes fought between navigating the vehicle and watching the provocative, gone erotic fare, gyrating in his backseat.

"I'm cool, no worries."

"Hmmm, you don't look cool, David. Quite the opposite."

~⁓~

In the beginning of her liberation, Ariel's sexual desires had wavered between insatiable, to becoming physically nauseous at the thought of sex. Presently, she felt greedy, and wolfish, and needing to be orgasmic. She required a remedy for her lustful arousal before her attempts to attain her dream home. Well-nourished, was without a doubt, the status she wanted to *embody* for her imminent negotiations. Desperation could be detected if one had the right skill sets, and she did feel breathlessly desperate. She had no clue about the abilities of the owners, but she intended to be at her best. To get there, Ariel's prowess needed skin to skin contact, nothing else could appease her hunger.

Ariel leaned forward, her face bumping her lips along David's neck, until she reached his left earlobe, and whispered, "Have you ever had oral sex with a famous person before, not counting your fantasies? Don't answer unless you're good at keeping a secret."

Sitting back, Ariel held a finger to her lips, until she caught the driver's glance. He had not budged nor turned his head, his eyes were searching the view, almost a mile ahead.

"I, uh, my lips are sealed, I mean they're available for whatever you'd like, uh, when I'm not behind the wheel, of course." Clearing his throat, he lowered his voice an octave. "What happens in my ride, stays in my ride. I can pull over anytime, just say the word."

The finger slid into her mouth, and she sucked it sensually, as she considered her next moves. Having lived in a *sex-filled prison* most of her life, it was challenging to live without daily sex, and human touch. She had learned how to engage escorts, which could remedy her desire for a night, but since freed from her master, she had not tried "recreational sex" with a regular person.

Decision made, Ariel leaned back, opened her blouse, and tweaked her nipples. Exposing both breasts, she murmured, "Word."

The driver put on his blinker and turned off the highway, slowing as he looked for a safe place to pull over.

Is this really going to happen? She wants me?

"I aim to provide the best customer service, Miss." *Thank god I took a shower before work!*

Ariel's whisper was barely audible, "I need it, I can't wait another minute, and no one can know. I mean to use you young man, so keep it simple, just sex."

Lost in her want, she brazenly masturbated, needing to come into contact with some kind of *strange.*

"I'll need to find some cover, so no one rolls up on us, I'll stop over by those trees."

"Hurry, I'm urgent for your touch," her hand reached for his thick hair, and tenderly pulled, then it slipped down onto his neck, over his shoulder, and back to her own body.

The gravel sounds under the tires, worked like an aphrodisiac for both. Their clothes fell off as the car rolled to a stop. David was ready to do everything or nothing, whatever she wanted. Just seeing her flawless skin thrilled him, and he had a fresh box of condoms on hand, if she offered more.

Ariel with barely a year of *normative social influences,* and a scant amount of non-enslaved sexual experiences, had struggled with "curbing" her sexual appetite ever since the action interview at the Bath House. Focusing on survival had kept her from making risky choices. Rather than overthink it, Ariel decided to take the gamble. In therapy, Ariel learned she needed to allow herself the *freedom* to discover her sexual identity, *if* she was ever going to be comfortable in her own body.

She had managed to limit herself to self-stimulation, but with her lower parts on fire, she knew she could wait no longer. David wormed himself over his seat through the opening, into her bare arms.

"Yes, cum here, I need to feel the caress of lips and tongue," *preferably those of an experienced woman, but this willing driver will do.*

When at last his hands found her pleasure places, she thought of the beautiful woman at the postal store. Visions of the Asian beauty electrified Ariel's lust. Her exquisite face reminded Ariel of Lily, the one who taught her about the animalistic pleasuring of men, and women. The one who had shown her love and taught her to dream of freedom. Knowing Lily had been removed from the master's service, meant she had been killed, but Ariel still loved her. The sensations David was giving, and the thought of the look-alike re-birthed her old yearning. Blissfully cognizant of the moment, a song lyric danced in her head.

If you can't be with the one you love, love the one you're with.

The peach-faced, fledgling driver was attractive. His vanilla life, readily seen in his public social media posts, had given Ariel the faith to trust him. He was too innocent to be involved in anything that could bring trouble to Ariel. The idea of having a "fuck buddy or two," had swayed in her recent fantasies. She pulled herself from make-believe, deciding to be present, if only for a fleeting fifteen minutes. The firm callow flesh against her own, sent off waves of endorphins. Ariel accepted the ephemeral backseat tryst, as medicine her soul needed, and she held nothing back.

"Here we are, safe and sound, Miss. We made good time, even with the brief, uh detour. I hope you were comfortable. No regrets?"

"Yes, you have made me very comfortable. You have done a great service for me. No regrets. Truly, you have been a divine distraction. Thank you, again, David. I hope you don't mind cash; it keeps the paparazzi guessing."

Seeing the bill in her hand, he was embarrassed he had not gone to the bank for tip change. Any good driver would not be without some bills, just in case someone waved a large bill, but could not give it all.

"Uh, well, we don't carry money, I won't have change to give you, but I could put it toward your next ride, if you'll need another ride?"

"To be honest, my current situation came at an unexpected time. I was about to leave for a trip abroad, as you can tell, I'm packed. Now, I have a last-minute meeting here, but I have no idea how long I am going to be."

"If you want, I can wait for you? I need a break anyway. You can call or text when you're ready, I've got nowhere to be until tomor-row morning at six o'clock, my other job."

"You are so kind. I will accept your offer, but only if you keep the meter running while you take your break. I insist."

"Customer is always right in this business. And do you want me to hold on to your bags as well?"

"David, again, you are divine! I only need one with me, it's my office on wheels. The mid-size one, if you care to pull it out for me?"

"My pleasure Miss."

Oh my God, am I dreaming or has my world turned upside-down? I think I'm in love.

The unexpected happenings in front of the dull painted office building, caught the attention of the male receptionist inside. Typically, the only thing that roused him from his monotonous routine was browsing social media, his phone never left his hand, his eyes never left his phone. Yet, with fifteen minutes remaining of his dinner break, his phone became a stepchild to the car that was parking on the curb. The blacked-out windows piqued his interest.

The sighting pushed him to his feet, "What the heck is going on in front? Chauffeur? Suitcase? Oh, my gawd, is that who I think it is? That's the blue-blond bob from the *Ghost* video, right? Could it really be her?"

Ariel's over-sized sunglasses clung to her face, keeping her new admirer wondering about her finite features.

CHAPTER 35

THE SNOOPY BANDAGE

"What do we live for, if it is not to
make life less difficult for each other?"
GEORGE ELIOT (MARY ANNE EVANS)

The nursing staff shut off the medication drip on Donald's IV tube, and then began to remove one of the lines, he had them in both arms. The activity made Donald excited for the inevitable discharge. He squirmed like a kid.

"Please sit still, this should not hurt, if you keep still. FYI, you are not going home this morning, not before we observe you another eight or nine hours; at least that is what the doctor indicated in your chart. Even if you feel perky now, my guess is you'll be worn out after breakfast, and happy to sleep when I'm done checking you."

"Yes, Nurse Cindy, and thank you for taking one of these needles out, this other arm is jealous for your attention too. Question. Are we there yet?"

Donald was sleepy, but he was also tired of being in the hospital. He wanted to get home and get back to his regular routine, which would definitely include spying on the lodge. Cindy did not bite; she had become familiar with Donald's brand of humor. In the moment, she was focused on her task, and knew better than to encourage the witty patient. She had been honest about him needing more rest and she did not want him to become overly excited, especially while she was checking his pulse.

"Okay, stoic type. Question, times two. Can't a guy be hangry? And does this mean I get real food today?"

"I'm glad you're feeling better. Sorry to say, I have bad news, times three. First, the line in your other arm stays in until doctor's orders change, second, breakfast is not for another two hours, and third, you are on clear liquids until the doctor changes the order."

"Ha, I thought you were the ambassador for wellness, instead I get the diplomat for depression, can't you give a guy a break?"

"Drink your water, and I'll be your eviction emissary. I will let the doctor know you've got your appetite back."

"Ahhh, well done, Nurse Cindy. Not like my meat. Because if cow is on the menu, I'd be taking mine blue, crispy burned on the outside, blood rare in the middle!"

"Another reality check, there will be no cow on your menu any time soon. I will grab you a couple jello cups. It will have to hold you over. And, do not get your hopes up, you're likely going to get bone broth and more jello for breakfast. I will make you a deal though, if you get yourself cleaned up, a shower and a shave, within the next couple of hours, I can put a good word in for you for lunch."

"Oh boy, it is my lucky day."

"If you count hospital food as lucky? I don't think anything served under this roof comes close to your wife's cooking."

"You're not telling me anything that I don't know, she's got a gift."

"Speaking of gift, did you know she sent over a huge tray of fresh sandwiches, and cookies for all the staff yesterday. I've never eaten a better sandwich; and that's saying a lot since I've practically lived on deli subs since high school."

"Oh my gawd, and you didn't bring me a cookie? I almost thought you were a nice person."

"Stay still and I will be nice."

"Okay, please don't talk about my wife's food, and please do bring me something I can sink my teeth into, or else I will start a rumor about you having a bad day, cuz you won't stop needling me."

Donald's grin didn't lie, he was feeling hungry, and he knew that was a good sign.

"Oh, that reminds me, she called earlier, your wife. She wanted to know when you might be released. I informed her you would not need a ride before four o'clock, at the earliest. And by the way, that is subject to change if the doctor doesn't like your bloodwork. But I'll tell you what, since you are hungry, and your vitals are good, I can go ahead and draw your blood now to speed up the process, unless you would rather wait for the house vampire, who happens to be running behind this morning?"

"Well then, I appoint you, Nurse Cindy, as my get-out-of-jail consul, to protect me from running-behind-phlebotomists, and I, of sound mind, do give you my permission to take such blood samples, as needed, for proving to the medical powers that be, that I, *the* Donald Harrison, am no longer patient worthy, and therefore, I must be sent home."

Laughing at his humor, the nurse thought it would have been easy to keep flirting with the handsome man, she was enjoying the banter, and it was good to see his color return to normal. There were other patients waiting, she would get to them as soon as blood was taken, and his arm was taped with a cotton ball. She retrieved and checked the tubes needing to be filled, verified the patient information, then looked his arm over for the right vein. She added the rubber band to constrict blood flow and offered more chatter to keep her patient distracted from any discomfort.

"Your wife said she needed to clean up at home and had one other errand to run before she would arrive. Okay, make a fist, and just a poke, okay, good, okay relax your fist. Your veins are good, and you are hydrated. All good signs. Just relax, almost there now. Okay. I wish I had someone at my house cleaning up. Between you and me, I'm wearing the last clean uniform I own. Guess that means I have a date with the laundry mat this evening. How are you doing? Good. Okay, needle is out, bend your arm, hold it. There. All done."

"Thank you, Nurse Cindy, you made that look easy, and I barely felt a thing."

"It helped you sat still for a change. Okay, other patients await, so, there is a lunch menu on your tray, if you want to make your wish list, someone will come to pick it up, uh, rather soon. Okay, let's see that arm. Good. Here's your Snoopy bandage to make it all better."

"Ah, great, thanks. And thanks for the message from my Mrs., and yes, she's incredible. I suppose she went home to clean out the refrigerator, and God forbid I should go home to dust on the shelves."

"Huh, a clean freak, I know the type, my mother was that way too, well, you can count yourself lucky to have her, don't take her for granted. I'm guessing she is as good at laundry as she is making sandwiches and cookies. If only I could find such a person for me."

"I could never take her for granted, you have no idea."

Donald's mind raced to think of all the ways Debbi made him feel lucky. From his perspective, Debbi deserved whatever time she needed to do whatever she did for herself. Even before their union, Donald saw how generous she could be. She gave everything to her parents, stepping in to take care of all their needs, putting her own personal life on hold. The young nurse was new to the area. She did not know his wife's story, nor her faithfulness to her parents and the community. Donald recalled that she never once complained about not having time for herself. He was equally awed at how she honored them when they passed, buying them the largest memorial tomb in the Loyalville cemetery. Debbi's devotion to visit, clean, and maintain the potted flowers at her parent's resting place, was notable, and warmed Donald's heart.

Oh, that's right, I bet I know what errand Deb's running, probably going to replace flowers at her parent's memorial, it is about that time of the month.

Debbi was on a cleaning mission to erase every essence of the evils left by the unwelcomed men, and she had less than three hours to get it done. Dressed like a deep-sea diver, covered with rubber boots, and gloves coming up past her elbows, her Mrs. Clean whirlwind was about to begin. Hia's upstairs apartment, and the hair salon below, would be restored to its lovely charm.

Every surface must be smudge, dust, fingerprint, and DNA free. I start high and work my way down.

Debbi noted no marks on the ceiling, but the coiled bamboo hanging lamps had been ruined. The lovely turquoise colors were defaced with black ink, and food remnants, including condiments, and what appeared to be noodles. It seemed the men had tossed everything out of the refrigerator, making use of everything to cause ruin and havoc. Debbi scooped and tossed, and scrubbed, making note on her shopping list as she went. The beautiful Vietnamese textiles, knick-knacks, and vases would be exchanged with like items, Debbi would replace it all. Stopping a moment to drink some water, Debbi was eager to put the job behind her.

The kitchen, done, the living room, done. Now, the bedroom and the bathroom, and cleaning the bathtub is my highest priority.

The tub drain stopper was replaced with the new chromed parts Debbi had in her cleaning case. Hot water was run heavily to cleanse the pipes of all residues. The fixtures, mirrors, and floors, along with every surface was scrubbed until all gleamed. Debbi added a fresh smelling diffuser for the counter, another treasure from the cleaning bag, and bleach tablets in the toilet tank, for good measure. Debbi simultaneously used the washing machine and dryer to restore the washable things which were not ruined. She used fresh scented dryer sheets to give the laundered items that little extra feel-good smell. Later she planned to add a stylish glass bowl, filled with fresh lemons, and an attractive table-runner, knowing these smallish gifts for the dining room would delight Hia.

Hia's parking area was typically vacant of people when her shop was closed, since the neighboring businesses had front sidewalk entrances, and plenty of street parking. Even so, Debbi checked for visible persons before exiting. Every 25-35 minutes, Debbi stopped, looked, then took a garbage bag out to her car. She was meticulous in her arrangement of the bags, filled with a variety of items, they were destined for multiple locations. Mindful as she loaded them in the roomy trunk, she made the drop look careless, in case anyone came upon her.

The filthy cowards. At least they were smart enough to go down the drain and find their way to the sewer, where their kind belongs!

When she was satisfied in reaching immaculate perfection, she turned her attention to the bag of the men's personal items. The phones were her first study. None had as much as a password to keep her from seeing calls, contacts, and texts. It did not appear the men had close family relations. Other than work related communications, there were no sentiments to or from others. Even so, she made mental notes in case something came up later. Their phones did show a two-minute outgoing call happened about the time the duo were out buying beer the day before. The contact's name was Dave. Dave had called back, earlier in the morning, while Debbi was cleaning. She listened to the message, three times, and decided Dave knew too much. She could not leave loose ends. Her last related task was to ward off anyone who might begin a search for the missing men.

Using the same vernacular, and spelling, as was used, Debbi sent texts to the men's boss explaining the guys had woke-up in Mexico; making it appear two were looking for the other. In keeping with his evident swagger, Debbi added a "drunk-dial" text from Dien, saying, "Hey you shood hav bin heer, lots of mexi cherrys, all ripe 4 pikin BTW got any *jobs* further sowth? lol" With the coverup text sent, she was ready to perform clean sweeps on the phones. Stripping them of all personal information, and removing all possible DNA, she packaged them in a padded envelope, to be mailed to a non-profit organization in Mexico.

Nearly done with the necessary cleanup, Debbi stopped to call the hospital. If awake, she wanted to speak to her man; if he was asleep, she would leave him a message.

"I assure you, he's awake and can't stop talking about going home. I'll connect you."

"Hello?"

"Ah, my husband, you are awake?"

"Well, there's my smurf, I was starting to think you had traded my sorry ass for a floorboard full of dust bunnies."

Forcing a little laugh first, she played along, "Now you've caught me. No sense trying to fool you, and I admit, the bunnies are a tough crowd, lucky for you, it's you I'm craving; that is, once you are well."

Clearing his throat, "Ahhem," and adjusting his bed up, he added, "I'm well enough to get out of here! I got a Snoopy bandage to prove it. Ya gonna break me at four?"

"If they release you, I am all in to get you home safely, just be sure it is not too soon. I don't want you faking better just to get out of eating the jello."

He gave her his word, adding, "The last thing I'd ever want to do is be a burden for my little smurf. And besides, I think this group of nurses would know a fake if they saw one."

"Alright then, I should be there 30 minutes early to pack up your room. You, keep still and rest until I get there, you're a tough one, but you're not invincible."

"Love you Smurf, don't work too hard, you'll make me tired if everything is too clean."

"Love you Mr. Harrison, now rest, and I will call you in a few hours."

After hanging up, Debbi returned her cleanup gear to her parent's tomb, along with fresh potted flowers for the perimeter. From there, Debbi drove out to the old train depot, about twenty minutes out of town. The retired cars that sat rusting were a gathering place for the homeless who made the mountain range their home. Debbi knew the regulars, and they her; they called her *the bringer*. This time, like before, she kept her face covered with a medical mask. She brought a bag of coal, and a container of chicken vegetable soup from her freezer. Handing off the soup to the pot-man, *the bringer* filled and lit the barrels. The men's items were consumed in a matter of minutes, but she stayed to turn the ash. When Debbi was satisfied all had burned up, she went home to check on Hia, take a shower, then headed to the hospital.

What she would say to Donald, about Hia staying with them, had not yet been determined, she only hoped he would not ask too many questions; that went for Hia too. Debbi felt it was best for both, especially Hia, to be kept in the dark on the details related to the day's activities. Eventually, there would be an investigation on the missing men, and Hia was not a liar; Debbi knew it was best for Hia to be kept in the dark.

After two nights considering what the FBI had reported to him about Donald's wife, Bob, the chief of police, made an emotional judgment.

Given our lengthy friendship, I don't give a damn about the FBI's concerns about keeping their spying secret. Donald has been an incredible friend. He put his own life at risk to save my dog, the least I can do is warn him about his wife being watched. I gotta do this, I'd never forgive myself if he found out I'd kept this kind of secret. But I can't use the phone, I need to get to the hospital and tell him face to face. He's not going to be happy, but it is what it is.

Trying to soften the blow, Bob reasoned with the gray faced man, "Donald, as I said, they've tailed her, or tried, and the fact she keeps slipping away, clearly losing them on purpose, makes her suspicious. And there's another thing. There have been murders in the county, killed with poison. Finding the same poisonous plant growing in her garden, well, you said yourself, she doesn't grow anything by accident, she has a purpose for all her plants."

"There's a lot of poisonous plants growing in yards around here, bet you got some in your own yard. Maybe they should follow your wife around?"

"Look, it's just odd. And odd enough to make someone in the FBI think you might be in danger. I'm not saying I agree with 'em, but how could I not warn you?"

As serious as a heart attack, Donald spoke in hushed tones, "Bob, what are you suggesting? Do you hear yourself? While I appreciate you coming to me with this and keeping it between us, this is totally ridiculous. You're talking about Debbi, my wife. She's an angel to half this county. She would never hurt me or anyone."

"I know, this whole thing blows my mind too. Still, you gotta admit the video footage of her sneaking around the neighborhood makes it look like your wife may have, uh, secrets. And why were the FBI asking for details on your household incident, uhhg, unless it wasn't random?"

"The questions about Debbi's activities are unrelated, they are targeting a good citizen who helps people, anonymously. She is sneaking because she doesn't want credit. God only knows why they imagine she's involved with a murder case."

"I know, okay, calm down. I don't advise you getting all upset over this, remember, I wasn't supposed to tell you. Stick to being Donald and don't go Sherlock on me. I mean it. I know you. Just let me do my job, and like I said, if the feds show up, you don't know anything."

"I don't like it, Bob. Why Debbi? They have nothing. Circumstantial bullshit. And they got no business nosing into Deb's past. If someone thinks they can implicate one of the most loved persons in this community for any criminal activity," Donald stopped to catch his breath, and make a fist, "they better think again."

Plainly upset, Donald gasped for air, then began coughing.

"Sorry man, calm down, I guess it wasn't a good idea to discuss this now."

"No, I'm glad you did. I just hope you're not buying any of this bullshit."

"No, man, we go way back, but this is legit. Just understand, your wife, as neat and sweet as she is, might still be caught up in something messier than either of us would like to believe."

"Come on! They got nothing, but the damn FBI will frame anyone who fits their profile, then work to prove it. Don't you be naive Ropier!"

"Hey, it's FBI and above my pay grade. I only know by their questions, and their warning to watch out for you. There's been multiple murders by poison. Word is, they're looking for a serial killer, and how she got in those crosshairs, I have no clue."

The phone rang and Donald, expecting Debbi's call, felt guilty for having entertained his friend's concerns. He stared at the ringing phone, unable to move.

"Bob, I gotta get this call."

Okay, just remember, this conversation didn't happen."

"Agreed. Now, get on out there, find the bad guys, and make my tax dollars' worth something."

The chief turned and walked out with his hands in the air. The conversation had gone better than he expected.

I hate being the messenger of bad news, especially to my good friend Donald, but at least he knows. Now he can decide for himself what is best to do. Lord knows he's a decent man, but I wouldn't want to be those making accusations against his wee gal. When they get to the bottom of this, there will be hell to pay, that's if his heart holds up. If there's truth to it, it'll break his heart for sure.

The click of the door-catch signaled it was safe for Donald to answer the phone.

"Hello? Oh, Deb, it's you."

"Donald, are you okay? You didn't pick up right away, and you don't sound yourself. I'm on my way now, but tell me, why are you upset?"

"Not upset, Smurf. Well, unless you want to consider the fact that my hair is growing faster out of my nose and ears, than it is growing on my head." He coughed, and she waited for him to speak again. His tone became tender, "Why is it you always know when I need you?"

"No more than you know when I need you, my honorable husband."

Donald smiled at the exchange, then asked, "ETA?"

"Three, fifty-seven, with just enough time to get you in the car, and back home in time to let the steam off the pressure cooker. I made one of your favorites, short ribs, and the mashed potatoes are already done, so you better be hungry."

"Oh baby, you are amazing, and so very good to me!"

"Okay, please remind the staff that you will need the large-sized wheelchair, your legs are too long for the regular one."

"Thanks Nurse Smurfette, your smurfy wisdom is appreciated. See you soon."

Ropier's words were spinning in his head, but Donald was determined to dismiss them, "She has nothing to do with anyone's disappearance unless they happen to be dust bunnies."

CHAPTER 36

HOUSE GUEST

"The question is not what you look at, but what you see."

HENRY DAVID THOREAU

Donald Harrison was brooding over ghosts, the kind that cut wires and left footprints in the mud, the ones moving into the old lodge, and the ones putting his precious wife in a bad light. It had been six days since the late-night incident, and his health, poor at best, was keeping him from doing his own investigation. Having been in the hospital for two days, Donald was feeling stronger. Nevertheless, his limitations made him feel helpless. He had only enough information about the FBI investigating his wife to make him irritable.

Our home was nearly violated, and I still don't know anything of substance concerning the activity at the lodge. All told, this is what Deb would call bad juju, the stuff that happens before the really bad stuff happens. I just hope the worst is over.

With so much in his awareness, his growing guilt was the heaviest in his chest. His culpability for keeping the cavernous underground a secret from his best friend nagged like gas pangs after sauerkraut. He wanted to tell Debbi about the mountain's secrets, but he needed to delay it until he was strong enough to accompany her to the mountain. Given his health status, he had to satisfy himself with a distant view. As soon as Debbi began her morning routine, Donald was ready to begin his work, lurking the neighborhood, from his windowed perch. He looked again at the underground entry points; there were two.

Looks like the one has been tampered with, but it is possible it was done by an animal. The only way to know for sure is to go and check it firsthand. Not today old man, gotta be content with binoculars, for now.

The morning had been mostly uneventful, there was a security shift change which apparently occurred every eight hours, like clockwork. Donald saw the guard walking down the long driveway on his rounds. When Debbi emerged from the bathroom, he was prepared to give her the update. Then, the sound of a nearby vehicle shifted his mind. Locating the car in his glasses, he followed it up to the drive.

Hmmm, a new car, a black Lincoln, blacked out windows, wish I could see the plates. Where's that guard?

Like a hawk eyeing a rabbit, Donald followed the car as it wound up the drive. It stopped short of the front circular drive, then the rear window lowered. As it did, Donald caught the glimpse of a woman peering out.

Who she is? Dark glasses, scarf, and that hat, who wears a hat like that anymore? Oh. Look how quick she retreats. She must be famous, that move had to be practiced.

It was only a brief glance, then the tinted window glided back up.

Twenty something, maybe thirty? Red lips, an exquisite nose, a soft jawline, and the briefest of smiles.

Donald muttered, "The kind of face men dream about, and surely with a face like that, the body must be fantastic."

As sudden as it appeared, the sedan made a U-turn and drove down and away, quickly disappearing from view.

What? Leaving so soon? Maybe it was just someone who went the wrong way? Hmmm, now the driver in a hurry to get back to the main road, that was odd.

Keeping his glasses on the move, Donald scanned the valley, from left to right.

Nothing remarkable. Just a wrong turn and a little curiosity, right?

Debbi walked through the bedroom; she was about to change her clothes for work. Seeing his wife go into the master-closet gave Donald's imagination bravado. His guilty pleasure percolated. He could not help himself from spinning a fake news fantasy.

A gorgeous young actress, birthed from early fame. A parent's dream, but she wishes for a peaceful home away from the Hollywood limelight. Wanting privacy, she invests in a haunted house in the small city of Loyalville, until the next big script calls her back. After meeting the tallest man in town, Donald Harrison, she wants him for her next leading man. Mmmm, mmmm, those red lips would taste as delicious as she looked.

Donald, smiling at his own deviate and colorful pansexual imagery, inflated his lustful daydream.

Of course the beautiful woman has a small package, yes, she's an undercover tranny-pan, that's what she is. I would keep her secret. She would discreetly hide her appendage under layers of fabric, bringing it out only when she spent time with the man who would truly appreciate her uniqueness.

A quiet breathy whistle slipped out, before Donald could stop himself.

"I heard that, Donald. Do not tell me you're going to spend all day staring out the window? Your doctor said no strain of any kind, that includes stress." She came out of the closet with her shoes in hand. "That said, if something does happen up there," Debbi pointed to the lodge, "I want to know every detail."

Donald found his miniature wife utterly adorable. He knew she was just as nosy about people as he, and as fruitful as a pear tree in August. The morning had been a constant buzz. From his bed, Donald had heard everything from blenders to vacuums, the clinking of dishes to the squeaky sounds of her swipes on the glass doors. She, of course, had made him stay in bed, and brought his breakfast up to him, and she delivered it with a smile that could have melted Mt. Everest. And after all her home chores, she was still moving like lightening to get to work.

Dressed in her drab attire, she neared her husband to land a goodbye peck on the cheek. Donald obliged her kiss, by pulling his spy glasses away from his face, and bending low enough for her to reach his prickly muzzle. Keeping the sighting of the fancy-hatted woman in the chauffeured-car, to himself, Donald was not prepared to give up his fantasy. He would give the facts to her later. She paused with him for another glance out the window, then, he offered a half-hearted briefing.

"The landscaping crew is missing in action, I saw their equipment truck arrive earlier, with only a driver. He's still sitting there, at the end of our street, staring at his phone. Oh, and security had their regular guard change, right on time."

Moving toward the window, Debbi continued, almost calmly, "Good to know. Mind if I take a peek?"

"Uh, sure," Donald was not surprised with her interest, just with the timing. He handed her the glasses, "I love it, peeping Don and peeking Smurf, we make a great team, don't you think?"

Her laugh, close to natural, was still contrived. Donald did not notice.

"You're not usually so relaxed before going to work, does this mean you want to call off, and skip going postal until tomorrow?"

Waiting for the right moment to share her own briefing, Debbi first located the lone man in his truck. She looked hard at his shadowed face. He had his cell in front of his face. She decided he must be "Dave." She casually lingered on him.

Returning the binoculars to Donald's hands, she patted his arm and announced, "I will go by the shop, but Cookie is covering another morning for me, oh and, we have a house guest. She's downstairs in the spare room, likely asleep."

Not able to hide the shock from his face, Donald responded slowly, "Okay. Did not see that one coming. Uh, she? You know I don't need a babysitter, Smurf."

"It's more like you're the sitter. It's Hia. She was...attacked."

"What? Attacked? Is she okay? When and where did this happen? Why did you wait so long to tell me?"

"Calm down, Donald. I do not have all the answers, and I don't want to presume. It happened a couple of days ago. She called me. I collected her, and brought her here, while you were still in the hospital. I did not think she should be alone. She's been checked and given some sedatives. She says she will be alright, she just doesn't want anyone to see her, until the bruises fade. I told her you would be here, and that you would respect her privacy."

"Bruises? What about reporting it to Ropier? She did make a report, right?"

"Donald, I know this is hard for you, for me too, but Hia is not talking about what happened. Not yet anyway. I'm not sure we should pry."

Suddenly Ropier's crazy story seemed to make sense to Donald.

I knew Ropier had things messed up, it must be Hia who caught the attention of the FBI, bet it was her nasty cousin who messed her up, and now he's run off to avoid being arrested.

Making a concerted effort to lighten the energy, Debbi continued before Donald could think of what to say, "Actually, Cookie has been learning to distribute mail; Tom has been pleased with her. I think it has been good for them. She's there again today, so, I am going to go by Hia's first. I'll pick up a few things for her and clean out her refrigerator. When she's ready she will go home to a clean place, with fresh sheets. I'll head to work when I'm done."

"Ahh Deb, you are a jewel, and so practical. Nice of you to help Hia, I just hope she's not getting you into any of her troubles. And hopefully, she will be able to press charges, if she knows who attacked her. I won't bother her, of course, but what if she needs something while you're gone?"

"She has her cell phone at the bedside, and she knows she can call or text me any time, you too, for that matter. I will keep my phone handy. I know you'll spend the bulk of your time upstairs in front of the window anyway. I hope you don't mind her being here?"

"Mind? Hell no! It's just hard not knowing what's happened and at who's hand."

"I didn't want you to worry, you need your rest too. By the way, if you want to have a snack, there are apples in the pantry. Don't try to sneak cookies; save your sugar calories for the dessert I know you will want after dinner."

Wanting answers more than cautions about his dietary limitations, Donald put the glasses down. He felt a little relieved when Debbi curled her finger for him to follow, he didn't want her to treat him like an invalid. Like a good puppy he padded his slippered feet behind her.

"Don't forget your good shoes are in the garage. They are nicely polished after your traipsing through the dirt last week. For goodness sake, stay on the sidewalk. I won't have the neighborhood thinking I cannot keep my husband looking well. Donald, are you listening?"

"Yes Smurf. I should eat apples, stay out of the mud, and you do not trust Tom to teach his own wife how to deal with the mail, so you are going in to check on things. Okay? One question though, before you go. I look more like a *George Clooney* than *John Corbett*, don't you think? One of the nurses at the hospital said I looked like a mature *John Corbett*."

Smiling with a sparkle in her eye, Debbi winked, then sputtered, "Right now my honorable husband, you are even better looking than both. I'd say more like an *Indiana Jones*, well no, too young, more like *Harrison Ford* in *Six Days, Seven Nights*, only you're four inches taller."

"Ahh haa! And you're my smurf-sized *Anne Heche*, only four inches shorter, and more beautiful!"

Debbi smiled at his comeback, and then held her finger to her lips and closed her eyes.

"What? Was it something I said? Why the sudden sad look?"

"I'm sad for her family and her friends, she has passed away, it happened a few weeks ago, I heard about it in the shop."

"Oh, I didn't know. I didn't mean to be disrespectful."

"I know my dear man. I know. Maybe we can rent one of her movies soon. But for now, I do need to get going, and you need to get dressed, we have a house guest who is not used to seeing a naked man walk around. Oh, almost forgot, in the fridge, on the second shelf, the red containers, they are to be delivered to Bud and Nan. I'd do it myself, but Bud doesn't like visitors in the morning. You'll need some fresh air at some point. Do you mind walking it over in a couple of hours?"

"You mean you are letting me off bedrest, to walk on my own, down the street and back?"

"Yes, and shhh, I don't want you to disturb Hia. She needs quiet to sleep, and you will need something to do. The doctor wants you to keep up with walking, just not too far and not too fast."

The normal, fast-paced walk down the stairs was slowed for Donald's sake. At the bottom, Debbi stopped at the coat closet, and turned around to give her husband a sincere smile. He melted. Debbi reached in and pulled her jacket off the hanger, demurely handing it to him. He helped her to put it on, as if she was a queen. For the act, Donald received a peck on his furry chest, and a firm squeeze of his manhood. Her hand lingered, and both felt the rush of lust.

"Mmmmmm. If you really want to go, then you better leave now. Another minute like this, mmmm, and I won't let you go."

Debbi let go, but first gave a slight pull, then pressed her own form, fully into his hardening loins. Coyly withdrawing, Debbi's voice had become husky, "I don't want to disturb Hia, shhh, my handsome man. It's good to see you getting your color back. Please don't overdo. Save your energy. Do not worry about the things you can't control. Okay? Okay. I will see you later."

Donald was not alone for more than a minute, when his thoughts drifted back to *his* beautiful almost-make-believe "tranny" starlet.

I didn't tell Deb, the lodge had a visitor, and she was hot. Incredibly.

The sound of the garage door closing shifted his thoughts.

Nah, I shouldn't indulge such fantasies, especially with another woman in the house, one who was attacked, I'm such a dog. Debbi is a gorgeous woman, even if she downplays her attributes when out in public. Matronly is lovely, and when she strips it off, oh boy howdy, she knows how to treat a man. Had my share of women who assume the grass is greener in the big city, the type who went out looking to turn heads, and then drops her panties for the first young hunk that stops to flirt. Truly, I am a lucky man, no matter what Ropier says, they've got it all wrong if they think she is connected to any sort of criminal activity, all wrong!

CHAPTER 37

A SKI VILLAGE FOR GHOSTS

*"If we have no peace, it is because we have
forgotten that we belong to each other."*

MOTHER TERESA

Returning to the upstairs bedroom, long enough to put some clothes on, Donald was the rugged type, who only liked wearing cotton; jeans and crew neck t-shirts, and he only owned what would fit in his small four-drawer dresser. Debbi's habit of washing everything within an inch of its life, made his wardrobe soft, and comfortable, even if he did not like the fresh scent left behind by the dryer sheets. In that moment, he did not mind, he breathed deeply. He noticed that everything was better with his Debbi. Still, the act of getting dressed, tired him out. Rather than having a pity party over his failing heart, Donald sought to distract himself with something mundane. Then, he remembered the reason he had dressed, they had a house guest, a very sexy one. His thoughts ricocheted.

Jeesh, how can I be getting a hard on, knowing our friend was attacked? Down boy, down you go. Hard to believe anyone would hurt her, it must have been her slimy cousin. He's trouble. Hope Hia's going to be okay. What about our unsolved late-night incident? What's the FBI's story.

The pressure in his chest turned into coughing.

Damn, trying to stay calm ain't easy today. Hmmm. I'll think about our neighborhood ghosts instead.

Donald made his way to the downstairs office, closed the door softly, then he sat at the desk. Hidden behind a false drawer bottom, inside a number-key locked envelope, a file of notes and maps waited for his eyes only. He carefully pulled the documents from the folder to review the bygone details of the lodge. Systematically, the research drivel resurfaced.

The property had once been opulent. Near the end of 1969, the last landowners, quite wealthy, had begun converting the 1941 Victorian vacation home, and carriage house, into what they envisioned as the Grand Loyalville Lodge and Ski Village. The lowland area, between the lodge and the Harrison's subdivision, now closer to a ghost-town of partially built storefronts, was planned to provide additional business opportunities to draw seasonal customers to a ski resort. Hmmmm, a ski village for ghosts. I wonder what would have happened if tragedy had not drastically altered their plans?

The lodge on the mountain, unoccupied for years, sat as a backdrop to Loyalville. A short hike down from the lodge, where the hills flattened out, there once stood a large barn, with ample horse stables, and walking pens. Currently, the untamed landscape grew from the ashes of what once was the barn. On each side of the low rise, memorial stones were placed, representing the people, and the horses who died there. Further below, and sprinkled down the mountainside, large boulders, various other rock formations, and plant life, added much texture to the topography. These were efficient in disguising the stone huts, tucked on the left and right of the ridge. Beneath it all, the long narrow valley, stripped of its gold decades earlier, now defined the separation between the mountain and suburbia.

The man who designed and built those places was some kind of naturalist genius. Up there looks like Frank Lloyd Wright meets Where's

Waldo. It's a wonder you could build them, and still most folks have no idea they are there, thankfully.

Donald, needing to stretch, lifted his six-foot, five-plus inches to his feet. He took a long slow breath and walked over to the closet where storage boxes held other important paperwork. He located the portfolio he had placed on the bottom of his old papers. The folder, labeled "2009 Taxes," held other notes, and the maps he was making. Donald listened for any movement at the door, and hearing none, he sat back down and opened the file.

Last thing I'd want is for Hia to wake up and walk in here. If she saw this stuff, she'd have questions, and likely tell Debbi, and then Smurf would be on my jock with her own questions. Sorry Smurf, not yet.

An hour passed. Deciding there was no progress to be made today, he returned all paperwork to his hiding places, except for the parchment mapping. He considered heading out to check a few of his above ground markers if he could muster the stamina.

I'll tuck the map into the inner pocket of my dress jacket, for safe keeping. Okay old man, back up to your bedroom perch.

"One last look before performing my assignment today," Donald mumbled to himself as he picked up the binoculars.

Wow, there's a big crowd today, and a local black and white, good, bet they will tell folks to git gone.

Just then, Donald's phone rang, it was Debbi.

Hmmmm? Maybe she's worried about Hia?

He answered with a grin, but his face changed to ashen as he realized the reason for her call.

"If you haven't already noticed, there is a search party getting ready to go up the mountain. Donald, I know you'll want to help, but it won't do any good if your heart gives you trouble. I'm on my way home, I'll need to change my clothes."

"Yeah, I noticed a deputy, and a vanload of people just now arriving. What are they looking for?"

"It's Nan, she went missing sometime in the night. Bud fell asleep, before setting the house alarm. He's not sure when she left, he was asleep close to six hours. He thinks she may have tried to find her way, up to the fire memorial, said she's been having nightmares about the fire again. Are you looking up that way? Do you see anything? Donald?"

"Whuh, uh…"

A loud thud could be heard over the phone, as if the phone had been dropped, then silence.

"Donald? Are you there?"

Debbi hoped it was the signal that had dropped, and not her husband.

⁓

Nan, in and out of remembering her promise to keep the boy safe, made her way to the barn. She had reached the spot. The place she stood when the boy died.

Is it true, did it really happen, I didn't tell the father? Why? Wait. It's cold?

Awaking from her dreamy awareness, a panic was not far from reach.

"Where am I? This is the place. Why is he…gone? It's my fault, it's all my fault. They will be blaming me; they will punish me. They are coming. I've got to hide."

Nan knew of a place, and it was not far from where she stood, once again, she was a seventeen-year-old girl on the mountain. She knew the mountain's secret. She wished Debbi had not been taken, wished she had not let go of her friend's hand. She needed her friend, she would understand, no one else could.

⁓

As darkness fell on Loyalville, Donald stood and watched the flashlights lighting up the mountain behind his home. The search for Nan had brought in 50 volunteers, many who were volunteer firefighters and certified in emergency response, and some brought dogs. They were all over the mountain and nearing the lodge. Donald could barely cope with having to stay at home. He could see small groups of light, pointing and roving left, and then right, and some were moving toward one of the entry points for the tunnel. Donald had hiked up to it, before his hospital visit, and verified the interwoven invasive plants covering the door, were undisturbed. The ivy plant growth still hid the rock-like latch, and the inset steel keyhole.

Wait. Slow down. Damn this ticker, and this is not the time for another dizzy spell. I really want to be up there helping and protecting the mountain's secrets. I wonder where Debbi is, I'm sure she's one of those lights.

He dialed Debbi's cell phone.

"Hello Donald, are you okay? Is Hia okay? We are still searching."

"I'm fine, and Hia is asleep by now, I guess. I wish I could be helping; wish I knew which light belonged to you."

"Oh, I forgot you could see us from the bedroom window, don't stand too long."

"I'd rather be up there and helping, I know that mountain better than anyone."

"Of course you do, but thank you for staying home and staying with Hia. I know it's hard not to be helping, but your dizziness is telling you to breathe, stay calm and rest."

"I'm sorry about dropping the call earlier, I didn't mean to scare you."

"Are you still dizzy? If you are, you need to check your blood pressure again, and call your doctor."

"Yep, no worries, I'm steady and calm as a cucumber."

"Good, don't worry, I know we'll find her. Please sit and put your feet up. I've got to let you go; we've been asked to limit our cell phone use."

"Yes, I understand, love you Smurf."

Donald could see several groupings of light moving across the mountain. As he peered, scanning the mountainside, another lone light caught his eye. It was rapidly moving away from the direction of the group, making a beeline to one of the huts; the one with the underground opening into the mountain. Donald could not help but hold his breath as he watched the scene from his window.

Whoever that is, it can't be good. Nan where, oh where can you be? They need to find you before they find the mountain's secrets. Please be okay, please come home.

Donald did not want to panic; he tried to control his breathing.

It almost looks like that light knows right where to go, there, yes. "Oh fuck." *It's right on top of it.* "Damn it!" *It's too dark to see much, a single light, maybe. Still not moving away from the opening, in fact not moving at all. Maybe it's Nan? What? Could she know?*

CHAPTER 38

HERO OF LOYALVILLE

*"The world is a severe schoolmaster, for its frowns are
less dangerous than its smiles and flatteries, and it is
a difficult task to keep in the path of wisdom."*

PHILLIS WHEATLEY

This is nuts, I'm no hero," Donald was more serious than ever.

"Well, that is not true. You are my hero every day and today, you are going to be an awarded hero for all of Loyalville to see. And you deserve it my honorable husband. If it were not for you, keeping a vigil on the search, who knows how long it may have been before Nan was found."

Clearing emotions from his voice, Donald replied, "Ahem, uh, I'm just glad she had the sense to carry a flashlight, and lucky that her confusion caused her to turn it off and on, it was a lucky break, that's for sure. But this, about me, it's too much. Betty, and the Chief throwing a party at the diner?"

He swallowed back the growing lump in his throat and sat on a kitchen chair. Donald's wife, now at eye level, had that look on her face, which told him there was no use arguing.

"Yes, do sit down. I will get you a glass of water. Understand, it's not just Betty and the police, and the fire department, and the mayor, it's Bud and Nan, and all our neighbors and friends. They want to recognize you, just accept it. Even Hia is well enough to be there, and by the way, I told her to sit next to you, and to hold me a place next to her. I will meet you there, after I'm finished going postal."

He laughed, heartily when he noted she had not tried to make a joke. She took it well, then almost appeared apologetic.

"I'm planning on being there for the main event, but I have errands before and after, so it is best we go in two cars."

"What? My Smurf late for the party?"

"I am not certain of my arrival time. You do not mind having to drive yourself, do you?

"You're going to allow me to drive?"

"My dear husband, it is not just a party. You are being officially recognized for saving Nan's life. I would not miss this for anything. I'm so proud of you. And if I thought you needed assistance in getting there, I'd arrange a ride. You would tell me if you didn't feel up to driving yourself, wouldn't you?"

"Course I can drive myself, and nuff about me. How about you and all of the search party? I think every person that searched the mountain that night, deserves recognition. And what about Bud? He was the one to guess Nan went up there, and pointed the search there, not me. And what about the dog that helped her down the mountain? Now, he's a real hero, amid all the hectic voices, it was that hound that brought her back to her senses, you said it yourself."

"Yes, yes, you have the right to your own opinion. The fact remains, you are a hero, prepare yourself for the public honor."

"Yeah, yeah, yeah, I'm prepared."

"You don't mind taking Hia, do you? It's just the one way, she wants to stay at her own place tonight. She's feeling much better, although I think she's going to wait another day or so before she starts working in the shop again."

"Hey, clearly, the hero needs his arm candy. If I'm enough for a Smurf and Hia, figuratively speaking that is, I'm one lucky guy. And the way my luck is going, who knows, I may pick up another gone postal *gurl* before the day is past."

Donald chuckled and reached to hug his wife, proving it was her he wanted. His humor had a relaxing effect on Debbi.

"Oh, going postal." Debbi laughed, "I get it now."

Laughing, together, although both had dark worries brewing, hidden to protect the other. Each were scrupulous in stifling their genuine emotions, even if it meant having to keep secrets. The rest of their conversation was playful and light; word camouflage, to avoid the truths which could not be fabricated. They kissed good-bye, and Debbi left for the postal shop.

With a few hours to kill, before heading to the diner, and Hia getting ready in the next room, Donald decided to watch television. He sat down on the sofa, awkwardly, trying to keep his shirt straight and tucked into his pants, he had lost weight. Wearing the attire Debbi set out for him, he felt overdressed, and would have preferred wearing jeans and a t-shirt, then he regarded his polished shoes.

Smurf sure knows how to shine shoes, well of course she does, she knows how to put a shine on everything, even the underside of her car is clean!

Donald's thoughts were interrupted by a lively British voice coming from the television. His attention, now captured by an advertisement for "The Green Mountain Dog Resort and Training Center, located in Sparks, Nevada."

He had seen at least one of their ads before, he remembered it was the night Debbi came home late, acting weird. He tuned into the commercial.

"Many people find dogs to be their best companions as they age. And why not? A dog provides company and can help a person to stay active. Here at the Green Mountain Dog Resort and Training Center, we are more than just an upscale dog grooming hotel. We do more than train dogs to potty outdoors, fetch, roll over, sit, and stay. We teach pets everything from basic manners, to performing acts of service, such as fetching the paper on the lawn, or bringing you your cane. Those with greater service needs, may also qualify for a fully certified service dog. Here in our five-star training center, we are proud to have successfully facilitated service dog and companion matches for over a hundred families and counting. A service dog is more than a caring pet, it is an investment in security and happiness. If you are considering pet adoption, please give us a chance to share what we do. We wish to support you in making the best decision of your life. And when you visit, be sure to check out our pet boutique. We have many products to keep your pet safe and dressed well. This week we are featuring personalized faux leather coats, and paw boots, as well as hooded sweaters and thermal tees. And every customer who makes a purchase of fifty dollars or more, will receive this colorful pet scarf, made of virgin wool, while supplies last."

Donald caught himself smiling at the dogs modeling the boutique apparel. The idea of having a dog was not a new one, but Debbi's dislike of dogs had prevented him from getting one.

The right dog could win Deb over and change her mind about having a pet. For sure, this is the answer for Bud and Nan, I'm sure this is what they need. I know the doctors say I need to continue to moderate my activity, and they don't want me on my feet too long, but I'll be damned if I don't follow through on this. It's the right thing to do, even if Deb would say it was too much to take on. Heck, it's only an hour there and back, and another hour or so to check the place out. I was on my feet over three hours watching the search, I'd say my stamina is improving. I will find a time to go when Deb is smurfing and be back before she knows. I might even make it there today after the shindig.

∽∽

The crowd at the diner was proof of the many people who admired Donald Harrison. Donald was already deep in, surrounded by people who wanted to greet him. Although Debbi sporadically gave her husband a hard time for being a "Peeping-Don," she loved him for his motives, and she bragged to Hia, who she found as soon as she arrived.

"My Donald, he's really something, how he continually scrutinizes the neighborhood with his binoculars, for the sake of keeping our neighborhood safe. I am proud of him, look how handsome, he's the most handsome man here, even with all the uniforms in the room."

Hia readily agreed, adding, "You are most lucky married lady, your husband is big, impressive man, everyone likes him. I like the uniforms too."

Noting Sage, the *so-called* crossing guard walking in, caused Debbi's smile to drop. Hia was busy making eyes at the "uniforms" and did not notice. She continued giddily.

"They all are here to honor Mr. Donald. You are right being proud. He's a real gentleman."

Debbi replied sharply, "Of course he's a gentleman, you don't think I'd be with a creep or some lowlife fiends, like some dirty whore?"

"What? I don't understand why you are saying that to me?"

"Just kidding, can't you take a joke?"

Why did I say that? Why would I even think such a mean thing? She's been through a tough time. Look how lovely she made herself today, it is the first time she's looked happy.

Hia did not know what to make of Debbi's nasty tone, and condescending comment, she knew it was not like her to make jokes. Then, in the blink of an eye, Debbi was back to being all smiles.

"Hia, you look well, I'm glad you gave yourself time to rest and recover. And, by the way, your hair looks lovely."

Baffled by the dramatic change in Debbi's expression, Hia managed to reply, "Thank you, Debbi, I am grateful to have stayed in your home."

Debbi intended to say more to put Hia at ease, but the sighting of another person walking into the diner caused Debbi to lose her breath. In a flash, it was as if Hia, Donald, and Nan, and the whole diner had just been sucked into a vacuum, along with all the air. Debbi gasped from the shock of the feeling, then faked a laugh to cover it up, all the while never taking her eyes off the *vision* that had just entered the room.

It is Little Dove, the same who tried to hide herself with soot and coverings in the postal store, the new box owner, only now she appears to be male-ish on purpose. Oh look, there is Sage walking right up to her. They know each other? Is this some kind of trap?

The phony laugh was caught by Hia, "Mrs. Debbi, bless you, you okay? Your face looks like you saw a ghost."

Hia knew that something was wrong with Debbi, although she could not name it. Then, Debbi changed again. An artificial smile took over.

Murmuring mischievously, "No, I'm fine. I thought of something I forgot to tell Cookie to do."

Nan's movement interrupted the unorthodox whispers between Debbi and Hia. Standing next to her was Bud, holding her hand, and guarding her from the gathering. Nan's expression made her appear childlike, "Where's my friend, Debbi with an i? Debbi?"

Hia's odd look irritated Debbi, but she focused on Nan.

"Hi Nan, it is I, Debbi with an i, it's so good to see you. You look well. Nan, this is my friend Hia, and Hia, this is Nan and her husband Bud."

Hia smiled broadly, "Hi Nan, my name is Hia, that is Hi plus a silent A."

Debbi was struggling for her sanity. Heated worry decanted over her mind as if hot soup was pouring on her head. Bud reached with a hearty handshake for Hia. Nan moved behind him, meekly looking over his shoulder. For Debbi, the ground was uneven, air rapidly thickened in her throat.

Why is Little Dove here? And there, look, she seems to be avoiding women, looking only at the men and at Sage. She's acting. Maybe the monster has Sage watching that Little Dove obeys. Look how she is fixed on her. No air. No, breathe. I must focus on Nan.

Debbi smoothed her hair, almost like she was petting herself. It was an old habit, one she had given up, along with the other learned animal-like tics. A thread of reason held her back.

"Nan, Bud, your chairs are right here when you're ready to sit. Nan, may I sit next to you, on the other side?"

"Oh yes, let's sit together, then we can whisper if we have a secret."

The naive comment caused Hia to laugh. Her giggle was contagious. Everyone had some show of laughter, given they were celebrating Nan being found. Allowing for Nan's dementia, her emotional wellbeing was utmost on most everyone's mind, especially Bud's. He watched his wife with concern. He was thankful for the venue, however, because Nan was comfortable in the familiar place. She also had two full night's sleep after her long day lost on the mountain, which she did not remember.

When the laughter and the greeting rituals quieted, Donald and the Mayor joined Nan, Bud, and Debbi and Hia. The standing men prevented Debbi from seeing her ghost.

I cannot let my fear be obvious to Nan, I can feel Hia watching me closely too, as is Sage. Why is she staring at me? I must hear Little Dove's voice. Will she ever speak?

The merry-go-round increased its speed. Debbi swallowed hard, keeping her polite plastic smile on board. Waiting. Irrefutably, Little Dove began speaking to Betty's mother.

~~~

Ariel felt her heart in her throat the second she spotted Lily. She would have rushed up to her, except for everyone greeting her as she made her way in. Several patrons knew her as *Trin*, and made a point to make her feel known, including the super friendly woman who introduced herself as "the local crossing guard, Sage."

Wow, this really is everyone's favorite place. I feel so welcomed, like coming home, almost everyone has greeted me, except the one I most want to see, to hold, to kiss, my Lily. Why does she pretend not to see me? She won't even make eye contact. Oh dear, that poor woman looks unsteady, I should offer to stand.

"Excuse me, noticed you might need a place to sit, you are welcome to take my stool, I'm good with standing."

"Young man, you be new around here, ain't ya, well, thank ya kindly, but no, I cain't be sitting on no stool. I'd likely fall plum right over. But don't you worry none, my girl Betty has a place for her Mama. That's me, Mama. And what be your name?"

"Ooh I see, actually, now, I do see the family resemblance. My name is Trin."
~~~

"Nice to meet you Trin. That be short for Trinity? I had a second cousin named Trinity."

"No Ma'am, it's just Trin."

"Hmmm, that a family name? What kind of background you got there Trin?"

"Ah, no, not that I know of, uhm, I guess I'm European mix."

Mama rolled up on *Trin*, looking closely at *his* face, and then backing off a little, spoke freely, "Dang Son! Ya ain't got a stick of make-up, and you're still too pretty for being a man, but don't mind me, I know ya ain't be lookin' for my 'pinion."

"Mama, there you are, oh I see you met Trin, come on now, leave him be," Betty smiled widely, fully aware of how her mother spoke her mind.

Looking hard at *Trin*, who was still standing, Mama turned her walker to go in the direction her daughter was pulling, "Keep your seat young man, didn't I tell you Betty would have a seat for her mama, but you didn't say where you be staying? Now you let my girl know if you be needin' any friends, she'll steer you in the right direction. Nice to meet ya Trinity!"

"Nice to meet you too."

"Oh isn't she just the sweetest southern lady you'd ever want to meet, old school that one, she cares about all the singles. I'm single too. You are single, right?" Sage had moved into the gap left by Betty's mother.

"Uh, yeah, as far as I can tell, did you want a stool? You're welcome to mine."

"Naw, I'm too big for that little stool, but thanks, Trinity. You are going to stay, aren't you?"

Ariel had not been prepared for the personal questions being posed to "Trin," and the *friendliness* of Sage had become weirdly curious. The butterflies from seeing Lily had evolved into prickly cactus pears. It was a warning not to trust her.

"I had no idea how busy this place gets. Uhh, pardon me, Sage, uh, nice to meet you."

As *Trin* sought an escape route, Betty came rushing back, forcing an awkward change of places with Sage, saying, "Excuse me Sage, there's more chairs over that way, I'm sure you can land one, if you hurry." Then, kindly, "Don't even think about running, Trin, you're here. You might as well stick around and get to meeting more folks around here. As you can see, we have something to celebrate, it will be a kick in the pants. Stay. Coffee is on the house."

~~

Eavesdropping on the conversation, Debbi heard Little Dove was going by the name of Trin. She could feel the color draining from her face.

It's her. Why here, why now? It's a trap. He's found me. It was him who had eyes on me, but why use her? Why is she acting like a man? It's not much of a disguise. Where is Sage going?

The program had begun, but all Debbi heard was Lily's voice.

You'll need to go along with the new guy routine. Invite Sage too. Take them to the old train cars. Find out where he's hiding, then kill them before someone learns you are not Debbi.

Applause shook Debbi present. The mayor was speaking. He had produced a super-sized key.

"In light of the most recent crisis, I'm sure we can all agree, it was Donald Harrison's attention to details that saved this woman's life. Nan Gridley, here, with her husband, Bud..."

The mayor paused, noticing a new face among the familiars. He thought he was seeing *Halsey*, his favorite Pop singer. He hoped it was not a joke being played by Donald, who was the only one who knew of his secret crush. The mayor's cessation gave way to applause, for Nan and Bud. Everyone stood, Bud and Nan too. Bud was mortified with embarrassment, in his own humble way.

Nan squeezed Debbi's hand, and Debbi, knowing the childhood ritual, squeezed back three times. Momentarily satisfied, Nan thought Bud and Debbi's friend, the big man, was pleasant. The rest of the room represented a dizzying spinning-cup-ride for her.

What is that noise? Why can't they stop? They hate me, and why not?

I've hurt so many people, I hurt everyone. Except Debbi came back, and that makes me good. Bud wants everyone to be quiet too.

Nan squeezed Bud's hand and pulled it back a little, Bud looked over, and she felt relieved. Seeing her ease, Bud shot his free hand up to Donald's shoulder, a wordless thank you.

Donald had followed the mayor's eye, who was staring at the boyish woman across the room. The face was familiar. Donald tried to picture *him* in a fancy hat, looking out of the window in a Lincoln, then a momentary shoulder-tap from Bud, brought him back to his friends.

I'm nearly two years older, but Bud looks like he's my older brother. The man can't catch a break. This thing needs to wrap up, can't see a fella so broken and not find some way to help.

He turned around and pulled Bud into a bear hug, then reached around to touch Nan's shoulder. Nan followed his example and pulled Debbi into a hug. Abruptly, there was something unfamiliar about Debbi. Bud gave her a wink, and everyone sat down.

Picking up when the clapping weakened, the mayor dramatically continued, "Much like his best-loved childhood detective, Sherlock Holmes, Donald used abductive reasoning, along with a keen sense of observation to solve the mountain's mystery and save a woman's life. Now, Donald, I know, you aren't one to want any credit for what you do, but too late for squirming outta this one. So, without further ado, it is my great honor to present our Loyalville hero, Donald Harrison, with a key to our city."

Feeling warm, and cold at the same time, Donald called out playfully, "Hey Betty, how much pie will this key buy me?"

The crowd, favoring his wit, held their recognition to hear the expected banter between he and the diner owner.

"First tell me the difference between a unicorn and a free piece of pie? Oh wait, there is none, they're both fictional characters."

"Ah Betty, didn't you know a dog has more friends because he wags a tail, and not his tongue."

"Mr. Harrison, you know light travels faster than sound, that's why you appeared bright, until you started talking."

"Now, now, Betty, if I had a star every time you brightened my day, I'd be a guardian of the galaxy!"

After a riotous amount of laughter and applause settled down, the mayor introduced the chief of police, and the captain of the fire department, who stood to offer gifts to Donald. The first gift, an imported shark tooth, Sherlock Holmes Detective Hat, with Detective Harrison embroidered on the inner brim. With glee, Donald modeled the hat, while he opened his other present. It was a coffee mug with a quote. The captain called out for Donald to read it out loud.

Reading it to himself first, Donald smirked, then added just the right amount of sassy to his voice, "I'm not a psychopath, I'm a high functioning sociopath, do your research."

~~~

"Hello boss, great news for you, I've got both bitches in the same place, and they have no idea I've made them. They act like they are not together, but based on the eyes they made, they will be soon. I could try and grab 'em, but if you want a clean take-away, given their popularity, this ain't the place. Now if they separate, I can't stay on both of them. What would you like me to do?"

"Excellent work man, I knew I could count on you. Let's keep the two birds, one stone plan, stay with the China-bitch, and get a clean grab as soon as you can."

"Yes, Sir. I'll be in touch once she's in the bag."

~~~

The gifts drew more laughter, and a standing ovation for the man of the hour. As everyone stood, *Trin* took *his* leave. It was easy to duck out the front door.

I can't believe it. She is alive, and so am I, but we is never going to be. She is Mrs. Debbi Harrison, a wife, to a man. She hated men, but clearly, no more. It hurts, it hurts so bad, I can't think. She wouldn't even look at me. I know she saw me. I can't believe I've loved a ghost all this time. She has her world and by the look on her face, by the way she kept her eyes from me, I am dead to her. I should be happy she is alive. I should be happy for her. It is a miracle. She's more beautiful than ever, and she acts like a normie. But could it be otherwise? He didn't act like her Dom, but maybe he is? He had several women drooling over him and feeding his ego, as did she, I wonder if she has more than one lover? What the fuck! It hurts. Why? Why because I still love her, she is the only one I've ever loved. Maybe, I could follow her, and watch, and see where she lives? Maybe, if I can get her alone, she will speak to me. It hurts too much to think she no longer wants me. I can't give up now.

Ariel retreated; her eyes threatened by the lump in her throat.

～～

Debbi laughed politely. Nan cupped her hand up to Debbi's ear, and whispered, "Did they find our diaries? Do they know who set the fire? Did they find the boy's body?"

Bud did not hear what his wife had whispered, but he saw Debbi's face. He was sure she was not going to stay calm much longer. He noted Debbi was uncharacteristically sour.

That's not like Debbi, but she's got her hands full keeping Donald from overdoing it. I know he is not doing well, even though he puts on a good act. She does what she can to indulge Nan's dementia, but she must be weary of it after this event.

Before Debbi could decide how to respond to Nan, Bud leaned toward them, and said, "How about we get outside, away from the crowd?"

The change in Debbi's expression, said she was on board. Donald was busy with his ardent fans. Debbi leaned over and whispered to Hia, "Tell Donald I need to help get Nan home, and after, I'll come to your place, much later, if that is okay?"

Nodding she understood, Hia stayed faithfully behind Donald, and would wait until the three others had slipped away, and out of sight, before speaking. She was eager to have Donald to herself.

"Nan, Bud is going to take you home. How does that sound?"

"Debbi with an i, are you coming with us?"

Lily had asserted herself and would not let Debbi go, "No thank you Nan, another time."

Nan stiffened, "You are not Debbi, why are you pretending to be her?"

Suddenly, Sage was at Debbi's back, and she had heard Nan, "What is this, Debbi is pretending to be someone? But who?"

"That's ridiculous, I'm Debbi with an i, and you know it."

"No, you're a fake, what have you done with my Debbi?"

Hearing Nan's sincerity, reinforced by Sage, Hia immediately suspected Debbi was not the "real" Debbi.

Something's wrong, I feel it. She is a bad one, I know it, she is not who she says she is.

Bud heard Nan's words as he approached, he assumed she was sundowning. He took her arm and joined by Debbi, they found their way out of the diner, taking leave of Hia, Sage, and the crowd. He wanted to get Nan home before she became too agitated. It was nearing time for her medication, and if she became too upset, she would refuse to take it. They made it to the street, but Nan's eyes were terror filled.

"Debbi don't worry about it, Nan's overwhelmed by all the noise. I've got it from here. I'm sure you want to go back and join Donald. It's okay Nan, we are going to let Debbi go back to the diner. Her husband, Donald is waiting for her."

"Oh, she's with him? Does he know she is pretending to be Debbi, too?"

～{～

Lily didn't care that she had been *seen*. She was outside, and finally free to do her work.

Time to find little Mr. Trinity, I know you're his bait to catch me, but I will kill you and Sage before you have the chance to trap me. You could not have gone far. Then I'll execute Dave before he makes trouble.

～{～

The party dispersed when Betty announced there was a free piece of pie for anyone who wanted to help with dishes; her way of say-ing the event was over, and she was returning to business as usual.

Donald proudly shook the hand of everyone, except the one he most wanted to meet. In the chaos of the good-byes, it appeared the *he/she* had slipped out.

Oh well, no time for fantasy. My next stop, The Green Mountain Dog Resort, the best fix is getting them a service dog. I know Smurf won't like it, but it could be just the right situation to help her get over her fear, then maybe we can get a dog.

When the Chief saw Debbi heading to her car, he called out to her, "Hey there, Mrs. Harrison, hold up there a minute, give this old guy a chance to catch you!"

Limping with a skip, as it were, Bob rushed toward Debbi. His cast had been removed, and his leg deemed healed, but not enough to run on it.

"Of course, Chief Ropier, a formal inquiry? Since you're not using first names?"

Don't speak to him. Isn't it odd that he would approach you away from Donald? He's in on it too, keep your distance.

"Uhm, thanks, no, not formal, I just didn't want to appear too friendly when Donald's still inside. Ahhh, that doesn't sound right either. I, I, just saw you, ahh, rushing away."

He waited, allowing for small talk, but she just stood there with a fake smile. Unexpectedly, he could not think of what to say.

"Uhhhh, okay, I'll be brief, if you have a minute?"

Her silence forced him to continue, awkwardly.

"I, well, you know I keep my ear on the street, and I hear trouble for you might be coming along here, if it's not here already."

Nothing. Not even a blink of eyes? Should I spell it out to her?

"I don't know what you're into, or how deep you're into it, but the FBI, they came to me, with questions, about you."

Debbi had become a plastic doll, with no emotions.

"Debbi, Donald is my friend; I don't want to see him hurt."

Nothing, a blank slate stared back, hard. Bob began to wish he had not approached her.

Oh dear, what have I done?

"Debbi, are you hearing me?"

"Yes, I am listening with the intent to hear you."

"Are you, uhh, I mean, is there anything you want to report? I won't bother Donald with it, if you don't want him to know, I know he's still weak." She said nothing. "If you're in trouble, you can tell me. I mean I'd like to have you come into the office, there are questions we'd like to ask, about the night of your, uhh, security break."

"We?"

"Hey! Great job Chief, that was a real hoot, and bye Debbi, I'll be seeing you at the mail shop, ah but you already knew that…" Sage spoke as if she were leaving, but she moved towards Debbi's car.

The fire captain was next to interrupt. "Hey Chief, before you go, can we talk a minute? It's work-related."

Now's your chance to leave unseen, forget Sage for now, she's looking away. Pretend you're going back inside.

~

"Stanovich here, checking in Chief."

"About damn time. Where are you and what's all that noise?"

"I'm in Loyalville Chief, a local diner, and I've found the Ghost's runaway, she's going by the name Trin, and she's a transman, a pretty convincing one too."

"Well? What are you waiting for, let's get her in for processing, we need to locate our agents, and she's the key."

"Yes Sir. I am on it."

~

Hia had spied Donald becoming excited while staring at the strange new man in town, she looked and saw him stiffen in his pants. Uncertain of what made him excited, she wanted to believe it was her. She also wanted to warn Donald about Debbi being an imposter.

"Mr. Donald, oh you look tired, here, sit down. Yes, sit down. I want to ask you, did you meet the manwoman, he, I guess it's *he*, still looks like a woman, didn't you think?"

The topic was not expected, although Donald was always prepared to be probed for confirmation on town gossip.

"Hia, uh, no, I did not. But you know I am out of breath. I hadn't noticed. Guess I will just sit a spell before heading home. Speaking of home, is Debbi taking you there?"

"Mrs. Debbi didn't tell you herself? She is coming after getting Nan home. You want to join us? Yes, you come too?"

"Ahhh, well, I'm going to have to pass, but I'm glad you're feeling better. You know you can let me know if you want someone to go with you, to make a police report, uh, maybe tomorrow?" Donald could see Hia was disappointed, but his was a grave mission, and the hourglass would soon be filled.

Sage had made her way back inside, looking for Debbi, but she heard what her husband had just said to Hia.

"Pardon me folks, I couldn't help but overhear, Hia, I was wondering why your shop had been closed. Glad you're okay. I thought I saw some hooligans in your car too, is that what Mr. Harrison is referring to?"

At a loss for words, Hia did not wish to share her business with a busybody like Sage.

"Oh what? No, nothing, no bother." Her look to Donald explained her vague reply.

"Well, it looks like you need your rest Mr. Harrison. How about I give Hia a ride home? I'm going that way."

Speaking up before Hia could reply, Donald guiltily wanted nothing more than to get on the road, "That would be mighty kind of you Sage. Hia, you don't mind if I take my leave? And I'm guessing Debbi will be round your place soon."

With that, Sage made a show of guiding Hia out, she had many more questions in mind, to ask, and fully intended to wait with Hia until Debbi's arrival.

"Good, good. It is not only my pleasure, Miss Hia, but it would be my honor to see you home safely. Loyalville is filled with good people, to be sure, but someone as lovely as yourself, heading home to an empty house, certainly deserves to be escorted. Good-bye all!"

With that, Donald made his way to his own car, "Siri, take me to The Green Mountain Dog Resort, fastest route."

It is my hope that this story will bring more awareness to the human suffering caused by modern day slavery, and sexual exploitation, aka human trafficking, which sadly, continues for tens of thousands of victims every year. Although this is a fictional tale, many real truths are highlighted. Including, the truth that the majority of modern-day slaves are women, and the resulting impacts can be powerful and for most, lifelong. If you think you or someone else is being victimized, please seek help immediately. There are a number of organizations focused on providing support to adult victims of slavery, among them, *The Salvation Army*.

I believe in human resiliency, and although our psychology, our personal values, and beliefs, differ in response to victimization, I do intend to offer hope to those faced with such challenges. There are confidential hotlines, woman's shelters, emergency medical clinics, urgent care facilities, community support groups, spiritual counselors, psychotherapists, among other resources, which can help survivors find the support they deserve.

That said, my deepest gratitude goes out to all the overcomers, the great thinkers, the brave doers, and the courageous lovers of life, nature, justice, and freedom; your legacy in word and deed speaks for itself. Even centuries later, your posthumous inspiration is timeless. I prayerfully thank the following souls for their enduring contributions, of which I have utilized a brief quote to highlight the subtle, yet allegorical focus for each chapter: Charlotte Bronte (1816-1855), Elizabeth Gaskell (1810-1865), Louisa May Alcott (1832-1888), Jane Austen (1775-1817), Frances Hodgson Burnett (1849-1924), Mary Wollstonecraft Shelley (1797-1851), Eleanor Roosevelt (1884-1962), Walt Disney (1901-1966), Catherine M. Sedgwick (1789-1867), Eliza Leslie (1787-1858), Margaret Fuller (1810-1850), Elizabeth Barrett Browning (1806-1861), William Shakespeare (1564-1616), Emma Willard (1787-1870), George Bernard Shaw (1856-1950), H.L. Mencken (1880-1956), C.S. Lewis (1898-1963), Robert Frost (1874-1963), Dr. Seuss-Theodor Seuss Geisel (1904-1991), August Strindberg (1849-1912), G.K. Chesterton (1874-1936), Albert Einstein (1879-1955), Oscar Wilde (1854-1900), D.H. Lawrence (1885-1930), Emily Dickinson (1830-1886), Abraham Lincoln (1809-1865), Rumi (1207-1273), George Eliot, aka Mary Anne Evans (1819-1880), Henry David Thoreau (1817-1862), Mother Teresa (1910-1997), and Phillis Wheatley (1753-1784).